Praise for the Books of Nicholas Nicastro

On *Hell's Half-Acre*:

"Murder, mayhem, and deception stain the Kansas prairie in this historical novel of the Old West. In his latest novel, Nicastro (*Circumference*, 2008) fictionalizes the story of the Bender family, a gang of real-life serial killers who preyed on unsuspecting travelers in Kansas in the late 19th century. The narrative, told mostly from the perspectives of Kate Bender and Leroy Dick, one of her most upstanding neighbors, switches regularly between the family's murder spree and its aftermath and also addresses the childhood experiences that made the main characters who they are. Everyone has a secret to hide, and no one is quite what they seem on the surface. For the bloodthirsty, demon-worshipping Kate, murder is just a means to find her long-lost father, and she longs to give up such crime so that she can be with Leroy, whom she secretly loves. But the honest, compassionate Leroy has done his own share of killing in the past as a guerrilla fighter in Kansas, and when his neighbors' crimes are brought to light, he decides that it's his responsibility to track them down. The Benders aren't an ordinary family, but they do develop their own kinds of affection for one another, even as they make their livings by killing and robbing. Through his characters, Nicastro explores the very human desires that can turn people into monsters and the lies even ordinary people tell themselves and others to bury their guilt. By the time Kate asks, 'Have you seen what

I've seen? Do you know what suffering is?...Until you know the answer to those questions, who are you to judge me?', it feels like a question to readers as much as to another character. This meticulously researched, vividly told story marries an almost biblical poetry to the rough action of a Western. Readers who can stomach its violence will find a bleak beauty in this portrayal of one of the American prairie's ugliest stories.

A heavenly retelling of a hellish tale."

—*Kirkus Reviews*

"Nicastro has based this novel on the true crimes committed by the so-dubbed "Bloody Benders, America's first serial killers." Although the particulars of the gruesome murders, discovered in 1873 as if at a "Hell's half-acre," are well recorded, the Benders' origin and their subsequent disappearance are mysteries. Even the museum erected at the site has been taken down, replaced by a plaque. Nicastro has reconstructed Kate's story well, and although it's captivatingly written, with all of the details, prairie life, and dialogue of the period, its enjoyment requires suspension of disbelief. This Western's plot straddles the Civil War period, and the use of flashbacks keeps the mystery riveting. A surprise ending awaits readers. Recommended."

—*Historical Novels Review*

On *Circumference: Eratosthenes and the Ancient Quest to Measure the Globe*:

"Forget the myth of Columbus' daring in imagining a round earth. Nicastro not only traces the conception of a spherical world back more than a millennium before the seafarer set sail but also recounts in fascinating detail how the ancient Greek geometer Eratosthenes measured that sphere with astonishing accuracy. Though it would be thousands of years before his feat received appropriate recognition, Eratosthenes conducted his revolutionary science with nothing more complex than a sundial and a compass. With reader-friendly clarity, Nicastro explains the surprisingly simple calculations behind the earth measurement. But readers learn about much more than geodesy: Nicastro delivers the deeply human story of a multitalented genius whose tenure as the head of Alexandria's famed library occasioned remarkable achievements in literature, history, linguistics, and philosophy despite the political turmoil that periodically rocked the Ptolemaic world. Indeed, this polymath plays out his long career against a colorful backdrop peopled with a rich variety of conquerors and cosmologists, murderers and mathematicians. A distant yesterday still furnishes fascinating drama for readers today."

--Bryce Christensen, *Booklist*

"Propelled by the story of Eratosthenes's solution of an ancient puzzle-- how big is the earth? -- *Circumference* offers many unexpected pleasures along the way. With an amiable voice and a flowing style, Nicholas Nicastro brings historical places and people to vivid new life, from the shining city of Alexandria to the great conqueror for whom it was named. A real treat for lovers of history and science.

--Steven Strogatz, author of *Sync: How Order Emerges from Chaos in the Universe, Nature, and Daily Life*, and Schurman Professor of Applied Mathematics, Cornell University

"Given the paucity of material in English on Eratosthenes, anything is a welcome addition, but this book is much better than nothing. In its pages, historians of science will learn much about the ancient world, and historians of the ancient world will learn much about science."

--*Bryn Mawr Classical Review*

On *Antigone's Wake: A Novel of Imperial Athens*:

"Nicastro is an author who clearly relishes his subject. Each sentence bursts with juicy, nurturing historical detail and considered thought about the hopes, aspirations, ideals and troubles of those who lived in the distant past. We follow the triumphs and travails of Sophocles as he struggles to create his art and also be what Athens wants him to be—a brilliant general. Athens as a great civilisation is constructed in front of our eyes. Nicastro brings to life both the back-streets of the city and the sea-battle-lanes of its Empire. The towering giants of Western history, Sophocles, Euripides, Pericles—and his consort Aspasia—are, through his vivid imagination, given a voice. This book allows the reader to inhabit the Golden Age of Athens, and to taste its grit as well as its glory."

--Bettany Hughes, broadcaster and author of *Helen of Troy*: *Goddess, Princess, Whore*

On *The Isle of Stone: A Novel of Ancient Sparta*:

"With *The Isle of Stone*, Nicholas Nicastro joins the illustrious pedigree of Mary Renault, Valerio Massimo Manfredi and Steven Pressfield with great style and enormous panache. His hero's checkered life story is used to frame a dark and darkening history of Sparta between a hugely destructive natural disaster, a great earthquake in 464 BC, and a self-inflicted, man-made debacle during the prolonged and even more destructive Peloponnesian War. Nicastro knows his ancient sources intimately, but also has the born novelist's instinct to flesh out their bare bones all too plausibly. Nicastro's antiheroes of the isle of Sphacteria are the dark side of Pressfield's heroes in *Gates of Fire*: both demand and repay the attention of all lovers of expert historical fiction."

--Paul Cartledge, Professor of Greek History, University of Cambridge, and author of *Alexander the Great: The Hunt for a New Past*

"From its explosive first pages, *The Isle of Stone* draws you into the gritty reality of Sparta during the Peloponnesian War. Nicastro writes powerful prose, but this is no exercise in debunking. With drama, passion, and a sure touch for the facts, Nicastro reveals the heroism behind the humiliation of the shocking day when some of Sparta's unconquerable soldiers surrendered. His images of life and death under the Mediterranean sun hit you like the glare of a polished shield."

--Barry Strauss, author of *The Battle of Salamis: The Naval Encounter that Saved Greece - and Western Civilization* and Professor of History and Classics, Cornell University

"Reading one of Nicastro's books has the same fascination as staring at a terrible car crash. The scenes he constructs force us to grapple with the disturbing roots of our own cultural assumptions. Each of these characters spins into a series of bloody events far beyond individual control. Nicastro lays naked the complex web of collective motivations that shape the events of history. *The Isle of Stone* shows Nicastro's intimate understanding of this distant time and deeply foreign culture. By giving human faces to the dry bones of ancient battles, he goes a long way towards making ancient motivations somehow explicable. Once again, Nicastro proves his talent for capturing the attitude of historical times while spinning a passionate drama."

--Pamela Goddard, *Ithaca Times*

On *Empire of Ashes: A Novel of Alexander the Great*:

"*Empire of Ashes* is great historical fiction. Nicholas Nicastro paints an entirely believable portrait of the world of Alexander the Great, with the period detail and nuance that gives the reader a true feel for the time period. Even better, he resists simply regurgitating our common understanding of Alexander, and instead presents an unexpected and at times startling picture of a hero we thought we knew, but perhaps did not. *Empire of Ashes* is both fast-paced and scholarly, a difficult combination to achieve, but Nicastro succeeds beautifully."

—James L. Nelson, author of *The Only Life That Mattered* and *The Revolution at Sea* saga

"*Empire of Ashes* is a great read. I loved the style and thought the framing device of the court case was fascinating and gripping. The sights, sounds and social life of ancient Athens came to life for me in a way that few historical novels seem to manage. The characters were carefully and convincingly created and forced me to make various judgements about them, and then revise them, just as real people do. The action scenes were great too. Grim and gritty and vividly brought to life. All in all a great achievement..."

—Simon Scarrow, author of *The Eagle and the Wolves* and *The Eagle's Conquest*

"Nicastro describes life in ancient Athens with a vividness that leaps from the page...I was charmed by the notion of a teenaged Alexander with greasy hair and acne - an image characteristic of Nicastro's humanizing approach. He avoids both apologetics and exaggerated sensationalism, making *Empire of Ashes* one of the best recent novels on the conqueror."

--Jeanne Reames, *Amphora*

"*Empire of Ashes* manages to be many things at the same time. The book is a grand historical epic combined with a court-room drama and political intrigue. Believable characters rise off the page in clear, evocative language. Nicastro has a talent for capturing the attitude and motivations of historical times, and creating stories which tell us something about our current time and situation. The result is a captivating and compelling page-turner."

—Pamela Goddard, *Ithaca Times*

On *The Eighteenth Captain: The John Paul Jones Trilogy* **v. 1:**

"Nicastro takes you by the scruff of your neck and yanks you into the action of history. From the moment the spine is creased, you are there, on board the ship, like Jim Hawkins in the apple barrel listening to Long John Silver's most secret plan. . . . Kudos to Nicholas Nicastro and even more kudos to McBooks Press for adding this finely wrought novel to their armada of Maritime literature!"

—Eric Machan Howd, *Ithaca Times*

"This maritime historical novel fairly shimmers with furtive lustiness and wry humor. Embellishing John Paul Jones' early naval intrigues and sexual liasons, Nicholas Nicastro preserves the true spirit of a mercurial and moody hero."

—Jill B. Gidmark *University of Minnesota Professor of English*

“In *The Eighteenth Captain,* Nicholas Nicastro gives us a nuanced, insightful and thoroughly believable portrait of an American hero that few know beyond his saying "I have not yet begun to fight" which, in fact, he probably did not say. Nicastro does what the artist can do and the historian cannot; probe the inner mind of the historical John Paul Jones, guess who he really was from the empirical evidence, and then present that portrait in words and deeds that are on the one hand often fiction, but on the other true to the spirit of Jones. And he does it very well, showing us our American Tragic Hero, great but flawed, a conqueror brought down by his own faults. *The Eighteenth Captain* is beautifully framed by the fall-out of the French Revolution which represented the end of much that Jones loved but was a consequence in part of Jones' own actions, a lovely metaphor for the man's life and deeds. Carefully researched, accurate in tone and detail, *The Eighteenth Captain* is an insightful portrait of a man, a hero and his times, and what each of those things, in their essence, truly mean."

—James L. Nelson, author of the *Revolution at Sea* Saga

Ella Maud

Other Books by Nicholas Nicastro

Novels

The Eighteenth Captain
Between Two Fires
Empire of Ashes
The Isle of Stone
Antigone's Wake
The Passion of the Ripper
Hell's Half-Acre

Non-Fiction

Circumference: Eratosthenes and the Ancient Quest to Measure the Globe

Ella Maud

a novel
by

Nicholas Nicastro

Based on a true story.

Kinder Shore Books

Dedicated to Robert A. Thiel

for showing me all the tricks

Too much of water hast thou, poor Ophelia,
And therefore I forbid my tears...
—*Hamlet,* Act IV, Scene VII

Prologue

People wondered how Ollie spent her days. She knew this because, on the few occasions when she went out, she could hear them whispering:

"There's old Olive Cropsey. You know, the sister of poor darling Nell. Haven't seen much of her lately. Still unmarried, I hear. What *does* she do with her days?"

They called her "old", and she did not disagree. She was born in the year of Our Lord 1880. Her life, in the sense most people would call a 'life', ended on November 20, 1901. That was the night her sister left this world.

Everything since had been a kind of afterlife—a perfunctory addendum, unsought and unsavored. She rarely allowed herself the little gratifications of adult womanhood. She wore only the black crepe of first mourning, even on the long days she spent alone. There would never be a second or ordinary mourning for her. There was no color other than black, and she bought new clothes only when the previous wore out, or turned gray from hundreds of launderings. She had not changed her hair since the McKinley Administration, and it too had turned gray. She called on no one, and others had learned never to call on her.

When the milkman's son came to deliver bottles, he ran to and from her door, keeping his head down lest he catch a glimpse of the dark figure that haunted the parlor.

"The poor thing. She blames herself for everything that happened," people whispered. "A word from her, and maybe Nell would never have been alone on the porch that night with Jim Wilcox. She never would have ended up in that river! Can you imagine living with that?"

Ollie could not imagine living with that, because her inaction that one night wasn't close to the sum of her torment. Instead, she trod an ocean of regrets, was filled and suffocated by them. She dwelled on them as she buttered her toast in the morning—the things she'd said to Nell. The horrible, horrible things. They occupied the spaces between every tick of the clock. The smut of remorse adhered to her saucepans. Her regrets were the last things she thought about when she parted the bedclothes at night, and slipped her weary body between them.

It had been different once. The Cropsey girls were handsome, but also of modest means, which placed them in the position of being both resented and pitied. Once, Ollie responded with a furious kind of invention, constantly working to set herself apart. She always experimented with some accessory or another—some embroidery for her collar, or a bit of ribbon for her hair, or a shiny bauble to sew on her blouse. She took it as a personal failure to appear in public in the same exact outfit twice. One time when she and Nell were walking by the river, Ollie found a fishing lure that was so colorfully tied that she thought about sewing it into a hat.

"And if you're in the street and the fisherman recognizes his handiwork?" Nell posed.

"I would thank him for his compliment, and pass on!" replied Ollie.

"Yes, I believe you would."

Nell went to the other extreme: instead of adding more, she stripped all artifice from her appearance, all sign of useless ornament. She kept her colors simple, her lines straight. If she wore any jewelry, it was the best she could find, or nothing. No glass or stone was set in competition with her eyes, which showed violet during the day and split the spectrum under lamplight, as if fashioned from shards of broken crystal. To the judgement of her 'betters', she presented singularity.

Such memories were Ollie's legacy. They bubbled up at odd moments, as when she strained her tea, or dipped her hands in the washbasin. Memories and regrets with uncanny buoyancy—such as for poor Roy Crawford, who had been there the night Nell disappeared. Lord, to think of him! He shot himself in the temple in 1908. Poor hapless Roy, who had come to see Ollie, and had been courting her for months. But their relationship was a slight thing, based more on convenience than any true fondness, and it died in the aftermath, in the white-hot glare of attention he neither sought nor understood.

Her little brother Will followed; five years later, he poisoned himself with carbolic acid. It was an act as incomprehensible to her as it was heartbreaking, for Will was blameless. He was just a child when Nell was lost. In truth, his death had nothing to do with his lamented sister, but sprung from the branch of his own despair. Ollie could barely conjure an image of the adult Will, broken and frustrated by the downward arc of his life. Instead, she remembered him as a boy, delightedly grinning as he tore up his father's plantings with his scooter.

Ollie buried her father last week. He was put to rest at Hollywood Cemetery, and the funeral was the first time in years Ollie felt like removing her mourning clothes. Onlookers wondered—why had the family chosen to bury him there, all by himself, when the rest of the Cropseys lay in Highland? Why had he not been taken back to Brooklyn, to rest beside his beloved Nell? The thought of William Cropsey spending eternity near her sister filled Ollie with disgust. The onlookers wondered, but only she knew the truth, and would go on hiding it behind the drawn curtains of her parlor, and in her silence. *Video et taceo*—I see, and I am silent.

She had regrets, but not about letting her sister out on that porch in 1901. Nothing would have stopped Nell from doing so, if that was what she wanted. As it clearly was.

On fall days, when the sun stopped shining on the side of the house, she ventured out to trim the roses that ran along the trellis. She went out in her black weeds, in a black straw hat and gloves so old they lacked fingers. She worked carelessly, not caring if the thorns cut her. Sometimes she glanced between the trees at the neighboring property, and saw the boys playing there. They were pretend-drilling, like soldiers, with rifles carved from wood. Indeed, Ollie heard there was another war coming. There had been one a few years earlier, she seemed to recall, but it was over too fast for it to impinge on her thoughts. She didn't read the newspapers anymore. She had a bellyful of newspapers and their lies.

The milkman's son was on the porch. He fumbled with the box, and Ollie peered around the corner at him. Their eyes met, and she offered him a smile. It was a craggy, stiff thing, like a reptile poised to bite. To this gesture, and her appearance outside her house, he gaped in terror, and fled back to his father's truck.

"Smart boy," she said aloud, and sucked her bloodied fingers.

The Foyer

I asked myself— "Of all melancholy topics what, according to the universal understanding of mankind, is the most melancholy?" Death, was the obvious reply. "And when," I said, "is this most melancholy of topics most poetical?" From what I have already explained at some length the answer here also is obvious— "When it most closely allies itself to Beauty: the death then of a beautiful woman is unquestionably the most poetical topic in the world, and equally is it beyond doubt that the lips best suited for such topic are those of a bereaved lover."

— Edgar Allan Poe
"The Philosophy of Composition"

I.

"Papa, Nell is not here!"

Ollie stood at the top of the stairs, looking down at her father as she held the front of her dressing gown together. William Cropsey, who bothered with no such delicacy, stared up at her with eyes bleary and uncomprehending. He had just returned from a long sit in the privy.

"Nell is where?" he asked.

"She's not in her bed."

Cropsey checked the clock at the foot of the stairs. It was Thursday morning, it was chilly, and it was before dawn.

"Well, where is she?" he snapped.

"Last I saw, on the porch with Jim Wilcox."

Cropsey went to the front hallway. By the light of his finger lamp, he found the front door standing wide open and the screen door unlatched and wavering in the breeze. He almost tripped over an object—a parasol, it turned out—left on the floor.

He went out on the porch. The lamp's uncertain beams searched only as far as the empty porch, and a little beyond into the faint glow of the quarter moon. Further away, across the river, a few lights dipped their trails into the water. It was the kind of quiet that came in the late autumn, when the frost had killed the insects, and most of the leaves were down from the trees.

"Nell! Nell Cropsey!" he called.

Nothing answered but his own echo. He snuffed the flame, letting his eyes adjust to the deeper gloom. Now he could see the stretch of lawn in front of his house, and the scooter his son Will had left on it. But there was no sign of Nell.

"What's going on?"

Cropsey's brother Henry was at the door, tails of his nightshirt hanging.

"Nell hasn't come home," he replied. "and she's probably with that scamp Jim Wilcox..."

"Okay," said the other.

"...but we should probably check around here first."

"I'll get some drawers. And you should too."

They stooped and peered under the porch. Around back, they checked the privy and the root cellar. They peeped into the little shed Cropsey used as a storeroom and workshop.

When he came back to the front of the house he found his wife Mary. Ollie was clinging to her.

"Did you find her?"

"Does it look like I did?" he snapped. "Olive, are you sure you didn't see or hear from her since Wilcox left?"

"She came out with him before midnight. I never saw her come back."

It was too dark to make out his daughter's face. Yet Cropsey heard something in her voice—a brief hesitation, an evasive tremor.

He recognized it from the times she was a child and lied about eating an entire pie her mother had left warming on the stove, or bent the truth to cover for one of her brothers. He was about to press the matter when Henry interjected, "Best check the summer house."

They proceeded to the banks of the Pasquotank. There was no one in the summerhouse, and no sign anyone had been inside. Cropsey walked out on the dock. The river was calm, and blacker than the night above it. He was not one to ascribe human qualities to inanimate objects, but the degree of the river's obscurity now, like volcanic glass, struck him as malevolent.

"We're going to need to see Jim Wilcox."

The Wilcox place was about a mile away, on Shepard Street. They pounded on the door a good long time before a flicker of light appeared within, and the door cracked open.

"Yes?" asked the disheveled woman.

"Is Jim at home, Martha?" asked Cropsey.

"I think so. Why?"

Though the street was empty, Cropsey was loath to speak the words aloud—that he couldn't locate his daughter at such a delicate hour.

"May we come in?"

Within, Mrs. Wilcox offered them coffee. Cropsey declined, but Henry was about to accept, until his brother jabbed him in the ribs.

"We need to ask your son about Nell," he said.

Her brows flew up. "I see. Is she all right?"

"May we speak to him, please?"

She left them in the dark as she took the lamp upstairs. The brothers stood in the kitchen by moonlight, listening. They heard her open the bedroom door, and call Jim's name. After that her voice was lower, and all they could hear was an indistinct murmuring. Cropsey wanted to launch himself up those steps, to pull that boy out of his comfort and throttle the truth out of him. Had he ruined his beautiful daughter? Had he left her in such a state that she would do something desperate? As the torrent of thoughts tore through his mind, he grew agitated, scarcely able to stand still. He stepped to the window, forcing himself to be interested in the view of the empty street. He believed it would dip below freezing that night; he would have to see to the pigs' water trough before he went to bed. Cracked troughs cost money, he fretted. And he perceived the absurdity of worrying now, of all times, about such an inconsequential thing.

Martha Wilcox descended. She said nothing until she was directly before them, as if bearing a secret.

"He says he left her on your front porch," she said.

"When? In what state?"

"I'm sorry, Bill, but that's all I could get out of him. He works hard during the day."

"It sure would go easier if he'd talk to me now."

"I don't know what to say. He's a grown man. He makes his own decisions."

Ollie did not help her father and uncle look for her sister. Instead, she took to the parlor with cousin Carrie and her mother as they waited for the men to return with Jim Wilcox. Mary Cropsey, *née* Ryder, was beside herself with worry over the virtue of her sweet Nell, who was always the most popular of her daughters among the boys. Pretty Nell, with her fine features and blue eyes that danced. Nell whose hair was a curly, lustrous brown, like Mary's before her forty-two years and nine pregnancies. All her grown daughters —

Ollie, Louise and Lettie – perceived that Nell was their mother's favorite, and in their love for their tender, mercurial sister, did not mind. Cousin Carrie, who visited frequently when she was not at school up north, likewise bore witness to how popular she was among the boys, and could do nothing other than smile.

Olive Cropsey, known to all as Ollie, was only a couple of years Nell's senior but seemed older. Where Nell was small and lively, like a coiled spring of nubile energy, Ollie was longer, thinner, steadier, like an illustration in a dress catalog. She was widely regarded as attractive, but made a mature impression, embodying an ideal of womanhood that was already a decade past. Younger gentlemen dreamt of Nell, but older ones envisioned Ollie as a wife. Traveling salesmen mistook her for the matron of the house, and Mary Cropsey leaned on her in times of need. She was sitting just then on her mother's right, grasping her hand, interleaving her fingers and squeezing them.

The men returned after the clock struck three a.m. Along with Cropsey and Uncle Hen, Jim Wilcox was ushered within by Chief of Police Bill Dawson. Their faces were flushed, for it had indeed dropped below freezing that night.

"Had to get the law to drag him out of bed," Cropsey said.

"Jim, for the Lord's sake, where is Nell?" cried Mary.

"Mrs. Cropsey, I left her on the porch. We were out there only a few minutes. I gave her some of her things back, and she was crying. I had to meet Leo Owens before the saloons closed, so I left. You can ask him where I was at 11:30. On the life of my mother, I don't know what Nell did after."

"Did she walk to the gate with you?" asked Dawson.

"No."

"You say she was crying. Did she ever speak of...doing harm to herself?"

Mary Cropsey gasped at the articulation of this thought, and buried her face in Ollie's shoulder.

"Not in any serious way," replied Wilcox.

"How's that?"

Jim looked straight to Ollie. "Her sister was there. And Carrie, too. It was more than a month ago. We were sitting here talking about how we'd like to see ourselves end, if we took it in our minds to do so. Nell said she'd rather freeze than anything else."

"I remember that," said Carrie. She hastened to add, "But none of us took it seriously."

"That's a damn strange thing to be talking about with your girl," Cropsey snapped. He had been noosing up Wilcox with his eyes since they had entered the room. He made no secret that he'd disliked Jim Wilcox from the moment they met, and had never warmed to him during his long courtship of Nell.

"Is that true, Miss Olive?"

Ollie frowned. "Yes. But it's ridiculous to think my sister would ever...do that, on account of someone like Jim. I just can't believe that. No offense, Jim."

"Did you hear her crying?"

"I heard nothing from the time they went out."

"Hurt herself over me? She barely breathed a word to me for two weeks," Jim said. "That's why I returned her pictures. And the umbrella."

Cropsey glanced at Ollie at the mention of the parasol. She avoided his gaze.

"We're wasting time," she said.

"One more question, Jim," said Dawson. "Why didn't you see Nell inside, instead of just leaving her there, in such a state?"

"I told her to go inside because it was cold. She said, 'I don't care.' She wouldn't have listened to me then if I told her to get out of the rain."

"That's not an answer."

"Don't you think I would have seen her in, if I knew I'd be standing here now?"

This was the first thing he said that smacked of any common compassion. Mary Cropsey implored him with her eyes, while Ollie and Carrie stared as if seeing him for the first time. For there was something cold about Jim Wilcox that night.

Wilcox was indeed not himself: he was disgusted by the stink of accusation in the room. Had he not known all of them for the three and a half years he had courted Nell? Was he not a fixture in their house on Sundays, Tuesdays and Thursdays? How could they believe he would stand by and let anything happen to his girl?

Cropsey, Henry and Dawson resumed scouring the riverbank, this time with electric torches. It did not escape notice that Jim didn't move a muscle to help. It seemed to Ollie that he was trapped in some kind of terrible anticipation, as if he feared Nell had disappeared just to get him in trouble. He sat in the armchair beside the hearth, slouching and fidgeting exactly as he had hours before, when he had called on Nell and not exchanged a word with her. Nell had been cruel, pointedly ignoring him. Ollie had convinced Nell this was necessary: if she was ever to get rid of a man the likes of Jim Wilcox, she would need to be rude to him. And she was, in that perverse way of hers. Nell's mood was light, verging on giddy, as she plunged blades of indifference into him. Ollie almost felt sorry for him...then.

"Why didn't you get up when Papa came the first time?" she asked.

He started at the sound of her voice. Then he resumed fidgeting with the sleeve of the armchair.

"I wasn't awake. I barely remember what my mother asked me."

The Cropsey house was still in a furor at the first gleam of dawn. Every lamp in the house was lit. The younger children — William Jr., Fred, William Douglas and May –- had been roused, set to search the surrounding fields and outbuildings. Mary Cropsey passed from panic to a kind of inert shock; gently, with some trouble, Ollie managed to coax her up to her bedroom and under the bedclothes. Her mother stared into the ceiling, gibbering indistinctly, until simple exhaustion overtook her.

Ollie met her father on the landing. His pant legs were wet from wading into the river, his arms flecked with dirt from beating the reeds. He held the parasol he had almost tripped over in the hall. From her figure, he could easily distinguish Ollie in the dark —she was half a head taller than Nell, and towered higher from the way she piled her hair on her head, Gibson Girl-style. Unlike with her sister, Cropsey had never felt much of an urgency to protect her.

Father and daughter paused three feet apart, inspecting each other's eyes.

"Tell me," he said. "Now."

Ollie's gaze dropped to the floor.

"Come, then."

She led him to the bedroom in the back of the house the sisters shared. She could hear him breathing behind her—shallow with alarm—as she removed the key from between her breasts, and unlocked the door.

Being on the west side of the house, that room was still enveloped in pre-dawn gloom. Ollie led her father to the bed, to the human-sized mass under the blankets. She paused before pulling the covers aside, looking to him again, as if giving him a last chance to avoid the journey they were about to embark upon. His expression did not change.

She pulled down the blanket to reveal Nell's face. Cropsey's breathing stopped as he looked down on his daughter, who was too still to be merely asleep. Though it was dark, he could make out a black substance flowing from her left ear, down the gentle inflection of her neck, to pool on the sheets.

It was only then, for the first time that dismal night, that Ollie Cropsey bowed her head to weep.

II.

The same day Nell Cropsey disappeared, the Raleigh *News and Observer* reported the strange death of a sixty-five-year-old black man. Frank Jones was discovered lying face down in a small stream off West Street. As his fingers were curled into the muddy bottom, it was ventured that Jones "struggled when strangulation came on." The authorities concluded that he must have stumbled into the branch and drowned. Oddly, he died in a section of the stream that was only four inches deep. No further investigation of the incident was thought warranted, and nothing more about it appeared in the Raleigh papers.

The same day, the coroner's report came in regarding the death of one John W. Scott. Scott, "a young club and society man", had been discovered viciously beaten in a doorway in the west end of town, and died without regaining consciousness. The physicians concluded that he had been attacked "by a weapon in the hands of some person unknown". Though the newspaper reported that the affair "is exciting the greatest interest", nothing else was published about it, and the incident was quickly forgotten.

More outlandish, the *News and Observer* recounted the miraculous resurrection of James Wynn of Oxford, Alabama. Wynn had been pronounced dead more than forty-eight hours before his funeral. As he was about to be lowered to his eternal rest, "unwonted sounds" were heard from inside his coffin. The lid was opened, and the assembled mourners bore witness as the dead man's body "was seen to move." The casket was "hurried back to the home of Wynn, where he revived and is now under treatment." This incident—and hair's-breadth by which a man had escaped being buried alive—astounded all who heard it. Yet no investigation of the competence of the attending physician, nor those who prepared his "corpse" for burial, was reported.

By contrast, the vanishing of Nell Cropsey ignited a firestorm of interest that refused to die. Nell, after all, was reported to be a "beautiful girl", "winsome", "handsome", "the pet of her home", with "sweet, lively features" and—importantly—of "unsullied" character. Word of her disappearance flashed through the town. By noon on the 21st she was the first topic of conversation around work benches, across lunch counters, and over the bars of a dozen local saloons. "A right-looking girl, that Nell," folks said, and not just the men. "Saw her outside the Methodist chapel the other week, and she was almost worth a Sunday morning in church. Almost!" (Wink, wink). "She was at the racetrack last month with her sisters, dressed real fine," said someone else. "My brother the milliner waited on her," said a third, "and there was not a hat in the shop that looked bad on her head!"

At first, conversation settled on the beauty of Nell Cropsey, not her disappearance. She had, after all, been gone fewer than twelve hours. The mere fact that she was missing hardly proved the worst; it was not unheard of for young women to vanish from small towns in eastern Carolina. Some eloped. Some absconded with their boyfriends under less reputable circumstances. Some simply left abusive or unfulfilling lives with their families, seeking work in the big industrial cities. Everyone knew the story of Jenny Lattimer, a girl of eighteen who had disappeared from her parents' home on Pool Street in '99. The mother and father insisted on foul play; woods were swept, wells checked, properties in the Negro section of town ransacked—seldom with the occupants' assent.

Her fate stood as a mystery until a month later, when Chief of Police W.C. Dawson took a pleasure trip to Chicago. He went to Marshall Fields' with his wife. There, to his astonishment, he found Jenny Lattimer. She was in the store's uniform of white shirtwaist and black skirt, wrapping packages for customers. "Well hello there, Chief Dawson!" she chirped. "How is every one in Betsy Town?"

The story could have served a cautionary purpose—and would have, if Nell Cropsey had not been so much prettier than Jenny Lattimer. As noon chimed from the churches, scuttlebutt took a darker turn.

"Lucky bastard, that boyfriend!"

"You mean Jim Wilcox? He reported for work this morning at Tom Hayman's."

"Is that a fact? So where'd she go, if not with him?"

"Somebody should ask Wilcox. He always seemed shifty to me."

William Cropsey agreed that 'somebody should ask Wilcox'. Before Nell had been gone for half a day, he asked the judge to swear out a warrant for his arrest. Deputy Charles Reid fetched Wilcox right off the floor of his workplace at Hayman's. Though removed from the premises in plain sight of his co-workers and his boss, Jim cooperated without complaint. At the Chief's office, he recounted his story of the night before to Dawson, Mayor Tully Wilson, and (again) to the girl's father. There were no inconsistencies: he sat with Nell, Ollie and Roy Crawford for most of the evening, and asked to speak with Nell on the porch around eleven. Sometime during their conversation she became emotional. Jim left around 11:15, to meet some friends in town. He met Len Owens at 11:30, near the Ives place up Riverside Avenue. He was home soon after, and heard nothing from or about Nell Cropsey until hours later, when her father and uncle pounded at his mother's door.

"Can you say for a fact that she didn't follow you?" asked Reid.

"I can say for a fact I left her on the porch. What she did after that I can't speak to."

"What's that supposed to mean?" growled Cropsey.

"Nothing."

"My daughter did not harm herself. She would not."

"All right," said Dawson. "I want you to tell it again, Jim. Start at the beginning."

With a pinched expression that, for the first time, betokened some annoyance, Wilcox told his story again. Again, there were no inconsistencies.

"I'm asking you for the last time, Jim. Where's Nell?" Cropsey demanded.

"And I'm telling you again, sir—I don't know."

Fifteen minutes later Wilcox was released on condition of not leaving the county. Since a crowd had gathered in front of the Mayor's office, it was thought better to escort him out the back. William Cropsey, however, strode right through the throng, which was mostly composed of Elizabeth City's male, well-lubricated citizenry.

"Where's the girl, Bill?" someone asked.

"I don't know," said Cropsey, "but somebody does, and he's not telling."

"Is it Jim Wilcox who did it, Bill?"

"Somebody knows something," he said, and climbed into his buggy.

Though Nell had only been gone less than a day, Chief Dawson believed it was time for extraordinary measures. He sent a telegram to the town of Suffolk, Virginia, thirty miles away on the other side of the Great Dismal Swamp. There resided one "Hurricane" Branch. This was a man who had carved for himself a wide reputation as a detective and bounty hunter, and who made his prize bloodhounds available for manhunting purposes. His dogs, Sampson and Tiger, were not just good at following the scents of fugitives: in June of 1900, during a demonstration exercise, the 100-pound animals treed and almost killed their test subjects. As they were pulled away, the dogs turned on a bystander.

They had, however, proven their worth in—among other cases—the search for the escaped killers Walter Cotton and John Sears. Dawson was pleased to receive an almost instant response from Branch, who offered to come down by train the next day. He sent a boy over to Riverside Avenue to inform William Cropsey of the good news. To this, Cropsey made no response.

Branch and his bloodhounds showed up at the Cropsey home mid-day on the 22nd. It was one and a half days since Nell had disappeared. Branch came with Chief Dawson, Deputy Reid, and a straggling line of onlookers who had noticed the big animals being led down Riverside Avenue, and decided to have a look.

Hurricane Branch himself was not nearly as prepossessing as his nickname. Dressed in checked shirt and wool pants with suspenders, under a slouch hat, he looked like every other backwoods hunter or trapper seen in the Great Dismal. Sampson and Tiger did not lead him, but trotted calmly at his side, giving only cursory sniffs toward the air and ground. When Cropsey came out on the porch to greet them, the dogs sat on the sides of their haunches and tried to yawn through their muzzles.

It was a clear, sunny day, with the temperature warming into the fifties. William Cropsey came onto the porch in his shirt-sleeves, his napkin still in his collar from lunch. Only his son Douglas—held from school due to unfortunate events—came out with him. His eyes were glued to the lazy but fascinating beasts in his front yard. Ollie and his other sisters waited in the sitting room, expectant but also appalled that the search had so soon come to this. Their mother sat in the turret above, where she had lately installed herself, to keep vigil over the wide, indifferent river.

"Sorry to have to ask, but I'll need something that belonged to her," said Branch, in the soft tones he adopted for bereaved relatives. "Socks or some article of clothing."

Douglas went inside to fulfill this request. Cropsey pulled the napkin from his shirt, wiped his mouth, and pointed with his chin.

"Hope your dogs don't get stage fright."

Branch looked to the swelling crowd that had gathered on the road. A line of men stretched down Riverside Avenue into town, hands in pockets, cigarettes in mouths. A few boats had also anchored in the river opposite. Nothing had happened yet, but the promise of *something* beat the usual lunchtime lull. If that included a glimpse of a lovely girl's body, so much the better.

Branch was provided with a pair of Nell's stockings and her usual walking shoes—she had worn only slippers the night she disappeared. The dogs perked up the instant they saw these articles. As if in anticipation of his afternoon of work, Sampson lifted his leg and pissed on the porch steps. Cropsey looked afflicted by this, but said nothing.

Branch removed the hounds' muzzles. After burying their noses in the stockings and shoes, the animals' excitement mounted. Branch shouted "Whereaway!", and the dogs, thus released, whirled and sniffed their way down the front path, snouts sweeping, pendulous ears raking the ground. They barged forward as onlookers jumped aside, and Branch followed with a tight lead, giving them constant, inarticulate encouragement.

The dogs went to the center of the road, then began to turn in circles as if needing to regain the scent. From there they struck west, across the kitchen garden, shouldering the bean-poles aside. After proceeding fifty yards in that direction, they made a hard right, straight toward the river. The crowd buzzed and Mrs. Cropsey, with dread, rose from her chair in the turret. The hounds crossed the road and mounted the first pier on the river northwest of the Cropsey home—the one owned by Fearing's Marine Railway. Without the slightest deviation, they snorted their way down the pier, straight to the end. At the water, they sniffed the air, whined, and stared back at their master.

Branch came back to Cropsey on the porch. The latter was in a chair, face set skeptically. "You know that she went out on that pier almost every day, right?" he said.

"The dogs must follow the strongest scent," ventured Dawson.

"I don't doubt it."

The exercise was repeated, with the same results. The crowd dissolved into knots of men having the same argument. Was she abducted by boat? Or could she really have thrown herself into the river? Over the likes of Jim Wilcox? And for the first time, the public mood shifted from titillation to suspicion. Not a few asked whether there was an article of Wilcox's clothing available, to see if he had accompanied—or dragged—the girl to the end of that pier.

"Suppose you expect to get paid," Cropsey said.

"I will be, but it's not for you to worry about," replied Branch. Then he added, "I am sorry for your loss."

When Cropsey went inside he found his daughters Lettie and May had gone upstairs to comfort their mother. Mrs. Cropsey had taken it badly when she saw the hounds sniff the end of the pier. Only Ollie was left in the sitting room, with a handkerchief in her hands, fidgeting with the folds. She met her father's eyes as he looked in from the hall. Neither spoke, until Cropsey muttered "Tarnation waste of time", and went upstairs.

He found Mrs. Cropsey, Lettie and May standing at the foot of the stairs to the third floor turret. His wife—bleary-eyed from hours of staring into the distance— declared, "I don't care where those dogs tracked her, William. She wouldn't have drowned herself."

She used the formal "William" when she wanted to convey the gravity of her thoughts. He replied, "I saw her on that pier just the day before. There may be no fresh trail from the porch."

He turned away and shut the bedroom door behind him.

III.

The following day, a gathering was called of all citizens concerned about the disappearance of Nell Cropsey. Interest was so high that none of the town's churches was big enough to host the meeting. It was held instead at the Academy of Music, a theatrical venue that had been erected since the arrival of the railroad and the touring companies of performers the trains brought. The hall shared a stolid brick building that thrust its cornices over the intersection of Main & Poindexter streets. Downstairs was the Bee Hive department store, with its vitrines and floor displays and mannequins; upstairs, the Academy presented its slate of comedians and painted dancers and poetic declaimers. It was a grand space, the best in the region. The theatre's owners proclaimed that any sort of entertainment either had already been featured at the Academy, or soon would be. But no program quite like that of November 23, 1901 had ever been seen there before.

By the time the meeting was called to order, it was standing room only in the auditorium. The attendees—packed elbow to elbow— were almost exclusively male. The room's capacity was seven hundred, which worked out to a third of the adult men of the entire town. But it felt like there were more than seven hundred crowded into the place. The fire marshal looked down from the proscenium stage, and frowned.

When the town's steeples chimed seven, the thick form of Mayor and Justice of the Peace Tully B. Wilson appeared. Gazing over the assembled, he recognized faces from all the major professions of the burgeoning town. In the front row, some of the leading citizens, including the transplanted northerners Greenleaf, Turner and Winder. To his right, seated together, the pastoral contingent of the town, including the Rev. Dr. Lewelyn of the Episcopal Church, Tuttle of the Methodist, Ferrebee and Dunke of the Baptists, and their entourages of deacons, choristers, and organists. Behind them, sawyers and lumbermen from the logging camps in the Great Dismal; boatmen and dredgers of the oyster beds of the Pasquotank; the shipwrights and pilots and fishermen and ferrymen and all the others who kept the commerce of the waves, and the railroad men who kept it on the line of steel that snaked down from Norfolk. And, of course, there were the working men from downtown—the grocers, fruiterers, dry-goodsmen, bankers, stationers, druggists, clothiers, butchers, florists, milliners, bakers, cigar salesmen, upholsterers. Wilson had made his business to know all of them in his various campaigns for office.

It seemed everyone was there. All, with the exception of the prime suspect, Jim Wilcox, and the girl's father, William Cropsey.

"We might as well start," the Mayor said. And then he repeated it louder, until the room settled. "The purpose of this meeting is to inform you all on the progress of the investigation, and to organize the basis for further action. You probably all know the story. Ella Maud Cropsey is the daughter of William Cropsey of Riverside Ave. She is nineteen. She disappeared from her front porch last Wednesday night or early Thursday. The police have made inquiries all over town and in the surrounding counties. More than one hundred residences have been searched in this city alone. The last person to see her, Jim Wilcox, has been interviewed twice by Bill Dawson and Charlie Reid. He professes to know nothing of her fate..."

At the mention of Wilcox, a murmur went through the crowd.

"That she would have harmed herself has been dismissed by everyone who knew her. She is a happy, vivacious, innocent young woman. She lived in the bosom of a large family, and was popular with her friends and acquaintances in the Methodist congregation..." He nodded in the direction of Rev. Tuttle, who nodded back. "If you're anything like me, you are repulsed at the notion that a young girl like Miss Ella Maud could simply disappear off the face of the earth. If there is any function to the instrument of civilization, it is that the most vulnerable among us may live without fear of violence. For if that degree of basic safety is not assured, why should we bother with the contrivances of police and jails at all? Why not let us all descend to a state of barbarism?"

Voices rose in reply: "*No!*"—a resolute *no* to criminality, fear, and barbarism.

"At this juncture," the Mayor continued, "we must acknowledge that the needs of this investigation may exceed the resources of our peace officers. That said, and with the approval of Mr. Cropsey, I hereby call upon this community to form a special Citizens' Committee, for the purpose of ascertaining the fate of Miss Ella. The writ of this body would be to pursue whatever avenues necessary to get to the bottom of this mystery, without regard to privilege, party, or faction. And so, let the assembled show they stand in favor by a show of hands..."

Seven hundred arms shot into the air.

"Those opposed?"

Only two arms rose, but they were significant ones: those of Bill Dawson, Chief of Police, and his deputy Charlie Reid.

"The motion passes," Wilson pronounced. "And now the floor is open to nominations to this here Citizen's Committee."

The voting resulted in the installation of several local luminaries: H.T. Greenleaf (lumber and surveying), Roscoe W. Turner (lawyer), L.A. Winder (town inspector), W.M. Baxter (ice and lumber), A.K. Kramer (shipbuilding), and H.M. Hinton (schoolmaster). The body became known as the Committee of Five, though with the election of Hinton as 'alternate', it numbered six.

In his acceptance of the Committee's Chairmanship, Greenleaf mounted the stage and delivered a peroration on the solemnity of the task he and his fellows had, with heavy heart, taken upon themselves. "For we pledge before you this afternoon to leave no stone unturned in the resolution of this mystery. I have had the pleasure myself of knowing the young lady in question. Not in any familiar way, but as a valued member of this community..." In this way he described his sole encounter with her, passing her in the street with a doff of his hat and a nod of her sweet chin. "...And in that familiarity, we hereby shoulder the burden, no matter what the cost. As I trust all of us do, to the extent of his ability..."

With this cue, two satchels were passed around the room for the men to fill with cash.

By the time the meeting dissolved, and the men retired to the saloons, they had left behind the sum of $236 in coin, folding money, and IOUs. The immediate effect of this generosity was for many of the town's barmen to suffer requests for the extension of their patrons' tabs, for they had given away the day's drinking money for the greater good. Rarely was heard around the town such a high-minded excuse to drink on the house.

The collected funds were supplemented by private donations. The total exceeded $1400. The Committee's first acts were to hire contractors to expand the search: a detective to track down leads far and wide, and a dredging outfit to expand it below, into the dusky waters. As all the members considered themselves men of science, it was proposed to hire a diver to sweep the river bottom. They did this knowing full well that the river's currents might have deposited a body anywhere up and down miles of barren, uninhabited estuary. The Pasquotank, moreover, was a broad stream at the point of Fearing's Marine Railway—wider, in fact, than the East River in New York.

They knew these things, but had to appear to make all due diligence. An expert salvage diver, John M. Edwards of Washington, NC, was placed on retainer for the sum of $20. The dredging by Captain Williams cost $22.50, and the detective, the not-inconsiderable sum of $125. Their activities were set to begin immediately, for the mystery was beginning to preoccupy the town like nothing had before. Citizens were in the streets not shopping, not working, but standing around to discuss Nell Cropsey and Jim Wilcox. To the commerce-minded committeemen, the girl's disappearance was not only a moral emergency, but an economic disaster.

Police Chief Dawson shared their concern, but could not be persuaded to take the Committee's mission seriously. He refused to meet with the members as a group. Instead, Greenleaf, Baxter and Turner could only attempt to buttonhole him at odd moments, such as when he came out of the courthouse, or on his way to the cigar shop. Dawson was cold to them every time. He was opposed to sharing his duties with a gang of vigilantes, no matter how well-heeled, whether appointed by popular vote or not. To their requests for cooperation, he was vague. To their legitimacy, he was contemptuous.

By the 28th, Nell had been missing for a week. Ollie, who had shared a bed with her sister since she could remember, could not sleep alone. She found herself wide awake at 4 a.m., waiting for the light of dawn to filter through the curtains. At first gleaming, she rose, dressed and went downstairs to the dining room, where the cups and saucers had been set for breakfast the night before. She had tea, and poured it from the cup to the saucer to cool, but suffered a languor that prevented her from putting it to her lips. She stared at it, watching the curls of steam rise with the detached appreciation of a spectator watching a storm far out to sea.

That was when the first explosion shook the house. The china and cutlery rattled, and her tea spilled on the tablecloth. The dogs outside barked. Her father was suddenly down the stairs, dressed only in his long underwear. Dazed, he cast his eyes around the ground floor, as if expecting to find the source of the explosion there.

"What was that?" he asked Ollie.

"It came from the river."

Cropsey went to the window. With his back turned to Ollie, she saw the trap door of his drawers was unbuttoned, showing a considerable length of tufted crack. She averted her eyes.

The riverbank was only a couple of hundred feet from the Cropseys' front door. A few hundred feet beyond that, where the water was still shallow, there was a row boat with two men. As Cropsey watched, one of them stood up, braced one leg against the gunnel, and tossed something into the water.

In silence, an enormous spout of water erupted, and a second later the sound reached the house. The explosion shook the window panes, and Cropsey felt his innards recoil. He shut the curtains.

"The fools are using dynamite," he said.

At seven, Ollie arranged a tray with some bread, butter and a fresh pot of tea. As she carried it upstairs, the rattle of the tray's contents seemed deafening in a space that, since Nell was gone, had taken on the aspect of a funeral parlor. No one wanted to open the curtains. At the top of the second floor stairs she encountered her cousin Carrie, who ran her eyes over the tray and nodded her approval. She accompanied Ollie to the door at the foot of the garret stairs, and preceded her up. When she reached her mother, Carrie was kneeling beside her, cheek resting on her shoulder, grasping her hand.

"Look, Aunt Mary. Ollie has fetched breakfast!"

Mary Cropsey said nothing, and did not turn her eyes from the window. The day after Nell's disappearance she had taken up her vigil in the turret, which offered a clear view of the front yard and the river beyond. She had stayed there every minute of those seven days, with only brief interruptions to see to her most basic needs.

Her husband understood why she did this—at first. He had sat with her that first night. But he soon grew frustrated. From downstairs, the children heard one side of their argument, because only he was shouting: "What about the rest of us! Do you intend to...Of course!...Oh what complete nonsense...How could you think that?... You never cared for me!...And don't think I won't bring that up!... Yes, I said it...Well, then stay up here and rot for all I care, you damn cow!...Or join her down there! I don't care."

After that he no longer went up to see her, but slept in their bed alone.

The Cropsey daughters took turns with her. As she had stopped tending to her appearance, they brushed her long gray hair out over her shoulders, and emptied her chamber pot. They rigged up a makeshift shade to protect her eyes, which were glazed and wide open in the rude daylight. They kept up steady chatter with her, confining themselves to the most innocuous remarks. But when she responded, it was only to wax incredulous at the river. "It's so big," she would say, in a voice that grew weaker and more elderly each day. "Why does it have to be so big?"

Lately she watched the dredging barge towed into place. From that distance she could see the faces of the men on it. She could see them talking, and smiling, and dragging on their cigarettes as they worked the dredging lines. They tossed the butts in the water, which physically pained her, for they might have been despoiling the very bed in which her daughter slept.

And now came the men with dynamite. They didn't smoke, but they were high-spirited, as any young man would be when given permission to play with explosives. The turret creaked with every blast. Mary Cropsey caught her breath as she waited for the results—the dislocation of the body from wherever it was lodged on the bottom. Nothing ever came up, not even trash. But with each blast, it felt to Mary Cropsey as if less of her breath returned to her body.

That very moment, less than two miles away, Jim Wilcox was on his way to work. He was dressed in the usual uniform of a dockside manhandler: heavy dungarees, wool workshirt, kerchief around his neck. In a cloth sack, he carried the lunch his mother had made for him. He was a short man, but broad and thickly muscled, and he walked with a definite waddle, as if the robustness of his frame interfered with his gait.

Yet he was not unhandsome. His blond hair and mustache were striking; instead of wearing his kerchief like a child's bib, he tied it rakishly around his neck, as if he was a French artist embarking for the country to paint. He was used to women giving him second and third glances. He, in turn, liked to decorate his proximity with pretty girls. If pressed to give an account of himself, Jim would have said he was blessed, a happy man with an indefinite but bright future.

But that was all before the night of November 20th. When he walked the streets now, he was conscious of people avoiding his gaze. Housewives out sweeping their porches would abruptly go inside when he appeared. Children playing on sidewalks were suddenly called inside. Riders in buggies kept their eyes forward.

And then there were the young men who would actually call out to him. "Hey Jim, where's your girl?" they would say. "Hey Jim, why don't you help find Nell?" He mostly pretended these taunts were beneath his notice, unless they struck him in a particularly foul mood, and he would put down his lunch sack and challenge the heckler to repeat the question to his face. None ever did—for physically Jim was not to be taken lightly.

For his part, Jim had worn himself sleepless with thoughts of Nell. Half the time he agreed with Chief Dawson, that he should not have left her on the porch in such an overwrought state. The other half he resented her for disappearing. For he knew that Nell, who seemed so sweet to everyone else, had a cruel streak that had cut him many times over three-and-a-half years. He wouldn't put it past her to run off just to humiliate him. Indeed, he had come to realize that the one had enabled the other: if he had escorted her back inside that night, none of her ingenious spite could have been blamed directly on him. He had been stupid, and he was paying dearly for it now.

While Nell's perversity came as little surprise, he was bewildered by the way the rest of the Cropseys had turned on him. His courtship of Nell, such as it was, had begun mere weeks since the family had moved into the Fearing house, in '98. For more than three years he had been a fixture in their home. He was on easy, first-name terms with all the Cropsey daughters, and had given little thoughtful gifts not just to Nell, but to all of them. William Cropsey had never been overly warm, but the mother appeared to go out of her way to make up for her husband's diffidence. At no time had any of them made him feel unwelcome. Nor did he take anything less than tender care of Nell's virtue—even when he had her out late, without a chaperone.

And yet, the very night she went missing, when it was not even clear there was any crime or misadventure involved, the Cropseys seemed determined to cast him as the villain. Jim was a tough young man, loath to admit anything bothered him. But the blood suspicion of the Cropseys—so unfounded, so unjust—pierced him to the quick.

One thing was for sure: he would not gratify Nell by playing along. He would not take part in the idiot extremes the town had taken to find her 'body'. Despite his mistakes, he would not make a spectacle of his regrets. Instead, his public manner would be cool, like a man confident of his innocence. In his current predicament, with a storm of suspicion swirling around him, it was the only measure of control he had. For he was sure Nell was somewhere nearby—probably in the country, or in some house across the river, watching him, hoping he would crack.

"To hell with you, Nell Cropsey!" he said aloud. Too loud, in fact: he had just arrived at Hayman's yard.

"What was that you said, Jim?" asked Mr. Hayman.

"Nothing. Forget it," Jim replied, and hung up his overcoat on his usual peg.

"You okay?"

"Sure. Why?" he said, and gave a smile that looked more like a guilty grimace.

The dismal November ended. Over that time, Nell continued to be the favorite subject of conjecture around town. Just as interest would start to fade, a story would pop up in the newspapers claiming that Nell had been found. Bodies supposedly washed up at Sand Hills and New Begun. Live women answering to Nell's description were reported in Norfolk, Wilmington, Wilson, Hamilton, Baltimore and other towns, largely by the initiative of the people living there, who seemed as preoccupied with her disappearance as those in Elizabeth City. The detective hired by the Committee of Five was of little use in verifying these claims, as he had never met Nell and knew her only from the blurry photos kept by her parents. Inevitably, Chief Dawson or a member of the Committee would have to go up and confirm these stories. None of the girls turned out to be Nell. The Committeemen soon learned to dread these reports, which forced them to undertake a lot of fruitless travel, always at their own expense.

The dredging went on, covering one area of river before Williams' barge was disanchored and towed to the next. Edwards, the diver, donned his brass helmet and suit of canvas armor and slipped below; his assistant, meanwhile, sat in the boat, maintaining the air pump and smoking. Sometimes, he was seen to open the supply hose and blow cigarette smoke into it. This was apparently for Edwards' benefit. For it was dreary work, walking those dark, oily depths for such a grim purpose, and the diver had to savor whatever distractions he could.

And when neither dredgers nor diver were at work, the men with the dynamite took to the water. The theory was that the 'percussion' touched off by the explosions would free a corpse that had lodged on the bottom. If any of the good people of Elizabeth City were liable to forget the Cropsey tragedy, even for a day, the explosions were a constant reminder. The blasting dragged on for weeks, in the early mornings and evenings, shaking all the houses on the waterfront. Cracks appeared in windowpanes and masonry, causing much grumbling on Riverside Avenue. Yet no one complained. For who would begrudge any attempt to solve the mystery of the poor girl—least of all the men of other families, who also had daughters at vulnerable ages?

With the possible exception of Hurricane Branch and his dogs, the most compelling figure to enter the investigation at this time was Madame Snell Newman of Norfolk. According to her frequent advertisements in the Norfolk papers, she was "THE Renowned Clairvoyant and Business Medium" who "can be consulted at her parlors of all life matters; her tests are wonderful." Word reached the Committee of Five that Madame Newman had attained certain knowledge that Nell Cropsey was dead—abducted and murdered by Jim Wilcox. She let it be known that if she were given access to the environs of the crime, she would gladly lead the authorities to the location of the body. Her 'tests', she declaimed, would be offered purely on a *pro bono* basis.

The Committee paid for her morning train ticket down. When Madame Newman arrived at the Cropsey home, she was accompanied by Greenleaf and Winder, but not Chief Dawson or Deputy

Reid, who refused to encourage such nonsense. Ollie opened the door, and was greeted by an apparition in purple and black lace. She floated into the house like a taffeta cloud, filling up the space with her perfume and her eminence. She took tea in the sitting room until all the Cropsey adults and children were gathered from around the farm. All except for Mary Cropsey, who would not abandon her watch in the turret.

Audience secured, Madame put down her teacup and began the show. She sat with her eyes closed, breathing quietly at first, but then with more vigor. A low moan emanated from her throat, a sound that made the girls' blood caper. Then she stood up and left the sitting room. When she did so, she no longer heaved about like a shoal of flounces, but with the bird-like quickness of a certain nineteen-year-old.

"Sorrow! Such sorrow!" she cried as she regarded the dining room—the last space inside the house Nell was known to have been. "For I am in a dark place, and wet, and there is no one to mourn me!"

She drifted around the room, looking with mournful gravity at the settings placed for lunch. When she reached the corner closest to the kitchen, she stretched a quivering hand to smooth the tablecloth that had bunched up there. The act made Louise Cropsey seize Ollie's forearm—for this was exactly the kind of gesture the ever-tidy Nell would make.

"She has become Nell," Ollie breathed.

William Cropsey was less impressed. That public money had been spent to find his daughter bespoke the decency of the citizens of the town. But to waste a train ticket on the likes of Madame Newman struck him as vaguely back-handed. Who would they summon next? he wondered. A feathered shaman from the forests of Borneo? As the woman evolved around the room, Cropsey stood in the kitchen doorway with his arms crossed over his chest, giving her performance no reaction at all.

Nell, can I speak to you a minute?" Madame Newman said in a voice they all recognized as Jim's. She went out on the porch, to the right-hand section outside the dining room windows. There she leaned with her right cheek against the pillar, tears standing in her eyes—just as Jim had described Nell doing that fateful night.

Below the porch, the family and neighbors and reporters from all the nearby towns had gathered. To this throng she pronounced, "Nell is not in that river. She is in a much smaller place. A wet place..."

Cropsey suddenly went pale, and uncrossed his arms. But he was relieved when she went on: "After Jim Wilcox subdued her, he dealt her the fateful blow, and disposed of her in an old well. Oh perfidy! Oh horror!"

She gazed into the distance as she waited for them to absorb this news.

"If you wish, I will take you there."

The rest of the afternoon was spent in a tour of abandoned wells. The Cropsey family buggy, with Madame Newman beside William Cropsey in the driver's seat, led a procession of vehicles. Cropsey went along with the charade for the pleasure of watching the clairvoyant made to look foolish. But as each well proved not to hold Nell's body, she gave no hint of becoming discouraged. "Esoteric knowledge is not ordinary knowledge," she explained to her increasingly impatient audience. "It admits not of small notions, such as 'proof'."

Having toured ten wells, the party had no interest in an eleventh. Madame Newman was taken to the train station, and put on the 4 o'clock to Norfolk. As the train pulled out she opened the window and gave the crowd a triumphant wave; the crowd, made of decent people, waved back. But when she was gone, they dispersed under a cloud of disgust.

IV.

December unfolded dry and warm, with temperatures in the fifties and sixties. Nell was missed, but there came a time when they became accustomed to her absence. When she went up to visit Carrie in Brooklyn, she had been away for weeks at a time. It was just possible, with a little effort, to pretend she was still up north, sitting in on courses in design and homemaking at Pratt with her cousin.

In time, Ollie stopped expecting to see her in the mornings, seated at the dining table with her sewing, or on the porch with one of her books, kicking stockinged legs under the rocker. In these accustomed places she had become a memory--a fact that pained Ollie, and gave her fresh pangs of guilt.

Yet the fleeting shade of Nell would surprise her at odd moments. She would think she saw Nell out of the corner of her eye in the sitting room, at the window. Or just miss her as she came up the stairs and a slender figure disappeared into a bedroom. These were never really her--never really anyone, in fact--but the way the illusion struck her off-guard, when her thoughts were on something else, unnerved her. Once, when she was in the privy, she thought she heard her sister call her name. She heard the word so clearly she would have answered--but restrained herself.

After Nell had been gone two weeks, William Cropsey allowed himself to be questioned by a Norfolk reporter. To the surprise of those in the community who still hoped for the best, he said, "I am now convinced that my daughter is dead. That she would fail to communicate with us for so long leaves us no hope she may yet come home to us. I am positive that there are certain persons in this town who can throw light on her fate. Jim Wilcox can clear it up in about fifteen minutes. For lack of that, we yet hope justice is served, and those responsible will answer for their acts."

The rest of the Cropsey family was surprised by this declaration. Lettie and cousin Carrie loosed fresh tears. Uncle Hen frowned and took sudden interest in the buttons of his shirt. Ollie fixed her father with inquiring eyes. But when the reporter asked for her comment, she repeated what he said: "The time has come to face our loss."

Later, when they were alone, Ollie asked him, "Why did you say that?"

"I'm tired of the stories. If I have to hear another rumor that she's run off with some swell, I'll kill someone. Better dead than talked about that way."

He sent an open letter to the Committee of Five, which was reprinted in all the papers. In part, it read:

> *I shall always believe Jim Wilcox was instrumental in my daughter's disappearance and if she is dead I believe his hand or the hand of his hireling is responsible for her death. Sometime when this life shall cease and we shall stand before the presence of the great Judge I believe we shall learn how and when he murdered my daughter and that the justice he may escape will be dealt with then.*

The reporters tracked Jim Wilcox down at his job and asked for his comment. His outward reaction, it was said, was minimal, as if such dire accusations were daily occurrences. Pressed, he finally remarked "It is unjust. I've known the Cropseys for more than three years. I have nothing but the warmest feelings toward them. I am at a loss to understand why Mr. Cropsey would say such things."

It was the holiday season. Cousin Carrie--who also took dressmaking classes at Pratt--employed her skills with the scissor to make paper dolls in the shapes of angels and cherubs. The smaller children colored them, and hung them over the fireplaces. Ollie and Lett baked the components of a gingerbread house, and assembled them with molasses. The smells of their baking filled the house with a sweet perfume. It wafted up into the turret, to where Mary Cropsey kept her vigil. It made her smile a little, but no one was with her at that moment to see it. Since the public acknowledgment of Nell's death, no one had the heart to share it with her, and the family left her alone.

On Christmas Day, the family had its traditional meal of lamb, mint dressing and potatoes from their own fields. To everyone's relief, Mary Cropsey joined them. After, they all gathered in the sitting room to exchange presents they'd made for each other, or had purchased through catalogs. Uncle Hen got a fine 47 cents 'Easy Opener' knife from the girls; their mother, a shower bath yoke. Ollie brought out the presents Nell had meant to give but never would. When Uncle Hen got a silk handkerchief, embroidered with flowers by Nell's own hands, he was so overcome he left the room.

Later, he played the harmonica and Carrie accompanied him on the mandolin. It was strange to hear music in the house again. Nell was fair with the harmonica, but more enthusiastic to hear her uncle play. Sometimes, when he really got going, she would grab Ollie and they would do a jig together. Ollie was four inches taller than her sister, but Nell's vigor and enthusiasm made her the larger presence. Alas, that Christmas, there was not much taste for dancing.

There was a full moon that evening. William Cropsey quietly rose in the small hours, pulling on his boots and overcoat against the near-freezing night. Navigating without a lamp through the moonlit house, he went out the back door to the little shed in the yard. Moments later he came out with a large object over his shoulder: one of the heavy canvas sacks used to collect potatoes for harvest. This sack was filled not with potatoes, but a single object, and Cropsey struggled with its weight as he tottered out of the yard and toward the river.

After the holiday, the people of Elizabeth City were asleep in their beds, and the water was devoid of traffic. There were no witnesses as Cropsey went out on the Fearing dock and, with as little splash as possible, slipped the sack's contents in the river. He stood watching it for a while as, silvery in the moonbeams, it drifted on the current, toward the middle of the stream. Then Cropsey turned and, after a brief stop at the privy, went back to bed.

The next day was Friday, an ordinary work day. Ollie was having her morning tea in the dining room when her father came in with coffee in hand. Instead of sitting with her, he went to the front windows and stared out at the water. The purposefulness to his vigil made her wonder.

"Expecting someone?" she asked.

He let the curtains drop.

"Don't play the fool," he replied. "You above all."

She understood. And with that understanding, she shivered.

"So you say."

They looked at each other as the mantel clock ticked and the muffled thuds of the children roughhousing upstairs shook the ceiling. In that moment, under his frosty gaze, Ollie disliked her father. She looked at the stubborn cut of his jaw, and the bristling hardness of his cheeks, and hated what this ordeal had made him. She resented him with the passionate fullness of an ally who had become a betrayer, with the hatred that is love transfigured.

These feelings shocked and shamed her, and they passed quickly. Her father would not show it outwardly, but he was suffering as profoundly as his wife, with both the burden of his loss and of the truth. He was never an easy man to love. In many ways, he was a stranger to her.

Until now their shared secret had been theirs alone, and could be undone with a simple call to Bill Dawson. There would be an inquiry, of course, and probably an indictment. The public would resent them for their deception, and pour sympathy on Jim Wilcox for the calumnies he had endured. The Cropseys would be drummed out of Elizabeth City. But at least the lies would come to an end.

What her father was looking for out the window, she knew, was the point of no return.

That moment arrived on Saturday, the 27th. Just after sun-up, two men were on the river just across from the Cropsey place. The air had warmed up a bit, and a light rain peppered the water. The man at the bow hunched on his seat, collar of his oilskin coat turned up over his ears. He was keeping a close watch for good spots to fish, until he sighted an odd, dark shape floating midstream.

"Wait a minute, there. Come over that way."

Closer, and the shape resolved into a body. It was a woman, floating on her stomach, with clothes billowing and brown hair spread wide just below the surface. She wore a red shirtwaist, a belt of black leather, and black skirt. There was a slipper—the kind a woman might wear around the house, not outdoors—on her right foot. The other foot was clad only in a black cloth stocking, with one toe protruding through a tear.

At this sight, the man in the bow sucked in his breath, and looked to his companion. The other stared back in horror and wonderment. Both knew exactly whom they had found.

Neither would touch her. Instead, they sunk a spare oar blade down in the river bottom, which was shallow at that point. With a length of fishing-line, they tied the oar to one of the ankles, so the body would not float away. Then they rowed straight for the Cropsey residence.

As they approached the shore they saw a older woman come out to receive them. Unkempt, tear-stained, pale from weeks of isolation, Mary Cropsey had run down from her turret the second she saw the boat come in.

"You've found her! You've found my girl!" she cried, and seemed intent on charging straight onto the boat. Unnerved, the man on the oars, C.A. Long, pulled up just short of the waterline.

"We've found...someone," replied John Stillman.

"Bring her to me! Bring my sweet girl back!"

The men were relieved when William Cropsey came down, pulling a coat on over his open union-suit.

"Better take me," he said.

The rest of the Cropseys gathered as they rowed him out. Carrie and Ollie clung to each other as Cropsey leaned over the gunnels and pulled the body toward him. They saw him fumble with the weight of it, from the waterlogged clothes and the mass of matted hair. Neither breathed as he turned it over and looked at the face. They could see their father's shoulders droop, and even from fifty yards away they could discern his expression.

Ollie recognized the red shirtwaist she wore the night she had disappeared. That red shirt that made her seem so mannish, so modern and formidable in her burgeoning independence. Ollie had tried to talk her out of buying it. She never favored that look for herself, preferring the wasp-waisted profile of a decade earlier.

"That suits you, with your frame," Nell had told her. "It's not so good for me. I intend to be a twentieth century woman!"

She remembered those words as her father tied Nell's body to the oarlock. She heard them in her head as what remained of her beloved sister inanimately plowed the water. She heard that voice, and like that time she thought she heard Nell call to her, she wanted to plug her ears. But that would not silence a voice that lived only in her head.

"She is home!" said Mary Cropsey, beaming. "Nell is home at last."

A crowd gathered to watch the body come ashore. The people were silent, and not a few eyes were wet, as the drowned beauty trimmed in blood red was lifted into a hay wagon. Prayers were spoken as the impromptu cortege began its trip back to the Cropsey house, with the bereaved family behind, and the disconsolate, weeping mother—utterly exhausted—held up by her daughters.

With that, several young men broke away from the crowd, heading back up Riverside Avenue toward Hayman's.

"Where's everyone going?" someone asked.

"We're going to hang that sonovabitch Jim Wilcox!" came the reply.

The Hall

I.

Elizabeth City's development was delayed by the local geography, which begrudged settlement. To the east were the treacherous shoals of Eastern Carolina, notorious as a graveyard of ships. To the north, the Great Dismal Swamp— that "vast body of dirt and nastiness"— divided the lower Pasquotank region from populated areas around Chesapeake Bay. The Revolutionary War passed the area by, leaving its sparse population to fend for itself among a maze of small waterways. The few visitors from outside included ocean-going ships that dared the Outer Banks. The fresh water flowing out of the Great Dismal, peat-black and naturally full of tannins, was valued for resisting contamination over long voyages, if not for its acrid taste.

The obstacles of the banks and the swamp were finally overcome with the opening of the Great Dismal Canal. Dug entirely by slaves, the canal took a dozen years to complete. By the time it was opened, the area's resources of timber, fish and oysters exerted their pull on settlers from the north, many of whom settled near the point where the canal met the Pasquotank, and the river opened up to what became Albemarle Sound. The town was first called Redding. Then it became Elizabethtown, after the wife of the saloonkeeper who sold the land on which the town was chartered— or maybe Queen Elizabeth. Nobody was quite sure. In 1801, to avoid confusion with another Elizabethtown in Bladen County, the port became Elizabeth City.

The canal put the little settlement firmly on the map. Half the state's total import-export trade passed through Elizabeth City by 1829, rivaling the commerce of larger cities to the north. But its rise to greatness was seriously stalled by the Civil War. When the U.S. Navy confronted the local Confederate 'Mosquito Fleet' in 1862, the rebels were swept aside in less than a half hour, and the streets of Elizabeth City were occupied by U.S. Marines.

The occupation divided the population in a way that threw its entire future into doubt. Local secessionists swore the town would be better off burned to the ground than left in Yankee hands. Unionists, naturally, objected. When Col. Frederick Henningsen of the 59th Virginia Infantry set a fire that destroyed the courthouse and the residential district around it, half of Elizabeth City applauded. The other half joined U.S. sailors to put out the fire. A Union garrison patrolled the town for the rest of the war. But that didn't stop the low-level insurgency from simmering, or heal the political divide.

Elizabeth City continued to decline after the surrender. Neither the former Secessionists nor Unionist residents spoke of the rift. Yet the knowledge that one's neighbor had wished—and even helped—to burn one's house down did little for civic pride. By 1870 the city had dwindled to fewer than one thousand souls. Whatever vitality was left was contributed by new arrivals, so-called "carpetbaggers", from the North. Many of the families prominent in the town during the lifetime of Nell Cropsey— the Kramers, the Greenleafs, the Robinsons—arrived at this time, where for obvious reasons they co-existed uneasily with the divided locals.

The town was born again with the arrival of the Norfolk & Elizabeth City Railroad. In the scheme of things, this was rather late. The Rocky Mountains proved a lesser barrier to the railroads than the Great Dismal, as Sacramento, California was joined to the national rail network twelve years sooner than Elizabeth City. Transportation was liberated at last from the ponderous canal-boats and steamers, and the town tripled in population by 1900. Lumbering boomed, with camps and mills appearing even in the remotest backwaters. Oysters from the beds of Albemarle Sound were harvested in the morning and served by afternoon on plates in Washington, D.C. and Baltimore. The overheated commercial atmosphere, and large proportion of newcomers, made Elizabeth City more like a booming frontier settlement than other coastal towns—the westernmost town in eastern Carolina.

But prosperity did little to bring a sense of shared identity. The war was still within living memory, and an influx of entrepreneurs from Ohio, Massachusetts and New York brought tension as well as trade. It took another generation for an event that would finally heal the old divide. With the disappearance of Nell Cropsey, thirty-six years after the war's end, the people came together at last. "Never before has the people of this community been drawn so closely together by a common feeling," observed the *Charlotte News*. In blaming Jim Wilcox for the disappearance of Nell Cropsey, the good citizens of Elizabeth City were united at last.

II.

William Hardy Cropsey, of the old Brooklyn Cropseys, lived in Blythebourne. He was at this time a farmer without good land to farm. He supplemented his income with a job as a minor tax official, but feared his prospects for immediate advancement in city government were narrow. Brooklyn was crowded with other Cropseys, including his father Andrew, uncle Henry, brother Andrew G., the lawyer and judge. Almost all the good land was already improved, with prices spiraling above the astronomical rate of $1500 an acre. To make his way, he would have to borrow, either from the bank or from his family—prospects he loathed. For William Cropsey was not a man to suffer dependence.

Meanwhile, the reconstructing South was bursting with opportunities. Eastern Carolina, in particular, was growing fast on the strength of timber, fishing, canning, and shipping industries. The climate was milder than New York's, in soil so fertile it barely required much trouble to produce bumper crops, year-round. All those lumbermen and fishermen needed to eat, after all—as did the people of Norfolk and beyond. After much research, and a warm correspondence with his local contact, John Fearing, Cropsey decided that he would become a truck farmer in Elizabeth City. His family's future would be built on potatoes, raised by his own hand.

He announced his decision on a Sunday afternoon, at the dinner table. The only member of the family who wasn't surprised was his wife, with whom he'd shared his hopes until firm plans were laid. When he said it, "We are moving to North Carolina next month", the news was greeted with silence. Olive looked to Lettie, who looked to William Douglas, who stared at Nell, who gazed into her dinner plate.

Mary Cropsey finally broke the silence: "I told you they wouldn't like it."

"Children never do," Cropsey replied, and broke off some bread. He said this with a air of finality that wordlessly seemed to add "... but it is done."

"We are finishing the year at school first?" asked Olive.

"Of course," said Mary. "Our things will be sent ahead, so the change will be easy as rolling over in bed. Our house will be much bigger, and face the water. Think about how wonderful that will be!"

"You promised to take us hunting on Long Island," said William Douglas, who was only eight and tended to speak out of turn.

Cropsey frowned. "I did. And we will hunt, in the Great Dismal. There are a lot bigger things to shoot there than ducks!"

"But you promised."

"William Douglas, mind your father. He knows our best interest." said Mary.

At the far end of the table, a fork clattered to its plate. All eyes fell on Nell, who fixed her eye on William Cropsey. And then, with the calmness of absolute certainty, she declared, "*I am not moving.*"

The parents were so thrown by this utterance that they could only stare at her. Olive looked around as if planning her escape. Lettie looked at Nell with the remote pity of a spectator at a public execution.

Mary Cropsey recovered first. "Nell, you will apologize to your father."

"I will apologize to his heart's content. But I will not go to North Carolina. Nor to Florida, Panama or Patagonia, for that matter."

"You will not refer to your father by a pronoun."

"Mary, please—" William put his hand on his wife's to silence her. "Nell, you are not setting a good example for the others."

"I don't care."

"As long as you live in this house, you will do as you are told."

"I will not."

"Nell!" Cropsey bellowed, and pounded his fist. The force of it made the jam pot leap into the air, cartwheel and dump its contents.

Aware of what strawberry jam could do to linen, Mary Cropsey shot to her feet. But her husband, hand still on hers, yanked her down.

"I don't know how we've failed as parents, to have raised such a headstrong girl."

"You told me," Nell said, as if her father had not spoken, "that I may attend Pratt with Carrie when we graduate. How am I to do that from some town five hundred miles away?"

"It's not 'some town'. It's a handsome, remarkable town, that will do your brothers and sisters a world of good."

"Such selfishness!" grumbled Mary. "Thinking only of yourself, when the welfare of the entire family is at stake." And her eyes were still fixed on the spilled jam as it spread and stained and filled her head with Boschian visions of chaos and oblivion.

"I don't see how anyone's welfare is at risk," Nell replied. "We have a perfectly fine life here."

Olive hid her hands under the table because they were trembling.

"Should I get the switch, papa?" asked William Douglas.

"Hush!"

"Yes, should he get the switch, papa?" Nell mocked. "Would you like to whip my hands red, until I give in to this...arbitrariness?"

William Cropsey planted his elbows on the table and his face in his hands. "I beseech you, Lord, to tell me what I've done to deserve such a hateful daughter."

The charge of "hatefulness" had an effect on Nell. Her calm melted. Tears stood in her eyes, and she rose out of her chair. "The father who raised me," she said, voice quavering, "taught me to oppose injustice, no matter the source of it."

"Arrogance is what you have learned," replied Mary.

With that, Nell fled the table, toppling her chair behind her. The rest of the Cropseys listened as her footsteps ascended the stairs and the door of her bedroom slammed.

Of course, this protest had no effect on William Cropsey's plans: the lease with John Fearing was signed, and the packing of their belongings proceeded in anticipation of their move in April. But there was one surprising consequence. Instead of punishment for her outburst, Nell got a promise that she could return to Brooklyn in a few years to attend school. Nell told Olive about the arrangement as they were rolling bedsheets through the mangler on wash Monday.

"He came to me the next day, and made the promise. I will be a college girl after all! I didn't even have to apologize."

"Is that so?"

"It is. And I'd lie if I said I wasn't ashamed. He's more just than he knows."

"Funny that he never told the rest of us about it."

Olive was always thankful for a spirit of compromise in their home, but something bothered her about the incident. For she was sure that if it had been any other of the Cropsey daughters who had so openly defied their father, the consequences would have been far worse. If it had been one of the older boys, the switch would certainly have come out, and the rest of the children forced to watch. But Nell the beautiful child, lovely to look at and a delight to hear, got a promise instead of a beating. The double standard bounced in the pit of Olive's stomach, and made the edges of her ears burn.

That wasn't even the worst of it. What was worse was how oblivious Nell seemed to her favored position. If she owned up to it, perhaps expressed bewilderment, it would have been easier to excuse her, to chalk it up to the inherent unfairness of the world, and have a laugh together. But she showed no such awareness. Instead, she only seemed to grow more lovely, more entitled. Eyes flashing, she soaked up all good fortune. She sucked it out of every room, out of the very air, because she was fit by nature to take the lion's share of the blessings. Or so she must have believed.

Olive shared none of these thoughts with Nell. Instead, she continued to smile as she fed the sheets into the rollers for her sister to crank though the machine. Smiled, as she imagined the welts her father should have raised on Nell's porcelain skin. Smiled as she envisioned comforting her sister, her head on Olive's lap as Olive stroked those glossy locks. Ever gracious, she would lean down to Nell's ear, and pour comforting words into them. But she knew how the marks should have burned, and the quality of humiliation they would yield over the days they needed to heal beneath her skirts.

And in a secret place, Olive would have been glad.

III.

One of Elizabeth City's northern transplants was R.O. Preyer, who arrived from Cleveland in 1891. Preyer was a businessman who saw much potential in the timber business around Albemarle Sound. He soon became one of the top executives at Kramer Brothers & Co., and soon after that, built a fine house on 1109 Riverside Avenue.

Kramer Brothers was known for solid product. One of their regular customers at century's turn were another set of brothers, the Wrights of Dayton, Ohio. The bicycle mechanics purchased wood from Kramer Brothers to construct a camp at Kitty Hawk, just across the Sound on the Outer Banks. Some of their wood also went into a series of contraptions they were building, but the exact nature of their experiments were none too clear to the locals.

The finest quality wood in Kramer's stock went into the Preyer house. The design was Queen Anne, but with an eclectic hand. Onlookers admired its asymmetric but balanced impression, with the fine gabled section on the left, the notched, west-facing gable on the right, and the three-story tower anchoring the center, topped by a spire. There was a fine, double-story porch—alternatively known as the "piazza"— that extended across the front, adorned with intricate verge boards in the geometric style of Charles Eastlake. Another double porch caught the afternoon light on the west side. The gathering of dentils, spindles, beads and fish-scale shingle-work struck the contemporary eye as distinguished, demanding the kind of careful maintenance that betokened affluence. It was universally thought to be a fine addition to the row of handsome residences on the Pasquotank Narrows.

Preyer called the house Seven Pines. He and his family lived there for only a few years, until they decamped for Greensboro and the opportunities of the North Carolina Piedmont. The house came into the possession of the Fearing family, who rented it in turn to another family of newcomers.

The Cropsey children found their father's promises fulfilled at Seven Pines. They were indeed mere steps from the water, and there was a boathouse from which they could take a rowboat on the river. Summer lasted deep into September, and autumn lingered close to the holidays. There was a tropical closeness to the air that was strange to them, but also faintly exotic. Sometimes, when Olive stood on the balcony and the breeze came onshore, she thought she smelled the scented bowers of the Indies.

Cropsey seeded his first crop of Irish potatoes, and looked forward to reaping early in '99. While they waited for the crop to come in, the younger children wandered the pastures behind the house, and fished off the docks, and threw rocks in the river. The older ones attended a steady schedule of dances and revues at the theater. There was also rollerskating, and trips for ice cream, and races at the Fairgrounds, and promenades up and down Main Street in the evenings. And when the children turned homeward, they would find their parents on the house's magnificent porch—mother with her needlework, and Cropsey with his newspaper, rocking.

Olive and Nell took a rowboat out on the water some evenings. They would go out into the middle of the stream, cast in the rusty anchor with plenty of slack, and let the current play out as far as it went. The rocking from the gentle current was pleasant to read by, or to idle away the time watching the stars come out.

The river was unlike anything Olive had known up north: where the East River was brackish, and the North River seemed to flow cold from the heart of some glacier, the Pasquotank seeped black and oily. Though only a few feet deep, its opacity revealed nothing of what lay beneath. Rising from the vast swamp, it was like the black blood of some buried creature, bleeding from a perpetual wound. Years of hand-laundering had made the Cropsey girls keen judges of the qualities of water—soft or hard, sweet or salt, light or dark. When Olive slipped her hand in the water, the Pasquotank felt thick, a broth of soil and pine needles and decaying leaves. When she kept it there for a few minutes, her skin would come out faintly blackened, the color of weak tea.

The *entente* between Nell and her father spared the family further drama. Nell slipped into the domestic life on Riverside Avenue as well as any of the others—perhaps better. Olive asked her, "You seem happy for someone who never wanted to come here!" To which Nell replied, "I am happy because I know I'm going back."

The young men of Elizabeth City wasted no time noticing the attractive newcomers. Sometimes, in the evenings, the sisters would hear hoofbeats on the road. Looking out, they would see some local swain in his Sunday best, flower in his lapel, galloping his rig past their door.

The girls drew their share of glances during services at the Presbyterian church, which they noted but, of course, ignored. This had never been a problem in Brooklyn, but as there was no Dutch Reformed sanctuary in town, William Cropsey opted for this one instead. All the flirting, however, made him wonder at the morals of these Presbyterians.

It was only a few weeks into their residency when Nell met Jim Wilcox. She was with Olive, who had met her at school to walk her home. As they came up Riverside Avenue, they encountered Annie Mae Wilcox—a classmate of Nell's—chatting with a young man in his work clothes. Closer, and they could see the resemblance between the pair.

"Nell...and Nell's sister—sorry, what's your name again...?" asked Annie Mae.

"Olive. Call me Ollie."

"Nell and Ollie, this is my brother Jim. He works at the docks here."

Jim Wilcox was short, scarcely taller than Annie Mae, but broad in the shoulders. His hair was the blond of a sheaf of wheat—like his sister's—and his mustache framed a pair of full lips that curled at the tips. He was dressed in denim overalls smeared in tar. But when he reached out his hand to shake Nell's, his fingers and nails were utterly clean. Around his neck was a checkered kerchief that was likewise spotless.

"Pleased to meet you," he said, eyes flitting over her face and hair and bosom.

Nell, blushing, briefly touched his hand. But Olive could detect none of the coldness she showed at unwelcome male attention.

"Miss Olive," Jim turned to Ollie. When she touched his hand, his fingers were coarse. His eyes rested on her only for a second before they shifted back to Nell.

"Jim's going to take me roller-skating tonight," said Annie, in a tone of great accomplishment.

"I am indeed. And I'm happy to invite your friends too."

Nell glanced at Ollie, whose presence would be required at any such meeting. Ollie kept her face a mask.

"That's very tempting," she told him, "but we are engaged this evening."

"Engaged, heh? That's too bad," he said, eyes twinkling. "Well, don't be surprised if I ask some other time."

When they were out of earshot, Ollie remarked "What a lot of confidence in such a small package!"

"He's not so short," replied Nell.

"Goodness, he comes up only to my nose."

"He may have some qualities."

He soon showed one of those qualities: he didn't waste time. Just a few days later, he sent a note to Seven Pines requesting permission to call on Nell. She wrote a brief reply—"Yes, the gentleman might," and sent it back the next day.

The following Sunday, Jim showed up after they returned from church. He wore a suit of plaid wool, a pressed white shirt with starch collar, and work-boots, albeit shined to a high finish. His hat was already off, his blond hair appeared wet and dark from the pomade in it. When Nell opened the door, she was struck in the face by a wave of rosewater cologne.

"Miss Cropsey," he said.

"Mister Wilcox."

She invited him into the inner hall, and pretended not to notice a trio of eavesdroppers—May, Frederick, and William Douglas—tripping over each other to get out of sight.

"May I take your topper?"

"Please."

"Would you like something to drink?"

"That would be very nice."

She showed him to the right, into the sitting room. There she made him wait until she fetched her mother and Ollie. When they returned Nell bore a tray of tall lemonades and a sugar bowl. They found Wilcox seated comfortably on the sofa, arm slung over the back, legs crossed at the ankle.

"What a lovely trio of ladies!" he declared.

The ensuing interview lasted twenty minutes. In it, Wilcox was courteous, charming, confident, and perhaps a bit too familiar. He helped himself to three spoons of cane sugar for his lemonade, and informed them he was twenty-two years old. He lived with his family in town. When Mary Cropsey made the requisite inquiries into his profession, Jim did not dwell on his manual job at Hayman's. He did mention that his father, Thomas P. Wilcox, had once been sheriff of Elizabeth City.

"On what ticket?"

"The Republican." And when she made no answer, he added, "And now I think I've done it!"

Mary Cropsey laughed. "Oh, we won't hold that against you."

His father's prominence in the community seemed recommendation enough. When Mary Cropsey rose to leave, she gave Nell a look that, if thoroughly unpacked, would have said, "This gentleman is acceptable. But you may see him only under supervision."

Ollie stayed in the room but did nothing to fill the awkward silences. To her, it was not just that Jim Wilcox seemed common; there was something unserious about him, as if he was content to waste his time and Nell's on a courtship he knew would go nowhere. His interest in Nell was not odd in itself—she was, of course, a handsome girl—but the age difference did not sit well with Ollie. Louise at twenty-one or Lettie at nineteen would have been more appropriate choices. Or Ollie herself—if she had felt comfortable with a young man so much shorter than herself.

She became conscious of a strange sound. It was an intermittent chirping, like a bird's, and it came from the vicinity of the sofa. Had the cat brought another live animal into the house? She would have looked for it, but didn't interrupt Nell and Jim. They were making the most inane of small-talk, as Jim went on smiling and Nell sat and blushed and looked into the carpet.

"So how do you find Betsy City so far?" he was asking.

"I find it exceedingly fine," she replied.

At this lie, Ollie coughed into her hand.

"Compared to the big city like Brooklyn, it must be awful dull."

"It has its compensations."

"That it does. I've been here all my life, and have no plan to leave."

"Have you traveled up north, Mr. Wilcox?"

"Only as far as Norfolk. My boss hired a bunch of us to take a boat up there last year, through the canal. She was the sweetest little skipjack."

"How fascinating. Did you see any Red Indians?"

Jim laughed. "Not a one. But the fishing was good."

They went on like this until Ollie stood up to gather the service. This indicated that the interview had gone on for the appropriate time.

"I sure do appreciate your mother receiving me, Miss Olive," said Jim, taking his cue. "Miss Nell, may I call on you again?"

"Of course you may."

Nell walked him into the hall, and that strange chirping followed him.

"Nell, may I talk to you outside for a minute?"

Nell glanced to Ollie, who shrugged.

On the porch, Jim reached into his jacket pocket. From it he withdrew something Nell could not have expected: a live bluebird. It was a fine specimen, with plumage as blue as Nell's own eyes. She peeped with delight as he held the bird under her chin.

"He's yours," Jim said. "What would you have me do with this fellow?"

"Fellow? It's so beautiful, it must be a girl."

"Of course! How could it be otherwise?"

She looked into Jim's eyes with frank wonderment. "You had that in your pocket the entire time?"

"Well, I didn't exactly catch her in your parlor."

"You are a unique fellow, Mr. Wilcox. I think you know what to do."

Jim opened his hand. The bird stood on his palm for a moment, as if surprised it had not been eaten. Then it lit out with a fluttery blur.

From the porch, Nell watched Jim cross the front yard to the road. Jim, resisting temptation, did not look back, but kept walking with an easy, swinging gait that declared his good fortune to the world.

She was still watching him when her father came around the side of the house.

"So who's the bantam?" he asked her.

IV.

The dining room at Seven Pines was used for more than dining. Far from reserved for formal gatherings and holidays, it was a place for casual evenings. Strangers were shown into the parlor, where all the best furniture, curtains, rugs and bric-a-brac were on display. The dining room, however, was for household and friends. Equipment for play—checkerboards, chess sets, decks of cards—were kept there, as would the master's collection of pipes, and the family's musical instruments, and the sewing boxes of the women and girls. Meals were served, of course. But the time spent dining in the dining room dwindled in comparison to the time conversing, reading, playing, and otherwise entertaining each other, in the long nights before electricity.

The Cropsey dining room was entirely typical. It had a heavy mahogany table, lined with matching chairs. The sideboard did not match but was of the same heavy wood, with drawers for the china and the three kinds of tablecloths—linen for breakfast, finer linen for dinner, and oilcloth for messier activities. Two armchairs sat by the front window, with a little bookcase between them.

Most evenings, the girls gathered around the table, mending clothes, making alterations for the season, or doing ornamental needlework. When they had it in mind to make dresses, they covered the table so completely with paper patterns that their father complained there was not a spot to put down his newspaper. Lettie's contribution to industry was a wreath spun out of hair collected from everyone in the family. The project involved braiding the individual strands, and weaving in dried flowers and other bits of ornament for a keepsake that would be framed and displayed in the parlor.

She had done this work, and her sisters their sewings, by the light of oil lamps that were painfully dim. And indeed, few of the homes on Riverside Avenue had electricity yet. Even if they did, Mary Cropsey would have found the light of one of those newfangled bulbs painfully garish. To her, the amount of light in a house at night was a moral issue: too much was profligate, indicating misplaced priorities. Better a homemaker need glasses by thirty years old than declare her lack of economy to the world. And so Nell and Ollie went on with their needlework, and Lettie braiding her wreath, and resigned themselves to inevitable nearsightedness as the price for fine heirlooms.

Jim Wilcox became a fixture in the Cropsey dining room. He came over after work every Tuesday and Thursday, and Sundays too. He was there for Nell, but all the Cropsey girls came to look forward to his arrival. He brought them treats: fresh fruit, cakes, sticks of hard candy, shellfish from the docks if it was fresh. Nor did he neglect the brothers. Douglas got a fishing rod Jim used himself as a boy, and William H. a yo-yo carved out of whalebone. The children raced each other to the door when he knocked, thundering down the stairs and plunging through doors with a deafening racket.

William Cropsey himself never got up to answer Jim's knocking. In fact, other than a brief inspection during Jim's second visit, Mr. Cropsey paid scarce attention to this other adult male in his house. He never sat in the dining room on the evenings when Jim was there. If he was working in the garden outside or in the work shed at the back, and Jim offered to help him, Cropsey would never accept. Instead, he would thank Jim in such a perfunctory way it seemed to Nell to verge on rudeness. She told him as much—to the general discomfort of the rest of her family. But her father did not apologize, and didn't change.

Jim came to evenings at the Cropseys and took his usual chair by the window. He was unfailingly pleasant, speaking only in the most polite and general terms, and never dominated conversation. When Uncle Hen brought out his fiddle and Nell her harmonica, he would lean forward, beating the tune on his knee, beaming from ear to ear. Once he took a pair of spoons from the sideboard and joined in. This was as happy a moment as Nell could remember since moving away from Brooklyn. Alas, Jim never played the spoons again after word came down from the matriarch (indirectly, of course) that she did not appreciate her utensils being used in that way. It was—until the very end—the sole thing Jim did of which Mary Cropsey disapproved.

If he was allowed to stay long enough, he would pitch in to help the girls prepare the table for breakfast the next day. After laying on the morning tablecloth, they would put out the tea cups and the saucers, the napkins and egg cups and the brass tray with bottles of oyster ketchup, anchovy sauce, and mustard. And when that was done, Nell would turn down the lamps. Jim would watch as the light drained from her face, fading from yellow to red as her eyes flitted and glanced at him. Those last, dusky rays of light seemed to shine through her, lighting her from within, making her every inch the ethereal domestic angel of his dreams. To his eyes, she was as beautiful as one of those wild-haired sirens on the labels of soap wrappers and biscuit tins. This sometimes moved him to take liberties. But she would deflect him deftly, with a smile, and see him out onto the porch. There she would give him a kiss on the cheek, and see him on his way into the night.

Not so long after, the family's confidence in Jim rose to the point where they'd let him take Nell out for the evening. There were regular shows at the Academy of Music, where she particularly enjoyed the classical offerings and the legitimate dances. Jim preferred the comedies and burlesques, but he was gentleman enough to make it seem as if he enjoyed the odd concerto—especially when he subtly slipped his hand over her's, and Nell allowed him to caress her fingers. Ollie, playing chaperone, gave her sister a sharp tap on the arm. Jim withdrew his hand. But both he and Nell would sit with smiles on their faces, as if they shared a secret.

On nice days Jim took Nell (and Ollie, or Lettie, or whomever was chaperone) out in a rowboat. He would take them across the river to the Camden side, where they'd have beer and oysters fresh from the reef. On the way back, Nell would have preferred to float a bit, like she did with her sisters, but Jim wanted to keep rowing, to show his strength.

Sometimes during these wanderings Nell would remove a glove and let her hand trail in the water. When she took it out, her fingers were slightly discolored, and smelled of turpentine. The smell was not native to the river — there was a varnish factory on the shore that dumped its waste into the water. But Nell didn't mind. To her nose, the odor betokened a cleansing, antiseptic modernity.

There were horse races at the Fairgrounds, which were less than a mile south of Seven Pines. Nell went for the thrill of the event, and to see all the ladies of the town dressed in their finest hats and frocks. Jim liked the betting. He would try to get the Cropsey girls interested in the pastime, explaining what 'odds' and 'handicaps' meant and the various kinds of wagers. The girls understood it all, but feigned disinterest, because the activity seemed—if not disreputable—so thoroughly masculine. If they did bet, it would always be on the basis of which horse was the handsomest, or had a prettier name. Sometimes, this strategy worked better than Jim's sophisticated calculations.

In the summer, there was rollerskating at the town rink. Like the races, this was popular with the sexes for different reasons: for the ladies, it was the exhilaration of movement, as when the Cropsey girls formed a line and played "crack the whip"; for the gentlemen, it was the likelihood that the ladies would end up prone on the ground, their ankles and hopefully their shins showing.

Jim skated like he rowed: with a furious intensity. After he took a few slow turns around the rink with Nell on his arm and a sister on the other, Nell would sense his impatience, and turn him loose. Jim launched himself, orbiting the rink with his shoulders down and arms pumping like the cranks of a locomotive. He was fast, and delighted in his speed, but also graceful, never colliding with anyone. When he lapped the girls, he doffed his cap as he coasted by.

Nell watched him with a faint look of vicarious delight—with all her stays and undergarments and the weight of skirts around her legs, she could never hope to skate that fast. Ollie looked at the other townspeople, who observed Jim with an amusement that struck her as less than flattering. In fact, it seemed to her as if they were laughing at him. His exertions, far from conveying strength and grace, seemed in their eyes to be comedic. Instead of a charging bull, his hunched-over posture made him seem ever so chimp-like.

Ollie held public opinion in breezy disdain, but that only applied in the abstract. When her family was involved, she found herself utterly conventional. Jim, after all, was a native of the town, and was better-known around the rink than the Cropseys. If his reputation was that of a public clown, what might that do to Nell's, by association with him? Or to any of the other members of her family, for that matter? As Ollie watched Jim glide by, cap resting with mock solemnity on his heart, these thoughts assaulted her.

Jim had been courting her for three months when Nell at last asked her opinion. It was a Sunday night after Jim had left, and the sisters were in the bed they shared. In the faint, watery light of a half-moon, Ollie could just make out Nell's face, turned toward her on her pillow.

"So what do you think of our Mr. Wilcox?"

"You mean *your* Mr. Wilcox."

"You know what I mean."

Ollie rolled away, hiding her face from Nell. "What do you like about him?" she asked.

"He's sweet. He's good-looking. He makes me laugh."

"Those are good things."

"He's ever so strong, too. He lifted me into the buggy once when there was a puddle. I felt as light as goose down."

"Well, he does lift things as an occupation."

There was a pause as they listened. The windows were open, and there were frogs in the trees along the road. Somewhere on the river, a languorous bell tilted as a boat rocked at anchor.

"So you won't be plain with me?" Nell asked.

"I don't see how it matters what I think. But if it's that important to you—he's a fine fellow. We certainly can't fault his persistence."

"And his attention. I've never caught him looking at someone else."

"That's something," Ollie replied.

"Well, I know you don't like him."

"You know nothing of the kind. I like him fine."

The grandfather clock in the hall chimed midnight. Ollie knew it would have been better to let the conversation lapse, but gave in to temptation:

"I don't put any stock in what's said. And you shouldn't either."

Ollie wanted to snatch these words back the second they left her lips.

"What have you heard said?" Nell demanded. And when the other hesitated, she added, "Well?"

"Nothing. Just idle chatter. It's not worth a minute's sleep."

"I'm sure it isn't. What is it?"

"It's just...that he was the first one to court you since we moved here."

"And I should have broken some other hearts first?"

"Something like that."

Nell rolled over, so the sisters now had their backs presented to each other.

"And do you agree with them? That I should have rejected Jim just because he was the first?"

"Of course not."

"Good."

Soon the rhythm of Nell's breathing told Ollie she was asleep. In all their years sharing bedrooms, the younger sister had always slept easily. Ollie rolled on her back, and on her side, and back again. For lying, for reporting what she thought as general gossip, she sweated with regret. She lay like that, basted by self-loathing, until the clock chimed one. Then she muttered a single word into the darkness:

"Damn."

V.

I went down to de ribber, I didn't mean to stay,
But dere I see so many gals, I couldn't get away...

At sixty acres, the farm the Cropseys rented from the Fearings was one of the largest in the city. William Cropsey took a measure of satisfaction from this, and felt responsibility for making the ground productive. From the very first year of his tenancy, he was determined to take full advantage of every square inch of ground. His crop of choice was the Irish potato.

As the climate afforded the possibility of three crops a year, this entailed a lot of seed potatoes. Before a crop was sown, the Cropsey children were assigned—in addition to their other household duties—to prepare thousands of them for setting. In the yard, he and Uncle Hen set up planks on sawhorses for rude tables; the children had to stand at them (no chairs allowed) and cut the seed potatoes into pieces. Each piece had to contain at least two eyes—a condition Cropsey enforced by inspecting every one. Once approved, the pieces were left on the tables under canvas covers for two weeks, to cure.

The cutting was done with ancient, dull knives Cropsey kept in a bucket in the shed. They were dull on purpose, for the drudgery of the job, the hours upon hours of eye-finding and sectioning, put the children into a half-stupor that could easily result in cut fingers.

Ollie dreaded those days. To avoid the midday heat, she got up before dawn to wash, dress and help prepare breakfast for the family. She was out at the tables as the sun rose, and stayed there for at least four hours. She wore canvas gloves, because she had learned from experience that the roughness of the knife handle, and the repetitive motion of slicing and slicing again, would have worn her bare hands raw. Her father was always there, always ready with sturdy aphorisms like "One saves oneself much pain, by taking pains" and "No one ever plowed a field by turning it over in his mind." The first piece of poorly sectioned potato he would merely throw aside. If he found another, he would throw it in the cutter's face. There was rarely a third.

Despite his supervision, Ollie's mind wandered. On hot days, she wondered how few layers of clothing she could get away with—might she manage with just drawers, chemise and her dress? But of course her mother would notice the lack of petticoats merely from the way her skirts draped. Or else her brothers would, and delight in telling their parents when their sisters went out *sans pudeur*. As she sank into the monotonous, repetitive task, her mind assumed a state much like dreaming. She envisioned standing in the boat as Wilcox rowed Nell and her back from Camden, the breeze in her hair, which was suddenly loosed from its pile on her head and left to fly. The sensation of her hair against her neck was alien to her. She had been told she had a handsome head of it, black and lustrous like the body of a grand piano. She imagined her hair spread on the surface of a piano, pouring over the stand and among the ivories—and blushed at the indecency. But she also felt her blood quicken.

Such silly thoughts. At night, in the dark, she would sometimes grab a handful of her hair and clasp it over her nose. She liked her smell, a floral hint mixed with straw and sweat and soap grease. She never did this when there was a chance Nell was awake and might see her. Once, her curiosity got the better of her and she leaned over Nell. The latter's breathing was slow and deep, so Ollie bent down and buried her nose in her sister's tresses. To her surprise, Nell's personal perfume was different—it was sugary, like gingerbread, though it was not the holidays and they had done no baking that day. She lingered there for too long, until Nell suddenly turned over in her sleep and Ollie almost swooned with mortification. She bolted back to her side of the bed. Whenever she thought back on this incident, as when she cut potatoes, she felt that humiliation again, as it ripened into a pang of shame.

When the seedlings were all cut and cured, Cropsey let it be known around town that sowing had come. Gangs of free workers—mostly blacks—gathered at dawn in front of the farm. Ollie would peep out at them from behind the parlor curtains. In the warm season, they would lie on the riverbank with shirts open, taking the breeze. On cooler days, they would gather in little knots, sharing cigarettes and tossing dice. Some leaned on shovels they brought themselves: the best, long-handled picks and spades, because many landowners, Cropsey included, provided short-handled ones.

When a large enough gang of twenty or thirty men had gathered, Cropsey went out wearing his sun hat and riding boots. To Ollie's eyes, her father took on a different character as he inspected the applicants. As he dismissed the ones who had been laggard or insufficiently pliant in the past, he seemed to swagger. He shut his ears to all the sad stories of the rejected men, who begged for another chance because they needed the work. When they wouldn't leave the premises, he clapped his hand on a club he kept at his side.

The rest of the men were put to work in the fields digging furrows, twelve inches deep and—all told—miles in length. The job took all day and into the next, hard sweaty work that forced them to strip down to bare skin even on chilly days. To keep them productive, the Cropsey boys were sent out with buckets of water. At noon, they brought a luncheon of bread and cheese and whichever fruit was in season, which the workers had to eat standing in the dirt. Though it would have been easier to have his daughters distribute these, Cropsey never let them out of the house with so many shirtless men of low means on the property. For the time being, this made Ollie and Nell and Lettie and the other girls into prisoners.

Sometimes, as the sun began its long descent to evening, the Negro gangs drifted into song. They did it softly at first, as if seeking the landowner's permission. If he didn't object, more and more of the workers would join in, and the songs would get louder, until Ollie could hear them from any room in the house. They were not spritely tunes, but they were never purely sad. Instead, they seemed born more of loneliness. As she sat and listened, Ollie would think "Now here's a thing"—a Brooklyn girl like herself transported to the doorstep of the South, as plainsongs of endurance sifted through the walls. They made her blue even when she couldn't hear the words, and not always because of the men who sang them. Ollie, after all, had a flair for self-pity, and for some obscure reason it made her cry to think of how her life had changed.

One morning during the summer sowing the family was gathered around the breakfast table.

"Has anyone seen Nell today?" asked Mary Cropsey. "May? Lettie?"

"Shouldn't you ask Ollie that?" Douglas suggested.

Ollie appeared, bearing a pitcher of cream. Of Nell's whereabouts, she frowned: "She wasn't in bed when I got up."

"You have no idea where she might be?"

Ollie shrugged.

The mystery was solved inside the hour. There was a lot of whistling coming from the workers in the fields. When Mary Cropsey went to the window to see why, she saw Nell out among them. She was striding through the furrows, not looking at the men as they stared and stumbled to get out of her way. She was dressed in her crimson riding dress, with a black picture hat the width of a barrelhead, hair full of curls on her shoulders and a basket of flowers on her arm. Her face was still, with a faint smile brushing her lips. She ignored the whooping and hollering from the white men – the blacks would never dare such a thing – but the commotion befitted her, as if she were some blood-daubed pagan priestess of the open fields.

Her mother met her on the side porch. She concealed her fury until Nell presented her with the basket.

"The wildflowers near the racetrack are so pretty..." she began.

Mary Cropsey slapped Nell across the left cheek. The blow was so hard it knocked her hat off her head. Shocked, Nell covered her cheek with her hand.

"How dare you!" said Mary.

The workmen averted their eyes—as did the other Cropsey children in the windows.

"You know what we told you," continued her mother. "What do you think your father would say if he found out?"

Nell's eyes were wet. Then they hardened like the marble eyes of some ancient statue.

"You'll regret that!" she said, and ran into the house.

Mary Cropsey stood for a moment longer, keeping her back to the others. When she turned to come inside, Ollie saw there were tears in her eyes too.

Nell's spilled basket of flowers and hat lay on the porch for the rest of the day. When the workmen left in the evening, and she was permitted to go out, Ollie retrieved them.

Nell didn't leave her room that day, not even for meals. Before bed, Ollie returned her hat to her.

"So why did you do it?"

"Because the flowers were blooming."

"Nell—"

"Why has no one done it sooner? Is it fair that we are stuck in this stifling place, just because strangers are around?"

"You know the rules."

"Yes, you are one for the rules, aren't you?"

"That is unkind," said Ollie.

To their mother's question—what would their father do if he found out—they soon learned the answer. William Cropsey had been away all day, buying lumber at Kramer's for a new fence. When he got back in the evening, the children watched for the explosion, but it never came. Instead, Cropsey ate his dinner silently, and didn't inquire about Nell's absence from the table. Whether to avoid another dramatic scene, or because Mary's rebuke was enough, he pretended it was all beneath his notice.

By the next morning all was back to normal, albeit with Nell's face still bruised on the left side. Ollie didn't want to see her sister suffer merely because of her high-spiritedness. But she could not help feeling that her sister had been treated differently again.

After the digging of the furrows it was time to set the seedlings. The potato sections were brought out tenderly, like heirlooms. They were pushed into the bottom of the furrows, about a foot apart and an inch or two down, and then covered with manure. Cropsey hired carts full of the stuff, because the family's animals could never produce enough. By this phase of the planting a rank odor filled the house—more so when pig manure was used. During the summer and fall plantings, on those humid days when there was no breeze from the river, the stench was staggering. The Cropsey girls developed a solution: they put a drop of perfume in a handkerchief, and tied it around their noses. Passersby who caught a glimpse of them through the windows might have thought the Cropsey residence was a plague house, with masked nurses and an odor not quite of death, but bad enough.

Into these occasions Jim Wilcox would genially waft. With his cologned face and aura of sweet tobacco smoke, he seemed to come from a place where manure was a thing of the past. He brought sweets, and news of ships at the port lately arrived from islands of spice. The children would rush through their chores just to come and sit with him. In time, even Mary Cropsey smiled when she heard Jim's particular rapping on the door. It was not thought odd that Lettie asked for a lock of his hair, to be woven into the family wreath.

One of the things done in that time was for boys to serenade their sweethearts by moonlight. Jim made his debut one summer evening in '99. Round midnight, Nell was drawn to her bedroom window by a sickly thin melody. Jim was below, sitting in a chair he must have carried down the street, playing the spoons against his knee. Behind him were two other men she didn't recognize—one with a harmonica, the other sawing on a fiddle.

After listening for a few seconds, Ollie rose up in bed.

"What ARE they playing?"

"I can't tell."

The indeterminate tune meandered for a while until Jim stopped, and rounded on the fiddler.

"Leo! Have you been drinking?"

"Early and often," came the smirking reply.

Jim jumped up to give chase. Leo Owens dropped his fiddle, and Jim put his foot through it. He did so with such force that it stuck there, and he wore the busted instrument like a shoe as he stumbled across the yard, flinging curses. The neck of the violin tore a swath through her mother's kitchen garden.

Soon the only evidence of this concert was an upturned chair, some broken plants, and the fiddle bow Leo Owens had abandoned. Nell closed the curtain.

"Well, it was sweet of him to try," she said.

"Yes, I suppose it was the best you could expect," replied Ollie.

They shared a more accomplished musical evening some weeks later, when Jim took Nell and Ollie to the Academy to see a show. It was the only Elizabeth City appearance of Hoover's Amalgamated Genuine Ethiopians, a touring troupe of minstrels who boasted of being authentic blacks from the deepest South.

Due to what was regarded as provocative Unionism, there hadn't been many minstrel shows in North Carolina since the War. Elizabeth City, with so many transplanted Northerners, had never kept them out, and so had become a regular stop on the Baltimore to New Orleans circuit. To Ollie, such shows were already old-fashioned, being more associated with the times of her grandparents. Sophisticated girls from Brooklyn preferred legitimate theater, dances or, at worst, vaudeville. But as Hoover's group boasted real blacks "straight from bosom of the old South", it promised to be more interesting. So off they went.

The hall was full when they arrived. The audience was almost entirely white, predominantly male, and seemed to hail mostly from the outlying quarters of the city. A smoky pall draped the room, half-concealing the stink of body odor. When the girls edged into their seats there were cat-calls, but no one dared meet Ollie's eyes when she looked for their sources.

Though drinking was forbidden in the auditorium, there was a lot of pointless laughing from spectators who had arrived drunk. Jim saved his fortification for the main event. With an air of accomplishment, he pulled a pewter flask from his waistband and showed it to the girls. Ollie quickly looked away. Nell shot him a reproving glare that wasn't very sincere.

The show began with a cakewalk, with all members of the company jumping, twisting and high-stepping to the sound of fiddles and tambourines. Ollie wouldn't have thought it necessary, but most of the "genuine Ethiopians" were nevertheless in blackface. Only the host, a light-hued mulatto, was untouched by cork:

"Ladies and gentlemen, gather 'round as we regale you with the genuine sounds of a world sadly missed, an idyllic place, a glory to her people, betrayed by cruel war, lost in time..."

"If ye got the time, dat iz!" injected the minstrel at the end of the line.

There were songs, and moments when the performers could not contain their joy, and jumped up and danced. The host, who was dressed in an ill-fitting suit, puff tie and spats, tried and comedically failed to give the proceedings an air of class, to which some of the audience hooted "He's a show horse, ain't he?" and "Tell 'em Senator!" A heavily inebriated gentleman rose from the audience and shouted "God hang you monkey-faced, purse-thievin' dandy darkies!". The crowd erupted in applause, and the other Ethiopians laughed and slapped their knees as if they were in on the joke.

"I assure you, sir, I come from a distinguished family," replied the dandy. "My brother climbs mountains. He climbed the Himalayas last year." Then he pointed at one of the end-men, and asked "What mountains have your brother ever climbed?"

"My brudder? Him-a-layin' in bed every chance he get!"

The first act was topped off with a rendition of the old favorite, *Jump Jim Crow*, by a singer in ill-fitting rags. He feigned a gimp as he danced–

Come listen all ye girls and boys, I'm from Tucky-hoe
I'm gonna sing a little song, my name's Jim Crow.
Weel about and turn about an do just so,
Ebery time I wheel about I jump Jim Crow

Oh, I'm a roarer on de fiddle, and down in old Virginny
They say I play de skyentific like Massa Paganini...

Wilcox made a display of enjoying himself. He laughed overloud, turning frequently to Ollie and Nell to make sure they were laughing too. Between guffaws he bent his head down to his knees to take nips from his flask. To Ollie, his conduct reflected weakness of character, as if he felt compelled to descend to the level of the rest of the audience. It bothered her so much, she found it hard to enjoy the music, which was—truth be told—better done than most all-white troupes. A Negro fiddler with face painted black as a railroad tie performed some of the best bowing she had ever heard.

During the first break Nell got up to visit the powder room. When they were alone, Ollie turned to Jim:

"Are you just going to sip on that, or finish it like a man?"

He regarded her, surprised. Ollie met his gaze, not flinching.

Jim was never afraid to take up a challenge from his co-workers and his peers at the saloon. So why would he shrink now, from a woman?

He downed the rest of his whiskey in a dozen hearty gulps. Then he wiped his mouth with his sleeve, and stared back at her, triumphant.

It didn't take long for the extra liquor to show on him. As the three of them sat through the second act—which included a long, malaprop oration by the dandy on the absurdity of women's suffrage—Jim suddenly had trouble keeping straight in his seat. His head lolled on his shoulders, and he slumped, and began to mutter under his breath.

"James Wilcox, are you intoxicated?" asked Nell in a voice loud enough to be heard throughout the hall.

Jim heaved a sheepish laugh. Someone from the audience chimed in, "Yeah Jim, ain't ye drunk yet?"

"Ollie, let's go!" said Nell, red-faced and struggling to collect her things. As the ladies departed, the Ethiopians all rose to their feet, and the dandy doffed his cap.

Later, on the porch at home, Nell fumed.

"I'd never begrudge a man a drink or two. But to be falling-down drunk while escorting two women in public. It's disrespectful!"

Ollie kept silent, nodding her head but otherwise letting Nell's pique run its course. If she felt at all guilty for goading Jim, it dwindled beside the fact that he was liable to be goaded in the first place. Yet she felt compelled to add, "I might have suggested he finish his bottle or get rid of it..."

"To think he believes he's with his low waterfront pals when he's out with me!" Nell went on, not hearing or not caring what Ollie said. "To think that's the kind of conduct this family would approve...!"

"I wonder what Ma and Pa will say about this."

At this thought, Nell fell silent. She sat in the glider. Her thoughts seemed to try her as she stared across the river.

"I don't think it would help to tell them," she finally said.

"I wouldn't be much of an elder sister if I didn't."

"No, I don't think you should. Promise me."

"Nell—"

"I said promise me!"

"It's only your happiness I have in mind," said Ollie. "But don't ask me to keep more secrets about him. From this day on."

"You won't have to. You have my word."

She took Ollie's hand, and they sat together looking at the river until someone put out the dining room light.

VI.

The Methodists are worth considering; they are nearer the soil. Their religious emotions can be transmuted into love and charity. They are not half bad; even though they will not take a drink, they really do not need it so much as some of their competitors for the seat next to the throne. If chance sets you down between a Methodist and a Baptist, you will move toward the Methodist to keep warm.

--Clarence Darrow, *How to Pick a Jury*

Jim had been game for any sort of entertainment for all the years of their acquaintance—until September of 1901. That was when the celebrity evangelist George R. Stuart came to town for a ten-day revival. Nell had read about him in the newspapers, and wanted Jim to escort her to his sermon at the Baptist Church on Sunday the 29th. But to her surprise, Jim turned her down flat.

Stuart travelled far and wide on a campaign of temperance sermons that electrified and appalled the nation. Electrified, because he filled every house he spoke at, to the extent that hundreds of would-be attendees had to be turned away at the doors. His revivals were the despair of fire marshals, who had to countenance auditoriums packed shoulder-to-shoulder. In Dayton, Ohio, so many people came to hear him that he was obliged to deliver his sermon three times—once to the crowd in the sanctuary, again to those gathered in the basement, and a third time to the ones outside. In Portsmouth, two thousand people filled the largest hall in town, pressed so tightly that Stuart was unable to reach the stage. After the cry went up to "Lift him!", he was raised on the shoulders of the people and invited to crawl to the pulpit over their very bodies.

For all this anticipation, his crowds were never disappointed. Listeners, whether regular churchgoers or not, were reduced to states of reverent ecstasy by his words. Hundreds of hard-drinking men swore to Christ and Methodism after hearing just one of his sermons. It was not uncommon for business to plunge at the saloons in the towns he visited—at least for a whole day or two.

Yet some were appalled by his popularity. Stuart, in fact, was no mere chapter-and-verse preacher. His fiery orations against Demon Alcohol were illustrated not only with examples from the Bible, but juicy stories ripped straight from the yellow press. Faithless wives, corrupt politicians, drunkard sons and husbands, thieves, whores, murderers and divorcees all figured in his parables. To certain old-school critics, Stuart's ministry smacked more of titillation than righteousness.

On the basis of his "off-color" and "unchaste" language, an Asheville newspaper called for his censure by the Methodist conference. In Chattanooga a judge swore out a warrant for his arrest, so he might face the consequences of asserting, in front of three thousand voters, that the public servants of their city were in the pockets of saloon-keepers. Stuart skipped town before the sheriff could fetch him.

As much as appreciation for his eloquence, there was a thrilling sense that Stuart might say anything, no matter how sensational, to win souls for Christ. This proved to be an irresistible draw for the citizens of Elizabeth City—except for Jim Wilcox.

"No matter how long I know him, I'll never understand him," Nell complained after Jim had turned her down.

"Never mind. I'll go with you," said Ollie.

The Baptist sanctuary on Main Street was the biggest church in town. It was already full to bursting when the sisters arrived. The attendees were almost entirely gentlemen, and they courteously cleared a path for the young ladies to come forward to a section near the pulpit.

Within moments of sitting down, Ollie felt unwell. The commotion of the audience, which seemed to press in and buzz like a crowd at a racecourse, gave her a headache; the smoke from hundreds of cigars and cigarettes made it hard to breathe. Worst of all, the building's new electric lights were not working that day, so the place was lit by combustion. The smoke from the Church's two kerosene chandeliers collected among the rafters like a bank of sickly blue clouds.

"Why don't you untie your hat?" Nell said.

Figuring this would be inappropriate in a church—even a Baptist one—Ollie shook her head.

"Well if you won't I will..." declared Nell, who not only untied her hat but removed it. The appearance of her uncovered head, and her chestnut hair tied in a chignon at the nape of her neck, drew whistles behind her.

"You shouldn't have done that." said Ollie.

"Tell Mother and she'll find out about a certain novel under your pillow."

"You are evil. You don't belong in a church."

There were no formalities when the program began—no introductions or trifling announcements. A tall man in a black suit and tie simply strode to the pulpit and commenced to speak.

Stuart's face was narrow, with deep, angular features and a spray of laugh lines at the corners of his eyes. His brown hair, parted on his right side and breaking in wave-like abundance to his left, made him tower still higher. Ollie noticed his hands: they were large, with spindly knuckles and fingers long enough to envelop her whole head. They found their way around the edges of the lectern with complete ease, as if he had preached from that spot every Sunday.

"I hold in my hand the Word of God," he declared, and held up a Bible clad in well-limbered leather. "It is the source of the Wisdom of God and all subjects: moral, social, business and political. I shall take from this book tonight the statements of God concerning our nation..."

He read some Old Testament verses, which Ollie did not hear because she was so compelled by the sound of his voice. The weight of it sank into her as if she was made of mere smoke. And yet it was not frightening or portentous—there was an ease about it that evoked the prayer before a quiet Sunday dinner with family. Nell, too, was affected: she reached for Ollie's hand and clenched it.

"Now I like to think I am a godly man, but not a smarter man that any of my brothers and sisters assembled here in this holy place. It doesn't take much to put something by me, trusting as I am in the grace of the Lord. Shoot—the first time I read the good book I did it with God's Word in one hand and a dictionary in the other, so few of the words did I know!"

With that word, "shoot", a tremor went through the audience. It was not an exclamation Ollie had ever heard from a pulpit. And yet, with that vernacular eruption, Stuart's audience relaxed. Here, they thought, was a man who spoke their language. Here was the edgy, dangerous preacher they had heard so much about. And when he smiled, and unfurled teeth of unblemished white, it was with the assurance of a veteran performer—an actor who knew he had his audience where he wanted them.

"And so, when I speak to you tonight about the scourge of liquor, it is not because I have any special insight, any pretensions to sagacity. I say what I say because I am enlightened by the Word of God, and have eyes to see. I have a mind to judge, and a mouth to proclaim the truth. No more, and no less."

From there, Stuart's talk went in a direction Ollie would never have expected. Instead of denouncing the liquor trade solely in moral terms, he made a hard detour into the economic:

"Now I am going to show you that money spent on liquor is not just 'commerce', but burned up as surely as if it were thrown in an oven. I do not ask that you have a first-class mind to see it. I can show it to a fellow with half-sense..."

He paused to let the audience laugh at this, and went on, "Do you know how much it costs to make a gallon of liquor? Some of you ought to, you have drunk enough of it!" [More laughter.] "It costs about twenty cents a gallon to manufacture. They used to sell it in my State for twenty-five cents a gallon. Do you know what it sells for over the saloon counter at ten cents a drink? It sells for about four dollars a gallon, not taking into account the licorice and tobacco and other devilment put in it. Now let us see where this four dollars comes from, and where it goes. If you would see where it comes from, stand at the door of the saloon and watch the men come and go. They are the laboring men, the mechanics, the wage-earners, whose families need every cent of their wages.

"Now let us see where it goes. Twenty cents of the four dollars goes for apples and corn and rye and other materials out of which the stuff is made, and to pay the few men used in the manufacture of the stuff. This goes back into the legitimate channels of trade. Five cents on the dollar, then, you see, goes back into legitimate trade.

"Where does the rest of it go? One large bulk of it goes to the United States Government to pay the great army of officers to look after this business and pay the other expenses of running this murderous and expensive traffic. I believe the United States Government ought to be supported from the luxuries of the rich and not by the bread and meat and clothing of the families of the poor!" And he paused again for an outburst of applause. "Another bulk of the money goes into our big city corporations to pay extra policemen to take care of drunks and brawls and fights and to quell the mobs created by this traffic and to lay the streets in front of the palaces of the rich. The poor rascal out there who cannot build a front gate to the cottage of his home is plunking down his money upon the counter of the saloon to pave the streets of the great cities!

"Another bulk of it goes into the hands of the brewers and distillers of this country to make up the millions of dollars which are used by the great liquor organizations of this country to buy our politicians and law-making bodies, to subsidize the American ballot, and to dig down the very pillars of American liberty. The meat and bread and comforts of the poor drunkard's cottage turned into the corrupting fund of our country! Another bulk of it goes into the hands of the thousands of diamond-studded gamblers, who, with velvet hands and elegantly clothed bodies, have their rooms in the saloon buildings of this country, who do not work, but gather up the money of the saloon crowd and buy their clothes, their diamonds and their fine horses, with the bread and meat of the poor. No wonder the middle classes of this country are in such a distressed condition today!"

Stuart displayed a coin in his slender fingers.

"I hold in my hand a silver dollar. That you may see clearly what I mean, I will spend this money before your eyes. I drop it on this pulpit and—Lord help me—I call it a saloon counter..."

He dropped the dollar on his hymnal with a hollow *thunk* that was audible throughout the hall.

"That dollar buys a quart of liquor. Now I will take the saloon end of that dollar, and then I will take the home end of it, and see what becomes of the dollar. As I have shown you, five cents of it goes back into legitimate trade; and the ninety-five cents remaining is distributed to the United State Government and to the big city corporations and big brewers and the diamond-studded gamblers, and nearly all of it, as you see, is drawn out of the hands of the common people, and does not come back. So far as the masses of the people are concerned, that money is gone.

"Now let us take the home end of it. I drink the quart of liquor and start home to the drunkard's cottage. My wife, Sallie, meets me at the door, surrounded by her hungry, wretched children, and says 'John, what did you bring home?' 'I brought you a quart.' Now if the ladies in the audience will pardon me, I wish to ask what the quart of liquor in the poor drunkard's stomach is worth? I say that the dollar is burned up at the home end; not only is the liquor worth nothing to the poor old drunkard's home, but it burns up his body, burns up his mind, burns up his soul, destroys the happiness of his wife and children, ruins his business or trade, disqualifies him from making another dollar, hurts the community, hurts everything. Do you see where the saloon dollar goes?"

He paused again as a thousand men leapt to their feet. Ollie turned to the faces behind her; intoxicated by sanctimony, they pulled hard on their cigars as they spewed smoke and acclaim. Many of them, she noticed, bore the blotchy redness of the habitual drunk. Some even stank of liquor. Yet the men stood and cheered for Stuart, who stood back and nodded into the crowd.

"I'd think the government bureaucrat buys *some* bread with money from those liquor taxes," she remarked to Nell.

Nell was in no mood for petty cynicism. She sat silent for a moment, as if to let Ollie's objection dissolve, and then declared "I've never heard the liquor question treated that way. This is modern. This is scientific preaching."

"While Sam Jones and I were in Houston a few months ago, I made this argument with reference to rents," Stuart continued. "The pastor of the Methodist Church said: 'O George, your speech about rents called to the minds and hearts of these people that we have just had it sadly illustrated. The daughter of one of our preachers married a good man, who, after his marriage, began to drink...'"

"Maybe she gave him good reason to drink," Ollie whispered in Nell's ear. With that remark, Nell stopped holding Ollie's hand.

"'...He lost his business, and walked the streets a drunkard. His wife was a member of my Church. I often visited her. I saw the blue veins on her face and her tearful eyes as she said: 'O brother, the rent-paying haunts me like a nightmare. I have to sew till nearly midnight to make the rent and pay for the little that my half-starved children eat. My husband came in and found me sewing the other night, and he said if he caught me working for a wage again he would kill me. But, O brother, I am obliged to sew.' The preacher told me that he had seen the little woman at one of the early meetings at the tabernacle. And the last song they sang was *We'll Never Say Goodbye in Heaven.* That very night, possibly making up the hour she had spent in worship, she was found by her husband stitching away at midnight, thinking of rent! Rent! RENT!!! Staggering into the room, wild with drink, he said: 'I told you I would kill you if I found you working!' Bang! Bang!! Bang!!! Three balls tore their way through her quivering flesh. As her little children came screaming around her, she sent her little boy of the preacher. 'And,' said the preacher to me, 'as I stooped over her dying body, she whispered, as her life-blood ebbed away: 'We'll never say good-bye in heaven, and thank God! There will be no rent to pay up there.'

"This is but one of the almost daily occurrences throughout the land. Shall we men, who hold the ballot of our country and the destinies of these poor women in our hands, suffer such cruelties year after year? God Almighty help us come to the rescue of our suffering women!"

It seemed hardly possible, but the ensuing applause was even more thunderous. Men bobbed their heads in assent and stamped their feet. But Ollie suspected it was that story that really thrilled them—the image of the "three balls" that "tore their way through quivering flesh." Such erotica, deftly juxtaposed with sentiment! Here was language hardly ever heard outside of trash novels. The kind of novels, in fact, that few of these men would let their daughters read. Ollie knew to never ask permission to read hers.

Stuart was rounding for home now. "Every person who has a handkerchief get it ready," he said. "I will tell you a handkerchief story. The day my dear wife told me Bowling Green carried for prohibition, I took my handkerchief from my pocket, and, waving it, while tears of gratitude ran down my cheeks, I said: 'Wife, the day is coming when the pure white banner of temperance will wave its graceful folds over the downfall of every saloon in glorious old America.' Those of you who will enter the battle of the white flag, work for victory, and shout in triumph, let us hail the oncoming victory by waving our handkerchiefs!"

A thousand hands waved, white cotton handkerchiefs flying in the lamp smoke. Reaching into the bag that was chained to her waist, Nell came out with one of her own. It was silk, and it was scarlet, but duly did it wave.

Nothing Ollie had heard convinced her that Stuart was anything more than a clever manipulator. But even she would have been compelled to admit the truth: the spectacle of all those white cloths flying, and Nell's solitary red one in the midst of them all, was one of the damnedest things she had ever seen in a church.

The newspapers said Stuart would be leading revivals in Elizabeth City all week. At home, Nell could not stop singing his praises. For the first time in her young life, she felt the exhilaration of discovering a cause beyond herself. Stuart's crusade had elevated her to a height where the air was cleaner and clearer. She talked of his "evangelical rationalism" at the dinner table, and at the wash tub, and in their bed at night. She spoke of throwing their father's liquor stash in the river. She kept Ollie up so late she begged her to stop.

When Jim next came over, Nell sat him down in the dining room and gave him the Full Stuart. Jim listened with a weak smile on his face, as if determined to humor her. But Nell never took well to being patronized.

"Is that all you have to say?" she asked. "Nothing?"

He tossed his head. "Well, I'm sure happy you enjoyed yourself. Not sure what it has to do with me. I'm not a drunkard."

"Look at your britches, Jim Wilcox. If you saved all the money you spend on rot-gut, you wouldn't need those patches."

"My mama didn't raise no prodigal. I'd wear these patches even if I had a million!"

"He is the first preacher of the modern era."

"I don't doubt it. But I'd rather spend my time with you going out, doing gay things. Not in a church."

"Ollie, he's impossible!" Nell cried. "Tell him for me."

Ollie looked up from her sewing. When she fixed him with her eye, Jim's face went white, and he became fidgety.

"Can't you spare an hour on this, Jim? Just for your girl?"

"It's the Lord's own truth, Ollie—I don't have an hour to spare this week. Four boats have to come out of the water, and there's the devil's own amount of tarring to do, and Hayman is already on me for the time I spend away..."

Nell was staring at the opposite wall, as if not hearing him. Her eyes were indigo now, blazing and burning holes in the wallpaper. After a few moments of excruciating silence, Ollie said, "Jim, I think it's best you go."

"Is that what you think, Nellie? Should I leave?"

She did not answer.

The following Wednesday Stuart spoke at the Methodist Church. Nell tried to convince the whole family to go, but the elder Cropseys were too tired, and the young professed no interest. Nell declared she would indeed attend, alone and without permission if necessary. Ollie forestalled that conflict by volunteering to go with her.

The theme of the night's talk was *On Strong Womanhood.* Stuart appeared at the lectern in the same suit, lofting the same pliant Bible. He began again with Scripture: Proverbs 31:10, "Who can find a virtuous woman? For her price is far above rubies."

He said: "How insincere, how full of shame, how full of deception, is the female character of today. There sits a woman with the appearance of luxuriant hair falling in flowing bangs about her forehead, but I do not know whether it is confined to her head by nature, or pinned on by hairpins. Over there sits a lady with beautiful rosy cheeks, but I don't know whether they came from a ruddy blood careering through her healthful system, or whether she got it out of a little box on the bureau. A woman's hair, teeth, lips and cheeks are not more treacherous than her tongue. I touch the subject with a degree of hesitation. I handle a woman's mouth like I handle a loaded pistol. You never know when it is going off."

"O, the insincerity of society's tongue! The insincere praise and flattery and condemnation. But an honest woman—a sincere woman. It is safe to buy a candle from her..."

When he said "there sits a lady with beautiful rosy cheeks..." she thought his eyes flitted in the direction of her and Nell. She wasn't sure, but the suspicion made her burn with self-consciousness. For she had indeed opened a little box on her bureau before going out for the evening, and her hair was not innocent of hair-pins.

"The strong woman industriously looks after her children. She knows where her children go, how long they stay, and what they do. It was not her girl you saw out on the street with that dude after midnight, the other night, returning from the opera. It was not her girl that you saw taking a moonlight buggy ride with that young man. It was not her girl that you saw encircled in the arms of that lecherous youth, whirling on the ballroom floor. It was not her boy you saw on the streets at night. It was not her boy you saw in the club room at the card table. The curse of our land today is that our mothers do not look to the ways of their children."

The strong woman, he declared, is the very bulwark of civilization. "A strong woman means a woman who makes some demands upon the opposite sex. God grant that the day may speedily come when our girls will think as much of themselves as the boys think of themselves, when a girl will stand at her parlor door and demand the young man who enters that as her company he shall be as clean in his life as the young man demands she shall be."

"In one of our Tennessee homes there lived a bright, cultured young woman, who put a womanly premium upon her own life and her society. A brilliant young lawyer was paying court at her shrine. He was young and bright and strictly moral, though not religious. He had won her love and gained her consent to her marriage. During the Christmas holidays, with a company of reckless companions, in an unusually hilarious moment, he was persuaded to take wine. Ignorant of the treacherous drink, he was soon intoxicated, and to the delight of his envious companions he was carried to his room drunk.

"The news was carried to his young lady friend, who retired to her room, buried her face in her hand, fought a battle and gained a victory. Late in the evening of the next day this young man rang the door-bell at her father's residence. She saw him coming and told the servant she would answer the bell. She opened the door and said to him: 'I have heard of your last night's conduct. You have taken my name and our relations into disgrace. You have shown your appreciation and your estimation of me. I cannot receive the attentions of a man who values so lightly his own character and mine. You may go back to your companions, and be my friend no longer. Our roads separate here. Goodbye, sir.'"

Stuart's vision of ideal womanhood landed harder in the crowd than his denunciation of drink. It was one thing, after all, to fulminate against the saloons, which would never close no matter what any preacher said. That was the kind of moralism any drunk could risk. But the company of fast women always seemed like a precarious blessing to the men of Elizabeth City. Young ladies were so suggestible, so weak, they might actually be persuaded to withdraw their favors. The prospect was chilling. There was no laughter at this sermon, and the applause after was more polite than enthusiastic.

The hall was so crowded Ollie and Nell decided not to brave the aisles until the men were gone. They were still in the pew when Stuart and his partner on the preaching circuit, Sam Jones, came out of the rectory. They were a mismatched pair—Stuart was long and elegant, but Jones was short, with the kind of handlebar mustache Ollie associated with lawyers and dry goods salesmen; where Stuart radiated serenity, Jones' eyes were darty, searching everywhere until they settled on the two Cropsey sisters in their seats.

"Well hallo!" Jones cried. "You'll have a long wait, young misses, if you intend to stay until the next revival!"

"A fair prospect, if we didn't have to be home soon," replied Nell.

"Much as I approve of a woman who knows her sphere, we welcome our sisters in Christ. Especially for preaching that so directly concerns them..."

Stuart, who had said nothing yet, extended a spidery limb to Ollie. Blushing, she did not shake his hand as much as tap it away.

But Nell grasped it without reservation, and shook it so hard that the soul-winner's arm jangled. He smiled, and they locked eyes on each other for a moment longer than the occasion demanded.

"A lovely child," said Stuart, in that molasses voice that seemed to pour through Ollie's ears and collect sweetly in the pan of her cranium.

"I warn you, there are hairpins under this hat," Nell replied.

"For lending us your presence, you are forgiven."

"And what did you think of the Minister's talk?" asked Jones.

"I've heard nothing like it before."

"That is a diplomatic answer," said Stuart, smiling, "that I will take as a compliment."

They spoke for only a few moments, until other petitioners lured the ministers away. But the sisters found themselves as charmed by Stuart's person as they were compelled by his oratory. He was a figure who embodied quiet, confident manhood, from the loops of his shoelaces to the farthest hair on his head. The tips of his mustache only flirted with gravity. His collar was tight enough for the setting, but loose enough to suggest he didn't care. There was nothing blustery about him, nothing that enforced his authority with coarseness. It pained Ollie to think of the contrast he made with the Cropsey men.

The meeting, in fact, left her wrung out, exhausted, and not a little irritated. Sometimes, even the most casual of social encounters left her feeling that way. And yet there stood Nell, not just surviving as Ollie was, but thriving. She seemed ready to exchange a hundred more quips. She seemed to grow taller, her eyes brighter. "How does she do it?" Ollie had asked herself a thousand times, as her energy flagged, and she sank into invisibility beside her younger sister.

They were picked up in front of the church by Uncle Hen.

"You're ten minutes late," he said as he pulled them into the buggy. "Your father will have words for me."

"Let him!"

"Nell, mind your tongue."

Nell was about to reply, but Ollie pinched her forearm. They were no longer ascending the heights of Mt. Olympus with Jones and Stuart. They were being pulled again into the Vale of Ordinariness, where men and women discussing great thoughts were subject to reproach for being ten minutes late. A look of distress came over Nell, of promises withheld and vistas denied. She didn't speak for most of the ride home, until they were a few moments from the house, and she turned to Ollie.

"I think I will go the Methodist Church next Sunday."

"Is that so?"

"I've never been happy with the Presbyterians. I never chose to go there.'"

"Don't you think that's a matter for discussion?"

"I am discussing it."

"And what if Ma and Pa disagree? Will you go alone?"

"Of course not," she said, and flashed a smile. "You will come with me."

Her gloved hand patted Ollie's, and she turned back to look at the river as they drove up Riverside Avenue. The water was so calm the bank seemed to end in a black chasm. The dock at Fearing's shot into the void like a bridge that was never completed, a fruitless construct reaching toward a shore as distant and unattainable as the half-moon above.

"What are you girls whispering about?" asked their uncle from the front.

"We're becoming strong women!" replied Nell.

"All right," he said. "As long as you strong women are indoors by nine-thirty."

VII.

After supper the next day, Nell was in the dining room, trimming one of her winter jackets with a handsome, self-colored fringe. The door-bell rang at about the time Jim Wilcox visited every Thursday evening. Nell didn't budge from her chair. The bell rang again. Ollie looked up at Nell; her expression was one of absorption in her task, but Ollie knew her sister well enough to see the annoyance in it. She was deliberately making Jim wait.

The bell rang a third time. Nell pushed her work away, rose, unfurled her arms in a long, time-consuming stretch. The bell rang a fourth time as she went to the front door. After a moment, Ollie followed her, but stayed in the parlor and tried not to be seen.

Through the glass, Jim watched Nell come down the hall and through the inner doors. From her slowness, he perceived she was distracted. When she opened the door she did not smile, and bowed her head only slightly when he came forward to peck her cheek.

"Is it a bad time?" he asked.

"As bad as any," she replied.

It was one of those sultry late September days, when the heat brought out the sickly odor of leaves rotting on the ground. Nell had not been outside yet, even to use the privy, because she was so engrossed in her projects.

She took one of the porch chairs now and looked at him. The hem of her gray house-dress rode over her ankles, and she was wearing a pair of natural rubber slippers over her stockings. His eyes flitted between her ankles and her face. Nell, meanwhile, was staring at the paper sack he was holding.

"There was a man at the station selling these," he said.

Jim opened the bag. Inside was a dozen small, round, lumpy fruits.

"Oranges," she said.

"Tangerines. From Georgia. First of the season."

"Thank you, Jim. I'm sure the children will enjoy them."

They plowed another furrow of silence.

"I get the feeling this is a bad time," he said.

"I would have preferred your company the other night, when I asked you to come to the revival."

"Oh, that again."

"Yes, that again. Would you say I've asked many favors of you, in the time we've known each other?"

"No."

"Have I been quarrelsome? A burden on you in any way?"

"Wouldn't say that."

"You *couldn't*," she said. "Yet the one time I ask a special favor of you, you deny me. How should I feel about that?"

"I guess you'd be sore about it."

"You'd guess I'd be sore! Perceptive as usual!"

Mocking his wits—this was something he was hearing too much of lately. It cut him, but he refrained from responding in kind. Instead, he took the other chair and stared out over the water. Just then, not far offshore, old Ben Shrive was heading out into the Sound. It was easy to tell which shad boat was Ben's: it had the sail with the long, skinny patch on it, a remnant blue as denim. Under the circumstances, Jim wished he was out on the water with him, splitting the swells, sharing the old man's cigarettes and his quiet.

"Look. I didn't come here to argue. If you want to know, I did my time in the pews. My maw was a regular customer, when her health was better. I heard every sermon with her. I heard it all. I only get a few times a week to spend time with you, Nellie. I'm sorry if I'd rather spend it doing gay things."

"I understand that," she spoke, softer. "But that's just what I'm saying. You haven't heard it said like this man did. It's like no other sermon you ever heard. There were plenty of gentlemen there, more than the ladies. He used the common language. It wasn't 'a dose of Scripture and up on your feet for a sing, fellows'. It was a new kind of preaching, and I wanted to share it with you. But you didn't even give it a chance. You didn't trust me."

"Oh for damnation's sake, why do you gotta put it that way, Nell?"

"Language, sir."

Jim reached into his jacket for his pewter flask. As he pulled on it, Nell became more irritated.

"Must you do that now, of all times!"

Jim laughed. "Is that your new kind of preaching?"

"I'm going inside—"

"No, wait," he said, grasping her arm. Indeed, he had always been free and easy in the way he laid his hands on her. It was never anything indecent, of course—never above the elbow, or below the small of her back. It was just a gentleman's casual mastery over female flesh. There was nothing like it between her parents, or between her sisters and their callers. She was never quite sure if she liked it.

"I never hid the fact that I like a drink now and then, Nellie. With the work I do, I'm thinkin' I deserve it. And to be plain, I don't like people telling me I'm damned to hell for it—"

"Language, again."

"Damn if you don't bring it out of me, every time. I don't know what I'm saying when you're like this—"

"You don't understand. In this church, you earn your redemption by what you do. You *choose* to be saved. The minister isn't there just to tell you your fate. He tells you how to save yourself. Why would you be be frightened of that?"

"Ain't frightened."

"I'm sick to death of them telling me I've got no say in where my soul is going. Based on what ignorant people did thousands of years ago! It's insulting. I'm sick of it."

"Uh-huh."

"Isn't it better to have the power in your hands, based on what you do?"

Anybody who spent as much time fishing as Jim heard his share of philosophic discussions. He reckoned the backwaters of the Dismal had hosted more such seminars than the halls of any college. Something about such questions always struck Jim as rhetorical, not really inviting an answer but instead the peaceful reflection of a man with a pole and a smoke and nowhere to be for the rest of the afternoon. He had sometimes enjoyed those moments.

But not this one. Nell was looking at him in a way that demanded a response. He shifted his feet, accidentally kicking over the bag of tangerines. The fruits scattered over the deck, one rolling down the six steps to the front walk. He uncapped his flask.

"For instance, you can throw that away," she said.

The suggestion caught him in mid-swallow. The whiskey hit his throat hard, causing him to choke and cough.

"What do you say, Jim? Will you do that? For me?"

She was gazing at him now with an new expression: eyes flashing, lips slightly parted, head inclined toward him – a look of implied reward if he bent to her will.

"Uh, I don't know what you mean," he said.

"You know. I want you to throw that flask away. Can you do that?"

"I can do anything I set my mind to, Nellie. But I don' see why."

Her eyes froze. "You don't see *why*? I'm asking you. Isn't that enough?"

Jim got up to retrieve the scattered tangerines. He got them all back in the bag—except for the one that had rolled down into the front yard—as he thought and cursed and felt Nell's eyes scorching his back. Then he turned to her, and slipped the flask back into his breast pocket.

"No," he said.

"No?"

"No, I won't. I don't know what devil has gotten into you today, but I won't be spoke to that way, with demands and such. I ain't yours to lord over. If I asked you to give up your books for me, would you do that?"

"That's different," she said. "Reading isn't a mortal sin."

"I say anything's a sin that takes away a man's innocent pleasures. Pleasures that ain't hurting nobody else!"

"So you not only refuse to escort me to the revival, Jim Wilcox, you refuse to do me this one small thing?"

"I guess. Yeah."

"I'm asking for the last time."

"I've given my answer."

"Then please leave. I won't look at the sight of you right now."

She then got up, and padding silently on her rubber slippers, left him alone on the porch. She shut and locked the inner door, and pulled the shade down.

Later, at supper, young Douglas came in with a sack he had found beside the front walk.

"Found these oranges outside!" he announced. "They were sellin' 'em for a nickel each at the station you know, and now we got a dozen for free!"

"They're *tangerines*," Nell said, biting off that last word in a way that struck everyone else as odd. Everyone, that is, except for Ollie.

Jim was furious as he stalked his way back to town. When he was angry, he was given to spitting, which he did in heaving, guttural fashion on the curb. People sitting on their porches watched him anoint their properties, and gave him a hard stare or cleared their throats to express their disapproval, which Jim ignored and invited again with the next expectoration a few doors down. He'd had enough of the petty prejudices of these Riverside Avenue folk.

He flushed anew at slights he wanted to forget. Once, when he came to take Nell and Lettie to a show, Lettie came out and asked, "No buggy? Why didn't you harness the horse for us, Jim?" Then Lettie and Nell laughed.

He was a patient man, a forgiving man, but that remark made him want to throw the bouquet of flowers he'd brought in Lettie's face. Yes, he'd harnessed the horses now and again, but he did it as a favor, not because it was expected.

"Because I have been lackey long enough," he replied.

Why did he keep coming to that place? It couldn't be for the sake of those favors most girls would do their beaus by now, three years into courtship. Nell was pretty—the handsomest girl he knew—but there was too much in her manner that said she understood her value. All the Cropsey girls had it, this lift in their chins, this ever-so-lofty distance. Sometimes he thought they were making fun of him, the way they stood erect when he was near, as if to make a point of how short he was. Lettie had it, and Louise, and especially Olive, whose eye-level made him feel like an insect. The father would barely have anything to do with him. The mother never made him feel more than adequate for her daughter.

He thought: it must have something to do with where they came from. From being Brooklyn Cropseys, where the name meant something, to here, where it meant nothing at all. Betsy City, where they didn't even own the property they lived on! The thought gave him a moment of satisfaction—those high-and-mighty-Cropseys, scratching out a living growing potatoes in someone else's ground. It made him feel so good that he laughed out loud. The driver of a delivery wagon was passing by when he did so, and gave Jim a puzzled look. But Jim didn't know him, and didn't care.

By this time he had reached some of the watering holes near the swivel bridge. These were no more than closet-sized shelters with room for a short bar and a few men to stand. Jim went in and ordered himself a beer. His fingers around the cool glass, and the prickly snap of the liquid in his throat, relieved the unseasonable heat. He began to feel better. The barman, who Jim knew slightly and went by the name of Cab, wiped the bar with the filthy towel. Jim lifted his elbows and his glass.

"Been down to see that girl?" asked Cab.

"Yeah."

"Lucky man," he said, and winked.

Jim finished his drink and drifted back into town. In truth, he didn't need Cab to tell him he was lucky to have Nell. Nor was she the first girl to tell her man not to drink so much. The scuttlebutt among his co-workers was full of such stories—of female brains filled with guff from the latest itinerant preacher to blow into town. Seemed to him these ministers of the Lord had stopped telling men they should be good, but dwelled instead on the sins of Demon Alcohol. Seemed the 'new religion' was all about making excuses.

He imagined the Cropsey girls in their rented dollhouse. How were they to have the breadth of mind a man might, who was out in the world and knew better? For all their book learning, what did they know of a hard day's honest labor, hoisting timbers and blacking hulls like Jim did? They begrudged a man a dram of relief, but took the gifts his wages bought, every time. They heard whatever some fool preacher said, and couldn't distinguish the gold from the pig shit. He began to pity Nell as he might a child. And who could stay angry at a child?

He rolled a cigarette as he walked, slowing for the tricky part of pouring the loose tobacco into the paper. Lighting it, he amused himself by blowing blue fumes straight into the air, trailing them behind like a locomotive, and thought, "Who am I fooling?" In truth, he loved every moment at Seven Pines. There was an air of pleasing civility about the Cropseys, an industry of constant improvement in mind, that he had never experienced in his home. Just being around them made him feel the rusty gates of possibility creak, crack, and begin to open on what lay beyond.

The girls were all beautiful in their ways, from Ollie's elegance to Lettie's steady, dimpled smile to the way Nell fit just so under his shoulder. Yet they were more than just pretty faces to him. Each represented a distinct inspiration, each the seed of a different future he might imagine for himself. He envisioned how the long lines of

Mrs. Olive Wilcox would reflect well on him, coming to the door to welcome their guests. A half-dozen children surrounded him on the lawn with Mrs. Carrie Wilcox, as she unpacked roast chicken from a wicker basket. And he imagined Mrs. Ella Maud Wilcox filling their cab with packages from the shops of St. Louis. Out of breath, glowing softly with perspiration, she would lean in to kiss him, and ask about his day.

His reverie ended when he reached his mother's house. He found her at the stove, boiling hunks of bread in a cast iron pot. He gave her a kiss on the cheek and joined her as she stared into the roiling water.

"Testing again?" he asked.

"There's a plaster taste in everything that bakery makes," replied Martha Wilcox.

He broke off a piece and took a bite. When she stared at him, expecting his opinion, he just grinned and kissed her again.

"You're a damn fool," she said. "I don't know what that girl sees in you."

"Language, dear mother."

After their quarrel Nell didn't see Jim for the rest of the week. Roy Crawford, a boy who had lately began to pay court to Ollie, came over twice. They sat in the parlor, batting pleasantries between them. He was a quiet presence, polite and chivalrous and without any of Jim Wilcox's sharp edges, and she felt she should be nice to him. He worked at one of the oyster shacks on the other side of the river, so his hands always smelled of shellfish, and he had bandages on his fingers from cuts he got handling them. He brought iced buckets of oysters to Seven Pines on Saturdays.

Nell stayed alone in the dining room at her needle and thread. Ollie kept one eye on her, watching as Nell's languor deepened and she left off sewing altogether, just gazing out the windows. And when she could take her sister's bereft mood no longer, she politely dismissed Roy.

"Lose something out there?" she asked Nell.

"I don't know where I get my certainty. And I definitely don't know where it goes when I need it."

She approached Nell from behind and retied her sagging chignon. "You know, there are other boys in this place. I bet any number would love to come over here."

"Do you think I was rude to him?"

"Was he rude to you?"

She looked at Ollie over her shoulder, brow arched, blue eye frosty.

"Wouldn't you know?" Nell asked. "You were listening, weren't you?"

Ollie felt her arms drop, letting Nell's hair fall loose. She blushed.

"Of course not."

"Oh don't be a ninny. I don't care. Just tell me: was I wrong?"

Being caught out like this so mortified Ollie she could barely speak. It took her a moment to get her mouth working again, during which she felt the impulse to atone by saying the opposite of what she wanted.

"Not rude. Maybe you put him in a position where he could nothing but refuse. As a man."

Nell turned back to the window: "Of course I did that. I even knew it at the time, but I kept on doing it."

The sisters fell silent, and Ollie went back to tying Nell's hair. But before she could finish, Nell spun about and hugged her.

"What's this for?"

As that gingery scent filled her nostrils, and Ollie felt the softness of Nell's neck against her cheek, she felt herself sinking. She pulled back instead of letting herself linger there.

"It is for being my sweet sister," Nell said.

They didn't speak of Jim until the following Sunday. After supper was done, and the plates washed and put back on their shelves, and the leftovers wrapped and placed among the blocks in the icebox, Ollie slipped outside and behind the work shed. There, under the cover of a magnolia, she found Nell standing high on her toes, studying the remains of one of the blossoms, a cigarette dangling from her lips.

Ollie took the butt from Nell's mouth and leaned against the wall. She took long drags, letting out profuse puffs because she didn't fully inhale and liked to watch the smoke distribute on the air.

"Did Jim come by today?" she asked.

"Why are you asking me? Wouldn't he be here to see you?"

"You'd think. But he's been paying more attention to Carrie these days. I suppose he wants to make me jealous."

They laughed—until the sound caught in Nell's throat.

"He's so obvious," she said, "but he's trying."

"If he wants to be with Carrie, let him. Why must you take his bait?"

"I'm not taking it."

"Take this from your elder sister: you'll never get anywhere if you don't stick to your decisions. You must stay strong. Sooner or later, he'll understand what's best."

"I know. But..."

"There's always a 'but' with you."

Nell took back the cigarette and fell against the shed. There was an inquiring look on her face that made Ollie self-conscious.

"What is it?"

"I don't think I noticed until now," said Nell, "that you are getting to be more and more like *him*." And the way she flicked her eyes toward the house, she knew that by "him" she meant their father.

Ollie soon learned the extent of Nell's strength. Coming back from downtown, she turned into the yard at Seven Pines and drew up short. For there, sitting on the porch together, were Nell and Jim Wilcox.

They lounged in adjoining chairs. Nell had her arm slung across Jim's lap, and Jim was stroking it as one would a contented cat. It took Nell a moment to notice Ollie, but when she did she quickly pulled her arm back and straightened up. She wore a chagrined look as Ollie approached.

"Well hello there, you. Buy anything nice?"

Ollie glanced at Jim as she mounted the steps. Jim stared back with a faint smile that seemed just on the right side of the line between polite and defiant. He wore no fancy cologne today; as she passed, her skirts brushed him, and wafted up the distinctive smells of turpentine and grease.

"Afternoon, Miss Olive," he said.

"Afternoon, Jim," she replied, nostrils pinched.

She went inside without acknowledging Nell.

That night, Olive went to bed early. Nell joined her, and lay staring at the ceiling for a while. She could tell from Olive's breathing that she wasn't sleeping.

"I know what you're thinking," said Nell.

Ollie was silent.

"You can upbraid me if you want," the other went on. "I deserve it. I was weak, I own it. He came here with a piglet. A piglet! And he'd dressed the little thing just the way he dresses himself, with that kerchief. Well, when I saw that little piggy Jim, what could I say? 'You're right to see me like this,' he said. The damn fool, he knows exactly how to talk to me. What could I have done?"

Ollie fought her impulse to answer, but lost.

"You could have stuck with what we agreed."

"I know, I'm sorry. Just don't be mad at me for not being as strong as you."

They lay silent for as long as it took for the horned owl in the magnolia to hoot three times. Then Ollie reached back and patted Nell's hand.

"It's all right," she said. "Go to sleep."

Yet it wasn't all right. The entire affair upset Ollie, and dominated her thoughts in a way that she resented—which in turn made it preoccupy her more. It should have been such a small thing, to brush this irritant away, this boy who was so unsuited to Nell. Girls rid themselves of boys all the time, didn't they? And yet here he was, reclining on her porch, flashing impertinent looks. If she had been a conniving person—a truly calculating villainess—she might have come up with more creative ways to discredit him in Nell's eyes. But she was nothing like that. All she had was to appeal to her sister's rational nature.

"At least I will not hear of any quarrels for a while," she told herself. When Nell and Jim had reunited in the past, it was usually followed by a few months' peace, as Jim reverted to his best behavior and Nell was temporarily in a forgiving mood.

But this honeymoon lasted only through the end of October. That evening, before supper, Nell looked at her in that way that suggested they meet behind the shed. When Ollie got there, Nell was pacing.

"Do you know what he did now?" she asked.

Ollie shrugged.

"We were in town, outside the Bee Hive. I had to go into my bag, and do you know what I found there? *Do you know?*"

"I can't imagine."

"A frog. A disgusting, warty, wet *frog...*"

Ollie burst out laughing. She laughed so hard she felt her balance slip, and had to lean against the wall. Nell fumed as she watched her sister convulse.

"Yes, go ahead. Enjoy yourself!"

"I'm sorry," Ollie gasped. "I really shouldn't. I shouldn't—"

"No you shouldn't. I suppose I deserve it."

"I should say so! Did he confess to it?"

"Gladly! He thought it was ever so funny! To make me scream like that, in the middle of a busy street..."

Ollie would have indulged in her vindication longer, but she could see that Nell was close to the limit of her humiliation. She straightened.

"So what did you do?"

"I made him take me home."

"What do you want to do now?"

"It's not only what I want to do," she replied. "It's what you must do too."

Puzzled, Ollie shook her head.

"A man like that...isn't a man yet. And I can't very well wait for him to grow up. This time I'm going to drop him. It's time to do the necessary..."

Nell took Ollie's hand and pressed it to her breast.

"...and I need you to promise me: if I become weak again, I want you to stop me. Any way you can—"

"My dear, I can't. I don't want that responsibility..."

"You must! Argue with me! Divert me! Sit on me if you have to! You've always been strong."

Ollie withdrew her hand. She would not have denied a certain relief in being proven right, but this turn of things filled her with anxiety.

"I need you to promise me," said Nell.

"I...Nell..."

"Promise!"

"What *are* you girls doing out there...?" Mary Cropsey cried from the kitchen stairs. "I can hear you talking!"

Nell pulled Ollie close, their noses touching. "You will promise," she whispered, and squeezed her hand. Then she twisted away and was gone.

Ella Maud

The Shed

I.

Oh, swift flowing river, a secret you hold,
Way down in the depths of the waters so cold
Oh be merciful, river, hark to our prayer,
And tell us who gave to your pitying care,
The fair girl whose story so sad has been told,
Stole away in the night, a lamb from the fold.
Whose treacherous hand dealt the villainous blow?
The secret, oh river, you surely must know...

—from a poem by Jeannette Crapsey (January 8, 1902)

Mary Cropsey kept watch in the turret from the day Nell disappeared. The tower was like the rooftop platforms some architects put on top of seaside houses. "Widow's walks", they called them, though in truth she had never seen a widow or a wife of any kind cross those promenades, looking out for their husbands missing at sea. She objected to the term. To consecrate a mere piece of carpentry to such loss, to grief, struck her as indecent. Especially now, under these circumstances.

She hardly looked at the river in the years they had lived at Seven Pines. To a mother, it was either a byway devoted to commerce, and therefore the province of husbands, or a venue for leisure, which placed it in the sphere of her children. At the same time there had always seemed something hostile about it. Its syrupy water oozed from the swamp, impenetrable to light. The wind did not raise it, but furrowed its surface, making it darker still. Heavy creatures slid beneath, blank-eyed and oily. The thought of her dear Nell among them was unthinkable, intolerable. She thought of nothing else.

Thoughts were the least of the things she was prepared to sacrifice. When the horror struck, it was her first instinct to mortify herself. If Nell's absence was to be redeemed, it could only be by her mother's vanishing—in spirit if not in physical fact. If He demanded her eyes, she would give her eyes. If it was to be her life, she would shed a tear for her surviving children, but go forth gladly. There would always be time for her husband to marry again.

The single thing she begrudged the Lord was her recollection. Mary Cropsey was two months gone before it occurred to her that she would have her fourth child; where previous indispositions had assaulted her body, Nell had pleasantly manifested within her, warm and indistinct. When she was born, her beauty reduced all to inarticulate wonder. "Ah," said the doctor as he toweled the blood from her tiny face. "Oh," said her husband when she was presented, swaddled in down. When she drowsed and drifted away, the adults marveled at this accomplishment.

This is how she chose to remember Nell's infancy, in this twilit glow. She could do no more than this, still and watching from her helpless vantage, the river shuffling heedlessly to sea. The hours passed and the shadows swiveled around her. Her daughters came up to hold her hand, or to offer food. A chamberpot was left under her seat—by whom she did not notice—but her fast halted her functions, until not even her brief sips of water passed through her. Staring at the shimmering water, she lost all feel for her materiality, or that of the house, until she became no more than pure longing. She was sad and shattered upon the air.

She abruptly resumed corporeality when she saw them throw sticks of dynamite into the river. The explosions split the river's grape-like skin. Blossoms of vapor rose that seemed pretty until the concussions shook the turret. She screamed. Feet pounded the staircase, and she cried "What have they done to my poor Nell?" as they took her by the arms and tried to drag her down the stairs. She was weak, but would not cooperate. Her husband cursed her in the presence of their children. She still would not relent, until at last they gave up, and led her back to her chair, which she seized as if overboard and grasping the last piece of flotsam.

In the middle of December she woke to witness the season's first snow. Small flakes distributed over the land and water, falling in straight lines as if in a hurry to reach the earth. The far shore of the river dissolved in the crowded air; a crusty mantel formed on the ground, like the residue on the bottom of a pot left too long on the stove. A single pair of wheel-tracks marked the street, fading as the snow covered them.

Her brother-in-law, whom she followed the children in calling "Uncle Hen", came out in the early morning, wearing his boots and his nightshirt and no hat. He walked with a shuffle, as if reluctant to lift his feet, and paused at the side of the road. For a moment he gazed into the foggy expanse that hid the river. Then he raised his arms above his head. He seemed beseeching, enjoining God, and the gesture gratified her for a moment; she felt not so alone in her ordeal.

But then his hands clawed further into the air, and she realized his posture was nothing more than a morning stretch. Higher, and the hem of his nightshirt exposed the ropey cords behind his knees. When he was done, he turned back, stepping precisely in his own tracks on his return.

She could tell if it was freezing outside by the fog of her exhalations on the windows. Later that day the glass cleared and the sun came out. The residue of snow gleamed, until it dissolved into the sickly green of the winter grass, and she knew the temperature had risen. "Here one minute, gone the next," she muttered.

"What did you say, Mama?" asked Lett, who had been sitting behind her silently.

"*Yet you do not know what tomorrow will bring. What is your life? For you are a mist that appears for a little time and then vanishes.*"

"Oh Mama–"

She broke her vigil to sit for Christmas dinner. A table lined with expectant faces greeted her as she entered the dining room. Her regular place was waiting for her; William Cropsey regarded her from the head of the table, with no expression. When she took her seat on his left hand he indicated the blessing would commence by bowing his head. All the Cropseys joined hands–except for Olive and William Douglas, who were separated by the seat usually taken by Nell. It was left empty.

"In Thee, O God," Cropsey began, "we live and move and have our being. Thou didst create us, and Thou dost uphold us, and without Thee we are nothing. We bless Thee for this food, the token of Thy continued care for us. We take it as a gift from Thy hand of love, and we pray Thee for wisdom, that we may spend the strength it gives us in ways that will please Thee best..."

The boys released, expecting the end of the prayer. But their father continued, and they had to join hands again.

"Almighty God, Father of all things merciful, we do give Thee most humble thanks for all Thy goodness, though we are unworthy. Show those who have failed in Your sight to right the wrongs they have committed, for all the reasons our mortal hearts might chose to do evil. Let their evil be uncovered, and let its architects be struck down for their many falsehoods, though they may have sat among us. Just as our Lord Jesus Christ, all glory upon His name, was betrayed by him who sat beside Him at table, at that last meal partook in His mortal life.

"For whom but You, O Lord, might redeem such perfidy, such degradation of the free will You have gifted all men, in your wisdom? What greater sin is there than this, to join hands among the host of Thy children, with such evil at heart? What punishment is too harsh for them? What blackness may not be improved by Your fire? Almighty God, let Thy divine wisdom fix the means, but let retribution come to those who laugh now, and despise our suffering, so that they may be unmasked, and cast down, and erased from Thy creation like foul smudges upon Your divine parchment. Let Thy will be done.

"And if not by Thy fury, O Lord, may the author of our misery, Jim Wilcox, find the decency that has eluded him so far, to confess the sin he has visited upon this house. Let his heart swell with its natural villainy, that it may not be contained anymore, but burst upon him, and inspire him upon Thy mercy. And let us beseech Thee, give us that due sense of all Thy wisdom, that our hearts may be thankful; and that we show forth Thy praise, not only with our lips, but in our lives. Let us walk before Thee in holiness and righteousness, our eyes fixed upon Heaven, through Jesus Christ our Lord, in all honor and glory, all of our days, world without end. Amen."

There was rising unease around the table as Cropsey's prayer went on, until he included Jim Wilcox by name, and the tension burst in the open. Lettie let out an audible gasp at his mentioning. Ollie loosed a cold sweat. Mary Cropsey abandoned the threadbare expression of normalcy she had assumed on reaching the table, her face calcified by grief. When Cropsey was done speaking, there was a pause none of them was willing to transgress, until he grasped the serving fork and knife and, with a bit more brio than fit the occasion, flung forth the first portion of lamb.

Ollie looked to Nell's empty place. If she felt her presence since she'd gone, it was only fleetingly, and with guilt, for the presence of her ghost could only have meant that her body had given up her spirit. She would have preferred to sense nothing. But the spirit of her father's prayer was so detestable it would surely have drawn a rebuke from Nell, had she heard it. Ollie thought she felt a thickening of the atmosphere around her place, as if a strange energy was gathering in the room. She both dreaded and desired to hear her voice again, manifested out of the air, so thin it might break, bright with the gleam of her rightness. She stared at Nell's chair, engrossed, until she became aware of William Douglas nudging her in the arm, and saying "Hey. HEY! Pass the dressing over here, will ya?"

"You forget your manners, young man?" chided his father.

"No, my fault..." said Ollie, and delivered the bowl.

That very moment, less than a mile away at their house on the corner of Martin and Shepard Streets, the Wilcox family also gathered around their table. Jim's father Thomas was likewise at the head, holding forth on current affairs. For his part, the former Sheriff saw no need to dress his feelings in a dust-ruffle of piety.

"I don't know what you did to those Cropseys, Jim, to deserve the way they talk about you."

"Hmm," Jim replied.

"There's nothin' logical about it. It's not just that I'm your father. I've been around a few investigations, and I've never seen railroading as plain as this. There's something else going on. I know it as clear as I know my right arm..."

"Hear, hear."

"I swear it's not even about you. It's about the next go-round at the polls. They reckon this will keep a strong challenger off the ballot. Never good to see a Wilcox with a badge, they say. The usual dirty tricks..."

"That may be," warned Martha Wilcox, "but we don't swear at table."

"I'd be surprised if she was even dead. Wouldn't put it past Greenleaf and his gang to put her on a train to Chicago. Tell her to make the rounds at the shops on Michigan Avenue. She'll turn up back here buried in hat boxes."

"My friend Kate has an uncle in the ice business," Jim's sister Annie piped up. "She says he said that the Cropseys are taking more than their share of block ice these days."

Wilcox stared, and slowly began to nod.

"Is that a fact? Well that's interesting. Do you think he'd testify to it?"

"I don't know him personal."

"Well, if we had a halfway competent sheriff, instead of wee Willie Dawson, there'd be an investigation. And the papers would have something else to talk about, instead of what comes out of old man Cropsey's mouth."

"Think you might stand again, Pa?"

"I've a mind to," he replied, wagging his head in a manner that said that if he did, it would be a sacrifice done wholly out of civic duty, not personal ambition.

"I can't see how this is the right kind of table talk," Jim spoke up.

As all eyes turned to him, he went on, "I can't speak to what Dawson's after. But I can't blame Cropsey for being beside himself, what with a daughter missing. I'd say just about anything if I were in his shoes. Paw, if Annie Mae were gone, would you be any better?"

The old man's jaw unhinged at this statement. When he found his voice he said, "That's awful broad-minded of you, boy, considering that it's your name—*our* name—they're dragging through the mud."

"That may be. But I got nothing to do with it, so why should I concern myself? The truth will come clear. And if I can content myself with that, why can't you?"

Thomas Wilcox was going to respond, but Martha spoke first: "Oh, let it be. Can't Christmas be one day we don't talk about Nell Cropsey?"

"Yes, please. They talk about nothing else around here!" declared Annie Mae.

"I seem to be out-voted," he said, and with a heave of resignation, turned his attention to feasting.

II.

After they got Nell to shore, they placed her on a cart. Ollie met them with a blanket to wrap her body—the very one they shared in bed. She managed to hold off tears until her father took the blanket from her. Then, as they rolled Nellie away, her legs weakened and she fell to her knees.

It seemed indecent to leave her outside for all to see, yet also unfitting to exhibit the waterlogged remains in the parlor. Instead, they brought her around back, into the shed, and laid her on the workbench, face-up and feet toward the doors.

They shut the shed in time to shield her from the crowd that gathered. It was maddening to William Cropsey, how quickly these layabouts and rubberneckers got wind of a spectacle unfolding. Did they not have business to attend to? It seemed to him the very essence of what was wrong with the world: too much idleness, too much prurience. He went out with a pistol and banished them all to the lines of the property. To Ollie, who gaped as he returned, he declared, "She was violated in life. I won't see her violated now."

The first official to arrive was Sheriff Dawson. He seemed to have come right from his breakfast table, in suspenders with shirt-tails hanging out. When he saw Nell's body in the shed he sucked his lips in disappointed fashion, as if he were hoping—absurdly—that the body, like so many others in recent weeks, would turn out not to be hers.

"I'm so sorry, Bill," he said.

Cropsey muttered. Dawson couldn't make out what he said, and didn't ask.

The coroner, Dr. Isaiah Fearing, came out next but stayed only a few moments.

"Be back presently."

"Are you fetching a jury?" asked Dawson.

"I need two more doctors to assist."

"Are you sure we shouldn't call someone in?"

"Come again?"

"I don't know, Ike. She's been in the water a long time. Maybe someone who's seen a case like this or two?"

"I think we can manage one autopsy," the other retorted.

Soon the crowd swelled to what seemed like thousands. The more nimble climbed trees for a better view. Others brought opera glasses to get a glimpse of Nell's splendid dead form. Dawson summoned every full- and part-time deputy he could to keep the throng back and under control. But the mob was already simmering with outrage; Jim's name was heard, frequently attached to profanity.

"That poor girl. Someone should give it to that goddamn Wilcox."

"I'd give cash money to see that bastard hanged!"

"Shot!"

"Shot and then hanged!"

Fearing returned by ten o'clock with two other men. Ollie, who was watching from the window, did not recognize them, but could guess their functions from what they carried: a doctor's black bag, and a stenographer's notebook.

The coroner faced the crowd and asked for volunteers to serve as jurors for the inquest. A hundred arms rose, and Fearing picked six men to serve.

They gathered in front of the closed doors of the shed and lit cigarettes for each other. The temperature rose beyond fifty degrees, and some of the men removed their jackets. None of them seemed in a hurry to get to their task. Nor did any member of the Cropsey family come near. The closest was William Cropsey, who was helping to hold back the crowd.

A last man arrived: the Cropsey family doctor, Dr. Wood. He gave a curt nod at the other attending physicians: "Ike. Dr. McMullan."

He then wished the jurors a "good morning" without thinking about how, under the circumstances, those words sounded.

With that, Dawson opened the shed doors. The space was tight and windowless, and smelled of sawdust and old fodder. The men crowded around the bench where the body lay, gazing at it. Dawson would have closed the doors after them, but Fearing stopped him.

"We'll need the light, Bill."

"All right," replied the other. Then to his deputies—"You fellows! Form a line!" And his men assembled at the open door, facing outward, to block the crowd's view of what would happen next.

Fearing opened his bag and withdrew a pair of rubber gloves and a scalpel.

"Who will dictate?"

The doctors looked blankly at each other until McMullan shrugged.

"I will," he said. "Mr. Sykes, are you ready?"

The stenographer nodded.

"*Subject is Ella Maud Cropsey, a nineteen year-old female...*" McMullan began.

"Twenty," corrected Wood.

"*Correction, twenty. She is dressed in a red waist with plain brass buttons, collar of same color, black leather belt, and a black skirt with—*" And he flipped up the hem of her skirt—"*black stockings. She is wearing a single rubber slipper on the left foot. The right foot is unclad. There is a bandage on her right big toe. The clothing appears to be in good order, no evident tearing or stretching...*"

Fearing undid the bandage and showed the toe to McMullen.

"*The bandage covered a corn on the right large toe. Injury is not connected to subject's death...*"

After rotating the body to confirm the condition of the clothing on her back side, the doctors commenced to strip her naked. The six lay jurymen watched this with sheepish fascination. J.B. Ferebee, a barber, remembered when he had last seen her—on Main Street, walking with one of her sisters. She was a fine-looking filly, fit and proud and far beyond the kind that would ever glance twice at a mere tradesman like him. Yet here was that magnificent girl now, prostrate and stripped to the skin before his eyes.

They left the stockings on her. The doctors did so without needing to agree on it, as if it were the most natural thing in the world. Wouldn't they want to check for bruises or whatnot on her legs? It seemed like they should. But Ferebee was only a barber, and lacked the confidence to raise his voice.

"*The body is waterlogged but generally in a good state of preservation,*" McMullan continued. "*There is no bloating. No saponification. There is no evidence of scavenging, not even at the extremities. The skin is entirely intact, not split, with no evidence of violence or trauma...*Does the skin tone appear normal to you, Dr. Wood?"

"It does not."

"*The skin tone is dark, perhaps due to long exposure to river water...*"

Fearing placed a hand on her forehead, as if he were about to tousle her hair. A transparent sheet came off on his fingers; when he grasped a tuft of hair, it all came out in his hand.

"*The epidermis separates from the dermis, as expected in such cases...*"

Fearing took up his scalpel, and as the jurymen held their breath, cut into Nell's abdomen just below the breastbone. He drew the incision down, to just above her pubis. There was, of course, no spurting of blood, the tissue parting like a somewhat overdone pudding. Two of the jurors looked away.

Upon pulling her apart, Fearing reached in and, after much cutting, withdrew a body in the shape of small, red purse.

"*The uterus is of normal size and empty. The hymen is...?*

Fearing pried between her legs and nodded to McMullan.

"*Yes...it is intact.*"

Thus assured of her chastity, they proceeded to the other organs. Fearing cut open the stomach and found no water, just a small amount of semi-digested food. After extracting the breastbone, he found both chambers of the heart empty. The lungs were collapsed. Fearing cut away a piece the size of a small book and put it into a bowl of water. It bobbed like a cork. Then he took another piece and pressed it between his hands, expelling some air and a small amount—no more than a teaspoon or two—of bloody froth.

"Why, she's as dry as a bone," remarked Wood.

"*No ecchymose in the lungs. They are of normal color. The lack of water in the stomach, heart, lungs or pleural cavity do not support drowning as the principal cause of death...*"

Fearing probed further, but less than a hour after they'd started, he was at the limit of his expertise. The doctors and jurymen stood around nervously; to the question they were all asking, "Did she throw herself in the river or was she murdered?", the body offered no clear testimony. Her virtue was not violated. She was not assaulted—at least in any way that would leave a mark. And yet the lack of water in her system hinted that she was dead before she entered the river. Or did it? The doctors struggled to remember pages of textbooks they had studied years ago. As he separated Nell's aorta from her heart, Fearing wondered if should have reviewed the relevant pages of Taylor & Reese's *Manual of Medical Jurisprudence* before he arrived. But where did he leave it now—in his office, or on his home bookshelf?

"I'd say she's no more drowned than I am," he declared.

"I wouldn't swear to that, Ike," replied McMullan.

"Isn't there something odd about her head?" Ferebee asked.

The doctors looked at him as if a rabid animal had slipped into the room. But Ferebee wouldn't be silent this time: in his profession as a barber, he had experience with heads at least.

"What do you mean?"

"Her left temple looks...I don't know...*swollen.*"

"Show us."

Ferebee stepped forward and pressed his index finger against Nell's temple. The impression his fingertip made did not spring back.

The coroner turned the head back and forth.

"That's completely normal. We expect a body in the water that long to show evidence of dropsy. Look here..."

Fearing poked at Nell's left aureole. The flesh yielded and stayed depressed.

Ferebee shook his head. "That doesn't seem quite the same to me."

With that, the autopsy was declared complete. Mr. Sykes shut his notebook, and Fearing put his tools back in his bag. When the men emerged from the shed, Sheriff Dawson hailed them:

"So what's the verdict, fellows?"

"There's still some discussion," replied Fearing. In fact, he was still preoccupied with the whereabouts of Taylor & Reese.

When he got to his home he found the text in his book case. He sat at his desk for some time reviewing it. There were twenty-one dense pages that addressed cases of drowning, and as he read them he became more and more dissatisfied with the morning's work. He had, in fact, only performed two post mortems before this one, and never on a victim who had drowned. Obviously he needed to examine the body again. But would that amount to an admission of incompetence on his part?

Around one in the afternoon, Charlie Reid came to his rescue. Standing in his foyer, hat in hand, the deputy reported that the jurymen were making the rounds of the saloons, complaining that the autopsy had been a waste of time. He seemed apologetic, but keen for Fearing's response. To his surprise, the doctor reached for his coat.

"Well, we ought to go back, then. I believe we did a thorough job, but we can't leave the public in any doubt."

It took until three p.m. to reassemble the doctors and the jury. By this time the crowd outside the house had dispersed, and there was only one deputy guarding the shed.

"Back for more?" the deputy asked.

Inside, Fearing had them reverse the body, so they could get more daylight on the head.

"Now let's see about this..." Fearing said.

Starting on the right side, he cut around the crown of Nell's skull. When he reached her left temple, blood coursed down her ear and onto the table. He completed the incision and, with a firm tug, removed the entire scalp.

Ferebee gulped. He had been around heads and hair all his life, but seeing a person in this condition, scalp of chestnut hair in a heap, blue-white dome of the skull exposed, made him feel he had never truly seen a human body. The sight was so discomfiting that he barely heard McMullan vindicate his suspicions:

"The left temple is markedly contused. There is a small but significant amount of blood suffused into the tissue. It is likely that the blood was circulating when the injury occurred. There is an approximately two- by two-inch discoloration of the meninges. The skull itself is undamaged..."

"Well, we seem to have discovered the telling lick," remarked Fearing.

"Proceed," said Dr. Wood, his face as still as Nell's.

With his saw, Fearing opened the cranium. Metal teeth ground on bone until the cap came loose—and the room was filled with a prodigious stench.

"Good lord!"

So far the body had seemed as fresh as if the girl had died that morning. The brain, however, had taken on the consistency of loose oatmeal, and lacked the solidity to remain in the skull. As the men watched, it ran onto the table and puddled in the creases of the canvas beneath the head.

"*The brain is much corrupted,*" continued McMullan. "*There is a strong odor suggesting a stage of decomposition well beyond what is apparent in the rest of the body...*"

Fearing probed what was left of the brain. This took enough time for Ferebee and the other jurymen to despair of their lunches. Just when the barber resolved he absolutely must duck outside for air, Fearing looked to McMullan and shook his head.

"*As much as can be told despite the severe state of decomposition, the brain is not physically damaged. No vascular irregularity. No sign of bleeding. No tissue atrophy. It is unlikely that was cause of death.*"

With that, Fearing put down his tools and removed his gloves.

"Well, gentlemen?"

"The bruising on the head tells the tale," said Wood.

"Yes, without a doubt. She was struck before death, but the blow was not penetrating. Some sort of padded instrument, I would think..."

"...And then she entered the water."

"But did the blow itself kill her," asked McMullan, "or was she rendered senseless and then drowned?"

Fearing frowned. "Difficult to say, after so much time. But I think we know this was no suicide."

The crowd had dispersed after the first autopsy, but not because the people were satisfied. The conversation on porches and street corners was invariably about hapless Nell Cropsey and the villain who had so cruelly undone her.

"That son of a bitch Wilcox!" was heard on Main Street: "If he were here now I'd give him what for. I swear it!"

"There's not a body in this town that would stop you," came the answer.

"Why'd he do it, you think?"

"She came to her senses and dropped him."

"And he didn't like that, did he?"

"I'm not a violent man...unless it's somebody like Wilcox, and he deserves it."

"They knew how to deal with the likes of him, once."

"Whole world's gone soft!

"I know for a fact Wilcox is not in town."

"Where is he?"

"He's fishing up on Frog Island, just as happy as you please!"

"The cold-hearted bastard."

"Then again, if he happened to disappear in the swamp, who'd miss him?"

Laughter all around.

The peace-loving citizens of Elizabeth City would gladly have taken their cogitations to their local places of refreshment. But when they got there, they found them all closed. On the doors, signs were posted:

CLOSED BY OFFICIAL ORDER
T. B. Wilson, Mayor
(Go home to your wives.)

That day, around noon, Sheriff Dawson had gone to Mayor Wilson with a warning: now that Nell had turned up murdered, and out of an abundance of caution, the gin joints needed to be closed.

"Won't that make folks even more angry?" asked the Mayor.

"Better angry and sober than angry and drunk," replied Dawson.

So the order was given, and as the citizens of the town gathered in the streets, sober and slow to go home to their wives, it was widely agreed that—for the sake of their dry throats at least— Jim Wilcox was a dead man.

Wilcox only heard about the discovery of Nell's body when Charlie Reid came out to to collect him. He had gone to his uncle's place a few days before, as the mood in the town had gotten so hot that he decided—and the Sheriff agreed—it might be better for him to stay out of sight for a while. Not having to go to work wasn't exactly a sacrifice, either; it had been too long since he had had some time to himself. That, and the fact that Mr. Hayman had fired him three days previous.

"Gonna have to let you go, Jim," Mr. Hayman told him as he arrived that Tuesday morning. "You need to know, I ain't never had anything against you. Never heard as much as a single complaint. But you know how things have gotten around here."

"Yeah, I know," said Jim. "I don't suppose it matters if I swore to you I'm innocent, does it?"

Hayman sucked in his cheeks and shook his head.

"Afraid it doesn't. But if that's established as a fact, you've always got a job here. Deal?"

And Hayman stuck out his hand for Jim to shake. For a second, Jim thought about leaving the hand there, hanging and unshaken. But he supposed he understood the dilemma Hayman faced. So he shook his hand and took payment on his salary for the rest of the week.

His uncle's farm was down near the Big Flatty Creek, southwest of town. He spent the first couple of days lazing about with a fishing rod in his hands, not really caring if he had the right kind of bait or whether it went anywhere near a fish. He was pensive at the dinner table, and his aunt and uncle didn't disturb his peace. He was thinking about Nell—not about her disappearance, but about how he had truly lost her, long before that. Should he have put that toad in her bag? Would it have been so bad, after all, if he had gone to hear that preacher?

"You should take the Sharps and go for that woodchuck who's tearin' up my pasture," his Uncle finally said. "You'd be doin' me a service."

"Maybe I will."

He did. And he was out there for two solid days, sitting out on a little hill with his uncle's ancient rifle and a jug of applejack. By noon of neither day was he in decent shape to hit a cow, much less a rodent.

Morning of the third day he saw a figure approaching from the farmhouse. Closer, and he recognized Deputy Reid—and understood exactly what that meant.

"Any word on Nell?" he asked.

"They just pulled her out of the river, Jim. She's gone."

Jim nodded slowly. Then he reversed the rifle and offered it stock first to the Deputy.

It was close to twenty miles back to town. Elizabeth City didn't own a covered police wagon, so he was driven in an open buggy through the streets. He was seared by a thousand burning eyes; he heard cuss words out of mouths of women and children, and men spat on the ground as he passed.

"Did she drown, Charlie?"

"Appears not."

"How long was she in the river?"

Reid gave him a look that asked, "Shouldn't you be telling me?"

Nell is dead, Jim thought. Dear sweet Nellie is no more. The words made sense to him, but not the meaning. How could she be gone, he wondered, when she was so young? How could she, when it felt as if he had just seen her? And just at that moment, he felt remorse at thinking she had intentionally went off, just to cause him trouble. How petty he could be with his suspicions! He was disgusted, and thought he would join in the contempt everyone was showing him, had he been standing in the street watching himself pass.

But Jim wasn't one to parade his misgivings. When he was worried, he was wont to smile; when he was frightened, he hummed a tune. At his great-grandfather's funeral, when he was ten, he had sported a new set of playing cards and performed card tricks on the pews. His apparent indifference struck some as disrespectful—but it was just his way.

Thus it was widely reported that Wilcox looked "well pleased with himself" and "without a care in the world" as he was driven to jail. To most onlookers, it didn't look like the confidence of an innocent suspect expecting to be exonerated. It looked like the maddening indifference of a depraved man.

The county jail was half a block north of the courthouse. As the buggy crossed the square, there seemed like a lot more people gathered there than on a typical Friday afternoon. Many of the men had liquor bottles in their hands.

"What a commotion. Did they close the saloons or something?"

"In fact, they did," replied Reid. "Now let's see if we get through this mob with our skins."

Jim turned up his collar and lowered his head as Reid told the horses to get up. Every face turned to Wilcox. For a moment, the buzz among them was suspended, and it seemed like the encounter was poised on a razor's edge between calm and chaos. Halfway across, Jim dared think calm had prevailed.

But then—from somewhere out of the crowd—a liquor bottle arced toward him. It was a good throw, missing him only by inches. A torrent of invective was suddenly uncorked:

"God damn Jim Wilcox to hell!"

"You'll suck that river water soon, Jim!"

"Don't think that jail will keep you safe, *murderer*!"

Reid whipped the horses, splitting the scrum as they passed the Fire House and up Pool Street. Jim was sure a few men must of been trampled by their hooves, or clipped by the buggy's wheels, but he didn't hazard a look back to see.

The report of the Coroner's Jury was released to the newspapers the next day:

> *We, the coroner's jury, having been duly summoned and sworn by Dr. I. Fearing to inquire what caused the death of Ella M. Cropsey, do hereby report that from the investigation made by three physicians of Elizabeth City and from their opinion and also from our personal observation that Ella M. Cropsey came to her death by being stricken a blow on the left temple and by being drowned in the Pasquotank River. We have not yet investigated or heard any testimony touching as to who inflicted the blow and did the drowning. We are informed that one James Wilcox is charged with the same and is now in custody. We recommend that an investigation as to his or any one else's probable guilt be had by one or more magistrates in Elizabeth City township and that said Wilcox be held to await said investigation.*

III.

William Cropsey telegraphed news of Nell's discovery to his brother the day she was found. The reply came in an hour: Judge Andrew G. Cropsey—Carrie's father— would be on the next train from Brooklyn.

The Judge appeared on their porch twenty hours later, holding a carpetbag. Inside, he greeted every family member in turn with a tighter-than-usual embrace, replete with due sympathy. When he encircled Ollie she smelled the odors of cigars and oysters. His brush mustache scratched her lip, and his spreading belly assaulted her midriff.

"This is difficult," he whispered.

"Yes, it is."

"Have you been taking care of your mother?"

"We all have."

"It's all we can do. Until justice is served."

Uncle Andrew spoke frequently of justice. In appearance he was shorter than his brother, but more substantial—the thick gray stump to his brother's gangling tree. Something about him brooked no defiance, even before he opened his mouth. No one thought to argue otherwise when he announced, "Now I will see your mother."

Mary Cropsey had given up her vigil when Nell was brought in from the river. Her condition before had resembled a nervous breakdown, but now that Nell's death was certain her inner turmoil seemed to manifest physically. When she was unfortunate enough to be awake, her hands writhed around each other like wrestling snakes. The whites of her left eye were bloody now—the consequence, Dr. Wood speculated, of a burst vessel.

"What's all this got to do with blood vessels?" demanded Cropsey.

"If that's the worst of it, Bill, I'd thank my stars."

Ollie didn't go in to watch Uncle Andrew greet her mother. Instead, she waited in the parlor until he and the other Cropsey men came out. Uncle Andrew fell upon the sofa with a sigh. Her father took the rocker, and Uncle Hen stood in the doorway, leaning against the frame.

"I take it you had her chaperoned whenever she was with that fellow, Wilcox?" asked the Judge.

"Of course."

"In my profession I've seen these types, time and time again. When these boys get it in their heads to do something rash over matters of love, Lord knows what they're capable of."

"Yes."

"Judging from the coroner's report, it's obvious she wasn't drowned. She never talked about harming herself, did she?"

He was looking at Ollie.

"No, never."

"Then by process of elimination, there can be only one possibility. She was abducted by this young fellow. Her state of preservation testifies to nothing else. She was abducted and held somewhere. Isn't there a swamp around here?"

"The Dismal." said Hen.

"Exactly. So as the noose tightened around Wilcox, the boy panicked. He had her killed, probably no more than a couple of days before she was found. Then they threw her in the river to make it look like suicide."

Dyspepsia washed over William Cropsey's face. The Judge thought little of it; it was the typical reaction of a man who didn't like to be lectured by his elder brother.

"The hole in your theory," William said, "is that Wilcox has been watched since the day Nell disappeared. How was he supposed to be keeping Nell captive while the deputies were on him every minute?"

"Obviously, he had accomplices. And perhaps a system of signals to communicate with them, like placing classified ads in the newspapers."

"Accomplices? And he paid for their services, and their silence, with what? His great fortune? Knowing the state of Jim Wilcox's schooling, I doubt he could properly address an envelope, much less concoct secret messages for the papers!"

"Bill, I know you are in grief, but you are making a damn fool of yourself. I've been around the criminal element my whole life. If you wish to debate the merits—"

He was interrupted by Ollie who, unable to hear any more, shot to her feet with a muffled scream.

All eyes fell on her as she stood there. Her face throbbed red as she feared her deception was exposed. Uncle Hen cleared his throat. Uncle Andrew looked exactly like what he was: a judge interrupted in mid-pronouncement.

"I'll check on Mama."

The men were silent as she left the room. She heard her uncle resume: "...debate the fine points of criminal investigation with a seasoned officer of the court..." as she shut the parlor door.

The funeral of Nell Cropsey took place at the Methodist Episcopal Church at Church & S. Martin. One and a half thousand people gathered that drizzly Sunday afternoon to bid goodbye to the girl few had ever laid eyes on, and almost none knew.

Ollie helped pick the dress Nell was buried in: a traveling suit of brown serge, with white silk chemisette and sleeves trimmed in bands of velvet. It was a dress, Ollie imagined, that Nell would have worn on one of the trips she dreamed of making.

Her body had been stitched back together by Dr. Fearing. The discoloration of her skin was concealed by arsenic paint on her face and hands that made her glisten faintly. As her hair never looked the same after the scalp was removed, she wore a lace burial cap that Lettie and Carrie had spent the night before embroidering with tiny daffodils. Ollie would have helped, but with eyes bleary from grief she couldn't manage such fine work.

The embalmers had seen fit to paint Nell's lips blood red. They were too bloody for her father's taste. When he approached the casket to bid her farewell, he used his handkerchief to wipe the color away. He made a mess of it—the red paint smeared into the arsenic, making her look clownish. After the service, Ollie took the undertaker aside:

"You won't let her go into the ground like that."

"Of course not, my dear."

Nell reposed to the right of the altar. Her casket was of polished black walnut, with white satin lining and silver fixtures, topped by four overflowing floral arrangements engirdled by white and green ribbons. The undertaker had picked the colors—respectively, for 'purity' and 'resurrection'. Ollie had sent to a greenhouse in Norfolk for asphodels, whose symbolism she hoped few of the other attendees would notice.

The crowd filled the church to capacity and spilled into the wet yard beyond. The rain came and went during the service, but as if in collective expiation, few bothered to open umbrellas. The town's prominent clerics took turns eulogizing her as the farthest mourners bent their ears. The preachers doled out their words a sentence at a time, so the nearer congregants could relay them to those too far to hear.

Pastor Tuttle gave the main oration. His tone started little different from the one he took for every funeral sermon. But so wide and indiscriminate was public grief for Nell Cropsey, the occasion felt like no other memorial. Significant sniffles, and the sounds of quiet sobbing, came from every corner of the church.

"A sad and mysterious Providence has come to a home in our community..." he began, ladling his munificent gaze down on the pews, to William and Mary Cropsey. "We thank God that the family has been sustained in their sorrow...We thank Thee, that she accepted Christ in this very place, just thirty-eight days ago, before being taken away from us...All deaths are sad, but oh how inexpressibly sad it is to be cut off in the bloom of young womanhood and like this, though mystery surrounds her death, we have this promise about her beautiful life: 'There is nothing secret that shall not be made manifest. Be sure your sins will find you out.'"

At this promise a murmur shot through the crowd. For it was known that Jim Wilcox was but a few blocks away, in the county jail. Indeed, it was the closest he had been to Nell since the night she disappeared. How easy it would have been for one or two hundred stout fellows—men with a thirst for justice—to take it upon themselves to break down the prison doors. In the church there was weeping, and there was hatred, often on the same faces simultaneously.

Neither emotion was on Mary Cropsey's face. Instead, she was blank with exhaustion. Her shoulders slumped in her seat, and she seemed physically shrunken. To onlookers, it seemed as if she did not comprehend what was going on around her. When she left the church, she lacked the strength to mount the steps to her buggy, and had to be lifted into it.

"I'll tell you this," Tuttle continued. "We hear the saloons have been closed as a protection to a supposed criminal...It is not interesting that the dry goods stores are not closed, the grocery stores, the jewelry shops and other establishments, were not shut up...? Only the liquor saloons, which on other days remain open to corrupt the innocent...Is this not as clear an admission as our civil authorities can make, that those places are inherently dangerous...? That they lie at the very root of the criminality from which they are sworn to protect us...? Indeed, does it take so much an effort of imagination to see the plot that brought us to this sad pass, hatched in exactly those places, by minds addled by alcohol...? They tell us that their revenues sustain our city. I ask you to look *there*, friends, to the beauty in that casket...There lies your profit! There are the wages paid this unfortunate family by the demon!"

He closed the sermon with the lulling familiarity of scripture—15 *Corinthians*. But the indignation he had abetted in the congregation did not subside. It buzzed as the members of the Committee of Five and William Cropsey lifted the glistening casket on their shoulders, and to the accompaniment of *Nearer My God to Thee* bore her down the aisle, out the door, and down to the hearse.

The crowd parted. The horses snorted and shook the black plumes on their heads, and Andrew Cropsey stood at attention as the casket was lifted into the back.

Many of the mourners followed the body the half mile to the Norfolk & Southern Depot. They watched as it was loaded onto the special train chartered for the journey to New York. Hundreds lingered as the engine gave a long whistle, and with a last exhalation of steam into the overcast sky, began Nell's journey home.

Two days later, on New Year's Eve, the lawyer packed his valise with the Cropsey autopsy report, depositions, and Jim Wilcox's indictment. He paused at the mirror to check that his mustache was straight, and swept away a flake of coal ash from his lapel. Then left his office on E. Main Street.

He stopped at a tobacconist on the corner.

"Afternoon Ed!"

"Afternoon Johnny. The usual please. And three packets of Duke's Best."

"Taken up cigarettes, Ed?"

"They're for a client."

"All on your tab?

"Yes, thanks."

"Do I know him?"

"Who's that?"

"Your new client."

"Have a good afternoon, Johnny."

On his way to the county jail he had to cross the square in front of the Courthouse. Four-man canvas tents—the kind not seen in these parts since the War—were pitched on the green, with weapons piled and sentries posted. In front of the tents, men sat talking, chewing tobacco and scratching. From the look of them, they didn't seem like regular soldiers: some were beyond forty, spreading bellies pouring through their suspenders.

He was halted at the corner of Mathews and Pool, short of the jailhouse.

"State your business," the picket ordered.

"Counsel for the defendant."

"Prove it."

He was at a loss. In Elizabeth City, everybody knew Edwin F. Aydlett, Esq., and he knew everybody else who was a lawyer too. The problem of having to prove his profession had simply never come up before. But the militia protecting Jim Wilcox from lynching was not from Elizabeth City.

"Where are you from, young man?"

"Currituck."

"Biting fish out there?"

"Like you've never seen."

Another militiaman came up and vouched for him, so they waved him through. Aydlett walked the last half-block in a curious state of solitude, with no other pedestrians and all the shops closed.

The deputy greeted him at the jailhouse.

"Morning Ed!"

"Morning Charlie. Any plans for the holiday?"

"Under the circumstances..." he replied, indicating in the direction of the cells, "Not this year."

"Sorry to hear that."

The cells in the Pasquotank County Jail were small—just seven feet on a side. They were engirdled not by bars but by lattices of flat steel ribs. There was one window, near the ceiling, that was propped open. There were ten cells in that block, but only one—labelled #19—was occupied.

Jim Wilcox was lying in the bunk, reading. The book looked like some kind of dime Western. When the key rattled in the lock he shot upright.

"Hey there Ed! Did'ya fetch the smokes?"

"Morning to you too, Jim."

Wilcox took the packs and tore one open at once. As he took his first puff, his face suffused with relief. He fell back against the wall. Then he opened his eyes and saw Aydlett watching him closely.

"Not much to do in here," he said.

"Stepping out now," deputy Reid announced. "Ed, if you need me I'm right outside."

"Thank you Charlie."

Jim fetched up a laugh. "Suddenly I can't be trusted alone with a body. You murder just one girl and look how they treat you!"

"That kind of joking ain't gonna help you, Jim. You need to knock it off."

The other tossed his head, took another drag.

"At least we've got some good news," said Aydlett as he reached into his valise. "The coroner's jury released a statement to the press."

He handed over a newspaper clipping. But Jim could not summon the will to read it; it was too painful. He handed it back.

"Good news, how?"

"This part: 'We are informed that James Wilcox is charged with the same and is now in custody. We recommend that an investigation as to his or any one else's probable guilt be had by one or more magistrates in Elizabeth City township and that said Wilcox be held to await said investigation.'"

"Sounds like the usual applesauce."

"Exactly. But when it's coming from town officials, and printed up in the papers, it can't help but prejudice any possible jury. They've practically convicted you *ex curia*."

"And how is that good?"

"Never seen anything like it in twenty years of practicing law. Wilcox's 'probable guilt'! That conclusion is practically a crime in itself. It's clear grounds for the judge to grant us a change of venue for the trial."

"Well, it would be nice to see the inside of a different cell."

"I think we should try for Norfolk. There's some sympathy there for the way you've been railroaded."

"My pap says you're a good lawyer, Ed, so tell me why I'm stuck in here. How come I can't post bond?"

"I'm afraid, Jim, that has less to do with your roots in the community than with your physical safety." And Aydlett tilted his head toward the door to indicate the general air of menace without.

Jim shrugged. He tapped the loose ashes from his cigarette into his water cup.

"So, you go to the funeral?"

"Yes."

"Good turnout?"

"I think you know there was."

"Yeah, I figured. I just wish I could have..."

He paused, took another drag, but didn't continue.

"Her uncle took her up north to be buried with her people."

The other nodded, bowed his head.

"Listen, Jim—I need to tell you something. Are you listening?"

"Aye-aye, counselor."

"I don't know what happened between you and Nell. I don't care what you did. Maybe you had your reasons, maybe you didn't. But I need you to be absolutely honest with me, and absolutely complete. So if there's something you're not telling me, I need to know it now. I don't want any surprises from the stand. Do you understand?"

"Yes."

"So let's go over the last time you were together. Is there anything that happened—anything that gives us a clue to her state of mind—that you've left out so far? I want you to really think."

Jim scowled. "If you knew how many times I had to tell that story..."

"And you'll tell it a thousand times more, too."

The other smoked and stared through the gaps in his cage, brow furrowed.

"Well, there was one thing I noticed..."

"Go on."

"I was about to leave, a little after eleven, when I asked if Nell would come out on the piazza with me. I looked right at her, you know, and said 'Hey Nell, would you come outside with me for a minute?' But she didn't look at me when I spoke to her. She looked at Ollie first. Then she got up."

"Did Miss Olive say anything to her? Did she give her a certain look?"

"Not that I noticed. She maybe just shrugged."

"Why didn't you say this before?"

"I don't know. Didn't seem important. Is it?"

"Maybe. Now tell me again how Nell reacted when you returned the sunshade and the pictures."

"The parasol was white and made of silk. I busted the mechanism on it sometime a while back. Damned thing was so delicate. I told her I'd fix it, but I bought her a new one instead."

"Did she thank you for that?"

"Did she!" Jim gave a sardonic laugh. "The one I got was worth twice the price. She kissed me on the cheek, and said 'Ain't you somethin', Jim Wilcox!'"

"So why'd you bring back the broken one?"

"After we stopped speaking, she let it be known she wanted her property back. So I obliged. I always oblige a lady."

"Did she put it inside the house?"

"Come again?"

"When you gave her back the parasol, did she go inside with it?"

"Not that I saw."

Aydlett nodded, then shook his head. He had been considering these details for days, and they gave him a headache.

"That's what I don't understand, Jim. They say the pictures were never found, but the parasol was found in the front hall. If Nell never came back into the house that evening, how did it end up there?"

Jim took a final drag and flicked the smoking butt through the steel ribs of his cage.

"I couldn't tell you, counselor. But whatever happened, I got a feeling it's my fault."

Jim learned about the militia the very day they arrived. The window in his cell, propped open to let out the cigarette smoke, let in sounds from the street. That afternoon, just after his lunch, he heard the crunch of marching feet, and the voices of the sergeants barking orders. Just after that, all sounds of wheeled traffic disappeared around the jail. It took a few moments for the implications of this to sink in. Then he proclaimed aloud, "So, this is what it's come to."

"Looks like the Governor made it official, Jim," said the deputy. "You're the most popular man in North Carolina!"

"You got to admit, Charlie: when I get in trouble, I do it right and proper."

Reid laughed, "You got that right."

Besides smoking and reading, he had a lot of time to turn things over in his mind as he sat in custody. The more he thought about how the Cropseys had wronged him, the more infuriated did he become. Setting that mob on him—so much for William Cropsey's dedication to law and order. The hypocrite! Wouldn't they like to think of him sitting there, quaking with fear? Wouldn't his accusers like to shuffle Nell's misery off upon him? For Nell was not the happy pet of the family that was described in the papers. He wasn't a Cropsey, to be sure, but he had known Nell for more than three years, and had seen her outside the house, out of the influence of her father and Ollie and that prying simpleton, Uncle Hen. He had seen her away from Papa Cropsey—the potato general—swaggering in his fields with a bullwhip, lording it over workmen too poor and desperate to tell him what a fool he was. Away from Ollie Cropsey, whom he was chagrined to remember once attracted him.

There were times in the seats of buggies or rowboats that Nell let him sit close. They said she was a proper girl and that was true: there was nothing about her that brooked disrespect. If he put a hand on her leg, she looked at him in a way that expressed neither disgust, nor reproof, but bemused surprise, as if were an overeager boy accosting a grown woman. Nell was almost six years younger than Jim. Yet she had a way of making herself the grown-up between them—which suited Jim fine, since he liked to play the fool. Over the years it had become a comfortable sort of game between them. Jim would let himself sound like an unlettered rube, and let fly with whatever malapropism or off-color remark entered his head, and Nell would get to smile at his naïveté, and correct or scold him, and say "You silly boy. Didn't your mother teach you anything?" At the age of twenty-five, Jim had already visited the brothels in the colored part of town, and was on familiar terms with some of the girls. When he glimpsed Nell's bare wrist, or a flash of calf, he was well aware of the shape of the territory beyond. He was not ashamed to admit he burned to explore it. In their reversed roles, Jim's experience was less threatening, and her lack of it was concealed.

But there were times when Nell sounded like the restless teen she was.

"Ollie was such a little witch today," she told him one day at the skating rink.

"Is that a fact?"

"She knew I wanted that piece of organza for a particular purpose, and she got up early just to take and use it before I could forbid it."

"Did she now!"

"She always hates it when I have something she doesn't."

"Sounds witchy to me."

"Don't think I don't know you're making fun of me. I've got a mind not to tell you anything, if you take that tone."

"What tone?"

And she attempted to push away from him, but because she was such a poor skater, she lost her balance and fell against the boards. Jim took her back in his arms, and brushed a loose curl of hair from her eyes, and felt her body so small and bent and lithe in his grasp, and had to say, "You know I adore you."

"If you adored me, you'd take me away from here."

"Is this place so bad?"

She stiff-armed him as she gathered her feet.

"There doesn't have to be anything wrong to want to get away," she said.

Once he had gone up to New York to visit her at school. It was his first time outside of North Carolina. He brought his best duds for the occasion, and enjoyed promenading down the Ladies' Mile in spats and yellow gabardine suit with such a fine girl on his arm. They plied Central Park Lake to the music of floating accordions. In Brooklyn, she showed him the Pratt Institute's fine library, with its book stacks flooded with daylight through floors made of Tiffany glass.

"Anyone who lives or works in Brooklyn can borrow books from here, from the scholar to the humblest workman," she told him, as proudly as if she built the place. Nell was not really a student, but Carrie took her to her classes whenever she was up for a visit, and the teachers at Pratt were happy to accommodate unofficial auditors. It was amusing to see how the college atmosphere excited her.

And indeed, the library was an striking place. It was a strange feeling to be walking on a floor made of glass, like a bug on the panes of an enormous window. But a man couldn't very well admit being impressed with such things.

"They got any dime Westerns?"

There was a show of the students' handiwork at the school that week, to which Carrie contributed a costume she and Nell had designed, cut and stitched.

After Jim was escorted through the throng of visitors on the third floor of the Ryerson Street building—dedicated to 'the Domestic Arts & Sciences'—he was confronted by a red boating dress with pleated skirt, white lapels and buttonholes piped in gold. The mannequin wore a straw hat festooned with swan feathers. It all seemed a bit much to him.

"So, what do you think?" asked Carrie.

"I'm imagining myself showing up at the docks in that."

"Pearls before swine!" declared Nell. "Come along, Jim. Let's get some hot chocolate."

He was disinterested in most of the exhibits, but was pleased for the Cropseys when the judges awarded their creation 'Honorable Mention'. For the sake of their beaming faces he refrained from wisecracks as they collected the certificate. When he noticed a reporter from the *New York World* was interviewing the students, he made sure he came over to talk to the girls. Under the reporter's gentle questioning Carrie's pride turned to bashfulness; she left it to Nell to describe the "basting" and "darting". The reporter listened to the details with a look of polite distraction on his face, and did not write them down.

Later, Nell pulled him close, as if to kiss him.

"Jim, do me a favor, will you?"

"Anything."

"Your accent. Maybe...if you talked less. In front of these other people."

"What's wrong with how I talk?" he replied, loudly.

"Nothing, Jim. Never mind."

He was left to ponder this exchange for the rest of the afternoon.

He didn't want to make a big deal out of this and other bits of disparagement. But he couldn't conceal a certain despondency when he came home after an evening at the Cropseys. It was beginning to be a habit—to go over there with gifts for the family, full of expectation, but return undercut and baffled. It was a pattern that didn't escape his father.

"I don't know how you put up with them," Tom Wilcox grumbled. "No pretty face is worth that."

"Be careful what you tell me to get rid of."

The old man glared at him as if Jim had swindled him. Then he muttered "Damn fool" and settled back into his newspaper.

But Tom Wilcox knew exactly what Jim was talking about.

When Jim was a boy, he saved the money he'd made doing neighborhood odd jobs and sent away for the pet of his dreams — a genuine, live falcon.

Ella Maud

He anticipated its arrival for weeks. He waited at the mailbox after school for the late delivery, hoping for the notice that his package had arrived. On the day it finally did, he practically hopped with joy as he made his way to the Post Office.

She was a duck hawk—also known as a peregrine. She arrived in a padded container the size of a hat box, with holes in the sides. When he got the top open, the chick was alive but caked in her own excrement; it took all the patience of an excited twelve-year-old to learn how to handle her, to avoid the beak and the tiny talons, as he cleaned her undersides with a cloth his mother used to polish the silver. For a mews, he used an old chicken coop in the back yard. After much thought, he decided to name her Tarheel.

His bird came with a booklet of instructions on falconry, "the sport of kings." Jim pored over these directions with a diligence he never paid to his school texts. He learned that his bird was female, because females (it said) were more tractable. To feed her, he hunted for worms, toads, and mice, or begged his neighbors for any unwanted ducklings or chicks. When he acquired these live, he had to break their necks and cut them up into pieces.

He fashioned a leather gauntlet for her to roost upon his arm, and a tiny hood—with a tiny tassel on top—for her to wear between lessons. When the bird was fledged at last, he was thrilled to watch her flutter away, trailing on the string he had tied to her leg, and then return to his arm. When he put the hood back on, Tarheel would dutifully close her hard, gem-like black eyes.

By the end of summer Jim and his companion had made a lot of progress. The bird was healthy and growing, and didn't fly away when Jim risked her first untethered flight. She learned to strike when he threw up the lure for her, and to return when he whistled. He envisioned a time, not long off, when she would hunt for him, bringing down pigeons or ducks, or plucking fish out of the creek for his dinner. He imagined using her to deliver messages to his future sweethearts.

Indeed, training Tarheel made him feel better about himself than anything he ever did, and ever would, for years. Jim wasn't the richest kid in Elizabeth City, nor the smartest nor the most athletic. But he was the town's sole bonafide practitioner of the sport of kings.

The brotherhood of falconers had its drawbacks. Jim was often seen that year with gashes on his fingers. Once, when he was foolish enough to try to feed Tarheel out of his own mouth, she nipped his lower lip. His father noticed the cut at supper that afternoon, and said, "What are you doing with that wild animal?"

"Raisin' it."

"Seems to me you have enough toys without endangering yourself with that thing."

Jim made no reply, and was thankful when the old man dropped the subject. But his kid sister Annie Mae was listening.

He came home the next day to a full-fledged furor. Dr. Wood was coming out, and gave him a pitying look as they passed on the front walk. Martha Wilcox was upstairs, in Annie Mae's room, wailing and weeping. And his father was downstairs, his heavy leather belt off his hips and stretched across his lap.

"What happened?" he asked, eying the belt.

"What happened," said Tom Wilcox, "is that your sister has been disfigured by that *thing* in the chicken coop."

"Disfiggered? How?"

"A scratch right across her cheek. The doc says it will scar for sure. Her looks are spoiled for good! And I told you I didn't want that thing around. Now you're gonna pay."

"But I told her to stay away."

"Come here, boy..."

Jim got such a thrashing it was hard for him to sit down. Worse, his father ordered him to get rid of Tarheel. He swore, "If it's not gone by tomorrow, I'll break its neck myself!"

Dread of this prospect almost made him forget the belt marks on his rear end. In bed that night, he imagined running away from home, a sack of his belongings over one shoulder and Tarheel perched on the other. But Jim was a practical sort, even as a boy; what kind of life he could provide for himself and his companion at such a young age? Where could he escape with his father—who was also a former sheriff—out looking for him?

When Annie Mae came down to breakfast, he got a look at the cut on her face. It was indeed hideous—a neat slice down the bridge of her nose and over her left cheek. An inch in either direction and an eye would have been put out.

"Hey stupid! Didn't I just get done tellin' you to stay away from my bird?"

"James Wilcox, you...will...not...call...your...sister...stupid!" his mother said.

"But what if she is?"

"Apologize to her. Right now!"

He decided the next best thing was to give Tarheel her freedom. It was a Saturday, so he was free to spend the morning preparing her. He fed her and groomed her, tenderly explaining to her why this drastic change was necessary. Her hard gaze was constant and empty and filled him with unendurable sadness. He put the hood on her head for the last time, for the trip down to the river.

The banks of the Pasquotank seemed the best place to release her into the world. A little ways out of town there was a swivel bridge where the river met Charles Creek. From there, he would watch her disappear out over the water, toward the freedom he had yet to taste for himself.

But Jim's errand didn't go unnoticed. As he went down Shepard Street, a handful of the local boys saw the strange kid walking down the center of the road with a large bird on his arm. The witnesses called others, and they called more, until there was a small crowd of a dozen boys trailing behind him. So oddly processional did the scene become, with Jim bearing his tasseled bird at the head, that it took on the air of a triumphal march, with the others skipping and gamboling behind him.

He didn't expect an entourage. But what harm could it do, he thought, for the town to give Tarheel a proper send-off? When they reached the river, Jim raised his arm, displaying his bird to the ragged throng. They cheered.

He removed the hood, and gave her a last look in the eye.

"Goodbye, loyal comrade," he said. It was a phrase he read in a book once.

He raised his arm and let Tarheel fly. She soared out over the river, just as he imagined. The witnesses fell silent, agape at the majesty of it.

But then she wheeled, and with a few powerful flaps, glided straight back to Jim. Jim was astonished as she hovered a few feet above him, talons extended as if to perch on his arm.

"Dumb bird," Jim said. "Get out of here!"

Tarheel flew away again, across the river. But she turned, and came in low, her wingtips almost touching the water. Then, with a graceful swoop, she was reaching for him again.

"Get out now! Shoo!"

The boys began to jeer:

"Having some trouble with your pet, Jim?"

"Is that a hawk or a chicken?"

Jim tore off some grass and threw the clump at her. She evaded it, and gave a plaintive screech.

"You're free! Go on! Light out!"

She ascended and milled around above him, as if confused. That's when the first rock was thrown. It was well wide, but Jim was astounded.

"Who threw that? Who threw that rock?"

"It was a piece of grass," someone replied.

"Liar!"

Now half the boys scrambled for rocks to throw; some of them brought out slingshots. Jim screamed for them to stop, but it did no good. He turned back to Tarheel, waving her away. But the more projectiles came at her, the more frightened did she become, and the more she tried to regain her perch.

The assault went on for a few more sickening minutes, as the falcon dodged dozens of stones. Jim dared think maybe they couldn't hit her.

"You sons of bitches! I'll get you all for this!"

That was when young Aloysius Spencer, the eight-year-old child of German immigrants, notched a smooth stone in his sling-shot. He pulled and released. The rock hit Tarheel dead center, in the breast. She spiraled out of the air and plunged, shedding feathers, into Charles Creek.

All the boys went silent as the magnificent bird fell. Slingshots fell limp at their sides, and stones were surreptitiously dropped.

There were no words Jim could utter in the face of this. He could only stare at her, floating in the stream befouled with sewage, and littered with old cigar wrappers and oyster tins. He wasn't aware of it, but the other boys saw him trembling with what might have been rage, or despair. Somebody pulled little Aloysius away and took him home, before something worse happened to him.

Jim used a stick to retrieve the bird from the creek. He took her home cradled in his arms, aware of the eyes watching from the houses around him. He kept his face a mask; he knew they expected him to show how he was feeling, but he refused to gratify them.

When he got home, he fetched a shovel. There was a quiet spot behind the bushes in the Wilcox's backyard—a place where neither his parents nor his sister ever went. He buried her there, good and deep.

There was a patch of sunflowers in the garden, standing sentinel over the vegetables. They were his parents' pride. He broke off the biggest, finest bloom with his bare hands, and laid it over Tarheel's grave.

When he went inside for the evening, his father was reading his paper in the dining room.

"Hey there, little man. Did you get rid of that bird?"

"Yes."

"Good. Now go up and wash those hands. I don't know what you get into, that you come in here so filthy..."

Jim never mentioned Tarheel again—until a dozen years later, when Tom Wilcox disparaged the Cropseys, saying "I don't know how you put up with them. No pretty face is worth that."

And Jim thought, "Maybe not." But he knew that courting such a comely girl, having her on his arm around town and lending her company only to him, made him feel better than anything since Tarheel died. He'd be damned if a few cuts on his fingers deprived him of that.

"Do you remember the last time you told me to get rid of something?" Jim replied. "This is one falcon you're not taking away from me."

IV.

The Pasquotank County Court convened on Monday, March 10th, 1902. The docket of Judge George A. Jones was crowded with the usual probate and eviction actions. There was also a dispute over a parcel of land in the Fairgrounds, the contested inheritance of a farm, and award of title to a stud horse. Among the criminal cases were nine charges of larceny, five for assault, one for 'nuisance', and one for carrying a concealed weapon. Folks around the nation were talking about just one case, however — the prosecution of James Wilcox for the assault and murder of Ella Maud Cropsey.

The Wilcox case was widely expected to dominate the two-week session. Out-of-town reporters had taken all the rooms at the main downtown hotel—the Arlington on Water Street. They were seen together at the bar, drinking, smoking, spitting, mostly among themselves. They so monopolized the town's lone Western Union telegrapher that regular townspeople had to wait hours to attend their messages.

The trial was not scheduled to begin until the 11th. Jones met with opposing counsel on the opening day of the session, however, and began on a jocular note.

"Don't look now, fellows, but we've got a hummer of a national event this time. Terrible circumstances, of course. But they won't be asking 'where's Betsy City?' anymore!"

"I hear this is the first time the trains are regularly running more full from Norfolk than to it," said Aydlett.

"I don't doubt!" Jones laughed. But then, as if aware that his humor might appear callous, he turned serious:

"Ed...George...I don't have to tell you the feelings that have been stirred up by this case. I'm going to bring down the gavel hard on either of you, if you turn my court into a medicine show."

"You have nothing to worry about from me," said George Ward, the county Solicitor.

"Your Honor, it's funny you say that, because that is exactly the point of our concerns—"

"I won't be drawn into that debate again, Ed. If you wish to make a motion in open court, that is your right. But I will not grant it. I will not tell the people of this county that they are unable to pass judgement on one of their own."

"Your Honor, with respect, that motion would never be construed as an insult to the people of this county. Any more than the Governor posting the militia at the jail was taken as an insult."

"What the Governor does out of an abundance of caution..."

"...might be taken in the same spirit, should you grant the change."

"I think I've made my position clear on this," said the judge as he rubbed his eyes. "If you want to argue the motion, I will give you all the rope you need. It will not change the result. Now, on to jury selection—"

Aydlett and Ward later found themselves walking together downstairs.

"I almost wish you won that argument, Ed," said the Solicitor.

"You could have said something. What prosecutor wants to see a verdict thrown out over the issue of venue?"

"Wishing you'd carried the point and helping you make it aren't the same."

They paused at the door to don hats.

"That boy's good as convicted already," said Aydlett. Then he tipped his brim and walked out into the sunny afternoon.

Opening day of the Wilcox trial saw the largest crowd of spectators attempt to enter a courtroom in the history of the town. As if for a hot ticket at the Academy of Music, a line formed in Courthouse Square two hours before the doors opened. The ground was still torn up after the departure of the Pasquotank Rifles, and the milling about of hundreds of more feet turned it into a moonscape. Yet everyone was equal in their muddy shoes and soiled cuffs—the whites and blacks, the men and women, the old and the not-so-young.

An elderly Negro sold roasted pecans for two cents a bag. For throats made dry by this, another man offered a single ladle of clear water for the sum of one cent. A boy—conspicuously not in school that Tuesday morning—sold copies of the *Weekly Economist*, which his patrons eagerly scanned for fresh news of the investigation. There was nothing about Nell or Jim in the March 7th edition, but much sympathy was raised by an unrelated item: the noted Ohio millionaire and philanthropist who was found dead nine days before. The body was discovered hanging in his office by a family member who went to call him to dinner. "Illness and the suicide of a favorite son, a Yale graduate, a year ago, made Mr. Perkins temporarily insane," the story read.

"Poor man," a woman cried.

"Mercy on that poor soul who found him!"

"How hard on that poor family!"

"Hey, there's the bastard!" someone shouted.

Jim Wilcox was being escorted to the front door. He was well dressed for his indictment, with short black coat, shirt pressed and starched, bow tie and shoes polished so high they gleamed. Jim had done the polishing himself, and believed he'd never worn a finer set of clogs. As he mounted the few steps to the door, he nodded amiably to the crowd.

"He looks guilty as John Wilkes Booth," a man said.

The main courtroom was grand but entirely typical: wide-plank floor, soaring strip-ceiling with chandelier, railing of carved finials. From the back wall, Abraham Lincoln and George Washington gazed over the judge's shoulders. The first row was taken by the fashionable women of the town, who had been escorted forward as a courtesy. The lack of ventilation forced many to fan themselves furiously. Despite the stuffiness, the women wore fancy hats that blocked the views of the men behind them. Because asking a lady to remove her hat was not a done thing, the men had to stretch to peer around the ostrich plumes.

Every inch of standing room was likewise taken. The white spectators jammed the front, spilling into the areas usually reserved for the clerks and witnesses. A hundred black faces crowded the back. To spur the civic education of the youngsters of the town, Judge Jones invited every boy who fit to squat at the foot of his bench. Next to the judge himself, these boys had the best seats in the house.

The buzz in the room faded as Wilcox was led in. All eyes were on him as he took his place at the defendant's table—except for two of the boys, who took turns whispering in each other's ears. Once Jim was settled next to Aydlett, Jones gaveled the court to order. Solicitor Ward rose.

"If it pleases the Court, we will arraign the prisoner in cell 19."

"Proceed."

"James Wilcox, please stand. Hold up your right hand."

Jim stood and raised his arm. To him, the entire tableau seemed like a dream; when he looked to his right, the hand there seemed like it belonged to someone else. He repeated the oath mechanically. His awareness of what Ward was saying faded, until he perceived his name being spoke, and heard "...the jurors of the State, upon their oaths, present that James Wilcox, of the county of Pasquotank, State of North Carolina, on the 20th day of November, 1901, with force of arms, at and in the county aforesaid, feloniously, willfully and of his malice aforethought, did kill and murder Ella Maud Cropsey against the form of the statute, in such case made, and provided, and against the peace and dignity of the State."

"How does the defendant plead?"

Aydlett rose. "My client pleads not guilty, Your Honor."

A hiss went through the crowd. Jones paused for it to subside, fingers lingering on the handle of his gavel.

"How will you be tried?"

"By God and by country!"

"When does the prosecution think it will be ready to go to trial?"

"Thursday, the 13th."

"What does the defendant say?"

"Well, Your Honor, we don't know," said Aydlett, feigning haplessness. "We will try and be ready by Thursday, but cannot say. I think it very probable that we will be ready to go by Thursday noon."

"Your Honor, the defense has had no less time to prepare for this proceeding as the State."

"There are witnesses for the defense that are not yet ready to testify, Your Honor, due to the intensity of the bias against my client in the community..."

Sensing that Aydlett was about to bring up the matter of venue in open court, Jones almost rose from his chair—

"Fair enough! Let the jury be impanelled here by Thursday at 12 o'clock."

He brought the gavel down again, and the first day of Jim's trial was over. With that, one of the boys at the foot of Jones' bench turned to the other and asked out loud, "Is that it?"

As they led Jim out, he sighted William Cropsey among the onlookers. Every inch of his long form was clad in black, and his expression was one of withering contempt. It baffled Jim, this hostility—it was almost as if by this, the pure force of his malice, Cropsey believed he could make Jim into a murderer. But Jim was nothing of the kind, and he was sure Cropsey knew it. And indeed, when Jim held his gaze, Cropsey's eyes lowered.

This little victory sustained him all the way through the jeering mob and back to his lonely cell.

On Thursday Jim got his first look at the jury. That he was to be judged by his exact peers was never in doubt: the jury was entirely male and overwhelmingly white. Of the twelve, he recognized two only slightly, and could not put names to their faces.

Ward called the first witness for the prosecution: Dr. J.E. Wood, the Cropsey's personal physician and member of the coroner's jury. Solicitor Ward began:

"How long have you been practicing medicine?"

"Since 1869."

"What college did you graduate from?"

"I graduated at the Washington University of Maryland, now known as the College of Physicians and Surgeons."

"From your experience as a practitioner, and from your learning as a physician, do you consider yourself competent to give an opinion satisfactory to yourself on medical matters?"

"I do."

"Objection!" Aydlett rose. "Whether the witness can offer an opinion satisfactory to *himself* is irrelevant."

"I will rephrase, Your Honor," replied Ward. "Dr. Wood, from your experience, do you consider yourself competent to give an informed opinion on medical matters?"

"I do."

"Is that acceptable, Mr. Aydlett?" asked the judge, in a bemused tone.

"Withdrawn."

"Are you able, from your learning in practice of your profession to form an expert opinion as to the death of a person, whether it was caused by drowning or otherwise?"

"If the body is preserved, generally."

"Objection! Prosecution has offered no evidence that witness is expert in post-mortem examination."

"That competence is implicit in his credentials," replied Ward.

"Mr. Aydlett, if you are going to object to everything State's witnesses say, do us the courtesy of informing us now. The Court will apply to the Legislature for funds to pay for a two-year trial."

There was a smattering of laughter around the courtroom.

"The defense will make no promises, Your Honor."

"You may take your concerns up on cross. Objection overruled."

"Exception."

"Dr. Wood, are you competent in this regard?"

"I believe I am, sir."

On his examination, Aydlett did not pause for pleasantries.

"Dr. Wood, is being a physician your only profession in this town?"

"No. I also run a drug store on Main Street."

"And how much time would you say you spend on that occupation?"

"I don't know. A good part of the day, but not all."

"I see. And have you ever had the experience before this, in examining a body that was claimed to have been drowned?"

"No sir, I have not."

"Then you have never made before, an autopsy of a person who was claimed to have been drowned?"

"This is the first one I made."

"Then doctor, how did you get your information regarding the drowning of people—from what source?"

"From the authorities."

"What authorities?"

"Taylor & Reese."

"Are Taylor & Reese standard authorities?"

"They are so considered."

Aydlett went to the defense table and lifted four heavy books.

"Doctor, how many works are there that treat upon the subject?"

"I don't know."

"Hammond is one, is it not?"

"I don't know."

The lawyer dropped Hammond with a *thunk.*

"Wharton is one, is it not?"

"Yes sir."

Thunk.

"Hamilton is one, is it not?"

"I don't know."

Thunk.

"Is Champman one?"

"I don't know."

Thunk.

"Then the only authorities you have examined are Taylor & Reese?"

"Yes."

"I have a copy of Taylor & Reese here," said Aydlett, holding up the text. "The section that treats of drowning is a single chapter in length, chapter 38. Is it your testimony, Dr. Wood, that a man's life should rest on the expertise of a part-time druggist, based on information gleaned from a mere twenty-one pages of a single source?"

The doctor blanched. "That was just plain mean, Ed," he said.

Judge Jones pounded his gavel. "Mr. Aydlett, contents of the town library notwithstanding, the competence of this witness has already been accepted by the Court. His testimony is admissible."

"Objection, Your Honor."

"Overruled."

"Exception."

Ward resumed his examination. After an exhaustive review of the circumstances and proceedings of the autopsy that left half the crowd appalled and the rest yawning, Wood testified to its finding.

"If the jury should find as a fact," stipulated Ward, "that the body of Ella Cropsey did stay in the water thirty-seven days after she was stricken on the left temple with a blow, and that there was a tablespoon of dark fluid blood underneath the skin of the left temple and diffused by the muscular substance, and the membrane of the bone thereunder was injured, and should further find that there was no water in the stomach, no blood in her heart on either side, no water in her lungs, no water in her pleural cavity – how, in your opinion, did this woman come to her death?"

"I should think that the woman was knocked on that temple and stunned and while in that condition, put into the water."

"So it is your conclusion that she was murdered?"

"She was murdered."

Ward paused to let this statement sink into the minds of the jury.

"Thank you, Your Honor."

"Your witness, Mr. Aydlett."

"Dr. Wood, you explained you found no marks of violence on her body and face, did you?"

"We found no obvious marks on first examination."

"And that was your decision when you left there and returned to town after you and the other doctors made that examination?"

"That is correct."

"So you are saying that the bruise was too subtle to be noticed, or that your examination was not thorough enough to notice it?"

"It was obviously thorough enough, because we found it."

"Belatedly so. Can you testify as to whom on the coroner's jury first noticed the wound?"

"I don't recall."

"According to his written statement, Mr. Ferebee, the *barber*, was first to notice a swelling on the left side of her head. Is that your recollection?"

"I don't recall."

Buried among the onlookers, J.B. Ferebee held his head up a little higher.

"You have testified that Taylor & Reese are the sole authorities you consulted, correct?"

"I have."

"Doesn't Taylor say this: that blood in the heart is no positive evidence whether a person is drowned or not?"

"Yes sir, it says it is not positive evidence."

"You say the lungs had no water in them?"

"No water, correct."

"Doctor, isn't a fact that about one-half of the people who are drowned have no water in their lungs?"

"Yes, sir."

"Isn't it frequently the case that water is not in the pleural cavity when one is drowned?"

"Very frequently."

"In fact, isn't it very seldom that water is in the pleural cavity when one is drowned?"

"It is found about half the time."

"Now as to the stomach. Do you always find water in the stomach when a person is drowned?"

"No sir."

"In fact, do not Taylor & Reese say the following—"*The absence of water from the stomach cannot, however, lead to the inference that the person has not died from drowning, because in some instances it is not swallowed, and in others it may drain away...?*"

"If that's what it says."

"Is that a 'yes', sir?"

"I mean I don't recall the exact wording."

"Well, Dr. Wood, you'll have to indulge me because I am confused. If your sole authority states that neither the condition of the heart, nor the lungs, nor the pleural cavity, nor the stomach are determinative of whether a person drowned or not, how do you come by such a definite conclusion, that Miss Cropsey was struck and put into the water?"

Wood swallowed.

"Any one of those conditions alone may not be definitive. But taken together, an opinion may be formed. Including the bruise on her head."

"Regarding that—the place where the body of Miss Cropsey was found is near a railway bridge, isn't it?"

"Yes."

"And there are sawmills nearby, and therefore scraps of wood and pilings and such?"

"I suppose there are."

"Based on your expertise, doctor, could not this bruise have appeared by the body getting into a position that it could have rested upon some hard or rough place, such as a stump or piling?"

"It is very apt to cause the bruise on the outside."

"But it could have produced the damage internally?"

"Not without showing an outside scratch. There would be—be apt to be—some external evidence."

"But do not Taylor & Reese say the following: '*Even marks of violence on the body must not be too hastily construed into proofs of murder...*'?"

"Objection," said Ward. "Counsel has not proven the witness was 'hasty'."

"Sustained. Jury will disregard that question."

Aydlett continued: "Was the body decomposed, doctor?"

"Only to the extent of producing enough gas to raise the body."

"Answer the question. Had decomposition set in?"

"Only at that point."

"What about scavenging from fish and such, doctor? Would you expect to see evidence of such after such a long time in the water?"

"Perhaps."

"Did you note any?"

"No."

"So is it plausible to you that a body may lie in the river for thirty-seven days, and show little evidence of scavenging?"

"It depends on circumstances," said Wood, shifting in his seat. A fine sheen of perspiration now stood out on his forehead, but he did not take out his handkerchief to mop it.

"What circumstances?"

"Ambient temperature. The condition of the water. The river from the swamp contains much juniper, which is acidic. That might have discouraged scavengers. That the body was heavily clothed may also have delayed scavenging."

"Miss Cropsey was clothed, but her hands and left foot were fully exposed, were they not?"

"Both feet were clad in stockings."

"But you testified that the left toe was exposed."

"You're quibbling," said Wood.

"Did you see any evidence of scavenging upon those exposed members?"

"No."

"Would you therefore agree, Doctor, that you present no definitive evidence that Nell Cropsey was drowned, or struck on the head, or indeed was even in the water for thirty-seven days?"

"Objection!" Ward jumped to his feet. "Witness has already testified as to his conclusions."

Jones hesitated, drumming his fingers. "Overruled."

"Taken in isolation," Wood said, "none of the details compel any particular conclusion. But taken together, I believe the truth is clear."

Aydlett yielded back to Ward.

"May I borrow that book?"

"Of course," said Aydlett, handing him the text.

"Dr. Wood, while we are reading from Messrs. Taylor & Reese, is it not true that on page 429, they state: *A medical inference of drowning is founded upon a certain series of facts, to each of which, individually, it may be easy to oppose plausible objections; but taken together they furnish cumulative evidence as strong as is commonly required for proof of any kind of death...*'?"

"I believe they do."

"Thank you. No further questions."

After a one hour break for lunch, it was Ike Fearing's turn. The young coroner did not look composed on the stand; as he recited his credentials, his eyes kept shifting over to Aydlett.

"From your study and practice of your profession," asked Ward, "are you able to form an expert opinion as to whether the death of a person was caused by a wound on the head, or blow, or bruise?"

"Yes, sir."

"And your conclusion?"

"The victim was rendered unconscious from a blow to the head, and then put in the water in that state."

"Thank you. Your witness."

Ward took his seat. Aydlett did not rise to begin his examination, but remained seated next to Jim. Wilcox had procured a piece of gum during the lunch break, and chewed away with a strange placidity.

"Doctor, did you ever examine a body claimed to have been drowned before this?"

"Yes, I have."

"Made an autopsy of it?"

"No sir, not an autopsy."

"Then you did not make an examination as to the condition of the parts of the body internally?"

"No, sir."

"Then, as I understand, you have never examined a body internally except this body, that was claimed to be drowned?"

"Yes, I have since then."

"When?"

"Last January or February; I forget the date."

"Where?"

"At Possum Quarter Landing."

"Then you examined one body since. Then Doctor, where do you get your information from if you have not had personal experience?"

"I got it from observations and that autopsy since then. And I have read some authorities."

"Which authorities?"

"Taylor & Reese," Fearing said, sullenly.

Laughter erupted from the back of the courtroom. Jones pounded his gavel.

"Continue, Mr. Aydlett."

"Then that is your information, from an autopsy conducted after the fact, and your reading of one authority?"

"Yes."

"Your Honor, defense has no further questions on the matter of Dr. Fearing's fitness to testify as an expert."

"Thank you, counselor. Based on examination, the witness is acceptable to the Court."

"Objection!"

"Overruled."

The prosecution pursued the same line it had with Dr. Wood. The clinical details became numbing to the onlookers; as terms like "osmosis" and "peritoneum" were uttered over and over, the eyes of the jurymen wandered.

"Dr. Fearing, if the jury should find that this body had been there in the water thirty-seven days, that the body had been put into the water, or gone in the water, not dead or unconscious, what in your opinion would be the condition of the stomach as to its contents?"

"Objection!"

"Overruled."

"Exception."

"I should expect to find water in there," replied Fearing. "Still, there might not be."

"And if they should find that this body had lain in the water thirty-seven days, and that it had been put in the water dead or unconscious, what, in your opinion, if any, would be its effect upon the stomach as to its contents?"

"Objection!"

"Overruled."

"Exception."

"I should expect to find no water in it..."

The pattern of questions repeated with respect to the heart, lungs, and pleura, with Aydlett objecting at every turn. So regularly did he object that it became a game in the drinking establishments of Elizabeth City: every time he leapt to his feet, look-outs would relay it to the saloons, and the patrons would cheer, toast and drink.

"Then it is your conclusion, Doctor, that Miss Ella Cropsey found her death by murder, not suicide?"

"That is my conclusion."

"Thank you. No further questions for now."

"Your witness, Mr. Aydlett."

"Dr. Fearing, it is correct that you were the one who physically conducted the autopsy?"

"It is."

"And it is your contention that you conducted a full examination?"

"That is a fact, not my contention."

"I see. But tell me, are you aware of the research of Dr. Riedell on the subject of drowning?"

"I recognize the name."

"Then can you summarize his main findings?"

"Objection!" cried Ward. "Counsel is not entitled to test the witness."

"Sustained. Mr. Aydlett, that horse has left the barn."

"Your Honor, the question bears directly on the conclusions on which the State's case is based."

"If you have a specific point to make, get to it."

"Yes, sir. Dr. Fearing, you are aware that Dr. Riedell's experiments on drowned animals showed there is one incontrovertible sign of death by drowning: the presence of a mucous froth in the air-passages and lungs?"

"I don't recall those words exactly."

"They are in all the textbooks, including Taylor & Reese. Page 427 of that book reads: *Dr. Riedell regards the presence of a mucous froth as a constant sign of this kind of death. In all his experiments and observations he states that he found a frothy fluid in windpipe, bronchii, and lungs; after death it gradually disappeared from the air-tubes by exomosis, but not from the lungs. The fluidity of this froth is, he contends, a distinctive character of death from drowning, and is not met with in any other case.*'"

"I found no such froth in the lungs. Or very little."

"So you have said. Dr. Riedell says it might be found in air-passages. Did you examine the windpipe?"

"I did not."

"Why not?"

The doctor scowled, looked at his feet. Jim Wilcox paused his gum-chewing as the court awaited his answer.

"It was an oversight on my part. But it is my firm belief that if we had examined it, no mucous froth would have been found so long after death."

"You say that, Doctor, but you don't know it as a fact."

"I know it."

"But not as a fact. Yes or no?"

"No," Fearing replied, tightly.

"Dr. Fearing, you have testified that the injury on Miss Cropsey's temple indicates that she was struck on the head before she entered the water. Correct?"

"That is correct."

"Did you see the lick struck?"

"No sir."

"Do you swear it was struck?"

"I swear that somebody struck it."

"Then you did not see a lick and won't swear any lick was struck?"

"No—"

"Then your explanation is based upon the idea that the lick was struck?"

"Yes sir."

"Then, if there was no lick struck, your explanation would count for nothing?"

"I don't know about that."

"Perhaps it is like the condition of the windpipe—you simply know the truth without any evidence."

"Objection! Argumentative."

"Sustained. Please restrict yourself to questions, Mr. Aydlett."

"Thank you, your Honor. Nothing further."

V.

The trial's second day left the town in an unsettled state. Of course, Wilcox was still guilty. But the vigor of the defense could not help but arouse begrudging admiration.

Aydlett's evisceration of the doctors encouraged those inclined to give Jim the benefit of the doubt. The town's Republicans grumbled over the Democrats' conduct toward the son of a former Republican sheriff. Certain preachers raised the subject from the pulpit: "I don't hesitate to say that I believe the prisoner is innocent," declared Rev. Lewelyn. "I will say that I condemn some things in his past life, and had he been a member of my church I should probably have censured him from the pulpit. But now I believe he is innocent of the dark charge that hangs over him." In general, the town split along both denominational and political lines, with Republicans and Episcopalians inclined to withhold judgment, and Democrats and evangelicals—a fair majority—certain of his guilt.

Though it scarcely seemed possible, the courtroom was even more packed on the morning of the 17th. The temperatures outside had risen into the sixties, and with the windows sealed, it was twenty degrees warmer inside. Men fanned themselves with newspapers and hats; women dabbed their glowing foreheads with lace hankies, and suffered.

The throng fell silent as the Cropsey family processed into the courtroom. Ollie led the way—a willowy figure in black, her face concealed by a breast-length weeping veil. They took the row of seats reserved for them behind the prosecution, and Solicitor Ward turned to greet them in turn. When he got to Ollie, who sat on the center aisle, he leaned in to whisper in her ear. Ollie nodded, the crepe of her veil dancing over her features.

The first witness of the day was Mr. C.A. Long, one of the boatmen who found Nell's body in the river. He recounted the story of how he found her floating not far from the Cropsey residence, how he had secured the body and alerted the family, and the condition of the corpse when he found it. As these facts were not in dispute, there was no cross-examination.

William Cropsey was the first direct relative of the victim to take the stand. He was clad in an ordinary black suit, with black bow tie. Where his eyes had been on the back of Jim Wilcox's head for almost every minute of the trial, they unaccountably wandered once he was called to testify.

"Mr. Cropsey, I think I speak for the entire court in our sympathy at your loss," said Ward. "We hope to detain you no longer than necessary."

"That's all right."

"Can you recount for the court the events of early morning of November 21st?"

Cropsey repeated the story of how he woke up after midnight to use the necessary; how Olive told him Nell was missing, and the immediate search for her; the early morning trip to the Wilcox house to talk to Jim.

"How would you describe the defendant's manner when you spoke to him?"

"He seemed unconcerned. When Mr. Reid brought him to our house, and my wife begged him to tell her everything, he was cold to her."

"In what way 'cold'?"

"He was more interested in excusing himself than reassuring her."

"And did he take part in the search for Miss Nell?"

"He did not. He never made a single move to do so. It was genuine strange."

"Did his manner convince you that he had some hand in her disappearance?"

"Absolutely not, sir. All I wanted was the whole story. When there was talk of lynching, they came around to ask what I thought. I told them to let the law take its course. If I had any hostility toward Wilcox, all it would have taken was one word from me."

Cropsey stared at Jim. This time it was the latter's turn to look away.

"But you soon came to believe your daughter was dead."

"After enough time, a parent just knows. Nell was a sweet girl, a loving girl. She would never set her family to unnecessary worry. If she'd have run off, she would have gotten some word to us."

"To your knowledge, was Ella Cropsey suicidal?"

"No. Never."

"Can you describe the morning her body was found...?"

Jim procured and folded a piece of paper into a neat, tiny square. Then he unfolded it and used the creases to tear it into small sections. At one point, he yawned.

"Finally, Mr. Cropsey, can you tell the court the effect this affair has had on your family?"

"My wife's health has declined. She requires constant medical care. To this day, she is barely able to move about the house. The children have been strong, but anyone can see the burden it has put on them. To think one of our own can simply vanish from the face of the earth, and from such a quiet, ordinary community. How could it not shake anyone's sense of security?

"All we ever wanted was the truth," he said. "That's all we want, even now."

"Thank you. No further questions."

Aydlett rose. "I too, would detain you only as long as necessary, sir."

Cropsey nodded.

"You say the defendant was 'cold' when you fetched him. But he was not under arrest at that point. He did come voluntarily after all."

"I don't regard the circumstances to have been 'voluntary'. The deputy didn't give him much choice."

"Can you attest to your own good feelings, if you were pulled out of your bed in the middle of the night? Pulled out of bed, and accused of complicity in a crime?"

"Objection! Hypothetical!" interjected Ward.

"Sustained."

"I would never have been in that position," said Cropsey.

Aydlett fetched up a bitter laugh. "I submit Jim Wilcox would have said the same, before all this..."

"Mr. Aydlett, you are warned again to watch your tone," said the judge. "This is a bereaved father."

"Understood, Your Honor. Mr. Cropsey, the defendant allegedly returned several personal items to your daughter that evening. Did you search for those items?"

"We did. We scoured the house and the grounds outside for days. The pictures never turned up."

"And the broken parasol?"

"It was on the floor in the hall. I almost stepped on it in the dark."

"On the floor, you say. Any idea how it got there?"

"No."

"Any theory?"

"No."

"Let the record show that the witness displays a definite lack of curiosity about this question—"

"Objection!"

"Sustained. The record will note no such thing. Do you have anything further, Mr. Aydlett?"

"No, Your Honor. But the defense reserves the option to recall this witness should the need arise."

The bailiff called Miss Olive Cropsey. If anticipation made a sound, it was heard loudly in the courtroom that morning. The correspondents in reporters' row got to scribbling the moment she rose. "Ollie is a tall and graceful girl," appraised the *Raleigh News & Observer*, "twenty-one years old, with soulful, sorrowful blue eyes, a mouth that expresses volumes of tenderness and sympathy: a face of classical contour, fair-haired and flushed. Her raiment of black emphasized her beauty."

Presented with the Bible, she removed her gloves. When she said "I swear", it was in a small, wavering voice.

Mr. Ward rose and came in close, head lowered, as if approaching a skittish horse. "Miss Cropsey, you are Ella Maud Cropsey's older sister, yes?"

"Yes. We call...we called her Nell."

"She was a small thing, was she not? Can you show us her height, relative to yours?"

Ollie stood up and held a flattened hand at the level of her veiled nose. "She came up to about here," she said, then took her seat again.

"Thank you. Can you tell the court something about Nell, as you knew her? Would you say she was a good and proper girl?"

"She was as kind and sweet a sister as anyone could wish. She was a joy to her parents, a pillar of love and support for all of us. She was the soul of our family."

She is well-rehearsed, thought Aydlett.

"Can you describe for us the history of her relationship with the defendant?"

"We came to Elizabeth City on April 4th or 5th, 1898...may I lift my veil?"

"You may," said the judge. "Bailiff! Open the windows!"

Ollie took the hem of her veil and folded it over the top of her hat. Chairs creaked as their occupants leaned forward.

Her face was pale and shone with perspiration. Said the *Raleigh News:* "When she exposed her sweet features, the spectators heaved an involuntary sigh of relief...the jury itself was visibly impressed."

She spoke softly as she began, but gathered strength as she went on—except when she faltered, and looked down to gather herself. Her tone, sad yet resigned, struck onlookers as the ideal embodiment of the tragic heroine, like in certain performances they had seen above the department store.

"We knew Jim Wilcox in June that year. He came to our house and met Nell. He seemed to show her attention from the first—"

"Is that the man?" asked Ward, indicating.

Ollie glanced down at the defendant, nodded. She would not look Jim in the face, but Jim's eyes never left her. There was a sardonic twist to his mouth as he anticipated a torrent of falsehoods. Most onlookers took this for a villain's mocking smile.

"He used to come to see her every Sunday, Tuesday and Thursday, and later he came most every afternoon. He paid her much attention. They would walk and ride and sail together, and Jim took her to all the shows. Twice when they went sailing they got back late at night. He bought her flowers and presents, some very nice ones — a silver dish, a gold ring inscribed 'July 17'. That was her birthday. He gave her pictures of himself.

"Last fall they quarreled. It was September when I heard them having little spats. I heard Nell say to Jim, 'If you're going to act like this the rest of the season, you can stay home.' Nell went to religious meetings and joined the Methodist church in October. Jim used to wait at the church door and walk Nell home.

"For a while they did not speak. Carrie came to visit us and they began speaking again. On November 7th, when we had a house guest, Jim came to visit. When he got up to leave, Nell said 'Pull!', as if she were spurring a horse. She said it in front of this house guest—"

"Did the defendant make any response to this?" asked Ward.

"He just got his hat and left. After that time Jim came two or three times a week, but Nell would never go to the door with him. She would talk in front of him about what fun she would have in New York, when she finally enrolled at school. That Tuesday before she disappeared, Jim came. Nell and I sat on the lounge and Jim sat nearby. He said to Nell, 'I suppose your toe is getting better?'—meaning the corn she had on it—and all she said was, 'A little.'

"The next day Jim took Carrie to the skating rink. He had started to pay attention to her instead of Nell, when Nell had turned cold on him. When they got back Nell was writing. Jim and Nell never exchanged a word during his half-hour's stay. Jim had brought some apples, but when he offered one to her, she refused to take it.

"Jim tapped me on the shoulder and said 'You're a nice girl.' I suppose he meant I was nice compared to a certain other girl. I said, 'Yes, I'm mamma's angel.' Nell and Carrie played together on the harmonica and the mandolin, and Uncle Hen came in and joined them with his fiddle. Jim just sat and listened. Nell said, 'Here I go to dance with my old lame foot.' Carrie passed the apples around, but Nell still wouldn't take any."

"After that we just sat around talking. Somehow the subject of how we'd like to die came up—"

"Did Nell raise that subject? Or the defendant?"

Ollie frowned. "I can't remember. It was just one of those things we talked about, like what foreign countries we'd like to visit, or which period in history we'd most like to live. It was just something to pass an evening."

"I understand," said Ward. "Please continue."

"I said I'd like to drown most of all, because I'd read somewhere that the moment of...of *passing* was a pleasant sensation. It was said to be, an almost ecstatic feeling. But then Nell said—"

There was a catch in her voice, and she had to stop. Into that pause, that space of grief, no one made a sound.

"—Nell said that she would rather freeze than drown. She said that water would make her look a mess, because her hair would fall out. Where if she died of cold, she would be preserved as she was. Carrie said that between freezing and drowning, she didn't care, but that she would never want to burn to death, because that was the most painful.

"Then Jim boasted he could put his hand under the kettle that was boiling on the stove without burning himself. He lifted it up and got some smut on his hand and put it right on the iron. He held it there for a long time. Then he put some of the smut on my face and gave Carrie a smudge on the end of her nose. Playfully. He didn't do it to Nell. I got a corn cob and rubbed it on the stove to put some on his face. We all laughed, except for Nell, who didn't say anything when Jim did his trick with the stove."

"Miss Cropsey, was the defendant angry at the cold treatment he received from your sister?"

"Objection!" shouted Aydlett. "Witness could not possibly know the private feelings of my client."

The judge scratched his nose. "Sustained."

"Rephrasing," said Ward. "Miss Olive, in your opinion, did Mr. Wilcox *appear* to resent his treatment at the hands of your sister?"

For the first time, Ollie looked directly at Jim, who stared back from under raised eyebrows.

"I would say, yes he did. I'm sorry, Jim—"

"Please direct your statements to counsel, Miss, or to the bench."

"Yes, Your Honor."

"To continue, Miss Olive," said Ward, "can you describe what happened on the night of November 20th?"

"That night we were all in the dining room after supper—"

"Who was there?"

"Myself, Carrie, Roy Crawford, and Nell. Someone was at the door, and we all knew it was Jim from how he rang the bell. Nell was fixing the lining on the coat she was going to wear on the trip to New York—it was cold on those Old Dominion steamers that time of year. She didn't get up to answer the door. Carrie said, 'I'm getting tired of poor manners,' and went to let him in.

"Jim sat on the rocker by the hall door. He was very still, continued to look at his watch and compare it with the wall clock. He and Nell did not speak. He spoke when spoken to and managed to talk a little, but was very still. Nell played the harmonica and when Uncle Hen came in, he played a tune or two. Then he got up to go upstairs, and Nell said, 'Oh, you are too stingy with your wind.'

"Jim asked if there was any water in the pump. I said there was a little, and got him a glass. He said he did not want it because it might be poisoned. It was strange thing to say, and none of us had an answer to it. Jim kept taking out his watch, checking it five or six times. After a while, Jim managed to tell us that Miss Barrett was going to be married. After that conversation died out, no one said anything. Carrie said good night to us all and went upstairs.

"Then Jim got up, took out his watch again, and said 'It is eleven o'clock and my mama said I must be in at eleven tonight.' I said, 'Jim, you must be getting good.' He rolled a cigarette, took his hat from the the back of the rocking chair, and put it on. He stepped out in the hall and turned around and said, 'Nell, can I see you out here a minute?' Nell didn't answer, but got up and went with him. She went outside as soon as he made his cigarette. I heard them talking in the hall, and heard the screen door close. I looked at the clock: it was 11:05. That was the last time I saw my sister alive."

With this, Ollie bowed her head and wept in silence. Muffled sobs were heard from the gallery. Grown men welled up in the jury box, and the pencils of the reporters surged into motion.

"The auditors, sad-faced and sympathetic, drank in the strong feeling which stirred this young woman's breast and remained immoveable but for heaving bosoms and wet eyelids," gushed *The News & Observer.* "It was a scene which comes only once in most people's lives. The eloquence of Clay, Webster or Calhoun, or the efforts of an emotional star at a stage climax could not have produced the effect made by the words and demeanor of this beautiful girl..." At this point the correspondent alluded again to her "heaving bosoms", but his editor removed the repetition from the published version.

To the wonder of court officers, the eyes of old Judge Jones reddened, and he pulled a handkerchief from under his robes to cover them. Aydlett was stunned. He wanted to object—but how did one object to the tears of a judge?

Jim Wilcox, for his part, spat his gum in a crimped piece of paper, and did not resume chewing. It did not escape notice that he looked pale for the rest of Ollie's testimony.

"The court recognizes how difficult this must be," said Judge Jones in a funereal tone. "Does the witness wish for a brief recess?"

"I will go on," she said, and wiped away her tears with a glove.

"When it got to be 11:30," she said, "I told Roy it was time for him to go. After making a cigarette and putting on his coat, he went out in the hall. I followed to let him out. When we got to the front doors, they were wide open and the little screen door was flapping. Neither Jim nor Nell were there.

"On retiring, I saw that Nell was not in bed, but I didn't think anything of it. I went into a doze, but was awake and heard the chimes ring for 12:30. Then I realized that Nell was still not there. I got up and went into the hall, and saw my father there. I told him Nell was missing, and the search started.

"Papa went over for Jim, who came later with Mr. Dawson. He went into the parlor and took hold of the curtain while Mama came in and said 'Jim, for my sake and your mother's sake, tell me where Nell is.' Jim replied, 'I could swear and kiss the Bible that I left her on the piazza. I gave her back her parasol, and Nell said 'I know what this means.' I told her to go in, she would catch cold. She replied, 'I don't care.' I went on over to town, leaving her leaning on the post, crying..."

The prosecution yielded. As Aydlett rose, Ollie clenched the gloves tightly in her right hand. But her anxiety was wasted: he had no intention of conducting a serious cross-examination. Holding a coroner's feet to the fire was one thing; harrying the victim's bereaved sister was very much another.

Aydlett did not even encroach upon her. From the remoteness of his chair, he said, "Your Honor, the defense wishes to convey its sincere condolences upon the witness in her loss. We have no intention of detaining her today."

"So noted," said Jones.

"Miss Cropsey, in his testimony your father William Cropsey testified as to the condition of the front hallway that last evening. Do you recall what he said?"

"I do."

"He said that there was a parasol lying on the floor. A white silk parasol, that the defendant said he had returned to Miss Nell. He would have done so around 11:15 p.m. Do you remember seeing that parasol when you closed the front doors for the night?"

Ollie stared at him for a moment.

"No, I don't."

"Mr. Cropsey said he almost tripped over it. It must have been very obvious."

"I'm sorry, Mr. Aydlett. I don't recall noticing it."

"Thank you, Miss Olive. No further questions for this witness."

After lunch it was the turn of Carrie Cropsey. She was also dressed in full mourning, and likewise a striking figure, but the correspondents, having exhausted their superlatives on Ollie, did not go into descriptive raptures about her.

"Miss Cropsey," Ward began, "you are the daughter of Judge Andrew G. Cropsey of Brooklyn, New York, are you not?"

"Yes, that is true."

"And you are a resident of that city?"

"Only when I am in school. Otherwise I live in Nanuet, New York."

"Where are you a student?"

"I attend Pratt Institute."

"What do you study?"

"Art and design."

"It was Miss Nell's intention to study there as well, was it not?"

"Yes. She very much looked forward to it. She would come to classes with me when she was in town. All the teachers and students remember her fondly."

"To improve herself as a woman and a wife," said Ward, "Alas, it was an ambition she did not live to realize—"

"Objection! Relevance, Your Honor?"

"Overruled. Continue, Mr. Ward."

Carrie was invited to recount her memories of the night of November 20, which she did in terms much like Ollie's. Her testimony became more compelling when she was asked about certain conversations she had with Jim Wilcox in the weeks before.

"When Nell stopped going out with Jim, he asked me to go with him. I didn't know anybody else in town other than my relatives, so I went. It also didn't sit well with me, how cold they had become with each other. Jim kept coming, so I thought at least somebody should be nice to him—"

"You felt sorry for the defendant," said Ward.

"Well...I guess."

Jim frowned.

"I asked him once, 'Jim, why is it that Nell dislikes you so much?' He answered, 'Why don't you tell me?' So I said, 'You haven't quarreled, have you?' He said, 'No, but she won't come to the door to meet me and I am going to drop her.' And I said, 'You mean she will drop you.' 'That's about the size of it,' he said."

"Another time, he told me 'You're a nice girl.' So I asked him, 'What's the matter, Jim?' He said, 'Eavesdroppers never hear any good of themselves. Last night I was out smoking, and I heard what you all said about me—'"

"What was he referring to?" asked Ward.

"He had brought me home from the rink, and I happened to mention that I felt like I towered over him when we were in our skates. So Nell said, 'I guess we should call him Squatty.' And I guess we all laughed at that."

"You guess?"

"We laughed."

"And the defendant said he heard himself being ridiculed?"

"Yes."

"And what was your impression of his reaction?"

"He seemed amused. But I could tell it bothered him."

Ward yielded to Aydlett.

"Miss Cropsey, you spent a considerable amount of time with Jim Wilcox, did you not?"

"I did. Second only to Nell, I'd reckon."

"Second only to Nell. And in all that time together, did you gather any impression of him as anything other than a gentleman?"

"Never less than a gentleman."

"Did he evince any personal cruelty? Anything that would convey that he was capable of serious crimes?"

"Well...he had a certain set to himself. He would never shrink from an argument. He sometimes talked about fights he'd been in."

"Did these stories strike you as anything more than youthful high-spiritedness?"

"No, never."

"And did he ever express animosity toward Miss Nell?"

"Animosity, no. Of their falling out, I would say he was more sad than angry."

"More sad than angry. Thank you, Miss Cropsey. No further questions."

Tuesday the 18th was dedicated to matters of space and time. That Jim had murdered Nell relied on the presumption that he had opportunity to do so, given where and when he was physically present. Leonard Owens, acquaintance of Wilcox and engineer on the packet boat *Ray*, was called.

"What is your relationship with Mr. Wilcox, sir?"

"We've known each other for a few years."

"Would you say you know him well?"

Owens tossed his head. "About as well as anybody I don't sail with."

"Can you describe what happened on the night of November 20th?"

"We landed at the Norfolk & Southern dock sometime after eleven on the 20th," he said. "It was 11:30 when Sherman Tillery and I left the boat. Captain Bailey didn't want to go, but told us to fetch a half-pint of whiskey. We went to Barnes' barroom on Poindexter Street and bought the whiskey, and also cigarettes. We were abreast of the Wilkins house when we saw someone coming. It was Jim Wilcox. We met near the Ives' place."

"How long were you with the defendant?"

"A few minutes. After that, I went home. The clock was striking midnight when my wife let me in."

"So when would you say you left Wilcox?"

"About ten to midnight."

"So you were with the defendant from sometime after 11:30 until 11:50?"

"Yes, sir."

The defense took its turn.

"Mr. Owens, you and Mr. Wilcox have not been strangers to the barrooms of this city, have you not…?"

Aydlett was leaning in, his tone comradely. Owens perked up.

"You could say that."

"You might even say you boys have gotten up to some trouble now and again, haven't you?"

"Now and again."

"Have you ever seen my client fighting mad? Angry in any way?"

"Yes."

"Would you say he's a violent man?"

"Well, no. He didn't make a habit of getting into scraps. But Jim wasn't one to hang back when the times demanded."

"What was he like on those occasions?"

"He would get all red in the face. And he'd seem to blow up to twice his size. In fact, we'd call him 'old puffer fish' because of that."

"Is that a fact?" exclaimed Aydlett, as if they were swapping stories in a tavern. "So you would say you're pretty familiar with old Jim when he's fighting mad?"

"I'd say so."

"Ever known him to kill anyone?"

"Of course not."

"All right, then. Please think back to the night of the 20th, Mr. Owens, and answer carefully: did the defendant behave unusually when you saw him?"

"No."

"Was he out of breath? Excited? Angry? Puffed up twice his size? In hot blood in any way?"

"No."

"Were his clothes in disorder? Were they wet?"

"Not so much as I noticed."

"It is the prosecution's view that my client had committed a horrible crime just a few minutes' previous to your encounter with him. He had supposedly attacked a young woman he had courted for some three years—a woman he knew well, if not intimately. The child of a fine Christian family that had trusted him with her honor. He supposedly attacked her in cold blood, striking her over the head, and then dumped her body in the river. He committed capital murder—his first, in fact. Would you say his conduct at the time supports that contention?"

"Objection!" stood Ward. "Witness is not on the jury."

"Prosecution just established that my client was well known to the witness," said Aydlett. "His opinion is germane."

"Overruled. The jury will hear the answer, but bear in mind that it is only the witness' opinion."

"He behaved as usual," said Owens. "He did not seem out of sorts in any way."

"Thank you. No further questions."

As Len Owens stepped down he glanced at the defense table. Wilcox gave him a little salute with his right forefinger, to which Owens blanched.

Next up was Ollie's gentleman caller, Roy Crawford. He was a tall man, with legs so long he had to angle them in the witness box.

Dressed up in bow tie and ill-fitting suit, he was nervous, barely able to make replies in distinct fashion.

"Mr. Crawford, at what time did you leave the Cropsey residence on November 20?"

"A little after [inaudible]..."

"Can you repeat that, please?"

"I said, a little after 11:30."

"And were Miss Nell or the defendant on the porch when you departed?"

"There was no one."

"Did you see them in the front yard, or on the road?"

"No."

"So whatever might have happened between the two had to have happened before 11:30. Would you say that is correct?"

"I suppose."

Asked Aydlett: "Mr. Crawford, when you left the house, did you notice anything lying on the hallway floor, or on the piazza?"

"I did not. But I [inaudible]..."

"What was that?"

"I said, I wasn't exactly looking. I was saying goodbye to Miss Olive."

"Thank you. No further questions."

Visibly relieved, Crawford edged his way off the stand.

"Better watch out for that Cropsey bunch, Roy!" shouted Jim.

Judge Jones pounded the gavel. "Order! The defendant will shut his mouth unless spoken to! Understood?"

"It is, Your Honor," said Aydlett, his hand on Jim's shoulder.

These were the first and last words Jim Wilcox uttered at his trial.

The morning's last witness was H.T. Greenleaf. As he took the oath, a map of the south side of Elizabeth City was brought out and erected on a stand.

"Mr. Greenleaf, you are a civil engineer, are you not, and engaged in that business for thirty years?"

"Yes sir, more or less."

"Are you familiar with the topography of the land in front of the Cropsey residence?"

"Yes sir. Surveyed all along there and been there a great many times."

"Mr. Greenleaf, what does that map represent?"

"The shore of the Pasquotank River, Riverside Avenue and the Cropsey house; Hayman's Shipyard, the pier running out from the railway into the river, cypress trees and site where the body was found. The fish house and all..."

"Objection! The defense has not have the opportunity to confirm the accuracy of this exhibit."

"It is part of public records, Your Honor," replied Ward.

"Overruled."

"Exception."

"Noted. Continue, Mr. Ward."

"How many feet from the Cropsey residence to the front gate?"

"It is 66 feet from the last step to the gate. On the street."

"How many feet from the edge of the street to a point in front of the river there?"

"From the north side of the street, down a little path directly from the house is 112 feet to the river shore. The whole distance from the steps to the river is 211 feet."

"How far is it from the little gate in front of the Cropsey house to the Ives' place?"

"About 2,700 feet."

"Did you ever walk it?"

"Yes sir, both ways."

"How long would you figure it took you?"

"Walking quickly, it would take about eight minutes. Walking slowly, ordinary gait, it would take about ten minutes to ten-and-a-half."

"Where on this map does Wilcox live?"

"It is labelled number eight, there."

"How far is it from the Cropsey gate to his house?"

"It is 4,500 feet. From the Ives House, 1,800 feet, or 600 yards."

"That is shorter than the distance from the Cropsey place to the Ives'."

"That is correct."

"So it should take less than ten minutes to walk it, at an ordinary pace?"

"I would say so."

"Mr. Greenleaf, the previous witness has testified that Wilcox did not appear near the Ives' place until after 11:30. According to several other witnesses, he went out on the piazza with the victim at 11:05. That leaves twenty-five minutes unaccounted for. Given the short distance between the Cropsey house and the river, would you say there was adequate time for Wilcox to have been at the river bank and still met Mr. Owens at 11:30?"

"Yes. More than enough time."

"Can you imagine any circumstances where a grown man would take twenty-five minutes to walk from the Cropsey place to the Ives'?"

"An able-bodied man? I cannot."

"Thank you, Mr. Greenleaf. Your witness."

Aydlett strode to the map.

"Mr. Greenleaf, you say it takes about ten minutes to walk from *here*...to *here*. Have you ever done that walk in the dark?"

"No. But I doubt it would make much difference. There was a bright moon that night."

"The defendant left the dining room at 11:05, but there is no evidence he left the porch until after 11:30, when Roy Crawford departed. In that time he had a conversation with Miss Cropsey. Can you tell the jury how long that conversation lasted?"

"I cannot."

"So in fact it must be less than twenty-five minutes unaccounted for, if their conversation lasted any time at all."

"I suppose that follows."

"Thank you. No further questions."

"Redirect, Mr. Ward?" asked the Judge.

"We have nothing further, Your Honor."

"Very well. Your next witness?"

Ward leveled his eyes at Abraham Lincoln.

"Your Honor, the prosecution rests."

An outbreak of whispering shivered the room. Jones pounded his gavel until there was silence.

"Very well. Defense may call their first witness."

"Your Honor, the defense moves for dismissal."

"On what grounds, Mr. Aydlett?"

"The prosecution has patently failed to provide any direct evidence of my client's guilt. No motive. No murder weapon. To call the prosecution's case 'wholly circumstantial' is an insult to circumstances!"

There were chuckles all around, especially from the press box.

"Motion denied," said Jones.

"In that case, Your Honor...the defense rests."

Jones' gavel could do nothing against the tumult that followed. The judge had to sit and wait for a lull in the uproar. The reporters wrote feverishly, writing variations of their headline:

'JIM WILCOX WILL NOT TAKE THE STAND IN HIS OWN DEFENSE.'

Jones bid counsel to approach the bench.

"Ed, I hope this isn't a poor attempt at a mistrial," he whispered.

"It is not, Your Honor."

"What about that boatload of witnesses you promised?" asked Ward.

"Your Honor, prosecution knows the intensity of feeling against my client, or anybody who might defend him."

"The defense exaggerates," replied Ward. "My own wife has sympathy for the accused."

"No objection here if the prosecution calls the Solicitor's wife to the stand."

"Pshaw!" said Jones. "Let's get on with this." He shooed the lawyers back to their seats.

"It's getting too late in the day to start closing arguments," he declared. "Court will reconvene at nine AM tomorrow."

No sooner had those words left Jones' mouth than the reporters bolted out the door. They raced out of the courthouse and down the street, bowling over pedestrians in their way, tripping and shoving, all the way to the Western Union office.

"All right, that's enough!" shouted the clerk. "Sort yourselves into a line! You've all got some waiting to do."

"The telegraphist, it turned out, had been busy the entire day. Some joker had tied him up in transmitting Webster's Dictionary—every word of it.

"The rat!" someone declared. "Why didn't I think of that?"

"Any other telegraph in this town?"

A last reporter strolled into the office with a cigar in his mouth. He was a little thing, young with prematurely thinning hair, and large round spectacles.

"Hello boys!" said the youngster, and then to the clerk, "Hello Sam!"

"Afternoon, Mr. Saunders."

Saunders reached into his breast pocket and unfolded his dispatch.

"Please tell your man to put the dictionary aside for now and send this..."

VI.

The next morning, at precisely nine o'clock, Judge Jones gaveled the court to order.

"The court will hear closing arguments," he declared. "To those in the gallery—please respect these proceedings by refraining from any outward reaction. If the dignity of this court is infringed in any fashion, I will empty this chamber without hesitation. Mr. Ward?"

The solicitor rose, straightened his jacket, and approached the jury.

"Gentlemen, you are about to embark on a momentous decision. Justice for the death of Ella Maud Cropsey is not just an imperative for her bereaved family, though their pain is foremost in our minds just now, and can't be imagined in its fullest horror by anyone fortunate enough never to have been visited by such misfortune. Nor is it only for the victim's sweet sisters, their youths now permanently blighted by grief. You also sit in judgment for young girls not yet ripened to full womanhood—and for girls yet unborn—that they may live without fear that ghouls in the night might take their lives.

"And yes, I used the word 'ghoul'. For how else might we describe a man who would so cruelly strike a defenseless woman, and dump her helpless body in the river like so much trash? What kind of mind imagines such a plan, let alone sets it into motion...?"

He turned and faced Wilcox. "By all evidence, *there* is your man. In the course of these last days, you have heard all the proof you need to convict James E. Wilcox of this crime. You have heard he had the opportunity: he was the last person to see her alive, with a full twenty-five minutes of his time unaccounted for. He had the means: his employer, Mr. Hayman, testified to his brutish strength, easily able to carry timbers heavier than poor Nell Cropsey across his shoulders. And he had the motive: Nell had tired of him, and wished an end to their courtship. He was in love with her desperately, and her love was growing colder and colder. The defendant made up his mind to conquer or kill her. The devil grew bigger and bigger in his heart, prompted by his own hellish pride. Which among us has not felt that sting, when our beloved has turned away from us? Who has not known their measure of heartbreak? The difference is, only the depraved give in to such passions.

"At risk of belaboring the obvious, let us review the facts, and the insights we have gained here into the character of the accused..."

Ward launched into an exhaustive review of the case that took an hour and twenty minutes. The jurymen slumped collectively as the oration went on, oppressed by the detail and the stuffiness of the courtroom. Judge Jones went through an entire jug of water, and ordered the bailiff to fetch another.

"We've heard talk of suicide," Ward continued. "The defense would have you believe that Nell was so troubled by whatever Wilcox said on the porch, she proceeded to throw herself into the shallowest corner of a dark, filthy river in the middle of the night. Troubled, they say, from separation from a man she barely spoke to anymore! Could any one imagine that light-hearted, happy Christian girl, who had just joined a new church, and who read Sunday school books and liked sweet music, destroying herself? Is there any person who could believe that a girl of her character, temperament and disposition, anticipating a pleasant trip to New York, committed suicide? By the sworn testimony of everyone who knew her, Nell Cropsey was incapable of such an act. To a person, all of them deny it was even a possibility. Who are we, utter strangers to her character, to say they are wrong? Who are we to convict her of self-murder, when she is no longer on this earth to defend herself from such calumny?

"Add to this the expert testimony of the finest physicians in this community. Ella Maud Cropsey was not drowned—she was struck on the head with a padded instrument. Ferrebee saw the wound on the head at the first autopsy. He is a barber and it is natural that he should have seen it before the doctors. The black blood in that bruise was caused by a blow. You know very well if you knock a hog in the head, black blood will settle under the wound. The condition of the brain attests to it, for it is usually one of the last organs to decay, but was in an advanced state of putrefaction when her body was recovered. The only possible cause is the injury inflicted by her murderer. The cause sits in the courtroom today.

"We have heard filthy intimations from the defense regarding the pristine condition of her body. Outwardly untouched by thirty-seven days in the water, still beautiful, how could she have been underwater for such a long time? Do not be fooled by idle speculation, gentlemen: the preservative qualities of Pasquotank River water has been noted for centuries. I have heard it said that fishermen had recovered leather articles from the Dismal Swamp that go back to the founding of our Republic. After a hundred years, they come up nothing more than slightly discolored. That quality, coupled with the coldness of the season, is all the explanation necessary to explain the condition of her corpse. Indeed, it might be said that God himself set the conditions to keep her intact—as divine testimony to the crimes of her murderer!

"There has been talk of a certain umbrella—a silk parasol—whose whereabouts the defense wants to make so much about. Why would Wilcox have bothered to return this object if it was his intention to murder the girl? In one respect, we all agree: it is difficult for a rational mind to apprehend the workings of a depraved one. Who is to say what the defendant intended by this gesture? It may well have been nothing more than a decoy, meant to put the victim at ease before enacting his heinous design. By all means, I say I know not why he returned the thing. But I further say, it changes nothing.

"Gentlemen of the jury, I suspect this is the most important trial ever held in Pasquotank County. Certainly it is the most momentous one. It has attracted much attention and large crowds, more even than the Cluverius case some years ago, in Richmond. The same Cluverius, you may recall, who was convicted and hanged for the murder of poor Lillian Madison, though there were only six minutes of time unaccounted for in his movements. *Six* minutes, versus the twenty-five Jim Wilcox roamed, murderous and at large in the dark!

"He sits there now, as cold as death and as relentless as the grave. That's the sort of man who carries weapons and makes midnight assassinations. Such men have got the stuff in them to commit hellish deeds and the same stuff sustains them on their way to the grave. It comes from Hell and thence it returns.

"Nellie did not drown. She was killed by a blow, a direct blow, on the head. That girl was murdered and there sits the man who delivered that blow. Look at him again, if you dare! Cold-blooded as a snake. Have you ever heard of a more atrocious, midnight murder? Because she would not make up with him before going to New York, he killed her. I ask you to weigh the evidence and if you turn him loose, set fire to your courthouse and jail and burn them down. For you will have no use for them anymore. If the women of North Carolina cannot be protected, we had best burn the law books and dissolve the legislature, and return to a state of barbarism!

"One last point, gentlemen. Presently, you will hear from the defense that the State's case is 'only circumstantial'. 'Only circumstantial', as in merely one of external details, with no direct proof. In this way counsel will attempt to sow doubt in your minds. I will therefore tell you something about 'circumstantial' cases that he won't: it is the way in which justice is served to those cowards who do their crimes in the dark, away from direct witnesses. It is the light of reason, vouchsafed to us by forensic science, penetrating the very citadel of ignorance. Cluverius went to his well-deserved death on the weight of circumstances. By such evidence, we banish the last refuge of the clever criminal—the careful choosing of when and where to commit his crimes. Circumstances are the great equalizers. Do not scorn them.

"Save your scorn for the fiend!" Ward exclaimed, pointing a crooked finger. "Respect his 'rights', yes. Weigh the evidence before you, yes. But by all means do what all of you know you must: solemnly convict him of murder in the first degree. Your community demands it. The family demands it. And most of all the soul of that poor girl demands it. She is in heaven now, but her body lies in a premature grave, five hundred miles away. Never again will she dance or play an air. Never will she know the joy of motherhood. Never will she know the satisfaction of seeing her children grow up, in a home as happy as that in which she was born!

"She cries out to us now—can you not hear her...?" And Ward raised his fists toward the ceiling, and pleaded unto Heaven, "For her sake, convict! Convict, for the love of God! Convict!"

As if he was spent, he let his arms fall to his sides. A thunderous wave of applause broke from the back of the courtroom, surging forward as the spectators leapt to their feet. Seated at the brunt of it, Jim and his lawyer could only hang on, red-faced and miserable. It was some minutes before the ovation died down enough for Jones' gavel to be heard. He had been pounding it the entire time.

"I will warn those in the gallery again: there will be order in this courtroom! Mr. Aydlett, your statement please."

Aydlett made the throng wait as he arranged his papers. Rising, he approached the jury box and took off his spectacles, folding and slipping them in his breast pocket. The eyes he exposed were red-rimmed and bleary.

"Thank you, Your Honor. Let it be said that the defense shares the State's sympathy for the family of the deceased. It might well be asked, what could be worse than to bury a child, especially one as universally beloved as Miss Nell? How inconsolable would any of us be if placed in the position of poor Mrs. Cropsey? Who could not but admire the courage of William Cropsey, bearing up with such dignity under such circumstances?

"I can think of only one other family that has suffered equally. Only one that deserves an equal measure of compassion. They sit in the second row, behind the defendant. I ask you, gentlemen of the jury, to cast your eyes with equal sympathy on Mrs. Wilcox, the boy's mother, Thomas Wilcox, father and former sheriff of this town, and his sweet sister, Annie Mae. Have they not suffered as well?

"The Cropseys, may God bless them in their loss, at least have the well-nigh universal support of the community. Who, I ask you, has sent flowers to poor Martha Wilcox? Who has given her son, who never knew a lick of trouble with the law until now, the slightest benefit of the doubt? How lonely the path they tread! How cold is the world they have known since last November! '*Reproach hath broken my heart,*' wrote the Psalmist, '*and I am full of heaviness: and I looked for some to take pity, but there was none; and for comforters, but I found none.*'

"It is not given to parents in their plight to wear black, like the Cropseys do today. But if the state has its way, they will have their chance, soon enough...

He paused, fished his glasses out of his pocket, and cleaned them with his handkerchief. Then he fixed them on the end of his nose.

"As an officer of the court, I have had occasion to hear many speeches by my colleague, Solicitor Ward. The great majority of the time, he is as eloquent as he is well reasoned. But this time—my, what a hysterical presentation! When the truth we all agree upon, that a young woman is dead, is bad enough, what need we of desperate hyperbole? Does he not trust you think the plain facts are bad enough?

"We teeter on the edge of barbarism, he shrieks. But you, gentlemen of the jury, ought to be concerned less with a state of barbarism, and more with the laws of the State of North Carolina. Those laws hold that it is entirely up to the prosecution to prove its case beyond any reasonable doubt. Beyond a reasonable doubt! That is our standard, for what is the alternative? Conviction by the mob? The elevation of mere happenstance to evidence of guilt? The prosecution has presented possibly the most flimsy case for a murder in the first degree that I have ever heard in all my years at the bar. No murder weapon. No real motive, except resentment for a few childish insults. A suspect autopsy, by physicians with no experience in forensic examination. If you convict on this basis, then I would be the first to agree with my colleague—burn the law books! Dissolve the legislature! For such a verdict would represent not the triumph of justice, but the very opposite.

"Some of you are no doubt wondering why my client did not testify in his own defense. The answer is already before you—there is no need for him to testify, because the State has presented no case! What man need be obligated to answer for mere calumnies, mere innuendo? What man need even bother, when the source of such 'evidence' is shrouded in shadow, and may never be exhausted? Ask not why James Wilcox does not rise to answer these charges, gentlemen! Instead, ask the motives behind the charges themselves.

"'Wilcox is indifferent,' they claim. 'He does not lend enough comfort,' they cry. Perhaps, by the standards of certain others, the defendant seems more calm in the face of tragedy than most. But that is not a crime. Nor is my client responsible for the faculties given to him by God.

"And indeed, given the depth of bias against him, what could he possibly have done that would not have been taken as evidence of guilt? If he wept, the prosecution would construe it as a confession. If he had found her body, they would say he knew where it was the whole time. If he didn't look for it, they would say he was concealing it. Every move of Wilcox was watched, every action criticized and even his face as he passed on the street was scanned and commented upon. Which of us—which of *you*, gentlemen of the jury—could sustain that kind of scrutiny?"

The town clock chimed eleven times. Aydlett pulled out his watch and sprung the clasp. As the jury waited, he adjusted the minute hand.

"Let us pass to the details of the case. It is the State's contention that Wilcox's whereabouts are unexplained for twenty-five minutes—from the time he left Nell on the porch, to when he met Mr. Owens on Riverside Avenue. This, I submit, is an utter falsity. Neither Mr.

Ward, nor I, nor any of you can have any clear notion of how long the meeting on the front porch of the Cropsey home lasted. The only fact we have is that no one was on the piazza when Mr. Roy Crawford left the home, sometime after 11:30. It is entirely conceivable that Nell and Wilcox spoke until just a few moments before Mr. Crawford departed. Nor can Mr. Greenleaf or anyone else speak with authority on the pace the defendant adopted on his way to the Ives' place. It was late, and it was dark. Perhaps he looked at the water. Perhaps he relieved himself behind some bush. What need had he to hurry?

"Mr. Owens testified for the prosecution. Yet he said that the defendant showed no outward signs of any struggle. His demeanor was normal. Does this sound like the aspect of someone who had just committed cold-blooded murder? Does this sound like someone who had just assaulted the girl he had patiently courted for more than three years? Mr. Owens stated his clothes were dry. But how could this be so, after the defendant supposedly had just finished dragging an unconscious body into the river? It seems that the prosecution not only holds that my client is a fiend—he also walks on water!"

This was a good line, but the gallery was in no mood to give an inch to the defense. There was only a smattering of laughter, which Jones hammered into submission.

"And then there are details that do not square with the others. The prosecution spent much time establishing that Miss Nell was finished with Wilcox, and about to drop him. She would not come to the door to answer his calls—she wouldn't even take a piece of fruit from him! But it is also established that Nell reacted badly to the return of the pictures and the parasol. He left her on the porch, sobbing. But if Miss Cropsey was indifferent, why did she sob? Why did she not take back her belongings, thank him, and go back into the house, pleased that her wish for a break had been granted at last? Clearly, the girl had deeper feelings for the defendant than some have suggested here.

"That is not the whole of it. William Cropsey says the pictures never turned up at the scene. In all likelihood, they are at the bottom of the Pasquotank. But the broken parasol *did* turn up, in the front entry hall. Think about this for a moment: how could this be so, if Ella Cropsey did not return to the house? If she was in the process of being struck over the head and drug to the river, what opportunity would she have had to go back inside? Clearly, gentlemen, something about the prosecution's account does not add up."

"It therefore gives us no pleasure to insist upon the obvious: on the night of November 20, 1901, Ella Maud Cropsey drowned herself. She had the opportunity, motive, and means to do so. James Wilcox was Nell's suitor for three years, and furthermore the only one she ever had. He had been loyal to her, and persistent in his attentions—until the arrival of Carrie Cropsey in the home, and his affections began to shift. Her coolness toward him—the petty refusals to answer the door—these were the transparent ploys of a ingenuous young woman to keep her lover's attention when she felt it slipping away. A young woman who was, by all evidence, a soul of deep feeling. She kept his gifts, the pictures and such, even as she pretended to be indifferent. Until the night when he returned her gifts. Now it was he who was indifferent to her! She was surprised, and mortified, and her mask began to slip. For who has not felt the pain of a broken heart? Who has not felt it to be the worst sensation in the world, if only for a brief time? Young Nell Cropsey had never felt it before—none of it. It overwhelmed her. It had to be escaped. And the river was so close."

At this story, Ollie resumed twisting her gloves. William Cropsey showed no reaction, preferring to look out the window.

"Does the defense have answers to every question?" asked Aydlett. "I assure you it does not. Alas, we don't have to explain all. It is incumbent upon the prosecution to do so. It is their responsibility to prove to you, gentlemen, that the simpler and more consistent story should be put aside—that Nell Cropsey committed suicide—in favor of a tissue of implausibilities. The fact that they have not should weigh in your determination that there exists some reasonable doubt—"

A commotion broke out at the back of the gallery. In unison, three entire rows of onlookers rose up, gathered coats and hats, and filed for the exit. Many looked toward Wilcox with undisguised contempt on their faces.

"What is this?" demanded the judge. "Order! ORDER! Spectators will remain seated...!"

More rows joined the walk-out. Aydlett stood dumbstruck. Wilcox, after a peek at the exodus behind him, turned back bemused.

Jones tossed his gavel on the bench in disgust. The interruption went on, as the less-committed of the protestors weighed the diminishing power of the demonstration against their curiosity to see what happened next. By the time the evacuation petered out, more than a quarter of the spectators had left the courtroom. As those who had left were entirely white, the black onlookers were left standing in the back with all the benches in front of them empty. None of them ventured to take the abandoned seats.

"Well, that is unfortunate," said Jones. "In all my years on the bench, I have never witnessed such a shameful display. Does anyone else wish to leave? No? All right then: bailiff, the doors will remain sealed for the balance of the defense's statement."

He bid Aydlett continue.

"Er, as I was saying...what was I saying...?"

"'*It is incumbent upon the prosecution...*'" said the court reporter.

"Yes, it is incumbent on them to prove their story...as provided by our laws...which protect the rights of the accused...as Sir Blackstone so notably wrote: '*it is better that ten guilty persons escape, than that one innocent suffer...*'"

As Aydlett rambled on, it was clear that the walk-out had rattled him. Where he seemed to be speaking *ex tempore* before, he now needed a sheaf of notes, pulling them out as the jurymen fidgeted.

"...the ingenuity of the prosecution cannot tear away the pillars of evidence which made it almost impossible for Wilcox to have done murder that night...if you convict on this basis, if you take away an innocent man's life...who is to say some Fury will not dog you for the rest of your life...?"

The air was split suddenly by the peal of an electric bell.

"Fire alarm," said the judge. "Bailiff, open the doors, please."

The depleted gallery emptied into the courtyard. The court officers waited behind the building as the fire wagon made the short trip from a block away. It took a while for the firemen to check every room in the building. In that time Jim stood in handcuffs, surrounded by police who kept an eye out for the lynch mob. Jim was the least concerned of them, letting the weak March sun warm his face. It was the first time in months he had stood in direct sunshine.

"Nothing. No fire," reported the Chief.

"Did anybody get a look at the party that pulled the alarm?"

"No sir."

When the court was gaveled back into session, the delay stood at thirty minutes.

"The citizens in the back of the room. Yes *you all...*" indicated Jones.

Not used to being acknowledged, the Negro attendees collectively gaped at the judge.

"Under the circumstances, there is no reason for you to loiter there. Find seats, all of you."

No one moved as a sudden frigidity struck the room. But gingerly, a fellow in a checkered suit and twenty-year-old stovepipe hat worked his way onto the back bench. Others followed, until they filled most of the seats evacuated by the walk-out. Some of the whites near them collected their things and moved away from them. By the time everyone had sorted themselves, the rows were neatly segregated.

"If any of you have complaints about the seating arrangements," said the judge, "You may address your complaints to those of your neighbors who have attempted to disrupt these proceedings. Not to gratify them with further delay, but I must say I am *disgusted* with the behavior of some in this community. If it results in miscarriage of justice—well, that is something they will have to live with.

"Now, Mr. Aydlett: I intend to give you the greatest possible latitude here. Would you like to start over?"

"That won't be necessary, Your Honor."

"Very well then. Please continue."

If the walk-out had slowed the defense's momentum, the false alarm broke it. A strange air filled the court that made its contours unrecognizable, its energies alien.

Aydlett was at half-strength now, voice quavering. As he floundered the expressions on the faces of the jurymen went from studied skepticism to dismay; some turned outright sympathetic.

"...it is manifestly obvious that Nell's order to Jim to 'pull' was not meant to be offending, and the defendant's statement that he was 'tired of being a lackey' was not addressed to the young lady but to her sister Carrie...sorry, I mean Lettie. On the contrary, he referred to the deceased several times..." and he checked his notes, "... as 'a true, noble little woman...'"

"And noble she was, in death as well as life. It is true that only the ones who loved her...and the ones she loved in turn — can speak to her significance to them. I saw her on the street, like many of you, but I didn't know her. Our horror at her death springs not from personal experience, but from a personal stake we all believe we have in her. For was it not Edgar Allan Poe who declared: '*When it most closely allies itself to Beauty: the death then of a beautiful woman is unquestionably the most poetical topic in the world.*' The Cropseys are Northerners, but many of us in the South understand the value of poetry. Some say it is all all we have left, after the War. Every death must have its reason, and the death of a beautiful girl, its poetry. But not every death is worthy of Mr. Poe, my friends. Some deaths have no rhyme, no meter. They are murky, and pointless. Not every Jesus has had a Judas. Let him who is without sin presume the worst of this poor wretch!

"Mr. Ward says that this may be the most important trial in the history of this county. On this, we agree: in the rows behind me are reporters from Philadelphia, Norfolk, Baltimore, St. Louis and beyond. They are all watching and, yes, many are doubting that in this fever of retribution, the defendant will even get a fair trial. Those hotheads below the Mason & Dixon line—how can they be trusted with the responsibility of upholding justice? The challenge is before you now, gentlemen, to prove them all wrong. Show them that we understand what the presumption of innocence means. Show them that we refuse to compound tragedy with outrage. Find the defendant innocent, for his sake, and for yours."

Aydlett sat down. There was no applause this time.

"Are you finished?" asked Jones.

"Yes, Your Honor."

"Very well. Court stands in recess for lunch, after which the jury will receive its instructions."

Aydlett spent the recess at a saloon down on the waterfront. The place was a cut below the kind frequented by lawyers: plank bar with gaps, working-class clientele, card-games prohibited, sawdust-strewn floor lumped with tobacco spit. But it was dark and out of the way, and he was seldom disturbed by reporters there. The barkeep knew him from years of court recesses, and never asked questions an officer of the court couldn't answer.

"Afternoon Ed! Hungry?"

"Starved."

"We got some ham steak."

"That would be swell, Charlie. And the usual."

It was an out-of-the-way place, but they were still talking about the case. The volume of chatter dipped discernibly when he walked in. It only rose to normal as he took a stool, lit a smoke, and minded his own business. The barkeep slid a bourbon in front of him.

As he regarded the glowing cherry of his cigar, he wondered if he should have some regret about how his closing statement had gone, but couldn't summon the will for honest self-recrimination. From his experience, what an attorney said at the end of a trial bore little relation to success. Some of his finest orations didn't stop his clients from being convicted; some of what he regarded as his least had swayed juries to acquit. The longer he served, his sense of futility grew, and the more he drank. This would be a three-bourbon recess.

"Hello, mister."

A boy of ten or eleven was standing behind him. He had his cap off, and he was barefoot in the sawdust.

Aydlett slipped a two-bit piece from his watch pocket and flipped it to the boy.

"You could have waited a little longer after that walk-out."

"Only if you wanted someone to see me," replied the other as he examined the coin.

"On your way then. But not too far away, just in case."

The boy gave him a one-finger salute and disappeared.

He was just finishing his ham steak—a bit too dry for his taste, but it filled him up—when a stranger took the stool next to him. It only took a glance for Aydlett to mark him as a reporter, and a lean and hungry one at that.

"No comment," he said before the man opened his mouth.

"Bill Saunders, *Norfolk Dispatch.* I haven't asked you anything yet."

"No comment."

"Well, maybe you can just listen for a minute," said the other. He signaled the barkeep for two more of what Aydlett was drinking.

"It's your money," said the counselor.

"What did you mean when you said the Cropseys were Northerners? Were you suggesting Miss Nell was a little naive to our ways here?"

Aydlett used his bread to sop up the juice from his chop.

"How about that walk-out? Ever see anything like that?" Saunders went on. "Strange how somebody pulled that fire alarm just a few minutes later. If I were a betting man, I'd say the two events had different causes. Maybe two different intentions."

The drinks arrived. Aydlett didn't nurse this one. After knocking it back in two swallows, he stood up and gathered his things.

"Don't know anything about it," he said. "If I didn't know you'd expense it, I'd thank you for the drink."

The alcohol made him slow with his coat sleeve. Saunders stood and guided his elbow through the hole.

"Thanks."

"Don't mention it. By the way, hard to see how he slips the noose now. Wilcox."

Aydlett smiled at this, and with a sudden urge to reciprocate, gave Saunders something better than the dictionary to telegraph:

"It's quite the opposite, young man. I think that walk-out saved that boy's life."

The decision went to the jury in the late afternoon of the 21st. As they filed out to their empty jury room, and to Aydlett's experienced eye, the jurors looked nervous, as if troubled by the magnitude of their responsibility. The judge had duly impressed upon them that although the State's case was circumstantial, their decision must be unanimous, and beyond a shadow of a doubt. But there was no anonymity at the county courthouse. Every face on the jury was known to everyone in the gallery, and in many cases their addresses, names of their businesses, their relatives and their friends. There were rumors of boycotts to come, and even bodily harm, if Wilcox was acquitted. The higher-minded among the citizens denounced the threats, deeming them unworthy of a civilized community. But no one could deny that someone made them.

As Jim stood up to have his wrists shackled, he said to Aydlett, "I had the most peculiar dream last night."

"What was it?"

"That I was hanging by a gooseberry bush," the other replied, grinning.

The accused was returned to his cell to await the verdict. When he got there a covered plate of food was waiting for him: a whole roast chicken and potatoes prepared by his mother and sister. He offered Aydlett a drumstick. The latter declined, and watched Jim disembowel the chicken without the utensils that he, of course, was denied by his jailors.

"I won't have much time to do it, but don't fear..." said Jim, mouth full. "I will issue invitations to my execution by two weeks before at the earliest. I won't forget you."

"If they take more than a day to decide, you are acquitted."

"How about a wing?"

Aydlett sat with Jim for a couple of hours, then went home without a detour to the saloon. He didn't take off his court clothes; he expected to be called back to the courthouse at any moment. He dropped off to sleep in the reading chair in his study. When he woke with a start, he was surprised to see sunshine streaming through the windows.

The decision indeed took more than one day. At nine-thirty p.m. on the 22nd, after thirty hours of deliberations, the jury reported it was ready to come out.

The court reconvened at ten p.m.—including a throng of two hundred spectators in the gallery.

"Has the jury reached a verdict?" asked the judge.

The foreman stood. "We have."

"The accused will stand."

Jim took his feet. He had no gum this time, and his shirt front was stained by fingers of chicken grease.

"What say you?" asked Jones.

"In the first degree," replied the foreman.

"You have not answered the question. Is he guilty?"

"He is guilty."

The crowd loosed a collective exhalation of relief. Chatter erupted, but the judge hammered it down.

"I will tolerate no more disruption," he said. "Upon further consideration of the events in the last few days, it is the opinion of this court that the behavior of certain parties has been utterly contemptible. Let it be known: if these acts were pre-planned, and if the names of the ringleaders ever become known to me, I will with no hesitation cite every man, woman and child for contempt. The good name of the people of this county requires nothing less."

He turned his imperiousness upon Jim. The latter was pale now, and could not meet the judge's eyes. Aydlett put a hand on his shoulder to steady him.

"The judgment of the court is that the prisoner at the bar, James Wilcox, be remanded in the custody of the sheriff of Pasquotank County, and that he be taken to the jail from whence he came, to be securely kept in solitary confinement until Friday, April 25, 1902, and that on the said day, between the hours of ten in the forenoon and three in the afternoon, he be conveyed to the place of public execution, in said county, and be hanged by the neck until he is dead, dead, dead.

"May God have mercy upon your soul."

As they led him out, Jim remarked loudly enough for the farthest person to hear: "That's a damned common jury, if they couldn't even get the verdict out right!"

The Bedroom

I.

The Cropseys moved out of Seven Pines in October of the following year.

"We are quitting this house next month," William Cropsey declared at Sunday supper, as if announcing a beach outing. "We will be renters no longer."

"Are we leaving Elizabeth City?" asked William Douglas, in a tone that was perhaps too hopeful.

"No we are not, young man. There is a house on Park Drive that is perfectly suited to us."

"Am I getting out of school?"

"Nothing else will change."

Later, over his evening dish of prunes, he deigned to explain more of this reasoning to Ollie. The new property, he said, was smaller, but had ample room for the family to continue farming. The cost of the mortgage was less than the rent for a waterfront residence.

"Yes...but considering what's happened, wouldn't we consider leaving?"

"We came to this city for a reason," he replied, "and none of those reasons have changed."

Three weeks later, a moving van arrived at their front gate. The two big percherons pulling it were let loose to graze on the front lawn. Assisted by the Cropsey men, the teamsters set to work wrangling the big pieces of furniture into the back.

It fell to Ollie to pack the contents of the bedroom she and Nell had shared. In all the months since, Ollie still slept on her side of their bed. The bottom two drawers in the bureau still contained Nell's waists and pantalets, the armoire her dresses, the foot chest her stockings. Heart heavy, Ollie folded them into a trunk. She waited until the very end—when the bed was gone—to take down the little shrine she erected to her sister: the pictures of Nell that Jim had returned that night, a little candle, a bowl of dried posies. An embroidery of a bluebird Nell had left unfinished. Dismantling it all made her eyes wet with the kind of tears that did not pour forth freely, but stood in her eyes thick and stubborn, like incipient blindness.

With no hankie at hand, Ollie dabbed her eyes on the window curtains. From there she gazed down on her mother as she supervised the loading. It was a warm day for October, so Mary Cropsey brought iced tea to the laborers. Then she chided them when the broadcloths were improperly secured and her furniture was exposed to scratching.

Though her mother seemed back to her normal self, the road had not been smooth. When Jim was sentenced to hang, she never took outward pleasure in the news, but left her bed to resume her household routine. Six months later the verdict was thrown out by the State Supreme Court—pointedly because of the disruptions at the county trial. As howls of outrage swept through the town, Mary Cropsey wept and fled back to her bed.

Jim was tried again, this time in a neutral venue in Hertford, Perquimans County. Everything had to be repeated, including the testimonies of their father, Ollie, and cousin Carrie. Ed Aydlett once again excoriated the slipshod performance of the coroners, and once again Jim made a show of his disinterest, this time by sucking lemons in the courtroom.

This time there were no walk-outs, no false alarms, and no need for the militia to be called out. Jim was still found guilty, but the circumstantial nature of the evidence troubled the jury; on his conviction for second-degree murder, he drew a sentence of thirty years. This sentence stood up on appeal. Jim went to the State Central Prison in Raleigh, and Mary Cropsey faced a choice: to accept that Nell was dead and her murderer was not; or remain in her own prison.

For the sake of her remaining children, she once again found the strength to move on. She remained fragile, however, leaving the rest of the family unsure whether they should ever utter Nell's name again. It went unspoken for weeks, until she finally cried out at dinner, "Why do you never talk about our dear sweet Nell anymore? God help us if we ever forget her!"

Ollie never recovered, and believed she never would. When Jim was sentenced to die, and her father and Uncle Hen broke out cigars to celebrate, she was lashed by guilt. When the conviction was voided, she was inwardly glad. But then she was afraid, because she was sure that the lawyers would never let her get away with that incomplete, misleading testimony a second time. There was no hiding behind that mourning veil now. And yet, to her disbelief, Aydlett again declined to handle her the way she deserved. He asked her about the parasol, and she again made the feeble excuse that she didn't remember. And he left it that.

She began to have trouble leaving the house. Her pitiful notoriety in the eyes of strangers was bad enough, for every member of the family had been transformed by their ordeal from unique individuals to bit characters in a piece of local lore. She was no longer Olive Cropsey now—she was just "the sister". Worse were the chance encounters around town with members of the Wilcox family. The Cropseys crossed paths with Martha and Annie Mae on the streets, in shops, and in restaurants. They never acknowledged her. But merely seeing them left her unsettled and unfit to finish whatever business she had gone out to accomplish.

The awkwardness threatened to boil over into an outright feud when Tom Wilcox filed an affidavit with the State Supreme Court, in support of his son's appeal. He alleged that the jury in Jim's original trial had been subjected to a determined campaign of intimidation. That reports on their debate—including the names of those inclined to acquit—had been written down and passed from the jury room windows to the mob below. That firm plans were afoot to lynch Jim Wilcox if he were exonerated, and that the jurors felt they had no choice but to convict.

The document never mentioned the Cropseys, but William Cropsey took it as an affront to his honor. It particularly galled him because he took credit for the fact that Wilcox got a proper trial at all. "If it wasn't for me he would have been hung from a tree last December!" he raged. "All it would have taken was one word. One word!"

When the appeals court ruled that Jim would get a new trial, her father went a step further: "If I see that son of a bitch again, I'll shoot him on the spot!" Fortunately for all concerned—and perhaps not by accident—Cropsey and Tom Wilcox did not cross paths again for many months.

At last, moving day arrived. John Fearing came for a final inspection. As the adults talked in the parlor, Ollie's little sister Mary took a pencil to the wall of the turret staircase and wrote:

Fearing found her signature later, long after the Cropseys had left and he was about to sell the house. He was not usually given to tolerate children scrawling on his walls. He went up with a cloth to wipe it away. But the family's sad story, and how the house had served as the stage for it, gave him pause. In the end he let the inscription stay. For it was at least in his power to make sure the memory of it—if not the girl herself—would never disappear.

The new Cropsey residence on Park Drive had at least one advantage: Nell's ghost did not haunt it. There was something about the new electric lighting, so copious and unflinching, that banished not only shadows, but memories. Never once did Ollie glimpse the arch of Nell's back as she rounded a corner, or glanced at the top of the stairs.

But she was still a presence. On the pretext of using them for hand-me-downs, Ollie opposed getting rid of Nell's things. Instead, she packed them away in the attic. Sometimes, she would go upstairs, open the trunk, and bury her face in her clothes, just to be reminded of how she smelled. Uncle Hen caught her doing this once, making her blush to the very roots of her hair.

There were other strange behaviors. She kept on wearing mourning clothes when the rest of the family had put them aside. Her father looked askance at her when he heard reports of Ollie coming out of Christ Church on McMorine St.. He worried to his wife, "Are we going to lose another daughter to some other congregation?" But it turned out she was only there to filch votive candles from the Episcopalians, which she used in the little shrine she had recreated for Nell in her bedroom.

The new house had nothing like the room for a big potato-growing operation. Instead, her father specialized in fancy vegetables he could sell at a premium. He entered his best cucumbers and squash in competitions all over the county, and often won prizes for them. Sometimes he would simply wander the neighborhood, pockets stuffed with produce, showing it off to whomever, black or white, would open his door to him.

Eventually he and Uncle Hen built a farm stand on the street in front of their house, from which they sold to housewives, picnickers and increasing numbers of day-trippers in horseless carriages. All the Cropsey children took their turns manning the stall, making bank out of oyster tins. Ollie did her part, sitting there in her widow's weeds, sun-hat tied with a bow around her chin. Sometimes, she heard the customers whispering to each other as they cast pitying looks at her. She ignored these for a long time, until one day she heard a mother and daughter muttering in a way that failed to be at all private.

"Yes, I am 'the sister'," she told them out loud. "I was the one who let her go. You don't have to treat it like a secret."

The mother looked to her daughter, and together they whirled around to go back to their automobile.

"You'll have to pay for that rutabaga!" Ollie called after them.

A different sort of encounter happened in the summer after Jim Wilcox went to prison. Ollie was at the stand, reading, when a young man with balding head and wire spectacles approached her. He glanced over the inventory with his hands in the pockets of his gray suit. Then he looked at her, eyes appraising with professorial detachment.

"You're Olive Cropsey, aren't you?" he asked.

"Who's asking?"

"I publish under the name W.O. Saunders. Maybe you've heard of me?"

"Can't say that I have."

"My, that's a handsome cucumber," he remarked. "I might just have to take this fellow home with me..."

"That'll be a nickel."

He produced the coin from the watch-pocket of his vest.

"My condolences about your sister," he said. "I was at the trials. Both of 'em..."

She just stared back at him. He went on, "We're all sure justice has been served. Some kind of justice, I guess. But a trial is never the whole story, is it?"

Her heart was thumping.

"I don't know what you mean."

"Nothing specific. But if you ever want to share anything—anything at all, like your memories of your dear sister—I'd like you to know I'm at your service."

He held out a business card. When she didn't take it, he laid it on top of the green peppers.

"You can contact me at any time," he said.

"I think I'd like you to leave."

"Of course. Thank you, my dear. Lovely vegetables!"

When he was gone Ollie retreated to the house. She was half-frantic now, stomach twisting, neck beaded with sweat. 'Why would this stranger feel entitled to ask me that?' she demanded of herself. 'Have I done something? What could he possibly know?'

Her father was waiting for her in the parlor.

"What did that one want?" he asked.

"The whole story!" she cried, and threw the business card at his feet.

"The whole story?"

"I told you. Didn't I tell you?"

"Is he a cop?"

"A reporter! "

Prying the hat off her head without untying the bow, she started up the stairs.

"Ollie, come back—"

"I told you!"

"Ollie, where is the till?"

"Still out there!" she shouted as she turned at the landing. "Don't ask me to go out there ever again! I've had it with lies! I won't be party to it!"

"I won't have you speak that way. Do you hear?"

No answer. Cursing, Cropsey retrieved Saunders' card and went out to shut up the stand.

Ollie never made good on her threats. She never called Saunders or anyone else to unburden herself. She kept Nell's fate a secret from the rest of her family. It remained something she and her father shared, both the most precious thing and the thing that could not be borne. In time, the guilt and the loss hardened into a tumor of misery—an intrusion that came to feel as familiar to her as her own reflection. A few years after the trial, she already spied gray streaks in her hair, and sprays of wrinkles where she furrowed her brow. Her taste for ornaments withered, as frivolous accessories did not befit a mourning that never ended.

Rarely seen on the streets, she drew no gentlemen callers. Instead, she served as chaperone for her younger sisters Mary and Carrie Elizabeth, and a severe one at that. Her presence, in her regular suit of black, cast a funereal pall; the girls begged to have anyone else along, even the embarrassing Uncle Hen, instead of Ollie and her silent reproofs.

A series of premature deaths, connected only by the Cropsey tragedy, seemed to confirm she was trapped in some kind of indefinite purgatory. In 1904, less than a year after Jim's second trial, one of the jurors committed suicide by cutting his own throat. The man, Lewis Felton, was said to be "well-known" and "highly respected" in the environs of Hertford. Believing himself to have been cheated in a deal over a horse, he became increasingly despondent; his body and that of the horse were found together less than a mile from his home. He had cut the horse's throat with a pen-knife and hung the bridle neatly from a tree. He then proceeded to cut himself so deeply that he severed the windpipe.

In 1908 she heard that Roy Crawford, the young man who had called on her on Nell's last night, was shot dead by his own hand. She had neither heard from him since the first trial, nor heard any details of his life after. Tongues wagged that he was more involved in Nell's disappearance than he had let on, and that he couldn't live with his knowledge of it. Ollie knew this to be nonsense, of course; she had not exchanged a significant word with Roy Crawford even when he was courting her. Why would anyone believe him to be privy to her most painful secrets?

Five years later the family was struck by tragedy again. The troubles of William H. Cropsey Jr., her younger brother by a few years, had long been known. Due to heavy drinking, he had drifted from job to job, and struggled to support his wife and daughter. His condition became so serious that his wife was forced to go to all the bars in south Norfolk, pleading with the saloonkeepers not to serve him. On his last night he came home drunk anyway. The couple quarreled. William retreated to the bedroom, and was seated in a chair when she went in to check on him. His head was bowed, and in his hand was a bottle of disinfectant.

"Will, what's the matter? Are you hurt?" she asked.

Without answering, and without looking at her, he tilted the bottle and downed most of the contents. His wife screamed, his five-year old daughter cried. A doctor was summoned quickly, but it was too late: Will Cropsey, the next youngest Cropsey child after Nell, was dead at twenty-eight.

Only her father, Uncle Hen and William Douglas went up to see to the arrangements. She and her mother were in no state for a train trip, much less to view the body. Ollie, at least, did not have to switch her wardrobe to black again.

After this, people began to speak of the Cropsey "curse". To the common mind, the accumulation of dead bodies could mean only one thing: something was not right with the way the case was resolved. Even if Jim Wilcox did it, others must have known more than they let on, and could not live with what they knew. Had Roy

Crawford seen something when he left Ollie that night—something so horrible that he was sworn to silence? Did Will Cropsey know something about the fate of his sister that turned him to drink?

Early in '08 an astounding story made the rounds in the out-of-town papers: William Cropsey was dead! Moreover, he had made a deathbed confession to murdering his daughter. When friends showed him these stories, Cropsey was too amused to conjure much outrage. "Goes to show you what they'll put in print!" he declared, and tore the papers to shreds.

And yet rumors continued to circulate much closer to home. Stories about heavy deliveries of ice to the Cropsey residence in the time before Nell's body was discovered. Accounts of an eerie light that had been seen burning, around the clock, in the turret of Seven Pines. Had Nell been kept prisoner up there, in punishment for defying her family over Wilcox? For Nell was such a pretty girl, and her father was a known hothead, and—well, decent folks left speculation at that. But out on the waters of Albemarle Sound, and in the logging camps of the Great Dismal, dinnertime talk often turned to the case, and the unspeakable ways it might have unfolded.

The burning lamp, of course, was easily explained: Mary Cropsey had been in the turret, keeping watch for her daughter. Of extra ice, William Cropsey shrugged. Let them gossip all they want. The man who had killed Nell—the party that was truly responsible—would spend most of his life rotting in prison. That was all that mattered.

II.

'We believe James Wilcox to be guilty of the murder of Nellie Cropsey, but we do not believe that he has been legally convicted of the crime. In other words, he has been sacrificed to the clamor of public opinion, and this is a very grave reflection upon the administration of justice in North Carolina.'

—*Petersburg Index-Appeal* (Va.)

After his first conviction, misgivings for the way Jim had been treated became utterable. Whether or not Jim was guilty could be a matter of debate, but few on either side felt the reputation of the town had been enhanced by the tragedy. "The feeling against Wilcox is cooling," observed the correspondent for the *Concord Times*. "Many leading citizens of this town would like to sign a petition to the Governor asking that the sentence be changed to life imprisonment. Some assert that the Cropseys would sign it."

A few months later this assertion was put to the test by the State Supreme Court in Raleigh. *The Economist* reprinted the full text of Chief Justice Furches' ruling on the appeal, which Ollie read with trembling hands:

'In reading the record of this case, it hardly seems possible that the jury could have given that cautious and vigilant attention to the evidence which the law required...In their immediate presence, one hundred people in their deliberate purpose to prejudice the rights of the prisoner, committed a great wrong against the commonwealth and a contempt of the court...Soon thereafter while the same counsel was addressing the jury, a fire alarm was given near the court house, which caused a number of other persons to leave. The court is of the opinion and so finds the fact that these demonstrations were made for the pur-

> *pose of breaking the force of the counsel's argument...The prisoner must not only be tried according to the forms of law, these forms being included in the expression, the law of the land, but his trial must be unattended by such influences and such demonstrations of lawlessness and intimidation as were present on the former occasion. The courts must stand for civilization, for the proper administration of the law in orderly proceedings. There must be a new trial of this case.*

The ruling once again tore the town in half. The critics believed themselves to be vindicated. The rest felt the dignity of the town insulted anew. There was talk that the saloons would be closed again (they were not). The final straw was broken when, shortly after the ruling, a note was found posted on the gate of the county jail:

> Get Jim Wilcox out of this jail by Saturday night if you don't want trouble.
>
> VOX POPULI

He was not moved by Saturday night, but there was no ignoring the writing on this particular wall. On the eve of the Hertford trial, the prisoner was transported to the train station by closed carriage. For the short trip, Sheriff Reid brought enough guards to keep order, but not so many as to attract attention. The Norfolk & Southern special was held until the carriage arrived, boiler stoked, spitting steam. The second the prisoner was aboard, the engineer released the brakes, and "Vox Populi" got its wish.

Applications for a governor's pardon of Jim Wilcox began as early as 1904, with the required notices in the newspapers. A petition, arguing that the case against him was circumstantial and the verdict preordained, drew a surprisingly large number of signatures from around the state. But the campaign gathered no momentum, being vigorously opposed by the Cropsey family and Uncle Andrew in particular. "The mere thought Jim Wilcox may get out of jail, when he has put in only one year of the thirty he was sentenced to serve, is enough to drive me distracted," Judge Cropsey declared in the papers. "If he serves one day less than thirty years there is no sense of justice."

Wilcox's application finally reached Governor Locke Craig in 1915. In the twelve years since his imprisonment in the old State Prison, Wilcox had contracted tuberculosis, and it was feared that he didn't have much time to live. The petition for pardon bore five thousand signatures from as far away as Pennsylvania; visitors from distant places like Cuba were inquiring about the case, being intimately familiar with the details of Nell's disappearance. Uncle Andrew, meanwhile, had passed away in 1911. Ollie—who was still reading newspapers at the time—refused to make any statement for or against clemency, and no other living relatives stood against it. Public opposition was therefore slight, amounting to only one letter.

Craig kept the world waiting for weeks during that early spring. He at last issued his decision on April 12: "I cannot say that in this case the judgement pronounced against the defendant that he be imprisoned for 30 years was any miscarriage of justice. I do not believe that the demand for justice would be satisfied by a punishment of 12 years' imprisonment for this atrocious crime...A great number of people have asked for his pardon. It is apparent that many of them have no conception of the evidence. There is only one voice raised against it, and that is the cry from a mother's heart that is always constant. She, with justice on her side, is the majority."

Locke Craig retired from politics when his term ended in 1917. The campaign to pardon Wilcox resumed with his successor, Thomas Bickett. In his first decision, Bickett wrote, "It has been suggested that there may have been mitigating circumstances and that James Wilcox has already suffered enough. If there are mitigating circumstances James Wilcox is the only man alive who knows what they were and he refuses to open his mouth. The plea before me is for mercy and not judgment; but repentance comes before salvation, and there is no suggestion that James Wilcox has in any degree repented of his responsibility for the death of Nellie Cropsey. For these reasons a pardon cannot be granted."

Yet Bickett was not as resolute as he seemed. More than a year later, a letter written by the prison superintendent, H.T. Peoples, arrived on his desk. "I have been connected with the state's prison for the past 18 years, and this is the first time I ever asked the Governor to pardon a prisoner," he wrote. "He has a clean prison record. I believe I would be safe to saying there never would be a prisoner in the state's prison [like] Jim Wilcox. I have known him myself for the past 15 years and I have never heard aught against his prison record. If a prisoner is due any consideration for a clean prison record I think Jim is due all you can give him."

A second letter, written by Jim himself, arrived during the holiday season of 1918. It made a deep impression. A message went back: Governor Bickett was sympathetic, but needed to look Jim Wilcox in the eye before reaching a final decision. He would therefore come to the work camp where the prisoner was held, to meet with him privately. Jim's fate would depend on what the Governor saw.

III.

It was remarked how close confinement agreed with Jim. The observation had a malicious implication, as if he were a born criminal destined for a cage. In fact, idleness and the meals brought by his family combined to make him plump; after missing his regular routine at first, liberation from work at Hayman's came to seem like not such a bad thing. As for the worst that could happen—he fretted over it, to be sure, but his certainty of his innocence made all that seem like such a remote prospect, it was just possible to put out of his mind. His biggest worry was not over himself, but the effect the case was having on his family.

Transfer to the state prison brought a different reality. The penitentiary in Raleigh was already old-fashioned when it was built a generation earlier. It had something of the appearance, and half the warmth, of a medieval castle. He now shared a cell with three other men, two younger and one very much older, and two of them were sick when he arrived. The old timer was a railroad man on a long stretch for pushing a colleague between two coal hoppers. He coughed up so much blood it was hard to understand how he had any blood left at all. His chronic hacking made it hard for Jim to sleep, until by some miracle it paused on the fifth night, and Jim was able to hear all the other sounds his coughing had hidden—the sounds of men self-abusing, and more distantly, of worse sins.

There were no more meals from his mother and sister, but instead a steady diet of institutional slop. Where idleness came as a relief in the county lockup, it quickly wore out its welcome in the face of a three-decade sentence. He was not up to the manual labor assigned the prisoners—digging fence-posts, clearing brush, moving rocks. He was reduced to collecting night buckets from the cells too old to have plumbing. As the prison 'stoolie', he got to know every inmate not from their faces, but by the quality of their bowel movements.

Then came that charmed day when the prison's fancy new electric light system went out. As lamps and candles were forbidden, the prisoners languished in the dark for days as the wardens awaited qualified technicians. Jim volunteered to have a look at it. The problem turned out be a simple short-circuit from rat-chewed insulation.

"You got any experience in the trade?" asked Hank Peoples, the superintendent.

"I fixed the wires sometimes at Hayman's."

"Fair enough. You're on the day shift, then."

With that, Jim was promoted from stoolie to house electrician. And for the next decade, the lights at the prison burned bright on his watch.

As the years passed, Jim came to understand that prison was not the end of life, but only another kind of routine. Before, he felt confined if he didn't get out on the river now and again. Inside, his sense of space altered, so that the fifty-seven steps from his cell to the mess hall, or the one hundred and twenty-two to the threshold of the yard, seemed like weekend excursions. As physical space contracted, the space between his ears expanded: he became capable of disappearing into chambers of his mind as vast and varied as a Vanderbilt mansion. His taste in reading grew beyond trash Westerns and detective novels; he sampled Twain, Poe, Sir Walter Scott. He toyed with the idea of setting pen to paper and composing his side of the whole sad story. But when the time came, he became discouraged. If nobody believed him when he told them he didn't murder Nell, why would he convince anybody writing it down?

He was widely acknowledged to be a model prisoner. Yet he was no tool of the wardens. His readiness to use his fists to defend his name did not go away, which in no small part explained why he never had to use them. He suffered, at worst, occasional remarks—murmurs in the chow line like "You get in her knickers before you clobbered her, Jim?" or "You should have married her, Jim. Then you could have killed her anytime!" He pretended these were beneath his notice. He was sent up for a crime only a little bit less reviled than child-killing, but he never had a serious fight in all his time behind bars.

Even as his memory of Nell began to fade, and he had trouble conjuring up an image of her face, she figured often in his thoughts. She would come at him abruptly, out of some dream, and rouse him with such violence that he would sit up and bang his head against the upper bunk. He saw her at her needle, face shining by lamplight, corona of curl-papers in her hair. Blanketed and furred, nestled under his arm for a winter's buggy ride, she laughed at something he said. "When's the last time you read a real book?" she asked. She tilted her head, piled her hair on one side, and let him kiss her neck.

Jim had not grieved over Nell since the morning her body was discovered. Suspected, reviled, he felt no room in his heart for the softer sentiments. But the luxury of time in prison turned him into a wet, palpitating wound. A year into his sentence, he woke up from a dream about Nell with tears in his eyes. She was at the rail of an Old Dominion steamer as it stood off the banks of the Pasquotank. She wore that red and white traveling dress she and Carrie had shown at the Pratt students' show. He ran into the shallows, calling to her, as she reached up and untied her hat. Then she grasped the ends of her hair and, as if feathering a chicken, depilated herself handful by handful. Blood ran down around her ears and down her cheeks.

He shouted, "Nell, it's getting cold!" When she answered, it was as if she was right beside him, and said...

He woke up as his bunkmate kicked him in the ribs.

"You were talking in your sleep," he said.

"What did I say?"

"You were saying 'Pull'."

His father visited him most often, several times a year. His sister and mother came twice, for the holidays and on his birthday late in August. They bore loaves of homemade bread and cakes and other savories, which the guards were obliged to inspect and confiscate if they were too tempting. There were also hand-sewn articles to keep him warm. Annie Mae went too far, embroidering little flowers on her gifts. If he couldn't tear these off, he had to throw the whole things away, because he couldn't be seen in the prison yard in a muffler sprinkled with pansies.

Seven years into his sentence he heard that his mother, Martha Elizabeth Wilcox, had died. She was only fifty-nine. The news seemed like some cruel joke—he had just seen her for his birthday the previous week. He only accepted it when he got a second telegram with the particulars about her funeral service. He requested leave to attend, but was denied: letting the reviled murderer of Nell Crospey back into Elizabeth City would cost the State too much for security.

And so, on the day his mother was buried, he was at his post in the generator room. His eyes rested on the switches in front of him, but his mind was consumed with the thought that his misfortune—indeed, his foolishness—had put his mother in an early grave.

His father followed five years later. This grieved him every bit as much, but by that time there was simply less of Jim Wilcox to hurt. Though he had always been short, he had been powerful, and rarely sick. He dwindled now to a mere one hundred and five pounds, and coughed up blood every morning. The prison doctor diagnosed tuberculosis, which struck him as mildly interesting but not worth his personal concern, like war news from Europe. He again requested leave to attend the funeral, and was again denied. Even his fellow inmates grumbled at the injustice of this: if a well-behaved fellow like Wilcox couldn't get a fair shake, what hope was there for them?

There was also less of him in mind. As his appeals for pardon were denied, notions like 'hope' and 'the future' came to seem like heirlooms left by some better ancestor. He would never live to see Paris, or Niagara, or the gorge of the Yellowstone. Thoughts of such losses were heavy—so he dropped them. He discarded them in various places around the prison, like moons of overgrown fingernail.

Soon the toll on his health was apparent even to his wardens. Hank Peoples, who by then had known him for as long as anybody outside his family, noticed the deterioration of Jim's health after the denial in '17, and worried.

"Jim, you need a change of scenery. How about you go up to mountain camp for a spell?"

"Thanks Hank, but I don't think I could handle that kind of work just now."

"Don't worry about that. We'll find you something to do."

Before he left, Peoples gave him a ball pen.

"What's this for?" asked Jim.

"It is for you to stop feeling sorry for yourself. Write. That's an order."

The next week he was sent up to the prison work camp outside of Boone, two hundred miles west of Raleigh. He rode in a carriage reserved for prisoners, with bars on the windows. He was not prepared at first for sudden exposure to the view outside, with the lowlands spread before him, or the scenes of regular life as the train slipped through the towns. The space and activity were unnerving, the changes since he went away, unfamiliar. There were now many more motor cars than buggies, and paved roads. And along the latter, tangles of wires strung from glass crosstrees stacked eight, nine, ten high. Men in olive uniforms loitered on the platforms. Beside them, young women wore dresses that exposed their ankles.

Peoples was as good as his word about the convict camp. Most of the men broke their backs pulling up stumps for roadbuilding, but he was assigned to the mess hall. For the next two weeks he did nothing more strenuous than paddle cauldrons of soup. For some reason—maybe because it was supplied by the local farms—the food at the camp was better too. Between that and the fresh air, he got some of his color back, and gained a few pounds.

His thoughts turned to what the Governor had said about him in the papers. Pardon was denied, he said, because Jim Wilcox had never shown any remorse. To which Jim wondered, "Remorse for what? Being falsely accused? Losing half a life on a trumped-up charge?" But in the clarity of his mountaintop vantage he understood that the facts were only half of what passed for justice. Maybe less than half.

He took out the pen Peoples had given him and wrote a letter:

Ella Maud

Governor Thomas W. Bickett
Governor's House
Raleigh

> *For 16 years, I have been unjustly punished and now, broken in spirit and health, I come to you asking for mercy.*
>
> *Although you may think I am guilty and viewing it from a direction other than my own, I, too, can see that the circumstances are against me, for it is a very mixed-up affair, but I do not know any more about it than an unborn babe, and were it my last words on earth, I still would protest my innocence, and would not be going before my Maker with a lie on my lips.*
>
> *For 15 years and seven months I have worked hard and been faithful, been submissive and obedient to those whom I have been under. That is what my prison record will show, and that is a record that very few ever attain. Fifteen years with nothing against it!*
>
> *And now, dear Governor, it is with the same spirit that you ask the Heavenly Father for mercy that I come and ask you for mercy, and should you see fit to grant me a pardon, I can assure you I will not cause you one regret for having done so. Of course I know you viewed the other side of the case in every detail, but now I ask you to do this. Just stop and think, 16 years unjust punishment. Mother and father taken away during that time, was not allowed to see them as others have done, broken in spirit and health, not much longer to live. I ask you, do you not think that I have been punished enough?*

He sent the draft to Peoples for his opinion. The superintendent didn't return it with comments, but immediately had his secretary type and mail it. When it reached the Governor, he telegraphed back *DID THE PRISONER WRITE THIS HIMSELF?* To which Peoples replied, *ON HIS OWN INITIATIVE.*

It was a chilly afternoon in mid-December when Governor Bickett rolled into the camp in a forest-green Oldsmobile. Jim was summoned from the kitchen to the manager's office. Coming in, he found the Governor sitting behind the desk, leaning back. There was no guard present—just the Governor and his assistant. Bickett's face was clean-shaven, mild, benign in that way perfected by politicians.

"Come in. Sit," said Bickett.

"Yes, sir. Thank you."

"I suppose you know who I am, and why I'm here."

"I know, sir. And I can guess the reason."

"I read your letter, and found much to praise in it. Did you write it yourself?"

"I did, sir."

"Honestly, I had my doubts. I've read the court documents, and nowhere were you praised for your eloquence."

"I suppose," Jim said, delicately, "there is some grace in innocence."

Bickett laughed. "Indeed! But of that, the courts have spoken. I'm here for a different reason. I wanted to look you in the eye and ask you the following question. Are you ready?"

"I hope so."

The Governor leaned forward and folded his hands.

"Tell me why you never defended yourself in court. You hardly opened your mouth. Not even at the second trial, when you knew silence only got you convicted. Is it because you did it?"

Jim said nothing at first. He looked down, straightening his cap from the knotted mess he had made of it. The Governor's assistant, a young fellow with a university look about him, was leaning against the file cabinets, staring. Bickett was staring. Even the sound of swinging picks and shovels momentarily paused outside.

"The first time, it was Mr. Aydlett who warned me against it. The second, yes, he changed his tune, and said I should testify. But I turned him down."

"Why?"

"I suppose, the situation being such a mess, and a fine young woman gone...I decided the books must be balanced somehow. If God wanted me to hang for it, that would be His will. Words would never bring her back. Nothing devised by Man will bring her back.

"When she first disappeared, I thought she'd run off. That's the Lord's honest truth. We all knew girls who lit out from Elizabeth City on their own. I was sure she'd turn up sometime, so there was no reason to look for her. Nell was always headstrong. She sure wouldn't be scared up by detectives—she would only come back on her own...on her terms.

"But when they found her in the river, I knew that I was as wrong as can be. I felt guilty for thinking the worst of her. I beat myself up pretty bad. I never wanted anything but the best for her, and when the time came...I let her down. I should have protected her, instead of thinking only of my feelings. I shouldn't have left her there on that porch, crying, just for the sake of Len Owens. If I'd stayed, she'd be with me now, or with somebody else. But she'd be alive..."

His voice was unsteady now, and his eyes unfocused.

"I said nothing because there was nothing to say. In the only important way, I was guilty. Not in the eyes of the court, but in the eyes of the Heavenly Father."

"So you were silent because you left your fate to the Lord."

"That was the idea."

"And did you kill her?"

"I did not."

"Did you have someone else do it?"

"No sir."

"Did you drive her to do it?"

"Honestly—I can't deny that."

Bickett rose to his feet.

"Come here, son."

The Governor took position right before Jim. He then looked to his assistant who, after a moment of not understanding what he wanted, approached the other two in the center of the room. Between the desk and the filing cabinets and the dictaphone machine, the three men joined hands. Bickett bowed his head and recited:

> *He does not deal with us according to our sins, nor repay us according to our iniquities. For as high as the heavens are above the earth, so great is His steadfast love toward those who fear Him; as far as the east is from the west, so far does He remove our transgressions from us. As a father shows compassion to his children, so the Lord shows compassion to those who fear Him. For He knows our frame; He remembers that we are dust...*

"Thank you for meeting with me today, Jim," said Bickett.

"It's me who should be thanking you, sir."

The Governor collected his hat. "You'll hear my decision before Christmas."

With that, he got back in his Oldsmobile and left. Jim returned to his paddle in the kitchen.

The next day he was ordered to pack his things for transfer back to Raleigh. The consensus was that this news could be very good for Jim, or very bad. Having been denied twice before, Jim didn't allow himself the luxury of hope. Instead, he drank in the light and the space of the world outside the train window, which seemed sweeter to him now than it did on the trip out.

When Jim's letter was reprinted in the papers, it was noted that this was the first time he had publicly denied his guilt, in his own voice.

IV.

On December 21, 1918, Jim Wilcox returned to his home town for the first time in sixteen years. The old Norfolk & Southern depot on Pennsylvania Avenue had closed several years earlier; he alighted on the platform of a new station on the city's west side. The change disoriented him. He spent a while standing around the place, eying the brick exterior and sweeping tile roof. When he went inside, he found two handsome, wainscoted waiting rooms—one for whites, the other for blacks. It was a Saturday, mid-afternoon, and there were a fair number of holiday travelers rushing in and out. But he recognized no one, and no one seemed to recognize him.

He was dressed in exactly the same clothes he had worn at both trials, and on the day he was remanded to Raleigh. He had five dollars in his pocket given to him by Hank Peoples. But he carried no luggage, and had no hat for his head. There was nothing in his prison cell he wanted to take away with him. He had come back with hardly more than he possessed when he was born, forty-two years earlier.

There was only one place he could go, but he needed a drink first. He sighted a bar across the street from the depot. As he crossed, he was frozen by a motor car swerving from nowhere, rubber tires screeching.

"Watch where you're going, old timer!" the driver yelled.

Jim didn't move. The car steered around him, the driver shaking his head. Jim was surprised by how fast those things moved, without the tell-tale clip-clop of hooves his ears were attuned to.

He came in and ordered a beer. The barkeep eyed him as he jerked the tap, appraising his suit.

"Just outta the hoosegow?"

"How could you tell?"

He smiled. "Just a lucky guess. That'll be two bits."

"What if I'm not done?"

"We pay as we go here."

Jim downed half his mug and glowered. He had come back to Elizabeth City without much thought of whether it was a good idea. To spend his first holidays as a free man with his surviving family just seemed like what he was supposed to do. He felt he should put more effort into envisioning a future for himself—maybe a fresh start up in Norfolk, or Baltimore, or New York. Someplace with the kind of dock-work he was used to. He remembered his time in Manhattan with Nell, gallivanting the shops in his yellow suit. The memory gave him a flush of pleasure—or was it the beer working on him? For he was a lightweight now.

"You take to the water sometimes?" he asked the barkeep.

"Now and again."

"Ben Shrive still set around here?"

"Sorry, can't say I know him."

"Len Owens? The Pastoreski brothers?"

The other shook his head. Jim drained his glass and pushed it across.

"Set me up again, doc."

"Jim Wilcox," someone said.

Jim turned. There was a man sitting three stools away, dressed in flannel shirt and suspenders. There was an empty mug in front of him, and a spittoon on the floor by his side.

"Do I know you, friend?"

The man turned. It was dark, but neither the gloom nor the passage of time prevented Jim from sensing something familiar about him.

"Yeah, you seen me," the man said. "I was on the jury."

"Oh," said Jim, turning back to his drink. "Well, no hard feelings."

The man fetched up a laugh, then loosed a bolus of black juice into the spittoon.

"I wouldn't think so. I argued for you for twenty-four straight hours. Wasn't for me, they would have convicted you in fifteen minutes."

"You don't say. What's your name?"

"No need to know my name."

From across the street, there was a long whistle as the train pulled out.

"Well, thank you for the attempt. Can I buy you a drink?"

"You know, I always liked the figure you cut, Jim. I never thought they had you right, saying the things they did. But can you take a piece of advice?"

"Sure."

"Get the hell out of town. Nothing's going to end well for you here."

After the man had gone, Jim finished his second beer. He had a mind to have another, but thought the better of showing up pie-eyed at his sister's.

When he stood up, the barkeep tossed his quarter back at him.

"I wasn't around here back then, so I didn't know it was you," he said. "I won't take your money—and not because I like you."

"Thanks for the hospitality."

Tottering out, Jim left the coin.

Annie Mae and her family lived in a little white frame house at 157 Baxter St., less than a mile from the train station. Knocking on the door, he met his brother-in-law for the first time.

"You Jim?"

"The very one," he replied.

"Sam Williams."

They shook hands, Jim withstanding his scrutiny.

"Got'ny bags?"

"I am as you see."

Annie Mae appeared out of the darkness beyond, an expression of ecstatic torment on her face. They embraced. The way she hung onto him threatened to wring tears from him, so he backed up a bit, grasping her shoulders. His little sister was a full-grown woman now, in her mid-thirties, of mature girth and worry lines. The scar she had gotten from Tarheel was fainter, but still puckered the flesh of her cheek. The way she beamed, covering him in filial devotion, made him uneasy.

"You're home now," she said.

"I believe I am."

"Come on in. We're about to start dinner."

Over roast chicken and potatoes, he met his niece and nephews: Oscar, 12; Betsy, 10; Samuel Hallett, 7; and Samuel Howland, 6. Both the younger boys were named after elders in their father's family. Having never had the opportunity to visit him in prison, the children stared at him in unabashed fascination. He didn't know how much their parents had told them about his past. Very likely nothing, he thought—though they could just as well have learned the story from their friends and neighbors. In any case, he chose to portray himself as a long-lost but entirely legitimate uncle, who simply happened to live far away.

Their father, meanwhile, was wary. His manner—cordial enough but no more—left no doubt about the real depth of his welcome.

"Did you come down on the 630?" asked young Oscar.

"I arrived more like 3 o'clock."

The boys laughed out loud.

"We don't mean what *time*. We mean what engine!"

"Oh, forgive me, fellas. I didn't notice the locomotive."

"It is true you had a falcon when you were a boy?"

"And is it true it *attacked* Mama?" said Samuel Hallett.

"Boys! Mind your manners!" cried Annie. "Please excuse them, Uncle Jim. They speak out of turn."

"'Tsall right. And in answer to your questions, yes, both are facts."

The boys looked at each other as if both had won a bet.

"Tell us!" they said in unison.

"Boys, please—"

"Annie, it's fine. Of course I'm happy to tell it, though I warn you it's not a story that ends happy..."

And so he told the whole tale of Tarheel, from the excitement of the early days when she first arrived to her unfortunate end. The children, from the youngest to the eldest, hung on every word. When he got to the part when their mother was cut, Samuel Hallett asked her, "Why'd you do that, Maw?" To which his mother replied, "Because I was a naughty child, just like you!"

"Paw, can we get a falcon?" asked Oscar. "Promise I won't be careless."

"Positively not," said Sam Williams.

"Any ideas where you might settle? Got a job lined up?"

"To be entirely honest, the last few days have felt like a whirlwind. But I think I'll look for something local."

"So you're coming back here?"

"Thought I might."

Williams glanced at Annie.

"Well that's splendid," she said. "We'll get to see you more often! Now when's the last time you had a good home-baked pie?"

That night, Jim slept in an ordinary bedroom, in a bed with carved headboard and softly laundered sheets, for the first time in almost twenty years. This simple luxury had seemed so unattainable for so long he had scarcely allowed himself to envision it. But now that it had become real, a strange thought went through his head: the way the bedclothes enfolded him was alien. The quiet of the house, without the sounds of sleeping men around him, was troubling. In some fashion he could not understand, he felt none of it was for him.

He hung around Annie Mae's through Christmas. Having no money he couldn't share in the gift-giving, but he did take the boys out to the river to look at the boats. Hayman's, he noted, was still there. But there seemed fewer fishing boats, and a general air of dilapidation. A number of the city's industries, Sam Williams explained, had moved inland, where the rail connections were better. Many of the jobs had gone with them.

It occurred to him that it had been ages since he'd shucked an oyster. He led the boys to the closest bar he could find—a good fifteen-minute walk—and sat them down on a bench.

"Name your pleasure, men. The Moses Pond? Topsail? Confederate Dollar?"

Oscar and the Samuelses pulled coordinated scowls.

"No?" said Jim. "I was handling my own knife when I was no older than two. That was about average for an Elizabeth City boy..."

He ordered a half-dozen, which arrived in a tin plate, recumbent on ice and already open. When he saw the boys looking dubiously at the soft brown contents, he seized one and showed them how it was done.

"These are some beauties here. When they were this color we used to call 'em Black Mammie's Cootch—but don't tell your mama I said that. So you take 'em by the shell here, and you put on your pleasure in condiments. I like tomato ketchup. But you can use pepper sauce or just lemon..."

He applied a dab of sauce and tilted the shell into his mouth. This one was sweet, and yielding, like it had never known a serious tide in its life. The pure concentrated essence of his childhood.

"...and you make sure to get all the liquor, because that's where the flavor is."

But much as he coaxed and cajoled, he couldn't make either boy partake. The best Oscar did was test an oyster with the tip of his tongue.

"Ugh, salty!" he exclaimed.

"They look like boogers," observed Samuel Howland.

"Well, I guess that means more for me," said Jim, and tugged the plate toward him.

They went out to the tracks to watch the trains. The boys knew all the locomotives, and could hold forth on the characters of each.

They walked the siding and picked up chunks of coal to throw around, spiking each other with soot, until their talk petered out and all of them suddenly seemed nervous.

"So is it true you went up the river for a long time?" asked Samuel Hallett.

"Shut yer yap, stupid!" said Oscar.

"Goodness, where'd you learn a saying like 'up the river'?" Jim shook his head.

"I'm awful sorry my brother got such a big mouth, Uncle Jim."

"Not to worry, son. Where'd you hear a story like that, anyway?"

"Our paw says you went away for killing your girl, years and years ago," said Samuel Howland. "My maw tells him to shut up about it, it ain't true. So who's right?"

And Jim thought: there it is.

"I guess you can say they're both right. My girl died, and I did get punished for it, for a long time. But I didn't do it. I've never lifted my hand at a woman in my life."

"That's what I thought," said Samuel Hallett, full of confidence.

The day Jim left, Annie Mae gave him a napkin tied up with an apple and a few sandwiches. When she pressed him to stay, he professed excitement at making his own way again.

"So you really are determined to stay in town?" she asked.

"I'm a regular bad penny. You can't get rid of me."

"Oh Jim, I wish you wouldn't talk that way."

They embraced on the front porch. Then Jim shook the hands of all the Williams boys.

"Come back anytime," said his brother-in-law, his eyes flashing "Never dare."

"I will," replied Jim, intending not.

There was a rooming house by the docks that offered beds for ten cents a night. As he had only two dollars and twelve cents left of

Hank Peoples' money, he decided to economize by sleeping outside unless it was well and truly cold.

The hay in any quiet barn was plenty warm, even when it was thirty degrees at night. He got comfortable doing this, rising before the owners came to tend their livestock. He bought a little breakfast—a roll or biscuit and some coffee—then went around town looking for odd jobs. He spent the first days of 1919 filling wheelbarrows with coal, collecting scrap iron, and mucking stalls. One of his easier gigs was sweeping up beard trimmings from the floor of a barber shop. That one didn't last as long as he would have liked.

By week's end, when he truly stank from the work and the manure of his quarters, he would splurge on an afternoon at the bathhouse. After soaking, he would look at the stick-thin figure in the mirror, and almost recognize the dude he used to be. He thought about visiting some of the cathouses. But then he would cough up his usual tablespoon of blood in his kerchief, and lose all inclination for such things.

Instead, he made the rounds of the drinking houses. Sixteen years of forced sobriety made him a quick drunk, plastered good after just three or four shots of watered-down rotgut. This went easy on his pocketbook. But he needed more than that to drive away the memories. He is fired by Tom Hayman, again and again. The judge trains that death sentence down on him, and strings of spit trellis the sidewalk at his feet. He and Nell walk arm-in-arm on a floor made of light. He gives her a topsail, and she downs the oyster with no need of a napkin, her blue eyes oceanic and engulfing.

Three months of this life and his purse still had less than three dollars in it. His visits to the bathhouse became less frequent, because there was drinking to be done. Once the most hated man in Pasquotank County, Jim became the most pitied. Citizens who had been in the crowds calling for his death looked upon him now, and declared "Sad how they treated old Jim Wilcox, wasn't it?"

"They convicted him just on the circumstances," others would say.

"Plain destroyed his poor family."

"Don't you just know that William Cropsey had somethin' to do with it?"

"That Yankee Jezebel wasn't innocent."

Now and then, he ran into people he once knew. Len Owens was still in town, retired from the river trade and manning the counter at a hardware. Just to prove there was no hard feelings, Jim went in and shook his hand, and Len looked about as sad as a widower. They spoke vaguely of a drink they never intended to have.

One day, toward spring, he saw Ed Aydlett walking down the other side of Main Street. In the years Jim was away, his former counselor had become something of a political force in the town. Jim was inclined to make greetings, until he saw Aydlett—the man who had defended him twice, with a passion that verged on tears—sink his head into his collar and walk faster. Jim obliged by pretending not to see him.

He was aware of the absurdity of his decision to stay on in Betsy City. Common sense, and the looks in every eye he passed, all told him that he needed to quit the place, to start over in a town without so many ghosts. But when the world gave him a nudge, Jim Wilcox was inclined to shove back. Common sense once told him to forget about the Cropsey girls, when they disparaged him. He was innocent, after all, so why should he give up the only place he had known his whole life? William Cropsey was the outsider, not Jim. Why didn't he leave town instead—and take his damnable clan with him?

It took until summer for Jim to get his first real job. Jerome Flora, who was a decorated veteran and much respected in town, was Fire Chief. Elizabeth City's fire company was largely volunteer, but there were two full-time positions at the station house behind City Hall. He offered one of the positions to Jim.

Jim took up his responsibilities as firefighter with the same seriousness he did as a model prisoner. He got a bunk on the second floor of the firehouse and a locker for what little stuff he had. He made the bed with military precision every morning, and kept its environs spotless. He took the care and polishing of the fire engines to new levels of fussiness. The boys in the fire company knew his history, and knew he liked a nip now and then, but they followed Jerry Flora's lead in giving him the benefit of the doubt.

The ritual of turning out was his favorite part of the job. The preparations, the urgency, the call to action at any hour of any day—these combined to give him a sense of importance he had missed. The heading out into the streets, with any number of possibilities waiting for them at their destination. Traffic parted for them as they careened and clanged; children gazed up to him on his gleaming perch, clad in his watertight armor, and begged him to ring the bell.

Most of the calls were false alarms, but there were a fair number of real emergencies. On those occasions he got no special attention, no second looks. No victims cared if the man breaking down the door to their burning houses once had some legal trouble. No one begrudged a horse saved from a collapsing barn. Only once, after about six months on the job, did someone recognize him as the infamous Jim Wilcox. He was an elderly black man whose modest house on the west side of town had gone up from an improperly insulated stovepipe. Out in the street, leaning against the wheel of the engine as he caught his breath, he fixed on Jim, and said in a hoarse, smoke-desiccated whisper, "Good lord, I know you."

"Do you?"

"Your trial was the only time I ever got to sit down in the courtroom."

"Glad to oblige," replied Jim. "But best think about covering that pipe."

Good as Jim was at the job, he saw no reason to stint on his pleasures. A steady paycheck meant a steady number of off-duty hours at the saloons, some of which even extended him a tab. Folks listened to his particular way of coughing up his lungs, and felt sorry for him.

"Never met a fireman with a cough like that," said one barkeep, "and I've met a few."

Jim said, "There's nothing a little smoke can do to these old lungs. I'm like a back-fired lot. Now set me up again, will you?"

Set him up they did, time after time. But the day came, perhaps inevitably, when he was at the saloon when he was supposed to be on duty at the firehouse. He had only intended to be there a few minutes—just long enough for the one drink that would take the edge off his nerves—when he lost track of time because damned if anybody kept a clock above the bar in those days. He was sunk down pleasantly on his stool when Jerry Flora came in and yelled, "Wilcox, what the hell are you doing?"

"What does it look like?" Jim snapped, not recognizing to whom he was speaking.

The saloon fell silent. The chief stood his ground for a few moments, until Jim understood the trouble he had bought for himself. Then Flora turned and left.

Back at the station, Jim found him at his desk, scribbling in the duty roster.

"Jerry, sorry about that. I didn't see you there in the dark—"

"Also seems you didn't hear the bell either. There was a hay-fire on the north side."

Jim was stunned. "And I missed it?"

"You missed it clean, son. Never happened before in the whole history of this department. We've had volunteers not show up for a call. But the officer of the watch missing an alarm? Never."

Head still buzzing from drink, Jim scratched under his suspenders. He was not sure how to proceed.

"I suppose you know you're out," said the other. That was when Jim realized he was crossing Jim's name off every column in the duty list.

"Fair enough," he said. "I'll be gone by the afternoon."

"See that you are."

As Jim collected his things, Jerry simmered down. He came to him as Jim was heading through the door.

"Sorry it had to be like this."

"You got to know I never meant to be away more than a few minutes," said Jim. "Was anybody hurt?"

"Nobody but a few hay bales."

"How I missed that bell I'll never know."

"You didn't mean no harm."

Jim's eyes wetted.

"I have to tell you, Jerry, that I hardly know myself anymore," he said. "I got myself broken somewhere along the way, like I left pieces spread all over the road on the way back. I know they're all back there, but don't know where to find them."

Flora put on a hand on his shoulder.

"Any notions on your next move?"

The other heaved a laugh. "Oh, you know me. There's always something next."

"That's great, Jim. You know it's nothing personal. You're always welcome to come around here, share a meal. You're still one of us."

"Thanks. I might."

Jim pushed through the door, his entire life's contents in the duffel around his shoulder. His immediate destination was never in question: he headed straight back to the same saloon, where he found the same seat waiting for him. The same barkeep was there, and seeing Jim's belongings at his side, poured him the same drink.

"Hell of a day's luck," he said.

"Nothin I don't deserve, Timmy," replied Jim.

"That one's on the house, Jim. But just so's you know, we're settling up tabs today."

Jim raised his glass. "Here's to you, bub."

And so it was back to odd jobs and sleeping where he could. After a couple of days, he took a job painting a fence. After that, he weeded out an old garden some widow wanted to put back into vegetables. He manned the cash register at the feed store, until the farmers complained about his bodily smell. There was just one thing he refused to do: one of the big potato planters hired a large crew to dig the beds, drawing itinerant workers from all over the county. The sight of them all, just like when Cropsey put the word out, was too much like old times for Jim. The money was good, but he steered clear.

In most respects, Jim had always been a cheerful sort. When he was provoked, he was quick to anger, but those storms passed quickly, leaving the usual sunshine behind. He was known to post drinks for men he'd brawled with the day previous. At Hayman's, a co-worker once dropped a two-hundred-pound crossbeam on Jim's foot. The impact broke two of his toes, and blackened four. Then all the nails peeled off, leaving him so tender that just putting on his boot was agony. But Jim never complained, and never blamed the man with the slippery fingers. Life was too short, and there were too many opportunities to seize, to dwell on past hurts.

In the days after he left the firehouse, though, he became conscious of a different mood overtaking him. He discovered a certain hopelessness. In time, it became almost a pleasure to think how worthless he had become—if idle familiarity could be called 'pleasure'. He would lie out under the stars, and it would occur to him that each of those uncertain lights would long outlast him. And it wouldn't matter a bit if he was there to contemplate his own insignificance. It struck him as a particularly deep sort of obscurity, the kind that was too insignificant even to note its insignificance. In his humor, he had always played at perversity. Now, for the first time in his life, he was no longer playing.

For what would the world lose when Jim Wilcox was gone? In the few decades since he had worked at the boat trade, most of what he did was now done with a tenth the number of employees, with machines. He was unwelcome at Annie Mae's. He was too ashamed to show his face at the firehouse. He was delinquent on several accounts at bars around town, and avoided those places. In every direction, he felt the circle of his prospects tightening.

There was one person on whom his existence had a profound effect, and she turned up floating face-down in the Pasquotank twenty years in the past.

He wondered, "Why didn't I marry her?" And then, like a bullfrog stealing his lure, his self-revulsion raised its warty head above the muck and croaked, "Fool question!" Did he remember nothing from the three years he had invested courting her? She was handsome, and she was lively, and a man could feel proud with having her on his arm. But a constant strain of conflict ran through their every moment. She had a way of reproving with the merest twitch of a nostril. He learned the vocabulary of her gestures—the skeptical eyebrow, the hair-tuck of embarrassment. That look over her shoulder when she wanted to be enveloped. She could eat a peach like a countess, and banish the pit like a magician.

He assumed what he felt was love. Her standards, alas, were too high for this world and the people in it. Pleasing her was a full-time occupation; before too long, he was infected with her unease, and looked with disdain even upon himself. Finding the comfort simply to exist with her, like with any ordinary soul, was hard enough that the idea of proposing marriage seemed like proposing a bridge over the ocean. Yes, it was love, because it was also fear.

And yet, the powerlessness of losing her, that way! If she'd run off with some swell, he could at least have had the satisfaction of hating her. But this. As challenging as Nell could be, there was one thing for sure: she was not disposable. Not like Jim Wilcox two decades later, whose lingering was only a prelude to his just, overdue end.

He had never fooled himself in believing he was a reflective man. In almost all things, Jim was content with his ignorance, if that was all the world required of him. But if the lost years had taught him anything, it was that unanswered questions killed.

They called to him through the thickness of his drunk, pleasantly engirdling. This unfinished business meant he had a last call to make at the Cropseys. It was not the most prudent place to show himself, and might get him a fist in the face or a bullet in the gut for his trouble. But it must be done.

"Pour one for yourself and drink to me," he said to Timmy. "For I am like unto Daniel, about to enter the lion's den."

V.

On Mondays, Ollie used the relative coolness of the morning to air the laundered sheets. She hung them on the line in the back yard, one by one, until a barrier was erected between her and the vegetable beds where her father fussed. When she was done, she stood staring at the cotton surface as it rounded with the wind, gently bowing like the belly of a dozing beast.

"I'll leave two of these on the table..." said William Cropsey, who appeared suddenly and made Ollie jump. He had a canvas sack filled with green peppers.

"All right."

"You awake?" he asked.

"As much as I care to be."

With a dubious shake, he left her. For it was his practice to go door-to-door early in the week, when the wives of the neighborhood might want fresh vegetables after the weekend. His rounds kept him away all morning, giving her several hours of blessed solitude.

It was not literal solitude—her mother was in the house. Mary Cropsey's inability to sleep at night, however, had worsened over the years, to the point where she was obliged to keep to her bed until after noon. Ollie brought a tray up to her every morning, with bread and a bit of cheese and a hard-boiled egg in a porcelain cup they had brought all the way from Brooklyn. The little vessel was the color of buttermilk, with cartoons of Dutch farmhouses and a windmill rendered in blue, and tiny human figures indicated with mere dashes of glaze. Having stared at this landscape at innumerable breakfasts since her girlhood, those squiggles of Dutch farmers had become as familiar to her as the lines in her own hand.

After delivering the morning's tray to her mother, she sat in the dining room with her tea. The clock struck eleven, and then eleven-thirty. The peal of the last train of the morning rose in the distance, and Ollie sipped. Her cup had gone cold.

There was a knock at the front door. Ollie listened. Her visitor knocked again, and a shiver went straight to her heart. Ollie recognized that rapping.

She opened the door.

"It is you," she said.

"Hello, Ollie."

Jim Wilcox looked apologetic standing there, head bowed like a naughty little boy. For her part, Ollie was only conscious of what she didn't feel: not anger, not sadness. Not even surprise.

"I guess you didn't figure on seeing me."

"We all heard you got out," she replied. "Do you want to sit?"

His eyes widened, and he peeped over her shoulder.

"Is that a good idea?"

"My father is out, if that's what you're asking."

She showed him into the parlor. The furniture there, he saw, was the same as decades before, the last night Bill Dawson brought him to Seven Pines. Ollie herself was still thin, still favored with a certain elegance, but worn and yellowed around the edges, like an old book.

"You're in mourning," he said.

"So I am."

To Ollie, Jim seemed to have aged twice the number of years he had been gone. His frame, so robust in its time, had withered, his gleaming head of blond hair dulled. His clothing was that of a roadside bum. When the stench of his body reached her nostrils, she said nothing, but rose to open the window.

"Would you like tea? Some water?"

"No thanks. I won't stay long."

"As you wish," she said, sitting and smoothing her skirt.

They stared at each other as the birds sang and the grandfather ticked. Jim, thrown by her equanimity, scarcely knew how to begin.

"How are your parents?"

"Well enough," she replied. "Mother doesn't sleep at night."

"That's a shame. Both my folks passed, years ago."

"Yes, I heard."

"And Miss Carrie? How is she?"

"Carrie is married and living in Rockland County."

"Guess I got back too late then!" he said, with a grin. Then he thought that, under the circumstances, that kind of joking was in poor taste. But Ollie only gave a faint smile, and a hint of a wink, and continued to regard him.

"I suppose you're wondering why I'm here."

She was motionless.

"I wanted to tell you—alone and with no reason to lie anymore—that I had nothing to do with Nell. It's what I said from the beginning, and it was the Lord's honest truth then, and it still is. I swear on the graves of my parents."

She tilted her head. "Well Jim, I wouldn't say you had *nothing* to do with it."

"Fair enough. I think you know what I mean."

"Yes, I do. And I know."

"You know what?"

"That you had nothing to do with it."

"You *know* that?"

"Yes."

She was tormenting him now with this reticence. He shifted in his seat.

"Then would you mind telling..."

"...if you're looking to be forgiven somehow," she interrupted, "you should know I'm the last person in the world who could give you that. Best you make your suit to the Almighty, in your prayers. Like I do."

"The Lord and I have been talking a lot, in the years I rotted in prison. I wonder if you can imagine what that was like."

"I have an idea."

None of this was going as he had expected.

"Well if you'll excuse me, but I'm hard put. If you know I had nothing to do with it, why did you swear that I did?"

"If you remember, Jim, I never testified that you were guilty. I only told what I remembered about that night—"

"Forgive me if I say that sounds a little lawyerly—"

"...and remember," she continued, icy, "you didn't exactly help yourself, the way you acted. I might ask you to explain yourself, Jim. I never thought you were capable of harming Nell, but you were so cold that night. So...callous."

Jim stared at the carpet. "I was pulled out of bed in the middle of the night. I thought Nell was playing one on me, running away. Believe me, the way she treated me those last weeks, I had plenty of reason to think so."

"Maybe you did. You might have said so—"

She stopped as a voice filtered down from upstairs. It was her mother, calling out "Olive! Olive!"

"What is it, mother?"

"I hear voices. Who is there?"

"No one. I'll be up soon!"

Jim started to speak, but Olive lifted a finger to stop him. Nothing more came from the bedroom above.

"It's probably best she doesn't know you're here," she said. "Speak softly."

"Does your father also know?" he half-whispered.

"I wouldn't say that."

"What would you say, then?"

"I would say that he is absolutely sure that you are responsible, in the final instance."

"'In the final instance?'"

"Correct."

"You'll have to excuse me, Ollie. I have only a high school education, so I don't know what you—"

He coughed, which triggered more coughing from deep in his chest, until he was doubled over. He pulled out a filthy handkerchief patched with old blood stains and hacked into that. Ollie watched until it occurred to her to cross to the dining room and return with a napkin. He waved her away.

When the attack subsided Jim fell back against the cushions, exhausted. Ollie stared at him, unused napkin in her hand.

"You're ill," she said, obviously but not knowing how else to acknowledge him.

"Appears. I'll take that water now."

She watched him drink and saw him with new eyes. Jim had always been small, but she also knew him as powerful, as when he put his hands around her waist to help her down from the buggy and she felt his grip. He handled her easily, lifting her higher into the air for her to meet his laughing gaze as he held her helpless, thin and insubstantial like a snared kite. He could snap her in half if he wished, and in a way she was loath to face; the knowledge filled her with a vague exhilaration.

No more. Now, his shortness looked like the consequences of a long, relentless grinding process. His hand shook as he held the glass. Even his clothes belittled him as they hung from his frame.

"Are you feeling better?"

"What do you think?"

"I know you loved Nell," she said, "so would you let me show you something?"

"Show me what?"

"Come with me."

She led him upstairs. As she preceded him, the chatelaine swung from her waist, jangling against her skirt.

They came to her mother's open door. She leaned in and closed it. "Who was that coughing?" Mary Cropsey demanded through the door. Ollie didn't answer.

He followed her, a thin black figure through the twilit hall, to her bedroom. It occurred to Jim that in the years he had courted Nell, he had never made this walk to his woman's bedroom. He was mystified.

She turned. "Are you ready?"

"Go ahead."

She opened the door so he could see what was within. It was gloomy, and it took a moment for his eyes to resolve what he was looking at.

It was a sort of shrine. On either side of a low dresser were two small candles, burning. Between them was a big framed portrait of Nell, garlanded with dried flowers. It was a picture he knew well: a three-quarters view, looking to the left, in a church dress with a high lace collar, hair pulled back. It was tinted, with her cheeks rouged unnaturally and her dress as yellow as a buttercup.

He came closer. Other photos—casual portraits, and pictures of her with her sisters and her cousins—stood in their various squares and ovals. Between the pictures was a miscellany of things Nell had once owned. A pair of kid riding gloves. A Methodist hymnal. A dish of hairpins, nestled in the center of which was a lock of Nell's hair tied with red ribbon. He lifted the latter and examined it; the lock was thin, so it was not exactly the color he remembered, seeming more blonde than brown.

A brochure of the Old Dominion Steamship Line. A thimble, and a work of unfinished embroidery. Leaning against the side of the dresser, the broken parasol he had returned that night.

"I've never shown this to anyone else," said Ollie.

"It is something," he said.

His eyes fell on an unframed picture. It was from the same sitting as the big portrait, likewise tinted, with Nell looking into the camera. Looking at it, it dawned on him that he had seen it before. And then he realized he had not just seen it—he had owned it. He picked it up and turned it over. On the back was an inscription in Nell's handwriting:

To my dear Jim, from his little bluebird.

This was one of the photos Jim had returned to Nell on her last night. He looked to Ollie, holding it up.

"So you did find these."

Even by candlelight Jim could see Ollie's face go pale.

"I...yes."

"Because I sat for weeks in those courtrooms, and know for a fact you testified the pictures didn't turn up. Your father too. He said you combed the property for them."

She only looked at him, her expression somewhere between panic and hopelessness.

"Ollie?"

"Oh dear," she said.

"Ollie, I do believe you owe me an explanation. What's going on?"

"Father will be back soon."

"I don't care," he said. "He can shoot me if that's his pleasure."

She held out her hand for the picture, and in the depth of his shock, he gave it to her.

"I'm so sorry I wasn't honest with you, Jim. You have to understand, there were other things to consider..."

"You're sor—you're sorry..." he sputtered, suddenly feeling more unwell than before. Nerves aflame, head swimming, he sat down on the bed to steady himself.

"Ollie, you didn't just lie to me. You lied to the whole world. You'd better start explaining, or there's going to be hell to pay."\

She folded the picture, stuffed it in the waistband of her skirt, and said, "I don't care about the world. I'm done with all that. But you're right, Jim—I owe you an explanation, at least."

She closed the bedroom door, and turned the lock. She was, at that moment, too afraid to come any closer to him, so she leaned back against the door. Looking into space, her features were still, but her face was alive with flitting shadows from the candles. In the gloom, her widow's weeds made her hands and face seem disembodied.

Then the specter began to speak.

VI.

"I think it's about time to retire, Roy."

Ollie and Roy Crawford were left alone in the dining room after Carrie went to bed and Nell and Jim went out on the porch. Roy was in the chair at the head of the table, looking awkward as he recrossed his legs every other minute. Ollie made small-talk with him for as long as she could stomach, until the effort of extracting conversation from livestock and the weather and his mother's health exhausted her.

"Yep, reckon I might as well get along..." he declared with arduous bonhomie.

Most of the length of the porch stretched in front of the dining room windows. Ollie couldn't see her sister and Jim out there, but she could hear an indistinct murmuring. At times, the sound crested into audible speech; she thought she heard the words "care" and "don't". But she didn't want to look like she was trying to overhear.

As usual, they parted in the hall. Roy flushed and fumbled for her hand, which she surrendered. He placed a kiss on it that was more scratchy mustache than lips.

"Good night, Ollie."

"Good night, Roy."

She noticed the front door was left open. She shut it after him, not bothering to check if Nell and Jim were still outside. Then she pushed the dining room chairs back in their places, snuffed the lamps, and went upstairs.

Her sister was in the bedroom when she reached it. Nell was sitting on their bed, head in her hands.

"Nell?" Ollie said.

The other shot erect, as if surprised. Her face was red, and in her eyes, that wild look Ollie recognized from other emergencies.

"He's leaving!" she cried.

Ollie shut the door. "Lower your voice. What are you talking about?"

"Jim says he's quitting me."

"So?" she asked as she sat next to her. "Isn't that what you wanted?"

"It's what *you* wanted! Never me!"

"You're out of your mind."

"I don't know what I was saying. You twisted my head all around!"

"Nell, calm down—"

"Don't tell me to calm down! Can you imagine the cheek of it, him telling me that? He doesn't leave *me;* I leave *him*!"

"You're just upset."

"I need to go after him. I want my shoes—"

"That would be the stupidest thing you could do," Ollie said. "Running after him. You would be under his thumb forever."

"I don't care. To be humiliated like that! I need to find him—"

She tried to get up, but Ollie held her arm.

"Let go of me."

"Nellie, please. Listen to me—"

"No! Let go!" she repeated, struggling.

"Remember that we talked about this. We knew this would happen. Remember what you told me?"

Nell managed to gain her feet. She was dragging Ollie off the bed now as she tried to break Ollie's grasp.

"Ollie! Stop it!"

"Remember you told me to sit on you if I had to. You told me not to let you go back to him. You said don't let you."

"You said that, not me," said Nell.

They were both on their feet now, pulling in opposite directions. Nell tried to pry Ollie's right hand from her arm as Ollie held onto the headboard with her left. They struggled in near silence for a few moments—until Nell broke away and hurtled backwards. She just managed to turn her head as it struck the corner of the dresser.

"Nell!" cried Ollie in a screaming whisper.

Her sister collapsed to the floor. Ollie rushed to her, cradling her in her arms. There was a welt on Nell's left temple where it had struck the corner. Ollie stared into Nell's eyes as she held her: the pupils were wide open, and she did not blink.

She managed to drag Nell onto the bed. Nell began to make a sound now—a low groan from deep in her throat. Ollie seized her hand and shook it.

"Nell, wake up!"

She didn't wake up. Instead, the groan grew louder and less human. Panicking, Ollie put her hand over Nell's mouth. The sound subsided. But then Nell's extremities began to shake, her body wracked with shivers. Her limbs commenced to thrash.

Ollie threw herself on the bed to hold her down. The bed jumped, the headboard slapping against the wall. The fit went on for the time it took for the downstairs clock to strike twelve. Nell's body gradually softened, and Ollie rose off her.

"Nellie? Can you hear me?"

Nell's eyes and mouth were open, but more in the manner of holes in some inanimate thing.

"I'm going to fetch the doctor," Ollie said.

From Nell's mouth there suddenly issued a gush of white foam. Soapy effluent poured over her chin and covered the pillow under her head. Frantic now, Ollie grabbed the first thing at hand—her own night dress—and used it to sop up the mess. But the torrent kept coming, and the material was saturated. Not knowing what else to do, she seized the blanket from the foot of the bed and threw it over Nell—including her head.

On her way out, Ollie almost slipped on a photograph dropped on the floor. Ollie picked it up, turned it over, and stuffed it down the front of her shirtwaist.

Outside, from the landing, Ollie saw her father downstairs as he returned from the privy. Then, without intending to deceive, or even thinking at all, she cried,

"Papa, Nell is not here!"

Eight hours later, with the morning light searching under the blinds, she and William Cropsey stood over Nell's body. He demanded an account of what happened, and Ollie told him plainly, with no effort to excuse herself. As she spoke, even as the room brightened, his face became darker.

"So this was all about Jim Wilcox?"

"She was out of her mind. She would have run after him. Oh God, what have I done!"

And she buried her face in her hands, thinking that now, at last, she could break down. But her father wrenched her hands away.

"This has nothing to do with you. It was *him.*"

"But Jim wasn't here."

"Don't say his name! Don't ever say it in this house."

"I...I don't know..."

"That son of a whore! That slough of shit! He twisted her brains with his lies and his presents and his flattery—!"

She felt her composure slipping again and covered her mouth.

"—It doesn't matter if he was here," he went on. "He's responsible, nobody else. He'll wear a noose for this!"

He punched the headboard hard enough to propel it into the wall, where it left a crack in the plaster. After examining his fist, he gazed at Nell. He placed a hand on her arm and left it there, as if assuring himself of her stillness. As it lay there, his hand trembled.

"Cover her up. Lock your door. And keep your mouth shut," he commanded. Then he left.

The next day, the 21st, felt like three days. Caring for her mother took her mind off the truth, but it was never far out of her mind. The charade of looking for Nell brought out a talent she didn't know she had. To preserve the big lie, she was obliged to hatch other, smaller deceptions that multiplied, each demanding its own care and feeding. Whether out of fear or shame, she turned out to be a good liar, keeping her swelling flock of falsehoods all moving in the same direction. She fooled her siblings, and she fooled her mother, and she deceived the Sheriff easily, steadily, with scarcely any compunction.

Sometimes, when she had time for doubts, she wondered where she had gotten the nerve of a riverboat grifter. And at her most self-honest, she knew that she had already been lying for a very long time. There was scarcely a moment free of calculation from the moment she realized that Jim was not the proper match for Nell. She was lying to Roy Crawford when she encouraged him to come around. She and Nell lied steadily to their parents when they smoked, or stayed out late, or read the wrong books. She even lied when she didn't have to, as when her monthlies left her indisposed, and she blamed it on "fatigue".

When she retired the very first night, utterly exhausted, she saw that Nell's body had vanished. Upon seeing William Cropsey the next morning, her eyes interrogated him, but he ignored her. "That is none of your concern," his diffidence said. Perhaps he is right, Ollie thought. Imagining her in some ice cellar somewhere, some chilly temporary coffin, made her fear her mask would slip. Her mere absence, on the other hand, made lying easier.

Mere deceit was one thing, but guilt was another. To her, her crime was so obvious it could be read on her face. The way she lit the stove proclaimed her guilt, as did the ways she filled the lamps and stacked the dishes. She misbuttoned her clothes like a murderess. She left the privy door open like a murderess. She kicked dustballs into corners like a murderess. When the deliverymen had to deliver more hard ice to their house than usual, it seemed as incriminating as publishing a confession in the newspaper. She caught Uncle Hen staring at her as she fretted at the window; had her father included him in their conspiracy? She dared not ask, and he told her nothing.

For along with Nell, Ollie lost her father that November morning. There was no small talk between them anymore, but only reproving glances and shared anxiety. William Cropsey had never been a warm man. Nell's fate ignited a fury in him that could be felt across a room. The pitiful circumstances—where justice would only lead him to lose another daughter—seemed to burn any trace of common sympathy out of him. He had no patience for her mother's incapacity. He could not tolerate Ollie's questions. The only thing that gave him satisfaction, it seemed, was to see Jim Wilcox suffer.

The final line was crossed that Christmas, when her father put Nell in the river. The wait for her body to be discovered was mercifully short—only two days. When they towed her to shore, she envisioned Nell rising from the shallows to point out her killer. It put her in mind of a poem by Poe, one of the few she had memorized...

I stand amid the roar
Of a surf-tormented shore,
And I hold within my hand
Grains of the golden sand
How few! yet how they creep
Through my fingers to the deep,
While I weep- while I weep!

O God! can I not grasp
Them with a tighter clasp?
O God! can I not save
One from the pitiless wave...?

...except, it had been her grasp that had assured that last grain of golden sand had slipped away. Her life was indeed a dream within a dream, of a contrived reality she despised yet from which she could not dare wake up. It took all her strength not to visit the end of Fearing's pier some dark night, cast herself into the void, and wake up at last.

She had to be alone with Nell one more time. The night after the inquest, she rose in the middle of the night. She stole downstairs, and finding the key on its usual hook, entered the shed.

Under the light of the full moon, she could see Nell's body on the table, covered by a sheet. Trembling, bathed in a cloud of her own exhalations, she rolled down the material. Nell's head was bald, her scalp pulled down in a heap at the crown of her head. Her skin was blue, her lips like black parentheses containing nothing.

Ollie bent and kissed her mouth. When she rose, some of her cold, eel-like flesh peeled away, and stuck to Ollie's lips. She knew she should have been disgusted by this, but was not. She rolled down the sheet, locked the shed door, replaced the key, and went back to bed with that bit of Nell still stuck to her.

The trial was the climax of her betrayal. She had been doing quite well at first—better than she imagined she would when she anticipated that cruel day. But when she got to the point in her story when she was supposed to have seen Nell alive for the last time, the misery came on suddenly, like a squall whipping up under a cloudless sky. She recalled that the ancients believed the wind came from caves at the end of the world. This was exactly how her grief felt—like a force blasting out of hard, empty chambers deep within herself. When she imagined these untouched places, the more hopeless she felt. For what was left of Nell within her was still there, lost in those shadows.

She cried because she lied, and because nothing she said was untrue. She cried for what she left out, for what Mr. Ward knew never to ask. And she cried for what that other lawyer, so without pity, would soon demand of her, when his turn came.

And yet, she survived this ordeal not once, but twice. She sinned against truth with impunity, but no thunderbolt came down on her head. No trap doors opened. Instead, she was admired for telling the story everyone in that mob had come to hear.

"The court recognizes how difficult this must be," the judge said. "Does the witness wish for a brief recess?"

"I will go on," she said, and went on playing her role, until there was nothing left of her faith. Questions posed and processes proceeded, and the cakewalk of sophistry. It occurred to her that none of the clocks in the courthouse agreed with each other. She would never marry, because she would never bring a child into a world where someone like herself was possible.

VII.

When Ollie was finished with her story, Jim was silent. The significance of what he had heard, its enormity, eluded his grasp. Every memory he had for the last twenty years was altered in light of it. Every choice had to be revisited. The task so daunted him that he preferred to believe none of it.

"No. It can't be. What can I have done to you, that you could do that to a man?"

"I'm afraid it is," she replied. "And you did nothing."

He looked at his hands. As he regarded the creases there, the scars of all the lost years, he felt his nerve cracking. He leaned over, face in hands, and suddenly, all at once, shed the tears he had long refused to show. He wept with relief, and outrage, and pity for his poor mother, who died far from him and would never know of his innocence. And he shed tears for poor Nell, whom he had lost so long ago and never truly mourned.

Ollie watched and could do nothing. She had no standing to comfort him. Instead, it occurred to her that Jim looked very much like Nell, head in hands, on that very bed, that night when Ollie found her in their room.

He dried his face with his hands and rose.

"Hand over that picture."

She didn't move.

He put his hands around her throat. He had wasted over the years, but the occasion brought back some of his old strength. He closed her windpipe, and met her eyes as she stared back, unresisting. Both of their faces turned red. Ollie, feeling an animal urge to fight him, clutched the doorframe behind her instead.

His rage withered in the face of her passivity. He let her go.

"You'd just like that, wouldn't you?" he said.

"It's what's coming to me."

He reached into her waistband and retrieved the picture.

"What's coming to you," he said, "is what you're in now."

He went direct from the Cropsey house to the nearest bar. Putting up a five dollar bill—half the money he had in the world—he told the man to keep the whiskey coming until it was gone.

On his third shot he took out Nell's picture, laid it on the bar, and looked at it. Was finding it good news or bad news? He was, of course, exonerated. But the years the Cropsey's lies had cost him were gone—and he always knew he was innocent. Proper vindication belonged in the eyes of the public, not his own. Yet how was he to proceed?

"That your girl?" asked the barkeep—one of the few in town who didn't know him.

"Yeah. Once."

Jim eyed him for a second. Then he simply told the man everything—his courtship of Nell, his last night with her, his indictment and trial, his incarceration, his pardon, and what he learned that very day. The barkeep's eyes became wider with every turn of the story, until Jim came to the end and he shook his head as if to say "don't that beat all?"

"I've heard my share of sob stories in my time, fella, but yours takes the cake." And he stood him an extra drink for this honor.

"Thank you kindly," Jim said. "But what do you think I should do about it?"

"How about gettin' some iron and airing out the father's guts?"

"The thought has crossed my mind. But I was thinking of something that doesn't involve murder."

"Well, you had a lawyer, didn't you? Why not ask him?"

And Jim thought, why not indeed? The next day, after a good sleep in a run-in shed by the tracks, Jim dusted himself off and went into town. His father had hired Ed Aydlett before, so Jim was not sure how to approach him now. He decided to try a direct tack, showing up at the lawyer's office on Main St.

"Do you have an appointment?" asked the young man at the desk.

"No. But he knows me."

The clerk's nostrils flared at the horse-stall stench of him. "He knows a lot of people. Would you like to leave a message?"

"Can I just talk to him for a minute? He'll want to hear what I have to tell him."

"I'm sorry, no."

"I was a client of his."

"He has a lot of former clients."

"I don't think you understand—"

"I understand completely."

"Just tell him Jim Wilcox is here. I only need two minutes of his time."

"I've already told you—he doesn't see just anyone off the street."

"I'm not just anyone, you fool!"

The other picked up the telephone. "I'm calling the police if you don't leave."

"Damn it, why can't you just shut your yap and listen...?"

The clerk started dialing. Then the door behind him opened, and Ed Aydlett stuck his head out.

"What's going on out here?"

"This man insists on seeing you without an appointment."

It took a moment for Aydlett to recognize the older, thinner figure in his shabby clothes.

"Jim," he said.

"I keep telling this nincompoop you'll see me, and he keeps telling me different..."

The lawyer came out from behind the door. He had long before entered his portly years, with his glasses perched atop his long, bald forehead. The glasses themselves looked the same.

"Of course I'll see you. But I'm on long-distance to Raleigh right now. Please make an appointment for tomorrow. okay?"

"I suppose."

The clerk opened his book. "Would eleven o'clock fit your schedule?"

The next morning Jim sat in a high-backed chair of red leather. He had fortified himself earlier with a couple of beers—just therapeutic enough to take off the morning edge. Aydlett, meanwhile, was slouched behind his desk, the photograph of Nell perched on his belly. As the sun poured and street sounds filtered up through the window, he stared at this face from his past with what seemed like pleasant distraction.

"She was certainly a handsome girl."

"Yes, she was."

Aydlett flipped the picture and read the inscription. His nostalgia evaporated.

"You should know I don't do this kind of work much anymore. Too many years of it."

"I might say the same," replied Jim.

"And you got this straight from Miss Ollie?"

"More or less."

"And how is she? She's not seen around much these days."

"A damn sight better than her sister."

Aydlett made an appraising glance at Jim, then laid the picture on his desk.

"Well, Jim, this sure is something. And remarkable that Ollie would tell you that story. In all honesty, I can't say I'm surprised. What do you imagine doing now?"

"I want my name cleared. And I want a lot of money."

The lawyer laced his fingers over his vest and focused on empty space.

"Well, taking the latter first—how much money do you think you could get out of the Cropseys? The father sells turnips door-to-door."

"They have a house."

"I am entirely certain the bank owns the house. And do you really want to throw a family into the street? From what you tell me, Mary Cropsey had nothing to do with it."

"What about the Brooklyn side of the family?"

"They also had nothing to do with it. They have connections in the legal world there, going way back. As your lawyer, I would be obliged to tell you your chances of success there are thin. Beanpole thin."

They sat as Jim glowered and Aydlett checked his watch.

"What about getting the conviction thrown out?"

"It was already thrown out. You were pardoned by the Governor."

"Yes," replied Jim, impatient. "But I should never have been sent up in the first place."

"You know I agree with you. I'm just not sure it is realistic to expect anything more."

"That sounds like a load of hooey."

Aydlett picked up the photo. "I'm sorry Jim, but this picture proves nothing. Any lawyer would simply argue that it was in your possession the whole time. That you took it with you the night of. When it comes down to it, it's still your word against the Cropseys'. We've already been down that road—twice."

Jim might have insisted that Ollie would testify to the truth. The words refused to come, because he could not swear to know for certain what Ollie would do. He once thought he knew her, but she was an enigma to him now.

"So tell me, counsellor: where do I go to get my twenty years back?"

As the clock ticked and the traffic signal chimed on the intersection below, Aydlett looked at him. There was affliction in his eyes.

"I hate to be the bearer of bad news. But you at least take some satisfaction in hearing the truth at last, direct from the source. Yes?"

"Yeah, I guess," said Jim. He leaned back, broke into a crooked smile. "It might have been better if I'd kept my date with that gooseberry bush."

The lawyer slid the photo back across the desk.

"So tell me, how are you keeping body and soul together these days?"

"Oh, a little of this, a little of that."

"You fixed for a place to stay...?"

"I'm getting along."

"...'cause there's a former client of mine who might have some space for you to set up, long-term. He runs a garage on the south side. I told him you were good with your hands, so there might be work too. Can I introduce you?"

Jim took the picture and stuffed it in his shirt.

"That's awful nice of you, Ed. Sure, a nice warm garage sounds good."

Aydlett's client was John Tuttle, proprietor of the repair shop on South Road Street. He was a pious, round-faced fellow whose heart was as spotless as his fingernails were permanently black with grease. For reasons he could not fathom, Tuttle concerned himself immediately with Jim's welfare. He wasn't interested in the details of his story; when Jim tried to account for his innocence, Tuttle waved him away.

Within a half hour of knowing him, Tuttle invited him to his house to meet his wife and three children. Over cow's tongue and cabbage—but no wine or liquor of any kind—they joined hands for the benediction. After the meal, they sang hymns and shared Bible verses. When it came around to Jim's turn, he shook his head.

"Sorry to say I don't have a favorite."

"That's all right," said Tuttle's wife Evelyn. "Let us all join hands and pray for our guest." And Jim had to sit through two solid minutes of silence in his honor. In that time his primary thought was when and where he would get his next drink.

Jim could not help but be touched by this hospitality. Yet he was also irritated by it. Tuttle was another in a line of benefactors, from Hank Peoples to Jerry Flora, whose largesse he had repaid by letting them down, time and again.

His quarters were in the back of the garage, set off by a plywood partition. There was a narrow bed, and a board stretched between two sawhorses, and a framed picture of a lion and a lamb lying together, cut out of a magazine. The room was windowless. Evelyn provided fresh linens and a blanket every Monday, but there was the persistent smell of rubber and oil from beyond the partition. The shop opened early, so he was often awakened by the sounds of car doors slamming and steel tools hitting the shop floor.

Jim made his drinking money by doing odd tasks for Tuttle. Out of respect, he tried to make this, his main preoccupation, unobtrusive. When he came back to the garage from the saloon, he straightened his posture, and made the slops on his back as neat as possible.

But as Tuttle rolled out from under a car and looked at him, anointed with God's grease, that look of sufferance on his face, Jim could see he knew what he had been up to. He knew, and Jim resented him for his knowledge. But most of all, Jim despised himself for his weakness.

When he could take this guilt no longer, he would wander over to Baxter Street to see his sister. When the kids were at school and Sam Sr. was working, Annie Mae would invite him to sit in the kitchen as she went about her housekeeping. If he stank of alcohol, or things worse, she put on a pot of boiling water with a stick of vanilla. When late afternoon rolled around, she became uncomfortable, as if worried he would still be there when the rest of the family came home. He took the hint.

The time came when his thoughts and regrets were so oppressive he drank up his last penny. He remembered that Annie Mae kept a store of drinkables in the sideboard. When she was outside with the washing, he sneaked to the dining room and examined this trove. There was a bottle of whiskey, and rye, and bourbon, and some fancy fruit liqueur whose name he couldn't pronounce. The whiskey and rye were at about the same level, so he guzzled about a third of both, then added water. He arranged the bottles exactly the way he found them. But she was too long getting back, so Jim went back and sampled the fruit stuff. It was raspberry-flavored and sickly sweet and made him queasy.

Annie Mae returned, calling his name. Jim replaced the bottle, but in his haste he forgot to shut it. He left the cork on the sideboard.

The next time he came over his brother-in-law was there.

"Hello, Sam!" said Jim, content and properly inebriated at ten in the morning.

"Good morning Jim. Can I help you?"

"You surely could, if you would inform my sister I am here."

"I will not."

"I'm sorry...what?"

"I'm telling you not to come back here. We don't host thieves."

"Thieves!" cried Jim. Of all the unjust accusations, he was used to 'murderer', but not 'thief.'

"You stole from this house. I found the cork. Do you deny it?"

Jim just stood there, dumbfounded. In fact, he wasn't sure he left the bottle open or not. He was a damn fool if he did so.

"I said, do you deny it?" Sam repeated.

Behind him, from the dark inside the house, Jim could hear Annie Mae weeping.

"I don't know," said Jim.

"Well, I do. Don't darken our door again. Don't bring your corruption around our children. Do you understand?"

"Sam."

"'Cause if you do, I won't answer for the consequences. Now get the hell off my porch."

He shut the door. Jim stood for a moment, confused.

"*But I didn't kill her,*" he muttered. "*I can prove it.*"

He took Nell's picture out of his shirt. It was creased now, and stained with his sweat. He smoothed it and pressed it against the screen.

"Here she is. You can see her," he said.

But no one came to the door. He looked at the photo again, admiring the blue of Nell's eyes. Were her eyes really that blue, like raspberry liqueur? She was so lovely, staring straight out at him with dimpled mouth and those eyes that were two. He stuffed the picture back in his shirt—an act that almost cost him his balance. He stood up erect and lurched off the porch. All the unpleasantness had cost him his precious stupor, and it needed tending.

He woke up the next day and remembered every detail. Loathing surged through him like an electric charge; he felt so low that he covered his head with his pillow, and didn't get out of bed until noon.

That was when he made his decision: from that day forward, he would not touch a drop of alcohol.

In the shop, Tuttle and his employee Gene Betts were hoisting an engine. Jim grabbed the chain without needing an invitation, and in his new resolution to clean up his life, found some of his old strength.

"Thank you," said Tuttle.

"I'm a new man as of today, Johnny. I'm off the sauce!"

"Well, that's great, Jim."

"Yeah, have one on me to celebrate..." said Betts.

To which Jim offered him the finger.

If Jim expected sobriety to make him feel better, he was soon disappointed. That very morning, he was afflicted with a severe headache that was only sharpened by his new clarity of mind. Colors, sounds, voices—all of them seemed a bit too loud. His damnable coughing was like hammer-blows to his temple.

Water didn't help, nor did black coffee. He was tempted to have a shot just to take the edge off, so he would have the strength to continue the struggle. But he knew this would be a mistake.

He took a day job spreading gravel along a railroad embankment. After an hour working in the sun, his head swam, and the shovel seemed as heavy as a keel. He sat. He was down for only a few moments when the foreman yelled at him,

"You! Get to work or take a walk!"

Jim, his skull splitting, flung the shovel to the ground.

"Guess I'll walk then!"

He marched away, dignity intact. But he only got fifty yards until he remembered his pockets were light.

"Hey there!" he called the foreman. "Can I get paid for the hour?"

On this way to nowhere, he drifted past a graveyard. He wandered inside and walked among the headstones. Flowers wilted on the recent graves, while others were so neglected that they were unreadable with coal soot. Trash from family picnics was scattered on the grass. He had always been more partial to adventure stories than romances, but he was not immune to the sentimentality of his times; he thought it might befit his state of mind to have a nap on one of the plots.

He stretched out on one with healthy grass and a clean headstone to a woman — "Eugenia Cobb, who went to the Lord in her twenty-fifth year, 1879." His rolled-up jacket made a decent pillow, and the sun was warm enough to keep him comfortable for a good snooze. He was out for some time—he wasn't sure how long—when he felt someone poking at him.

When he opened his eyes there was an old man standing there. He was leaning against a rake, staring down at Jim from under a hat so wide his broad, white mustache was the only feature visible beyond its brim.

"We like to keep visitors off the graves," the caretaker said.

"Oh, I'm sorry," said Jim, sitting up.

"It's all right. I don't think Miss Eugenia minds. Closest she's been to a man in years."

Then he pulled a flask out of his vest, tilted himself a swallow, and held it out. Jim looked at it for a moment, knowing full well that he should decline. But the man's kindness seemed to demand an agreeable response. Indeed, his head pounded so much, and he was only a mortal, and wasn't there always time to quit later?

Jim obliged.

And in that one irresolute moment, he was back on the sauce.

"How much will you give me for cleaning up all this trash?"

The caretaker looked around. "I don't know. Two bits?"

"Deal," said Jim, and creaked to his feet.

When he came back to the garage that evening he could barely walk a straight line.

"Hello there, fellows!" he saluted Tuttle and Gene Betts, who were working on the engine they had pulled that morning. Looking up at Jim, the latter smiled and shook his head. Tuttle, for his part, gazed on him with his usual resignation, and went back to work.

Something about that look rubbed Jim the wrong way.

"God damn you, John Tuttle," he said. "Your shit stinks, like everybody else."

Tuttle raised an eyebrow. "That's right, Jim. It does."

"Your Bible won't keep nobody out of Hell."

"Few of us are worthy."

"Well, see that you remember that," snarled Jim, and slammed his plywood door after him.

It was all Jim could do the next month to keep his routine: rise in the morning, scare up some work somewhere, drink until he forgot his name, wake up in an alley or under a bridge, stagger back to the shop, and sleep the dreamless sleep of the dead. If he still had headaches, he didn't feel them anymore. If his coughing was worse, he had the comfort of knowing it would not kill him first.

There was still the issue of money. On this score, his capacity for thought was scarcely impaired. He remembered hearing, during some round of barroom scuttlebutt, of a reporter in town who wasn't afraid to open his wallet for a good story. His name was Saunders, and he ran a newspaper called *The Independent* over on Fearing Street.

"He's a regular shatterpate," said Gene Betts. "I never agree with him, but—"

"...his rag is good for spreading under leaky cranks," injected Tuttle, who disliked the paper's attacks on certain evangelists.

Later, when they were alone, Jim made Betts a proposition: if he helped arrange a meeting between him and Saunders, he would pay Betts a commission of five dollars.

"What do you want to see him for?" asked the other.

"I think you know."

"Where's the five dollars?"

"The other guy has it."

Betts regarded him, appraising. Then he smiled.

"All right. Gimme the particulars."

Jim told him that he would meet the journalist at 3 p.m. the day after next, at R.C. Abbot's over on the waterfront. From there they would go by boat to some secluded spot on the river to talk. As he listened and nodded, Betts kept such a cheerfully dubious expression on his face that Jim wanted to punch it.

The next day Gene stuck his head into Jim's room: Saunders had agreed to Jim's terms.

"Did he give you the fiver?"

Betts plucked the bill out of his breast pocket and waved it. With that, he proved he was the only person directly to profit from Jim's misfortune.

When the time came to meet, Jim was sitting in a bar on Front Street, drinking cheap beer because he didn't have the money for anything stronger. The longer he sat, the more the skunkish swill sank him in a peevish kind of funk. For what did he have to sell the journalist, really? Everybody already knew Jim denied his guilt. As Aydlett had said, the photo proved nothing other than the Cropseys had lied about missing it.

And he thought: there's only one thing people will pay to hear. They want me to tell them I'm guilty. They want me to tell them I was against her going to New York, because I was afraid to lose her, and that I lost my temper on the porch that night, and knocked my sweet Nell in the head like I was slaughtering some animal, and dragged her body to the river and dumped it. And then that I was such a brute that I did all that, and had a pleasant confab with Len Owens, and then went home to kiss my mother's face, and go upstairs for a pleasant sleep. Because it was not accidents they wanted to hear about, or the regular kinds of misunderstandings that happened between people. It was horror they wanted to hear, and the face of evil they found most comforting.

In this way he managed to keep his seat until well after three, at which point he thought there was no use in going over and ordered another round.

When he staggered back to the garage Gene Betts was there to greet him.

"Why didn't you show at Abbot's? That reporter came here looking for you."

"He came here?"

"He says he covered your trial, way back when."

"Did he," said Jim, and steadied himself against a fender.

"Let me know if you want to set him up again. Only this time the commission is ten bucks. And you gotta pay up front."

"Aye aye."

His windowless room made it hard for him to judge the time when he woke up in the morning. More often he could hazard a guess by the sound of the work going on in the shop. When he came to the next morning, deplorably sober, he remembered he had lost his nerve with Saunders, and felt lower than an insect. No matter what he tried, it seemed he was destined to fail. "Pointless," he muttered, and got up to splash his face. He looked at himself in the little mirror Evelyn Tuttle had set up over the basin. "Pointless," he said again.

He shuffled over to take a pointless little piss in the garage's bathroom. While he was in there, he heard Tuttle calling him.

"Jim! You got a visitor!"

It had to be Saunders coming for him. The prospect was suddenly so terrifying he closed his pants too soon, wetting himself.

"Jim!" cried Tuttle as he rapped on his door.

The bathroom had a window. The glass opened only partway, forcing him to squeeze through a space as wide as his forearm was long. When he finally came free, he tumbled and jammed his shoulder against the ground. Yet he was up in a flash, and running from the garage with the front of his pants soaked, cradling his left arm.

Jim figured that in case the journalist waited for him, he should make himself scarce. He kept away all day and the whole of the following night. He woke up in a gutter on the west side of town, his cheek in a puddle of vomit. Jerking himself up, he was convulsed by a pain, intense enough to bring tears to his eyes, that shot from his left shoulder,. He had not just jammed that shoulder, but dislocated it.

Tuttle and Betts were next door when he got back to the shop. The door to the office was left ajar. Jim knew Tuttle sometimes kept a little bottle of brandy or schnapps in his top desk drawer, so he went in for a little fortification against the pain.

The infernal Tuttle, alas, had removed the stuff. But then Jim noticed the 12-gauge double-barreled duck gun on the rack behind the desk. He took it down and checked if it was loaded. It was not—but a box of shells, labeled 'No. 6', were sitting pretty-as-you-please in the top right drawer.

Tuttle and Betts were back when Jim came out with the shotgun.

"Whoa there, fella," said Betts.

"Watch me! I'm going to kill myself!" cried Jim.

Tuttle, with no hesitation, approached Jim with his hand out.

"Give me that."

Jim reversed the gun and held it under his chin. Then he jerked the barrel away from his head and fired. The shot—just one barrel—made a tight scatter of holes in the ceiling.

Tuttle wrested the gun out of Jim's hands lest he pull the other trigger. Jim shrank in agony as his dislocated shoulder was shoved in the struggle.

"Looks like he's hurt," said Betts.

They got Jim to lie down on his bed while the doctor was summoned. As he lay there he said nothing. Instead, he stared with animal hostility at everyone who came near him. If someone had asked him, and he had the inclination to answer, Jim would have said that he had passed the point of no return sometime that day. That point had come without him realizing it, but the conviction was no weaker for sneaking up on him.

Tuttle and Betts got back to work as the doctor tended to Jim.

"He wasn't serious," said the former. "He just needed help."

There was a muffled cry as Jim's arm was popped back into its socket. The mechanics ignored it.

When the doctor came out, Tuttle had four greasy dollar bills for him.

"Not necessary," the doctor held up his hand. "That didn't take long."

"Thank you."

"Your friend is in a bad way. He belongs in a sanitarium just for that cough."

Tuttle winced, and could only repeat, "Thank you."

"He's got a head for drama," he told Betts when the doctor was gone.

Despite his certainty that Jim lacked the courage for successful suicide, Tuttle shared the news of his attempt with his wife. Evelyn shook her head, "That poor dear. He was just in pain from that shoulder."

"I'll have to lock my office from now on," said Tuttle, in a tone that hinted nothing could be worse.

"We should take up a collection to get that poor soul to a sanitarium."

"Some time in the mountains might help."

Evelyn Tuttle did not make idle declarations. The next day, she sent notes to all her friends, asking them to suggest a good institution for Jim. She also phoned her minister to add his name to the list of unfortunates for whom extra prayers would be said that Sunday. She considered giving Jim the news about this coming bounty, but decided she better raise the money before getting his hopes up. For the moment, she would put on her hat and go to the market, with a mind to consoling him with a fresh-baked blackberry pie.

The next day, Jim's shoulder was still too sore for him to take any work. Instead, he drifted over to Annie Mae's house. He didn't knock on the door, but just stood outside on the street, wondering what was going on inside. Once he saw the parlor curtains sway, but only slightly, as if stirred by a puff of wind.

He opened the mailbox. Taking out his pen-knife, he wrapped it in his best remaining kerchief, and put them in there. Neither gift amounted to much. It just pleased him to believe his nephews would find them, and give them some use in the future.

As he made his way back to the shop, he passed two bars that were open at 11AM. Oddly, he felt no inclination to go in. It wouldn't have mattered if he did: he had no money, and no credit left in either place.

Back at the garage, he retreated to his bed and slept an indeterminate number of hours. When he woke, something about the quality of the shadows told him it was late afternoon. A feeble voice inside him told him to get up and make some use of what was left of the day. He wondered, simply for the sake of argument with himself, whether there was any purpose in him getting up. He could not think of a single one.

Next he opened his eyes, it was dark. He got up and looked out the door. The garage was shut for the night, Tuttle's tools put back in their places. He went to the bench and found a flat-head screwdriver. Testing the door to the office, it was, as he expected, locked. He stuck the head of the screwdriver into the jamb. The wood was soft, chunks of it coming out easily. The strike plate came loose, and the door clicked open.

The duck gun was in the same place, but the shells were no longer in the right-hand drawer. He searched for them, eliminating each possible place until he found them, hidden in the back of the bottom file drawer. He loaded the shotgun by the feeble light of the waning moon.

He went back to his room. Shutting the door, he climbed into bed with the gun. He lay there for some time, feeling the cool metal against his arm, suddenly in no particular hurry. Just having the means, so close at hand, was comforting. The sensation reminded him of the last time he hunted in the Dismal: it was a Saturday morning in October, '00. He remembered thinking it was unusually cold. Tassels of mist twisted off the water as the sun lingered behind the trees, and no matter how much he blew his call, the ducks would not be roused. He sat in his blind, contented, and thought that he would see Nell that evening and gift the family with a brace of birds, to which they would express delight and remark upon his prowess and ask him to dinner the next evening. Nell—as was her wont—would not overplay her satisfaction, but would look on him with smiling, half-lidded eyes. He would seem indifferent, as if his skill was a matter of course, but that look would warm him, and made him want to please her every day of her life. And in the sweet penumbra of that memory, he drifted off to sleep.

Gene Betts arrived at 8:30 the next morning. He had just gotten the garage door open when he heard Jim calling for him to "Come and see". Betts did not rush to respond. Jim called again, saying "Gene, you're gonna want to see this!"

Betts came. Opening the door, he saw Jim sitting on his bed with the shotgun propped under his chin.

"So, you still think I'm kidding?" he asked, a sneer on his face.

"If you're gonna use that," Betts replied, "then use it. I got work to do."

The bell sounded as a customer pulled into the garage. Betts went over to greet Mr. A.R. Luton, who rolled in with his head stuck out the window of his Plymouth.

"Hey there, Archie."

"Morning Gene. Got a few minutes to look after a leak?"

"Right now, got nothin' but time."

The two men stood looking at the front driver's side tire.

"May be a nail. Or a piece of glass."

"The roads around here really are in a state."

"Our tax dollars at work..." said Betts, setting the jack.

Both men jumped at the sound of a shotgun going off.

Luton mopped his forehead with his kerchief. “Somebody in your back yard?” he asked.

“It’s just Jim Wilcox shooting up the roof again,” said Betts as he commenced to raise the car.

As there was no obvious puncture in the tire, Betts dunked it in a pickle barrel full of water. Sure enough, a train of bubbles issued from a tight slit within one of the treads.

“Not a nail. Maybe glass or a sliver of metal...”

John Tuttle came in as the town clock struck nine. It had been fifteen minutes since they heard the shotgun blast. He joined Luton, bent over to watch Betts patch the tube.

“Nail?” asked Tuttle.

“I don’t think so,” replied Betts.

Tuttle nodded and went off to unlock his office. He passed Jim’s room on the way, but didn’t look inside.

He found his office door half-open. The screwdriver still on the floor, and there was a crunching sound as he stepped on fragments of wood.

“Oh for the love of Pete,” Tuttle exclaimed. And then, calling out: “Gene, did you see this?”

“See what?”

Checking within, there at first seemed to be nothing missing. Then he remembered the shotgun. Suddenly, he was filled with a deep, inexplicable dread.

Tuttle went to Jim’s room. The door was ajar, as Betts had left it. He pushed it open, and was stunned by what he saw.

Jim’s body was on the bed, the gun lying by his side. Half of his head was disassembled and decorating the wall, tracing lines of blood downward as they slid.

Head swimming, Tuttle fell back, only narrowly catching his balance as he brushed against a stack of motor oil cans. These crashed to the floor. Gene Betts noticed one of the cans roll across the concrete, into the shop.

"For God's sake, Jim..." he heard Tuttle moan.

Betts joined Tuttle at the door. Looking within, he felt his innards recoil. He was sickened, but also couldn't look away: Jim Wilcox's finger was still on the shotgun's second trigger, which had not been pulled. Pieces of his shattered skull littered a whole side of the room, but everything below his neck was free of blood. And on the half of his face that remained, he still wore the sneer that had challenged Betts in his last moments:

"So, do you still think I'm kidding?"

Word of Jim's fate spread quickly. By the time the Sheriff arrived, he had to cope with a throng of onlookers, each pushing to get a glimpse. Among them was W.O. Saunders, who grabbed his camera and rushed over the instant he got the news. Upon gaining entry to the scene, though, he took no photographs. Witnesses recalled seeing a thin, suited man in wire glasses behind the garage that morning, vomiting.

In his account that week in *The Independent*, Saunders described Jim as "the most tragic figure in Elizabeth City, destitute, sick, despondent and growing old [who took] leave of a wretched life in spectacular manner, protesting innocence of his sweetheart's murder to the end."

They found pieces of Jim's shattered cranium all over that room, gathering them in a milk box for the burial. These went into the ground on December 5, in Jim's solitary plot in Hollywood Cemetery. One unaccountably large piece, however, was found by Evelyn Tuttle weeks later, gathering dust in a corner. She refused to touch the thing. Instead, Gene Betts fetched it, tied it with twine, and hung it from the rafters of Tuttle's Garage.

There it remained for years, like some saintly relic suspended in the nave of a cathedral. It twisted there long after Tuttle sold the business, and memories of the Cropsey case faded. When he was asked about the strange bone twenty years later, the garage's owner shrugged, and said it was a piece of 'some murderer.'

Jim's last mortal remains found their final rest when the garage was demolished. The bone fell in among the rafters and roof slats and assorted debris, collected by backhoe and dumped. The pile was soon covered with weeds, indistinguishable from all the other mounds of detritus on the edge of town.

VIII.

The last time Ollie's father got sick, none of the rest of the family was able to see him. Almost the entire Cropsey clan had moved away from Elizabeth City—some farther west in North Carolina, most back north. William Cropsey was eighty-five by then, and frequently fatigued or in pain. The doctor used words like "interstitial nephilitis" and "arterioschlerosis", the gist of which seemed to mean "chronically indisposed". When the end came, only Ollie was at home, and her mother.

By this time Ollie had accepted her role as family helpmeet. For her, the status of wife and mother would remain forever unrealized. She had abjured them, pushed them away with both hands, as she had any of the less conventional roles outside the home. Her main occupations now were simply to make the house function—to see the bills paid and the groceries delivered—and to ruminate over the past. She became practiced at reliving her yesterdays in ever more precise detail. She was sometimes heard arguing with people who had been dead for years, demanding they explain what they had meant by some remark, or addressing questions whose answers had long since ceased to matter. Her brothers and sisters ignored these eccentricities. Ollie suffered from nerves, they said; different folks dealt with loss in their own ways. Inwardly they were merely thankful she cared for their parents, and left them free to live their own lives.

Ollie brought up a bowl of clear broth to her father, who sat up in bed because it made the pain endurable. He watched her eyes as she spooned the broth between his lips, not swallowing but passively letting the liquid process down his throat. She tended to him silently, as a matter of obligation; no words interrupted the rhythmic *scrape, tap, scrape* of the spoon against the bowl, and the ponderous tick of the grandfather on the landing.

She discharged this duty until he twisted his face to refuse the spoon, and with trembling resolve lifted his right hand to take her's. Ollie was surprised. She allowed him to hold her, shaking the broth onto the bedsheets, until she gently removed his hand and laid it at his side.

"Look here, we've made a mess."

"Ollie," he said, and lapsed.

"I'm going to have to change these sheets again."

"Ollie, what could I do?"

She wrung a cloth from the washbasin and dabbed at the stains. "What do you mean?" she asked.

"Ollie, what could I do? Let you go too? What could I do? What could I do? What could I have done?"

She stared into his eyes, gauging if he was in any condition to hear an answer.

"Don't fret about it. There's nothing you need say to me."

She would have left it at that. But something in her—something with a pretension to truth but more likely just malice—compelled her to add, "I'm not the one you should be speaking to. That one is gone."

He turned his head away and entreated the curtains, "What could I have done?"

"Hush now," she said. "It's almost over."

William Cropsey died in one of the few moments when Ollie was out of the room. That always struck her funny, his timing. People said the dying would wait until they were alone to slip away, to spare their loved ones the pain of watching their passage. She was not used to thinking of her father as considerate in that way. "Better late than never," she thought, and shut his eyes against the dawn light. She supposed that, in his way, he had always wanted to spare her.

It was her idea to bury him in Hollywood Cemetery, not far from where Jim Wilcox lay. She picked out a solitary plot for him, well away from any other Cropseys. He got a small headstone, no bigger than a footstool, that lay close to the ground, with no prayers or affiliations chiseled into it. It was the memorial he deserved.

She didn't make this decision out of any resentment—or at least none that she ascribed to him alone. When her time came, Ollie would be buried under exactly the same kind of stone. The three of them, Jim, William Cropsey, and she, would be forever united in the same ground, under the same terms. And nowhere near Nell.

IX.

In the fall of 1900, Nell and Carrie spent a Sunday afternoon at Coney Island. As the sun poured down through the leafy byways of southern Brooklyn, the girls walked to the station to catch the trolley. On the way they passed their school, Bath Beach No. 1, and showed their high spirits by jeering it together. Then they linked hands and skipped and sang like girls half their age, because Nell had always been more comfortable with her cousin than with Ollie, who loomed over her and adopted the superiority of the elder sister. They wore straw boaters for the occasion, with black felt bands that hung down among the curls of their hair, and comfortable shoes and knock-about dresses they didn't mind rolling around in. An afternoon at the amusements meant they would be spending much time off their feet.

"I've got a mind to enroll in fashion classes, no matter what *he* says," proclaimed Nell. "I'm made of more determined stuff than you!"

"Determined but still obedient!" Carrie replied, giving her cousin a light shove. "Daddy's little girl..."

"If I was 'Daddy's little girl' would I still be seeing Jim?"

"Maybe you shouldn't. There are some of those Brooklyn boys."

"*Swells*, you mean."

"Oh, pshaw! Not all of them."

"Oh really? Such as?"

Carrie smiled. "You can try, but I'll never say!"

They went on like this as they boarded the trolley, and were whisked away by electric traction. Settlement was left behind, the tracks leading among fields, and pastures, and farmhouses connected to trees by lines of fluttering laundry. With each stop, more passengers got on, many as high-spirited as Nell and Carrie. On this day of the week, at this time of the day, all of them were headed to the same place.

The towers of Steeplechase Park were soon visible above the trees. First, the Revolving Airship Tower, girdered and flagged like the younger brother of that more famous structure in Paris. Then the Ferris wheel, metal rim glinting in the sun, square cars rising and falling in their orbits. Whether or not the passengers had been to the Park before, they gaped from the windows, anticipation mounting. Nell and Carrie shared it, grasping each other's hands. And with the excitement, their first whiff of ocean breeze.

There was a byway in Brooklyn named after their family: Cropsey Avenue. As her Uncle Andrew never tired of explaining, the Cropseys were among the oldest Dutch families in New Utrecht, active both in the fight for independence and the building of its first landmarks. But to Nell and the other youths of the family, Cropsey Avenue was significant only for leading to the Coney Island amusements. This far from settled parts, the thoroughfare was a mere country lane. The trolley, elevated on its line of rickety pilings, followed "their" avenue, until they were mere minutes away from what —on warm summer days—was one of the most bustling places in the city.

"Do you know who had a hand in building the first hotel on Coney Island?" her uncle once asked her.

"I'm sure you will tell me," she replied.

"It was none other than James W. Cropsey, your great-granduncle on your father's side. So you see, our family started that too."

When the car stopped, the brakeman announced "Bridge Station!", and every passenger got off. From there the girls followed the throng across Neptune Avenue. Children in knee britches and sun hats ascended adult shoulders. Wheeled traffic was backed up for blocks as the surge of pedestrians crossed the street, horses stamping as their drivers glowered. The odors of popcorn and horse piss and creosote rose, as did the cries of sidewalk touts selling peanuts and roasted meats. It was always the same, and the sense of familiarity tempered the butterflies in Nell's stomach.

"You ladies on your way to Steeplechase?" a voice asked.

Turning, the girls found a young man walking just behind them. He was dressed in a three-piece brown and white seersucker suit, spatted shoes, straw hat, and an elegant ebony cane with ivory handle. The perfect outfit for an afternoon sipping Tom Collinses at Saratoga. In the brief moment she spared to inspect the dude, Nell found his face—clean-shaven, with dark, prominent eyebrows—not unhandsome. She shot Carrie a sidelong glance as they walked.

"We are going where everyone else is going," Carrie said.

"If I might be so forward," he replied, "I am well known to the management, and can get two pretty girls like yourselves through the gates for free."

"My, is he forward!"

"Where is your courtesy, dear cousin?" said Nell, who slowed to let the man walk beside them. The dandy took the opportunity to doff his hat.

"Charles Whittier, at your service. And your names, my lovelies?"

"Do you always accost young women in the street, Mr. Charles?"

He smiled. "Only at the most alluring provocation. But you should know that a male companion has his uses here. There are rough characters about, even inside the Park."

"And what do you expect for this chivalry?" Carrie asked.

"Nothing but what a proper young woman might extend a man like myself. Her company and her friendship. A companionable moment in a vast, impersonal city."

Nell looked at Carrie again, with an expression that her cousin knew well. Carrie, alarmed, shook her head, lips silently forming the word "No!". But Nell would not be deterred. Since her family's move to North Carolina, she had stopped seeing visits to Brooklyn as homecomings, and more as liberations. There were never crowds like this in Elizabeth City, never this sort of anonymity. And the dandy's brows were so fetchingly arched.

"My name is Evelyn," said Nell. "And this is my cousin, Carol."

Charles Whittier smiled.

The line at the ticket booth ran a hundred yards down the boardwalk. As the Cropsey girls and their new friend waited, he regaled them with stories from his time in Cuba, when he fought Spanish troops at Santiago. "The experience marks me still," he said, and unbuttoned his left cuff to reveal a long, deep scar across the back of his wrist. The girls stared; Carrie whistled. But in fact it was hard to tell if the scar was the result of combat, or an accidental encounter with a barber's razor.

A boy, dressed stiflingly in a full woolen suit, worked the line selling carnations from a bucket. Whittier called him over to purchase two pink blooms. He presented them to the girls, and Carrie followed Nell's lead in accepting them. For what else could they do, when so gallantly presented, and in front of so many people? Nell planted the stem through a buttonhole in her jacket. Carrie just held hers, looking troubled.

Whittier, gaiety exuding, boldly took hold of Nell's forearm, as if he were her regular beau. Carrie's eyes widened at the presumption. Nell let him lead her, a smile on her lips and a look of cool malevolence in her eyes. For he wasn't the first stranger to assume such liberties, in a crowd where it would be awkward to make a scene.

Why she might resent his attentions, she would have struggled to say. They clashed with her instincts, of course, which were properly modest. But she was also becoming conscious of a certain power rising in her—the kind that made strange gentlemen rein up in the street, and turn their heads to have a look at her. With each year, men seemed to be at greater pains to please her, though in her own mind she was just another girl who couldn't keep her pinafores clean. It was bewildering and exhilarating, and made her both pity the men who gave it, and yearn to know what it was they saw in her. For lack of clear feelings on the subject, she tended to a certain passivity—as far as propriety allowed.

When they reached the head of the ticket line, Whittier got them into the park by paying for them — 25 cents for 25 rides. So much, thought Nell, for him "knowing the management".

Visitors entering Steeplechase first had to negotiate the "Barrel of Love". This was a fifteen-foot-long rotating tube, through which adults had to pass in bent-over fashion. The challenge was to walk through without losing balance. This was the challenge but not the fun: most visitors happily failed to keep their feet, splaying themselves against the inside of the barrel. Young ladies and gentlemen would land on top of their friends, or find their legs and arms braided together. Girls would find their skirts thrown up, their stockinged ankles and even knees showing. Some ladies became so engrossed in defending their modesty they forgot to exit the barrel, going round and round as onlookers laughed.

Charles Whittier placed himself between the cousins as they entered the Barrel. Nell was in the lead, and passed through it in six smooth steps. Carrie was doing fine, suffering only a small bobble, until Whittier—with a theatrical cry of "Oh goodness!"—flopped in front of her, and she tripped over him. She was face-down over his lap as he made perfunctory attempts to help her. When she finally escaped, she came out bare-headed and red-faced. The smiling Whittier emerged with her hat. She snatched it back.

"I fear I will never master that!" he cried, triumphant in his failure.

The lines at the Steeplechase ride were too long at that moment, so they tried some of the smaller amusements first. Nell always enjoyed the Dew Drop, which required them to climb a gangway to the top of a fifty-foot tower. They slung down a spiral slide, which was smooth and fast from the passage of so many thickly clad bottoms. They were disgorged on a rubber mattress that, upon impact, gave a groaning fart. This time Carrie made sure she wasn't next to Whittier, and didn't get tangled with him. Nell, for her part, alighted from the slide precisely on her feet, and stepped off with not a hair out of place.

"How long do we have to stay with him?" Carrie whispered as they waited for Whittier to spiral down.

"Just follow my lead," replied Nell.

From the landing zone they proceeded to the concessions for sausages and beer. They enjoyed these standing up, as all the tables were jammed. The dandy, to his credit, paid for their lunch, and was more than ready to pay for more rounds of beer. But Carrie declared, "A bellyful of drink and a plunge down the Steeplechase does not a fine combination make."

"What makes a fine combination," the fellow replied, "is fun and friends. I know a fellow who'd dearly love to meet you girls. If you'd permit me to introduce you...?"

"Sounds divine," said Nell over her half-eaten roll. "Why don't you fetch him?"

"I will!"

And the dandy, after collecting his cane, headed off into the crowd. Then he turned, and with mocking admonishment, wagged his finger at them. "Now don't you go anywhere!"

"Wouldn't think of it!"

The second he disappeared, Nell grabbed Carrie's arm. They made straight to the ladies' powder room. There, Nell installed herself in front of the mirror, and removed her hat to check her hair.

Carrie needed the primping far more after her tumble in the Barrel of Love, but had barely the patience to glance at herself. She was about to mash her hat back on her head when Nell warned, "You better take your time. You don't want to run into him again."

"I don't know how you do it," said the other. "Can you lend me a pin, at least?"

Nell pulled one from her bun and handed it over. As she fumbled, Carrie looked into the mirror at Nell's face, which was bright from a sheen of excitement, and handsomely flushed under her cheekbones. Her blue eyes were dark as indigo, her chestnut hair aflame under the sunbeams streaming from the skylights. Carrie perceived, with an unsettling suddenness, that the cousin she had known for years, since they had hopscotched on the sidewalks of New Utrecht, was no longer just beautiful in the way of some children. She was becoming comely in the way of a grown woman.

"What are you staring at?" asked Nell.

"You're enjoying this, aren't you?"

"Enjoying what?"

"None of this is fun for me. This hiding out in toilets from strange men. It's not worth it."

"You didn't complain when you saved the money."

"When can we get out of here?"

"Patience...Carol."

When Nell thought the time was right, they emerged. There was a lull in the rush to ride the Steeplechase—a gravity-driven plunge on wooden horses down a thousand-foot track. Within ten minutes, they were whooshing along on adjacent mounts, simultaneously trying to keep their hats on their heads and their skirts down. The thrill put her in mind of one of Uncle Andrew's other stories, about how her grand-uncle, William J. Cropsey, rode in the Kings County Troop during the War. He pantomimed the thrill of the charge, sabres drawn, and about how his grand-uncle knew Robert E. Lee and Stonewall Jackson. He said a lot of things she didn't remember.

But the detail that delighted Nell the most was the fact that William Cropsey.'s uniform was so splendid, his epaulets alone cost forty dollars.

"Forty dollar epaulets!" she cried, delirious with velocity.

"What?!"

Distracted, Carrie nearly flew off her seat as she went over one of the 'jumps'—a quick up and down incline of the track. She had a clear vision of her death. Yet this scare, and her survival of it, made her reckless.

"Let's go again!"

"Yes, later. Let's try the big wheel!"

She followed Nell to the Ferris wheel, where they got a car to themselves. There they sat, arm-in-arm, as they ascended a hundred feet into the sky. The Park and the rest of Coney Island was spread beneath them, a great heaving mass of humanity and frivolity. The roar of it all disappeared as their car mounted to the top; it always impressed her how fast the cacophony faded with height. And just as they reached the apex, the wheel slowed to a brief stop, as it often did for children and old folks to enter or exit the cars—or to clean up the messes of patrons who had overindulged in eats and drinks.

Nell was gazing out at the ocean, over the glittering water and canvas triangles of ships rounding Seagate. Whence had they come, she wondered, and with what cargo? Would she ever sail on such a ship herself, to some far continent? And on her way to such adventures, would she look back at this giant, absurd wheel, taking its passengers round and round but never anywhere new?

So high did they ascend that Nell imagined she could glimpse her future. At the age of nineteen, and with a little luck, she could look forward to seeing the middle of the 20th century. She would have children—but unlike her mother, only four or five. In her home, she would enjoy a flush toilet. Train trips at a hundred miles an hour. Kitchen ranges run on electricity, and needles that threaded themselves. Horseless carriages run on coal. Buildings forty stories tall. Submarine excursions, and dirigible trips beyond the atmosphere and the Moon. Such a vast, exciting world, and somewhere in it, a place for her to watch it all.

"Nell, look here..." breathed Carrie.

Her cousin was gazing into the crowd below. And there, utterly distinct in his brown-and-white seersucker, stood Charles Whittier. He was looking straight back up at them.

"Get back, for God's sake, or he'll see you!" Carrie tugged at her elbow.

"He already has. Oh, look at that face! He's not a happy boy, is he?"

She blew him a kiss. The dandy's face darkened.

Nell plucked the carnation from her buttonhole.

"Here, take this!" she called to him.

She leaned out, and like Ellen Terry casting a boon from the stage, tossed the carnation. It spun, fluttered, and plunged stem-first, to land at his feet. Nell, at comfort with her cruelty, unfurled a smile so unabashed it made him forget his wounded pride. His frown vanished, and along with a circle of other men, he stood entranced at the vision hanging in the sky above.

Author's Afterword

The Nell Cropsey story is a familiar one today: an attractive, middle-class white girl disappears, triggering a frenzy of media coverage that culminates in a high-profile trial. In many similar cases before and since, the disappearances are less remarkable than the selective attention—by media and law-enforcement—paid to some and not to others.

But this sells this particular case short. Nell's story, in fact, is the mold out of which all the following instances were cast. It is an archetypal American story, set in a time when the mass media were assuming their modern forms, and when millions of young people were first tasting the freedom of industrial life. It is not without significance that Nell disappeared on the eve of a trip from North Carolina to Brooklyn; to elders unused to such casual mobility, to daughters no longer confined to home and local community, the freedom offered by trains and steamships had to be unsettling. In some corner of the American psyche, the fear grew that the family itself was under threat. Indeed, their worst fears have largely been proven justified today, with families atomized and local communities 'disrupted' by economic and technological forces far beyond their control.

This book is a work of fiction. I don't purport to know what actually happened to Nell on the night of November 20, 1901. The story presented here, however, is based on extensive research on the case, and represents one plausible solution.

For instance, that Nell's body could have been in the Pasquotank River for thirty-seven days, yet emerge in almost pristine condition, has long been a point of contention. On one hand, bodies were known to remain submerged in that river for as long as a month, until the accumulation of decay gases in the corpses made them sufficiently buoyant to surface. Deputy Charles Reid was quoted in the Elizabeth City *North Carolinian* as early as November 28—a full month before Nell was found— that "he had known bodies to remain in the river for thirty to sixty days before coming to the surface." According to forensic taphonomist Dr. Thomas Evans—who was gracious enough to review the facts of the case with me—factors like Nell's water-logged clothing, water temperature, tidal currents and salinity all may have contributed to keeping her down for weeks. As the river was an industrial area at the time, it is possible that her body was snagged on a piling or other piece of debris.

On the other hand, she was not wearing quite so many clothes as might be supposed for a woman of the time—just her underthings, skirt, top, stockings, and one rubber slipper. Moreover, her body had not putrified enough to emit the decay gases that might have brought her up. One of the most notable aspects of her autopsy was that her body (with the exception of her brain) did not smell of decay at all.

The experts in 1901 speculated that the cold water of the Pasquotank contributed to Nell's preservation. And yet—and notwithstanding the testimony of several witnesses at the Wilcox trial—it was not particularly cold in Elizabeth City in November-December, 1901. Department of Commerce weather records indicate that the average high temperature in December was a balmy 53.5 degrees F; the average low was above freezing. It was warmer still in November, with an average high of 54.6 degrees.

Most puzzling is that her body was utterly untouched by scavengers. The water of the Pasquotank River was rich in tannins, and it was heavily used by industry, but it was not dead. Oyster harvesting was a leading industry in the region. For a body to be submerged for more than a month, and suffer not so much as a nibble from a fish, with not so much as a snail found in Nell's hair or in her clothes, seems to suggest she could not have been down very long. That she surfaced almost exactly in front of her house on Riverside Avenue also seems strange, given that the tides should have washed her in and out dozens of times.

That she was immobilized on some submerged object could resolve some of these questions—but it doesn't explain the lack of scavenging. Moreover, the coroner noted no evidence that her body was hooked, snagged, lodged, or otherwise detained underwater. There was no damage to her clothing, no abrasions on her skin, other than the contusion noted by the barber Ferebee on her left temple.

If Nell wasn't in the river for thirty-seven days, where was she? Even at the time, townspeople speculated about lights burning in the turret of the Cropsey home, and extra heavy deliveries of ice in the weeks following Nell's disappearance. On December 5, the *Charlotte Morning Post* alluded to an odd passivity on the part of the family, noting "the Cropseys are not taking as much interest in the matter [that is, the search] as some other citizens..." This was followed a week later by the family's announcement that they believed Nell was dead—an announcement made a full two weeks before her body was discovered. Their resignation seems surprising, given that most families in their position would hold out hope for their daughter's safe return until the very last glimmer of hope was exhausted. This leads to the question of whether someone in the family knew more about her fate than publicly acknowledged.

As to Jim Wilcox's guilt, this writer is not alone in having his doubts. At the very least, his initial conviction and death sentence probably would never have happened in a modern context. That the state militia was called out to protect him from a lynch mob is all the proof necessary that he could never, ever have gotten a fair trial in Elizabeth City.

How Nell Cropsey died is unknown to this day. The responsibility for Jim Wilcox's death, however, is crystal clear: he may have died by his own hand, but he was killed years earlier. It was not his conviction or incarceration that ended his life, it was what happened after, in the town in which he was born, and to which he unaccountably returned after his pardon. Why Jim insisted on returning to the community that rejected him is as big a mystery as any in this story.

If Nell is an emblem of the future of social mobility in America, tied to no particular place, following opportunity wherever it leads, Jim epitomizes the opposite. His insistence on staying put is powerful testimony to the opposite current—to identify strongly with a place, to a locality to which one belongs. As noted in the work of geographer John Cromartie, this split has broken today firmly in favor of the former. Yet it continues to define the politics of rural vs. city, middle America vs. the coasts, well into our century.

In addition to Dr. Evans, the author also thanks Frank and Robin Caruso, the current owners of the Cropsey home on Riverside Avenue, for their hospitality and advice. The Carusos have been conscientious in their preservation of their historic home, using period records and photographs to restore it to a condition Nell Cropsey herself would have recognized. Thanks to them, I had an opportunity—both thrilling and eerie—to stand on the very porch from which Nell disappeared, and to visit the attic where Mary Cropsey kept her vigil. The inscription in the chapter "The Bedroom" appears courtesy of the Carusos.

Thanks also to Dave Elligers, historian of the New Utrecht Reformed Church in Brooklyn, for hosting me on a tour of the cemetery (currently closed to the public) where Nell is buried. Dave also helped me confirm that—contrary to almost all the newspaper accounts of the time—Nell was not nineteen years old when she disappeared, but twenty. Why the Cropseys allowed the fiction to propagate that she died at nineteen is puzzling. While a certain casualness with respect to birth dates was not unknown at the time, one wonders whether they believed portraying Nell as a teenager somehow played better to the public.

Archivist Paul Schlotthauer helped debunk another bit of mythology about Nell: that she was a college student at Pratt Institute in Brooklyn. While her cousin Carrie was indeed registered at Pratt, contrary to some reports in the New York City press, there is no record of Nell ever having officially studied at that institution.

Thanks also to Sarah and Gabriel Chrisman for their insights into everyday life during this period, and to the Registrar's Office at Pratt. I'm fortunate to have such perceptive and constructive readers as Selka Kind and Pete Reichert to help me shape the initial drafts of this book. Any mistakes are due not to the people cited here, but are entirely the fault of the author.

About the Author

Nicholas Nicastro has taught history, anthropology and psychology at Cornell University, Hobart-William Smith and Pima Community Colleges. He has published eight novels as well as short fiction, travel, and science articles for *The New York Times*, *The New York Observer*, *Film Comment*, *The International Herald Tribune*, and *Archaeology*, among other publications. His books have been translated into seven languages. He lives in northern Virginia.

Learn more about Nicholas Nicastro at his website, www.nicastrobooks.com, and at his Facebook readers' page, "Books by Nicholas Nicastro".

Made in the USA
Columbia, SC
30 January 2019